Nagasaki Six

Nagasaki Six

GUY STANLEY

POCKET BOOKS

LONDON · SYDNEY · NEW YORK · TOKYO · SINGAPORE · TORONTO

First published in Great Britain by Simon & Schuster Ltd
A Viacom Company

Simon & Schuster
West Garden Place
Kendal Street
London W2 2AQ

Simon & Schuster of Australia Pty Ltd Sydney

A CIP catalogue record for this book is available
from the British Library.

0-684-816164

Printed and bound in Great Britain by
Caledonian International Book Manufacturing Ltd, Glasgow

Other books by Guy Stanley also available from Simon & Schuster:

A Death in Tokyo
The Ivory Seal
Yen
Reiko

For Tom Humphrey

Acknowledgements

I owe thanks to many people but must mention Rob Burge and Mile Holtom for their technical help and others, like Dorothy Britton, Jo Rice, Graham Harris, Chris MacDonald, Ben Thorne, James Harris, Miranda Kenrick and Lew Radbourne, who gave generously of their time and knowledge of Japan. There were others, especially my wife Kayoko and my agent Peter Robinson, who gave me endless encouragement, and Tom Humphrey, whose experiences as a prisoner of war in the Far East inspired me to write this novel.

PROLOGUE

Approaching Haneda Airport, over Tokyo Bay

HANEDA RADAR:	NINA Three Two Eight. Contact Haneda Approach. One one nine decimal one.
CAPTAIN:	Roger. One one nine one
FIRST OFFICER:	Fifteen miles from runway. Wind's really strong now.
CAPTAIN:	Yes it is. I might have to take over. (*To Haneda Approach*) Haneda Approach. This is NINA Three Two Eight, passing four thousand feet. Radar heading two six zero.
HANEDA APPROACH:	Roger Three Two Eight. Continue descent to two one zero zero feet, heading two five zero to intercept localiser runway two two.

CAPTAIN:	Er, say again Haneda. Heading . . . er . . .
HANEDA APROACH:	Heading two five zero, NINA Three Two Eight, runway two two.
CAPTAIN:	Three Two Eight is cleared two one zero zero feet, heading two five zero, er, cleared localiser two two. (*To Engineer*) Initial approach checks. Twelve miles. (*To First Officer*) Reduce speed one seven zero knots.
FIRST OFFICER:	Flaps fifteen degrees, please.
CAPTAIN:	Roger. Flaps fifteen degrees. (*mechanical motion noise*)
ENGINEER:	Check altimeters.
FIRST OFFICER:	One zero two zero set.
CAPTAIN:	Confirmed and checked.
ENGINEER:	Speed brakes armed.
CAPTAIN:	Armed.
ENGINEER:	Landing gear next.
FIRST OFFICER:	Gear down please.
CAPTAIN:	Roger. Gear down. (*grinding motion noise*)
CAPTAIN:	(*to Haneda Approach*) Haneda. NINA Three Two Eight established localiser two two.
HANEDA APPROACH:	Roger, Three Two Eight. Cleared I L S. Contact Tower one one eight decimal one.
ENGINEER:	Set.
CAPTAIN:	Haneda Tower. This is NINA Three Two Eight, passing

	Arakawa on glideslope. (*To First Officer*) Er . . . fives miles at one one five zero zero feet. Check.
FIRST OFFICER:	Check.
HANEDA TOWER:	Roger, Three Two Eight, cleared to land runway two two. Surface wind two seven zero degrees, thirty knots, gusting forty.
CAPTAIN:	That's some wind out there. It's outside your limit. I'll . . . (*Pause*) I'll take over. I'll land it.
FIRST OFFICER:	If you're okay. Take it when you're ready.
CAPTAIN:	Okay. I've got it. Final flaps. Select thirty degrees. (*mechanical motion sound*)
ENGINEER:	Flaps thirty degrees. Final check list complete.
FIRST OFFICER:	(*to Haneda Tower*) Haneda Tower. Request wind checks on short finals.
HANEDA TOWER:	Roger. Presently two six zero degrees, Thirty-four knots.
CAPTAIN:	(*to Crew*) That's er . . . fine. (*Pause*) Fine. (*Pause*)
HANEDA TOWER:	Two eight zero, forty-two knots. (*Pause*)
UNIDENTIFIED CREW:	(*in Japanese*) Not again. (*cockpit and external noise*)
UNIDENTIFIED CREW:	(*unintelligible shouting in Japanese*)

3

| RECORDED VOICE: | (*Ground Proximity Warning System Recorded Message*) Glideslope, glideslope. |
| THE CREW: | (*unintelligible screams*) |

<u>1013 hours 22 seconds</u> – <u>TRANSMISSION ENDS</u>

'Smacked the ground hard,' Reginald Cameron said, shaking wet spatters off his jacket and dropping his umbrella into a wastepaper basket.

'Morning Reggie.' Alexander Bolton's eyes barely shifted from the bank of filing cabinets to greet his chief, or the Technical Director, as the head of British Underwriters International's aviation division was titled. The alarm had been triggered; the countdown was well under way. They called it the 'hot' phase. 'And some. The plane was almost vertical when it hit. There's a fax from Tokyo on your desk.' The two men were aeronautical engineers working as aviation accident investigators on behalf of the insurers of the world's aeroplane fleets. They were known in the business as surveyors and would arrive on the site of an aviation disaster at the absolute earliest opportunity. There were under thirty in Britain and BUI employed six of them. Smaller than their rivals in the aviation department at Lloyd's, their building in the City of London's Bishopsgate, housing the group's diverse insurance divisions, was a squat, functional block, a poor neighbour to the tubular edifice of Lloyd's Insurance in Leadenhall Market a short walk away.

Cameron had taken a call from an underwriter in BUI's Tokyo office at 3.35 a.m. British Summer Time, 11.35 a.m. local time in Japan, and another fifteen minutes later from the night officer at the company's monitoring unit in Reading. Called the BUI Intelligence Control Centre, it maintained a twenty-four-hour surveillance of aircraft movements and incidents around the globe. When he woke Alexander Bolton just before the hour he was able to tell him why he should pack for the earliest possible departure for Japan.

The last moments of the McDonnell Douglas DC-8-71, call sign NINA 328, were already flashing on live news information screens around the world minutes after the aeroplane, operated by NN Air of Japan, slammed to earth on the threshold of runway twenty-two at Haneda International Airport, Tokyo. Powered by four CFM-56 engines, the twenty-six-year-old jet, a DC-8-61 series – converted from passenger to cargo use – was on a flight from the Republic of Taiwan, four hours to the south in the Pacific. It had been diverted to Haneda, a mostly domestic airport jutting into Tokyo Bay, by a short-lived security shutdown at Tokyo's principal international airport at Narita, sixty kilometres to the east of the Japanese capital, near the Chiba prefectural coastline. A group of underwriters in London had reinsured the hull for 95 per cent of its US$20 million covered value, the small remaining portion of risk being met in Japan. BUI had taken a participation and was the designated hull leader, with its Aviation Department named in the policy as the loss adjuster of need. A surveyor's presence was now required, like yesterday, at the site of the incident on the other side of the world, to represent the insurers in the face of a claim the owners and the operator of the stricken aeroplane were already preparing.

Young money-market dealers from the faster professions scurried early to their City trading rooms through the squalls, and when the two aviation surveyors reached their suite of offices, almost simultaneously, it was not yet 6.30 a.m. Bolton lifted a slim folder from the cabinet and deposited it in a solid, broad pilot's chart case. He was tall, athletically rangy in a charcoal-grey suit. His light-brown intelligent eyes darted among the documents, sifting them through slender fingers. On the conference table with the case he had arranged the tools he needed at the site: a compact video recorder, a pocket calculator, a dictation machine, an automatic camera and a more complex Nikon with spare films. His laptop computer was collapsed, another piece of hand luggage. The aircrew were dead presumably, and there might be victims on the ground. And what was in the cargo? He reminded himself again that his protective gloves and face mask were packed in his case with a medical pack and a lightweight disposable overall. His innoculations against exotic diseases were up to date.

Cameron groaned loudly. He had slumped in a wing chair, rocking gently as he absorbed each new awful detail from a fax message, a two-metre stretch from Tokyo. Another awaited him, a terse message from NN Air, the Japanese operator of the stricken aeroplane. It had been generated from the instructions in a standard accident procedures manual and it formally requested the urgent attendance of BUI Aviation investigators at the site of the crash of its transport aircraft.

Cameron's office was minimally decorated, and furnished for business with bookshelves, cabinets, a ten-place conference table and a private fascimile machine. A broad-screen television and video unit, tuned low to CNN, filled a corner. The only hint at the profession of the occupant was the piece of fuselage from an African passenger aeroplane he had mounted on a wall bracket. It had looked like an accident but his persistence and experience had revealed the cause of the crash, and its lethal legacy still scarred the souvenir on Cameron's shelf: neat holes from the splintered residue of a rebel ground-to-air missile.

He was older than Bolton by twenty-five years, a veteran of crash sites on every continent, and his weariness was not only a consequence of last night's interrupted sleep. The real work, the hot phase of the investigation into the cause of an aviation accident, always began with a week of frantic activity: the dash to the site, hooked by fax and phone to brokers, lawyers, underwriters and desperate airline executives, followed by days probing, listening, stepping diplomatically around the official investigators, the local civil aviation officers, pilots, engineers and nervous rescuers while trying to prise records on the aeroplane, the cargo and the crew from an operator impatient for a quick payout. In trying to insinuate himself into the heat of the investigation, the agent of the insurers was an unwelcome interloper for the harassed authorities: he was not invited by them and he had no legal right to be there. Diplomacy was another skill the man on the ground needed in quantity.

'All yours,' Cameron said gladly, passing the faxes across the conference table. He had seen enough carbonised human remains, trodden through his last stinking mosquito swamp and found a child's scorched doll for the final time. He put responsibility for this small Japanese airline and its tragedy on Alexander Bolton, a senior surveyor in his team. But he'd miss the attention. The urgent aftermath of an air crash made the surveyor the most influential person in the investigation. His initial findings, his confirmation of the deaths, injuries, third-party damage and his opinion on the recoverability of the aircraft or its salvage, would decide the timing of the insurance payout. The owner, or the lessee operator, of the aeroplane courted him, entertained him, opened his heart and his books for him and then held out his hand to him.

A tall woman entered backwards, her arms cradling folders and loose papers. She placed them between the two men. Her eyes were alive with urgency. Cameron looked up and smiled. 'Thanks for coming in this early, Emma.'

'No problem.' She turned to Bolton, who was holding a pair of passports. 'No special needs for Japan. No visas, inoculations.'

'Great.' He kept two passports, one of them 'clean', free of sensitive visas that would prohibit him entry to certain countries. 'Have I got time to make some calls?'

She looked at the wall clock instinctively. 'Plenty. The first direct flight to Tokyo's at twelve twenty. Virgin. Gets you to Narita International at half past eight local time tomorrow morning. I'll book you on it as soon as they open for the day.'

Cameron was toying with the television's remote control when he spoke to Bolton. 'Cathy not too upset about your middle-of-the-night departure, Alex?'

Emma threw the younger man a knowing, sympathetic glance. She had once worked with Alex's long-time girlfriend and liked her.

'We split a month ago,' he said, stuffing papers roughly into the case. 'She moved out.'

The rain had eased and a break in the clouds funnelled rods of pale light into the offices. 'Better you than me on this one,' Cameron said, coughing awkwardly before swivelling towards the television as the brow of the Chinese-American presenter furrowed and her voice deepened gravely. 'And now over to Tokyo and the crash of that US-registered Japanese airplane.' Alex dropped the papers and Emma moved closer. They hardly heard her summary, or the shirt-sleeved Caucasian speaking from the perimeter fence at Haneda Airport. They already knew more than the news media and wanted to see the crash scene. This followed, courtesy of the jerky, long-range images from a helicopter in a holding pattern well outside the boundary of the airport, but the distance and the chaotic spread of emergency vehicles under a blanket of residual smoke and steamy haze ruled out any meaningful interpretation. The fax machine alert sounded and delivered another long message. Alex read it as it curled out, then tore it off and gave it to Cameron. Emma took a call. 'Guy called Suchida or something,' she reported, covering the telephone. 'General manager of Nippon Nagasaki Corporation, European Headquarters. He wants to come round. Says he represents NN Air's interests.'

'Tsuchida,' Cameron corrected. 'I've met him. He puts himself around the City. We know what he wants. Just tell him we're on the case but he should contact his broker in the first instance.' He swivelled towards Alex. 'Get to know NN Air but remember: we're not dealing here with just a straightforward aeroplane operator. They're part of one of those Japanese conglomerates. You know, like Mitsubishi, fingers in every pie.'

Between receiving calls, Reggie Cameron telephoned the company's lawyer, Jeremy Skipton, while Emma Healey sifted the files in his office to fill a checklist of documents. She was an able staff officer, an expert on the minutiae of aircraft intelligence and documentation. Alex had taken a folder of papers to his desk in the open office and was chewing on the lip of another plastic cup of machine coffee while specialist staff worked around him on the case of the wrecked DC-8-71. A young intense man delved into the computer database, searching for a reference to the NN Air fleet and its history, anything to help build a profile for Alex.

In the streets outside, the bankers, insurers, brokers, dealers and opportunist middlemen who made up the City's daytime population were reaching their trading rooms and offices in a light drizzle. Behind the patchwork windows in the buildings surrounding BUI's, the aviation insurance underwriters were deep into old files, their calculators primed to assess their portion of the loss for the hull, third-party damage, the freight and the lives of the crew. At 8.37 the important call came.

'Brian Levine on two for you Alex,' Emma called. Levine

10

was a broker in the aviation division of Matthias, Montague & Broome, a brokerage house whose origins were lost somewhere between myth and the City coffee house dealings in the seventeenth century. Levine had acted on behalf of NN Air when he broked the deal around the City of London for the reinsurance of six tenth-hand aircraft leased by the Japanese company six years earlier. It was to Matthias, Montague & Broome that NN Air rushed when their aeroplane went down.

'Pretty straightforward,' Levine said hopefully, after a short exchange. Alex had only a vague recollection of the broker's face but he imagined a desk piled with faxes and a small army of insurance underwriters queuing on an overburdened telephone board. Alex didn't know what a straightforward air crash meant, but the broker was under pressure to settle with his clients and it was in his interests to create a mood of normality, even for a US$20 million claim. But there wouldn't be a payout until the surveyor representing the underwriters' syndicate was satisfied, which was why Levine needed Alex. 'When are you leaving?'

'Around noon on the Virgin,' Alex said, shuffling some papers. 'Are you coming with me?' It went quiet while Levine wrote.

'No. I'll stay here with the London end. I've got a chap from NN Air's parent company battering at the door.'

'Name of Tsuchida,' Alex offered.

'That's him,' Levine sighed. 'He can wait. I'll talk to our Tokyo office now. You'll be met at Narita by one of my Japanese brokers. Guy called Yoshi Kanagawa. Probably someone from the operator as well. Do you need a hotel?'

'Please. Book me for a week at least. Tell your man I need somewhere with a secure communication set-up. My own fax if possible.' Cradling the telephone on his shoulder, his hands free to handle a folder, Alex pushed his chair backwards and lifted his feet onto the desk. 'I need to see the wreckage

11

quickly and without hassle. I imagine the Japs are expert at closing down the situation. Ask NN Air to use their influence to get me a pass for the site and any other authorisations I'm going to need. I don't want to have to battle the bureaucracy. And I don't want to talk to the Press. Tell them to get me through without fuss.' He gave Levine time to make notes. 'Who's my contact with the operator?' He heard the broker clear his throat.

'At a working level I don't know, but you're going to come across a chap called Hiroshi Miyamoto. He's president, chief executive, head of everything I hear, in the Nippon Nagasaki group. That includes NN Air. He's a very hands-on sort of person.'

Alex straightened and checked his watch. 'I look forward to it. Meanwhile I need a copy of the slip. Bring it with you and meet me in front of the BUI building at ten. You can come with me to the airport. It'll give you an hour's peace.' He hung up on the broker. Emma Healey was perched on a corner of his desk. She had collected his air ticket, a wad of yen cash and a book of dollar traveller's cheques and was delivering them at the moment Alex was itching to leave. The executive lounge at Heathrow beckoned as a monastery of calm.

'Counsellor Skipton on three,' a surveyor called with mock American courtroom solemnity, flourishing the handset from across the office.

'Latest from Tokyo,' Emma breathed, pressing a fax where he could read as he spoke. Alex leaned forward and readied a notepad. 'Jeremy. I was about to call.'

'Of course you were, dear boy,' the lawyer said pleasantly 'You might need me this time.'

'Reggie told you, did he, about the dive?'

'He said it sounded spectacular.'

Alex underlined a notation in the new message from Japan. 'We're hearing the plane was diverted to Haneda

12

because Narita was closed down again. Seems the local farmers bring in left-wing radicals to help them fight against their land being expropriated for a new runway. It can get very nasty. Home-made mortars have been used. It doesn't stay shut for long but the authorities are ultra-sensitive out there. Anyway, first reports from Haneda suggest the plane was hit by low-altitude wind shear or a downdraft or something. It was blowing really hard out there.'

'The pilot was American and the first officer and engineer Japanese,' Skipton said. 'The loadmaster was Taiwanese. That's a nice mixed bag of potential confusion.'

'Not unusual with emerging airlines,' Alex retorted. He could almost hear the pandemonium, the hellish bedlam induced by the proximity of certain death. Alex saw an image of twisted wreckage and charred bodies welded to the heat-seared metal. Mercifully there were only four known fatalities. His priority was to represent the insurers, to give them an opinion that would let them settle the claim that NN Air would already be preparing. Their London representative, Tsuchida, was already in contact with the broker and had made an appointment with Cameron, no doubt aware of the adjuster's role in adjudicating the claim.

'I mean the real owners of the old flying machine,' Skipton said in a high, imposing voice. 'NN Air leased it and five other planes from a Florida company.' He heard the silence. 'Yes. I thought that would interest you. South Miami Aviation, and it's still US-registered.'

'One of the usual suspects?'

'Can't be sure until we run a check through Oklahoma,' Skipton said. The Federal Aviation Administration's central files on all US-registered aircraft were kept in Oklahoma City. US registration and a Miami base told the lawyer and the surveyor that their request for details of the owner might lead them tantalisingly into a labyrinth of paper companies at off-shore addresses, nominees and entrepreneurs with a

13

singular approach to business. 'But it means of course that you'll meet your friends from the FAA and the other lot in Tokyo.'

'The National Transportation Safety Board,' Bolton added.

'Quite. It's an American show. It also means the crew should have an American Pilot Rating, the proper, certified regular medical checks and all that.' Another notation on Alex's pad. 'And the Japanese are devils about pollution. A splash of kerosene on a seagull could attract a suit. It sounds as though the plane came down inside the airport so we probably won't have problems with fuel poisoning the local water supplies and rivers, but take a good look around please.'

Alex listened to the lawyer's pitch with practised attention. It was repetitious, and a little tedious, but he liked to be reminded of the broad picture and his, Alex's, duty to look for third-party damage to buildings and people as well as the environment and anything that might attract a claim for damages against the aeroplane's insurers. Conversely, as he probed the remains of the machine and tracked back through its history and the record of the crew, he would be looking for evidence of negligence in maintenance or training, or some other contravention of the terms of the insurance policy, which if discovered would give the insurers a reason to consider possible denial of cover.

An intelligence officer called Mike caught his eyes and slid a small slip of paper in front of him. Alex's watch told him it was time to move on. 'I gather you're not coming with me this time,' he said.

'I'll come out if I have to. Give me an overview as soon as you can.'

'I'll fax you tomorrow night Japan time, Jeremy. I get into Tokyo mid-morning and should get to the site in two, three hours. Haneda's virtually in Tokyo. I land at Narita, fifty miles away. It was only closed for a morning.' He hung up, wrote a short note for Emma and crossed to her desk. She saw him coming and broke off her telephone call with an apology. 'Check this name through the leased and non-owned records, Emma, please,' he said. 'I think we're talking Miami.' She scanned the note and raised a thumb before returning to her call. Alex read Mike's short note as he crossed the office for a final briefing with Reggie Cameron and a support team. The aviation division of BUI produced confidential reports for the underwriters from a vast library of records and information and Mike had found a couple of trivial snatches on NN Air. They were not major incidents – neither had attracted an insurance claim – but the terse handwritten words documented two reports plucked from small-print news in esoteric trade magazines. Two years earlier an engine on an NN Air Boeing 747 cargo aeroplane was shut down on a flight to Hong Kong and a few months later one of the other two DC-8-71s had landed heavily and long down the runway at Seoul, its tyres bursting as the pilot applied maximum reverse thrust and brakes in order to stay on the tarmac. Alex logged the facts in his memory and slipped the paper into a file.

The surveyors met for a last meeting to lay down a survey strategy, most importantly a twenty-four-hour communication link with a site eight hours ahead of Greenwich and seven and a half thousand miles away. A man Alex did not recognise slid quietly into the room, cradling a beige folder wrapped with a faded red ribbon.

'You'd better get under way,' Reggie Cameron said after confirming they all knew their roles over the next crucial thirty-six hours. He extended his hand. 'Good luck Alex.' And with a grin he added, 'I don't have to warn you about the *geishas*.' The others threw him good-natured messages of farewell as they shuffled out past the newcomer. Then Cameron remembered. 'Alex. This is . . . sorry.'

'Martin. Martin Crawley. From Records.' The short,

greying man was a pale, bookish sort who spent his days among a hundred and fifty years' worth of records and archives. He had called Cameron earlier to request a few minutes with the surveyor assigned to the Japanese accident.

'Car's waiting,' Emma declared, her head appearing round the door.

'I don't have much time,' Alex apologised, sweeping a final document into his case and clasping it shut.

Crawley's eyes jumped nervously between the surveyors. He pulled the knot binding the folder and tried to speak to both of them. 'Can I ask you a small favour?' he asked, unsheathing a slim file of typed sheets and a flimsy, almost transparent, piece of paper attached together with a rusty staple. He passed them to Bolton. The typed sheets were dark around the edges but the bulk was intact: they were old but not often perused. The fragile paper was almost cut into three pieces along the creases where it had been folded and was covered with oriental-looking pictographs. There was something familiar about the flamboyant logo across the top. Curling above a pair of eagles, their wings spread imperiously around a globe, he read: NIPPON BRITISH INSURANCE LIMITED.

'We set up a company in Japan in 1920,' Crawley explained as Cameron stood at Bolton's shoulder. 'Changed the name to British Underwriters International after the war to mirror ours.' He sensed their impatience. 'To cut a long story short, these papers came to us last year from a solicitor in Cornwall. He's executor for the estate of a widow. They'd belonged to her late husband, Tom. He'd died years ago, 1957 in fact. Their daughter found them after her mother's death and really only out of interest wants to know what the foreign bits mean. The solicitor thought it through and matched the logo on this old Japanese document with ours and sent it to us. I'm afraid I've been sitting on it since.'

'So you want me to deliver them to our people in Tokyo,' Alex said brusquely.

16

Crawley's face creased. 'I'm not sure,' he admitted. 'I really didn't intend to do anything pro-actively but when I heard about the Nippon Nagasaki crash this morning it sort of triggered something about the old documents.' He put a finger gently on the fragile paper. 'The only English script in here is our Japanese subsidiary's name and these two bits in the middle of some squiggly characters.' Cameron and Bolton leaned closer. Among the rows of intricate and indecipherable hand-written Chinese-like writing they read 'Jonsson Nagasaki Kogyo' and two lines later 'Nippon Nagasaki Kogyo.' Crawley approached his extrapolation cautiously. 'I believe NN in the name of the airline involved in the crash stands for Nippon Nagasaki. There might just be a historical connection.'

'What's the Jonsson bit?' Alex asked. 'Sounds Scandinavian.'

Crawley shrugged. 'No idea. Perhaps the Japanese text tells us. I don't think there's any residual commercial value after all these years but it might interest somebody out there.' He jumped nervously. 'But only if you've got time.'

'You ought to be going,' Emma insisted.

'Okay, I'll look into it,' Alex said to the archivist, his mind somewhere ahead between the central lift and the company Rover waiting for him in Bishopsgate. He flipped the typed sheets. 'What are these?'

'They're old Tom's wartime diaries. He ended up in a prisoner-of-war camp in Japan.'

'But they're typed,' Cameron said suspiciously.

'The family had the original papers typed up years ago. Now they're lodged in the Imperial War Museum.'

Alex let Crawley pack the papers and the old letter. 'Why are they stapled together?' he said, unclipping his briefcase and making room for the new folder. He led Crawley towards the door.

'They were clipped together when the solicitor got them.

He doesn't know why.'

Alex hoisted his cameras over a shoulder and raised the heavy chart case. A volunteer made for the door with Alex's hastily packed suitcase and a travel bag. 'I don't know how I can help you with this one,' Alex said, with a touch of annoyance. 'I'm going to be pretty tied up with the air crash.'

'I'm terribly sorry to burden you with it,' Crawley said. 'If you could just put it in the hands of BUI in Tokyo they might have some old records. Or you could try Nippon Nagasaki. The old document at least might be of historical interest if it's about them.'

'I reckon Nippon Nagasaki Corporation have got enough problems for the moment,' Alex said as he left, his shoulders straddled with straps.

Brian Levine had the look of a hunted man as he hunched into the Rover. His mobile purred before they reached the Leadenhall Street traffic lights. 'I hope to have a preliminary indication from the scene of the accident about mid-morning tomorrow,' he told the instrument, looking with wide-eyed anticipation at Alex, who nodded back with a half smile. Levine depressed the short antenna and flicked the off switch. 'I need a break from all this,' he complained, and went to his briefcase. 'This is the slip for the DC-8 at Haneda. The copy's for you.'

The aviation market 'slip' was an insurance proposal summary prepared by the brokers Matthias, Montague & Broome, signed off by BUI as the leading underwriter and then taken to the market. Underwriters accepting these outline terms and conditions signalled their agreement with a simple initial. Later, sometimes months, the slip was replaced by a formal, detailed and complex policy of insurance. Bolton ran his eyes past the standard headings: type of risk, period, sum insured, premium, brokerage and the others, and fell on the additional information. The facts confirmed the

DC-8-71 was one a fleet of six, two other similarly converted DC-8s and three 747s.

'I see the planes are owned by a Florida-based outfit.'

Levine fidgeted with a file: a warning light had flashed. 'That's right. It won't be a problem, will it?'

The slip shook in Alex's hand as the car crossed a stretch of pitted road on the Embankment. 'Doubt it, but it means a lot more to look at. You know how it works. A US-registered hull brings in the FAA and the National Transportation Safety Board and there'll be all their regular checks and maintenance reports to get hold of, including the crew medical records. I'm going to need a lot of help from Nippon Nagasaki. Have you told them I'm on the way?'

'Yeah.' The broker scoffed. 'They seem to think you're bringing a cheque for twenty million dollars with you.'

'Did you tell them it doesn't work like that?'

'I said it might take a week.'

Levine produced a stapled batch of papers and he picked out the points he thought Alex should note with a red ballpen. It was mostly his file material on NN Air and their parent company. 'I await your reports eagerly,' he pressed, the Ark building glinting in a rare outburst of sunshine as they crossed the flyover at Hammersmith. 'And whatever you need from me, you only have to call.'

27 Feb. 1942 – On Board HMS Exeter, Java Sea

Left Surabaya Dutch Naval Base yesterday at 1900 hrs with another cruiser, the yank Houston, *three light cruisers and nine destroyers. Dutch Admiral Doorman in charge in the* De Ruyter. *Returning to port along north coast of Java and Madura when news came in of large force of Jap transports and escorts. Altered course 180 and sighted part of Jap escorts at 1620 hrs.* Exeter *engaged right hand light cruiser. Several hits seen and she turned away. Then we engaged the other light cruiser and after firing four or five salvos we were ordered by the Captain to engage two other heavy cruisers. Saw Dutch destroyer* Kortenaer *sink.*

About 1730 hrs Exeter *hit in B boiler-room. Two destroyers laid smoke screen for us and the* Houston *stood on our port bow. At 1805 hrs a Jap cruiser and two destroyers sighted off* Exeter's *starboard quarter and engaged with* Houston's *eight-inch guns.* Exeter *also engaged the cruiser which fired two torpedoes at us. They missed. Ordered back to Surabaya and arrived 2317 hrs. Rest of fleet fought on.*

20

28 Feb.
Disembarked bodies of 14 ratings killed yesterday. Heard that two Dutch cruisers sunk and Admiral Doorman went down with his ship. Exeter *oiled and provisioned and left at 1900 hrs with destroyers HMS* Encounter *and USS* Pope. *Orders were to proceed westward to Sunda Strait, get to Indian Ocean, then Colombo. Ship in first degree of readiness.*

1 March
First alarm at 0300 hrs when three suspicious shapes sighted. We turned away. Engineers got Exeter's *speed to 22 knots. Went to second degree of readiness at 0700 hrs so ship's company could get a meal. Back to first degree at 0800 hrs. We were trying to avoid action but were spotted by a Jap aircraft at 1017 hrs. Overtaken by four heavy cruisers with eight-inch guns and five destroyers. Not a very fair scrap. Our two destroyers sunk. We were hit in A boiler room and had no ammo left except practice shells. Captain ordered* Exeter *sunk and abandoned. I left my action station but could not get below. When I got to my abandon ship station I found my carley float had been launched. I went aft to the Quarter Deck but the Bolsa rafts had also been thrown over. I jumped overboard and surfaced near a large plank of wood. A stoker named Darley surfaced. He could not swim and was badly burned. I got him on the plank and we were joined by Signalman Rice and the Canteen Manager Mr Clements. I watched a Jap destroyer close on the* Exeter *and finish her with a torpedo. We were on the plank for four hours but Mr Clements left us. Two Jap destroyers picked up anyone who could reach them. I got on board just as she was starting her engines to leave. I had lost my wallet, bank book and photos of Kath and the children, but I found Reg Riggs, Jim Bishop and thirteen others. We had to*

21

*laugh because we were alive. We sat on deck and got a
small tin of warm milk and two biscuits.*

'I'm Tabata of Nippon Nagasaki Corporation,' the Japanese
man at the head of the carpeted ramp said when Alex
introduced himself. Bowing low from the waist he presented
a thinning scalp beaded with sweat. He was painfully thin,
his face gaunt and anxious, and he had been holding out a
stencilled card to passengers exiting the aeroplane. He
produced a wallet and extracted a calling card for the
Englishman. A dark-blue polyester suit, the trousers shiny
around his thighs, hung loose and uncomfortable on him. An
identification badge dragged on the lip of his jacket pocket.
'Please come with me,' he commanded, seizing Alex's chart
case and hobbling under its weight. They walked silently
through the departure lounges to the line of immigration
control desks. It was 8.30 in the morning and most were still
unmanned. Knots of passengers were gathering behind the
others. Tabata steered him past them to the end booth marked
for crew. He nodded at the officer in recognition, watched
him stamp the British engineer's passport with a short-stay
visa and walked him smartly into the baggage hall. Alex's
suitcase was already waiting by the conveyor. While the
Englishman loaded a trolley Tabata called out on a cellular
telephone.

Yoshikazu Kanagawa was waiting beyond customs in the
arrivals hall, his head bobbing and stretching behind a line of
greeters, his face beaming when he saw the foreigner with
the NNC man. He was forty but his smooth olive skin, trim
body and thick, jauntily unkempt hair made him look twenty-
five. He had joined the Tokyo office of the British firm of
brokers from university, defying his parents' pleas for him to
seek a humble, secure post with his own people to risk the
fickle managements of the foreign company. His outgoing
and cheerful nature was the natural cover for a tough

negotiator. His spoke English competently, with an exaggerated, practised American drawl. 'Call me Yoshi,' he demanded politely. 'How's Brian?' he asked amiably, seizing the luggage trolley.

'What's *his* role?' Alex asked after Tabata had gone ahead to call for the car. He was examining the business card. 'He's not from NN Air.'

They left the terminal as the crescendo of a departing jet rumbled along the building. 'Tabata? He's chief secretary to the president of Nippon Nagasaki Corporation, the operator's parent. You'll be seeing a lot of him.'

'Who? Tabata?'

'No, no. The big guy. Tabata's only the bag carrier for Hiroshi Miyamoto, president, chief executive, big chief.'

Alex breathed heavily, remembering the name through a haze of flight fatigue.

'He's absolutely hands-on,' Yoshi was saying. 'Every part of the NNC group. Aircraft, truck fleet, marine engineering. He doesn't delegate. Tabata will stick to you and look after you. Ask him whatever you want. He doesn't work for the airline but he'll know how and where to get information for you. Just remember that whatever you say and do gets back to Miyamoto.'

A black saloon with Tabata sitting next to the driver drew up to the kerb. The boot flipped open. 'What do I call this chap?' Alex asked, jigging his head behind the opened lid as he heaved a suitcase into the car. 'I didn't catch his first name.'

'That *is* his first name,' Yoshi said. 'And his surname. We always say it first and rarely use our given name outside the family. So just call him Mr Tabata or Tabata san.'

'What about "Yoshi?" That's not your surname.' He slammed the boot.

'A nickname for you *gaijin* to use. You always want to be informal. My full name's Yoshikazu Kanagawa. "Yoshi" makes it easy.' Alex opened the rear door for him.

'What did you call me? "*Guy gin*"?'

Kanagawa grinned. 'Right. It means foreigner, outsider, not one of us.'

'Do you want to go to your hotel first, Mr Bolton?' Tabata said when they were on the two-lane motorway, Tokyo still forty miles away, beyond the compact paddy fields spiked with young rice plants and the doubled-stacked houses, with orange and blue tiled roofs, of the farming hamlets.

Alex read the nervous man easily. Apart from a brief doze on the twelve-hour flight he'd been awake for twenty-one hours, but the imminence of his mission excited a renewed charge of energy 'Let's go straight to the site. We've got eight hours of daylight left at least.' He turned to his Japanese colleague. 'What's the situation at Haneda, Yoshi?'

'They can't start clearing up until the Americans have been over the site and the engine guys have had a chance to look at their wreckage. They're all on their way. Should be here later today, maybe on the site during the night. They're operating from second and third runways fairly smoothly meantime. It's called Tokyo International Airport, Haneda, but it's all domestic traffic.'

'Except the NN plane,' Alex said. 'And China Airlines I believe, for political reasons.'

'Of course. I'm sorry. The jet was diverted from Narita.' Kanagawa jerked a thumb over his shoulder in the direction of New Tokyo International Airport and told himself it was the last time he would try to get away with a sloppy answer for Alex Bolton. 'It sometimes gets closed down by fog and once in a while the radicals lob a home-made grenade into it.'

'What's happened in the last twenty-four hours?' Alex asked. Tabata twisted and counted off the events on his fingers.

'The four bodies have been recovered and identified. The cockpit voice recorder and the flight data recorder have been found and will be analysed by the experts.' He was pleased to be helpful and added, 'The tower's last words with the pilot have been reported in the press and on television.'

'And?' Alex snapped.

'In spite of the conditions, the descent's described as normal. No indication from the crew of a problem. The captain apparently took control shortly before it crashed because the wind strength was outside the co-pilot's operating limit.'

'Was it a bomb?'

Tabata's face hardened. 'My president firmly believes the aircraft malfunctioned,' he declared awkwardly. He'd learned enough in the last day about NN Air's insurance to know that a separate war cover policy was in place; Bolton represented the insurers who had covered the hull, third-party and passenger liability. It hadn't been easy for him to understand the detail in the policy but he had had all night to crack it.

His terse, tired monotone irritated Alex, but the nuance was clear. Alex said, 'I'm sure there's nothing to prevent a full payout on your company's claim.' Tabata's shoulders relaxed. Alex massaged the lids over sore eyes, reminding himself in the time it took that the aircraft had been contracted on a straight lease basis only. A lease-purchase agreement would have given NN Air a share of the indemnity based on the payments they had made to date. 'Of course this is just the beginning,' Alex said. 'The important thing is to get funds to the owners in Miami. They're still going to demand their monthly rent, whether the plane's in one piece or a million, until a proper settlement's made. Then we'll start looking for the cause of the accident and if we find there's been negligence in maintaining the aircraft or training the pilots the insurers will come down on you just as hard as if the fault was the manufacturer's.' Yoshi Kanagawa grimaced.

On a bridge, high above a broad river emptying into Tokyo Bay, Alex allowed himself a break, resting his head against the back of the seat. Metropolitan Tokyo unfolded in an endless spread of greyness in front and off to the right. Yoshi followed his eyes. 'A hundred and twenty-five million people in Japan,' he said. 'Most of us are packed between here and Osaka, five hundred kilometers away. Sixty per cent of the population on three per cent of the land and Japan's not much larger than Great Britain. The big difference is we're basically one long mountainous earthquake fault.'

Alex responded with a wide-eyed smile, grateful for the information. He realised he knew next to nothing about the country with the world's most dynamic economy and it irritated him. Once the Virgin jet had crossed the Japan Sea from Russia it had flown over range upon range of mountains, snow still covering the sheltered ridges of the scarred peaks that pierced the thin cloud cover. He had wondered where the people lived and now he knew.

They left the motorway shortly after the bridge dipped and eased into a lane of slow-moving traffic on a bay-side road that rose over canals and twisted between warehouses and clusters of plain, square office high-rises. They slowed at the approach to a toll booth. Beyond it the spans of an enormous bridge disappeared into the mist on the bay. 'The Rainbow Bridge,' Yoshi said. 'It saves us going through central Tokyo and puts us to the south of the city, not far from Haneda airport.' They circled the exit ramps on the west side of the bay and joined an elevated expressway signed for Haneda Airport and Yokohama. Yoshi pointed to an island of painted factory chimneys and wharf-side warehouses across the canal that ran beside the road. 'Manmade,' he said proudly. 'Like the New Kansai Airport in Osaka.' A distant twin-engined jet banked in the haze after take-off from an unseen runway.

Alex addressed the two Japanese. 'Am I cleared to enter the site?'

Tabata sucked in air, a noisy gesture which Alex was to learn often came with a pained expression and crooking of the head. It meant the speaker was embarrassed at the

26

possibility of failure and inhibited by custom from actually saying so. 'Perhaps not a problem,' Tabata said enigmatically, producing a badge which Yoshi helped Alex clip to his jacket pocket.

Traffic backed up along the sliproad to the terminals, a mix of genuine travellers struggling through the snares and delays and real rubberneckers with snack boxes and long-range lenses for their cameras. Police were everywhere, some of them in full riot gear, sweating in heavy helmets, the visors hinged upwards, their solid Perspex shields and long batons propped against their legs. They passed the first checkpoint with a minimum of fuss and pulled over to let a pair of ambulances, their sirens silenced, pass though the barrier. The black saloon cut between two All Nippon Airways hangars onto an access road lined with emergency vehicles in varying states of readiness. Checked again, they drew up to a high mesh fence between the outer buildings. Through it was an airfield panorama, with its clusters of hangars, terminals and sleek, multicoloured aircraft. A small village of open-sided tents teeming with officials blocked a view of the sea. The gateway was the last hurdle before the site of the impact. The massed ranks of the voracious Japanese media congregated around it, some of them having been allowed through to a briefing area closer to the site. A link of uniformed security guards along a cordon of blue and white ribbon strips kept them away from the nerve centre and the wreckage itself. Apprised of the implications of US civil aviation registration, they had been told to expect crash investigators from the Federal Aviation Administration and the National Transportation Safety Board as well as representatives from the aircraft and engine makers. Television cameras swivelled when Alex appeared and the mass stirred as one. He shunned them with practised politeness, acknowledging their presence only with a cool smile. The only way to avoid a misinterpreted quote that might affect the claim was to clam up completely. A couple of confident journalists threw questions at him in English and when his vision snagged on a flash of crimson from a hat he thought was making for him he ducked behind the opened boot of the NNC car. Draping his cameras over a shoulder and checking his dictation machine and notebooks, he followed the others in the pocket of the wedge they ploughed through the crowd.

'Let me speak,' Tabata said to Yoshi in Japanese, straightening his ID badge as he approached a short man in a dark blue fatigue uniform topped with an old military-type cap with chin strap.

'Ministry of Transport, Civil Aviation Department, Accident Investigation Department,' Yoshi said quietly to Alex as Tabata negotiated their entry.

Alex looked beyond the official, past the open mouth of a hangar to the outdoor command centre. He saw that the tents were erected on safe ground close to the nearest wreckage. They were really simple canvas awnings stretched between poles to protect the investigators and the papers they were accumulating on trestle tables. Through a gap he saw the rippled water of the bay, flaring under a cloudless May sky. Landing-light patterns sparkled on the two distant runways now taking all the airport traffic. But the forecast Yoshi had translated from the car radio had predicted a deterioration, with rain over the Kanto Plain by early evening, dragged in by the tail of the hurricane-level gusts that had buffeted NINA 328's final approach. Short-lived squalls stirred fresh kerosene exhaust and the lingering acrid traces from the charred and scattered wreckage.

He shaded his eyes and scanned the horizon. In five or six hours the site would lose its integrity, Alex realised. He clucked irritably. The ministry investigators expected at least three delegations of foreign investigators, and procedures to deal with them had been established; but the lone *gaijin* with no affiliation to official regulatory bodies was a problem, until Tabata urged the unhelpful official to consult the president of Nippon Nagasaki Corporation, who was somewhere on the site. A security guard turned and tapped into a mobile telephone and it was five minutes before he let them through. Reaching the command tents, Tabata acknowledged weary nods from NN Air staff as he indicated with a chopping motion the officials with an interest in the crash of a commercial aircraft: the Tokyo Metropolitan Police; a swarming delegation from various sections of the Ministry of Transport, principally the Aircraft Accident Investigation Committee; a sombre team from the Japan Airline Pilots Association and others representing engineers, the medical and fire services and the airport authorities. Salvage operations leaders, cordless phones and walkie-talkies pegged to their ears, came and went with the latest situation from the site of the crash. Taking in the broad view as his eyes followed Tabata's arm Alex thought he saw another flash of colour outside the makeshift encampment, beyond the dull and dark uniforms and suits. And was that a woman's voice, protesting above the subdued, reverent drone of the mostly male assembly?

Turning towards the sea, and the spread of the airfield, he saw the heads and caps of the emergency crews and the helmets of silver-suited firemen among the scattered blackened shapes. The tail of NINA 328 stood alone, weirdly upright, as still and lifeless as a statue as if frozen in time by the flame-retardant foam, two blistered green-painted gigantic letter Ns identifying the airline operator. He made towards it, for the open air.

'Please meet my president,' Tabata said desperately, motioning to a square of trestled tables and a stocky, flat-faced man in shirt-sleeves, staff bundled at his shoulders.

'Later, Tabata san,' Alex said. 'I want to see the wreckage before it rains.' He unslung the camcorder and left the cover of the temporary shelter. A light-duty crane rolled into view. 'And before they move it.' Tabata peeled away to report to Hiroshi Miyamoto, fielding questions about the tall foreigner as he threaded between the tables.

Yoshi and Alex followed a cordoned path making a jagged route between pieces of debris, bits of which were marked with numbered flags. Figures stooped and walked among the wreckage, clipboards and cameras ready. It was all too familiar to Alex: the heady smell of kerosene, unignited and soaked into the grass bordering the runway and airport threshold, and the acrid hangover from burned and seared aluminium. He swept the scene with the video camera, zooming in at times and then commenting into his dictating machine. His eyes followed the course of the doomed aeroplane's approach and estimated the point where its normal descent erupted into a few seconds of living, plunging hell. It was clear from the disposition of the wreckage, he told the machine, that it did not made a smooth dive into the terrain. If it had, the front section of the aeroplane with the cockpit might have snapped on impact, leaving it reasonably intact, the crew dead, badly mutilated, but still in a viable condition for autopsy. The shell of an engine, blackened, torn apart, lay close to an earth-coloured mound, which was the tip of the nose-cone. It was the largest single piece of wreckage from the front of the craft, which Alex calculated had been blown apart as an engine smashed it and kerosene from the wing tanks exploded over it. The old DC-8 had cartwheeled, Alex concluded, concurring tacitly with the report Yoshi had given him in the car. A wing tip had struck the ground first, the rest of the port structure collapsing under it and exploding, destroying the cockpit, the crew and their logbooks with all the vital information Alex needed to evaluate their qualifications and flying history and the maintenance status of the aircraft.

'It's going to be a tough one,' he said to Yoshi, clicking off and wiping sweat from his forehead with the back of his hand as he skirted another piece of unrecognisable wreckage. He stopped near a skeletal section of the fuselage. 'What are these, Yoshi? he said, puzzled, pointing at an expanse of ground spread with scorched, flattened strips of leather. 'Belts?' Yoshi closed in on the nearest, then remembered.

'Eels,' he said, sniffing the air.

'Eels?'

Yoshi allowed himself a half smile amid the devastation. 'They're in the cargo manifest. Live eels from Taiwan. We grill and eat them by the ton but have to import most of them. The NN Air flight was bringing in a shipment, among other things.'

'I hope you like them well cooked,' Alex said, skirting the mess. He didn't smile. 'Which reminds me. Get me a copy of the cargo manifest as soon as you can.' Yoshi made a note. Officials with clipboards looked up uncertainly at the foreign intruder who stooped, knelt, sniffed and juggled his still and motion cameras between short bursts of businesslike talk into a dictation machine. They skirted a section of fuselage, a black, yawning hole, its torn edges still dripping, like the carcass of an eviscerated whale.

'The crew died instantly,' Yoshi commented grimly when they stopped again.

Alex measured a distance upwards with his gaze. 'Absolutely unsurvivable,' he murmured. 'It wasn't particularly high but it came down at a very sharp angle, one of the wings hitting first. The explosion destroyed the cockpit. The wreckage is not spread that wide.' He dropped to one knee to take still, close-up pictures of a chunk of debris, when a shadow intruded across the image projected through the lens. Without detaching his eye from the camera, he flapped at the unseen body with his free hand. 'Step back a bit Yoshi,' he asked. 'You're in the way.' The shadow moved and Alex snapped his pictures. When he stood he was trapped in a semicircle of men, at least ten of them. Yoshi was on the edge of the group. Alex recognized Tabata and the man about to light a cigarette. 'Put that bloody thing out!' he ordered the president of Nippon Nagasaki Corporation. The others did not have to speak English to understand the foreigner. Tabata almost fainted at the insult to his supreme commander and was shaking when he stepped forward.

'President Miyamoto,' he stammered. 'This is Mister Bolton of British Underwriters International, Aviation Division.' Miyamoto's hand was firm, his face a blank, cold mask.

Alex tried conciliation, without apology. 'I didn't mean to shout,' he said, swiping at a patch of dampness on his trousers where he had knelt on the grass. 'There's kerosene everywhere. It's not evaporated yet.' Miyamoto's smile started from a shallow nod and it emerged slowly, reluctantly.

'Of course,' he said finally. 'I should have realised.' He turned Alex with a touch to an elbow until they faced a distant terminal. 'I thank you for coming here so promptly. This is the worst tragedy to face my company since my father created it more than sixty years ago.' They were walking steadily away from the NNC contingent. Yoshi had said when they were alone that Hiroshi Miyamoto was sixty-two but his skin was smooth, unblemished, his eyes alert in spite of the tension and twenty-fours hours without much rest. His hair was naturally black and thick, expensively trimmed, like the cut of his unorthodox, lightly chequered British-made suit. Alex thought he looked closer to forty. He had taken complete control of the Nippon Nagasaki empire in 1961 when he was twenty-seven, Yoshi had explained with unrestrained admiration. 'I was expecting this, you know,' Miyamoto said, turning and spreading his arms in frustration. 'These old planes.'

Over Miyamoto's shoulder, Alex picked out high layers of dark-bellied clouds out to sea, stacking to the south. On the ground a group of investigators had gathered round the corpse of an engine. It was forty metres from its wing mount, the blades twisted agonisingly. The wing was a tangle of mangled struts and torn blackened aluminium shards; two meters of the tip was sheared off and embedded in the earth bizarrely like the fin of an upturned shark. Alex made for the engine with Miyamoto and his staff trailing him. 'We won't know the cause until we've looked at every aspect,' he declared. 'The health of the crew and the condition of the plane and, of course, the instructions coming from the tower. The weather could have been a factor as well. I understand it was extremely windy at the time.' He turned to the imposing chief executive and cast a thumb at the makeshift headquarters of the investigators. 'They're going to come after the crew records, medical histories, maintenance logs and anything else in your files. It might be helpful to your claim if I saw them first.' He suddenly felt tired. 'As soon as possible.'

Whether from shock, exhaustion or mild dissipation, President Kaneko of NN Air slumbered soundly, his chin resting low on his chest, his body engulfed by the bulging, soft arms of a deep, mock-leather chair. He was an implant from the mother company, Nippon Nagasaki Corporation, where thirty-five years of loyalty had been rewarded with an unwanted and face-losing appointment to run six old aeroplanes which carried eels and bananas and were flown by malajusted white *gaijin* pilots and nasty Asians. 'President' looked good on his business card until the recipient noticed the 'Air' after 'Nippon Nagasaki', denoting the holder's status as a minor subsidiary company head in a prestigious conglomerate. His corporate chop, the tiny orange-ink seal of authority, was always affixed below a space for the supreme group president of Nippon Nagasaki Corporation, Hiroshi Miyamoto.

Men in groups of two or three stood with drinks and cigarettes, chatting earnestly. Others sat around the boardroom table, nibbling from plates of *sushi* delivered by waiters in white coats and stiff collars. Two Japanese underwriters brought into the NN Air insurance syndicate by Yoshi Kanagawa cornered their broker, probing for an insight into the progress of the *gaijin* investigator's deliberations. Pilots not on flying duty and engineers chattered to the functionaries Hiroshi Miyamoto had called to his executive suite at the end of day since the crash of NINA 328. It's for morale and therapeutic purposes, he had claimed when he had summoned them. Let's talk and drink together and share the pain of the disaster.

Seeing Bolton near him, he drew the only woman in the room towards him, introducing her as Yuriko Shimada, whose business card on its English side placed her in the president's office without formal title. Taller than her president, she wore a moderately sombre, thinly chalked business suit, a white silk blouse tucked into the short flared skirt. A cluster of bruised grey pearls hung from a silver chain between the opened buttons of the blouse. She rose on Ferragamo heels, with glossy hair parted neatly in the middle and drawn behind the ears of her slender, finely boned face. Her dark eyes were clear and intense, her full lips brushed in pale pink. Yuriko's English was fluent, Miyamoto explained in his own thick stacatto delivery, and, to her clear embarrassment, added with a smirk that her main role was to keep tiresome *gaijin* bankers and other visitors out of his hair. Not that Alex was unwelcome, Miyamoto quickly added, recovering the situation and grasping the visitor's shoulders, remembering that a short message from the Englishman could lift the dreadful cloud and trigger the release of twenty million dollars for the Florida owners of his downed aeroplane. Or it could withhold it. If there was any lingering resentment over Alex's rough reprimand about the cigarette, Hiroshi Miyamoto was putting expediency ahead of it. Yuriko would be the group president's mouthpiece, introducing Alex to key personnel from NN Air and the parent company and the anxious leaders of the Japanese underwriting syndicate he had summoned to meet the man from London whose word was the law. She would ensure he had access to all relevant documents and records and press for a meeting with the official Japanese investigators from the Ministry of Transport.

Alex sipped warily on a third Scotch, a second wind having cleared his head, but he knew his body would crack up before he finished it. He heard the involuntary slur in his voice and the faces of the Japanese he was meeting were slipping quietly from his memory.

He had stayed at the crash scene for five hours until the winds freshened ahead of darkening skies and the rescue teams began to drag tarpaulin covers over strategic pieces of wreckage and equipment. Stiffened with sweat and grime, his clothes were scuffing uncomfortably against his skin when he left with Yoshi Kanagawa in the same NNC's Toyota Celsior and in receipt of an invitation from its president to an informal evening gathering of *kankeisha,* – people involved in the matter, Yoshi translated. Thick wet mist quickly cocooned the car as it slowed behind a clutch of taxis on the entrance ramp to the Grand Kanto Hotel. Stooping against the damp, Yoshi slipped from the rear seat and into a cab for a brief separation from the Englishman. At the reception desk Alex was greeted with bows and a neatly folded batch of faxes. The lack of security at this stage was troublesome but inevitable. At least there were no journalists prowling the carpeted corridors.

The room was spacious, the bed low and huge, and the curtains slipped apart easily to reveal through rain-marbled windows the silhouettes of trees in a darkened park beyond the perimeter wall. Further out the multicoloured neons packing the Shimbashi entertainment district flared invitingly through the mist. He checked the door locks, found no suspicious attachments on either room or bathroom telephone and was pleased to note that the compact safe in the closet was opened by combination and not key, although of course it was arguably portable. He read the messages while the bath filled. Emma Healey had been busy with her runner check and the Federal Aviation Administration's Oklahoma registry office efficient and helpful in providing the profiles he needed from their records.

The wrecked aeroplane, call sign NINA 328, had been manufactured by McDonnell Douglas in 1969 and had by strange coincidence started its career where it had ended with such violent finality, flying in and out of Haneda as part of Japan Airlines' growing fleet of modern aircraft. It had carried the sign of the crane on its tail until 1981 when it began a South American odyssey. Bought by Aerovias Condor de Ecuador, it subsequently changed hands four times by sale or lease until it was sold to South Miami Aviation after a final year with Aerolineas Transandias de Chile. The Florida-based company, owners of aeroplanes for worldwide lease, converted the ageing aircraft to cargo usage, stripping out its seats and fuselage windows, upgrading the air-frame and installing state-of-the-art electronic and navigation systems. Repowered with four CFM-56 engines and now registered with US certifications, the transformed aircraft flew the emerging routes of Africa, under lease to airlines in Zambia and Kenya, and finally, after four months sitting idly in the dry, protective air of a Mojave Desert aircraft parking lot, it was packaged by South Miami Aviation and leased with two other converted DC-8s and three early-series 747s to Nippon Nagasaki Air of Japan.

The luxury of a hot bath revived him and when he had shaved and rubbed life into his scalp he sat in his underpants and set up his laptop computer for his first communication with London.

It was premature to make a firm statement on the cause of

the crash and it would be improper and dangerous to try. He was at the picture-making stage, picking up the pieces of a scattered mosaic and shuffling them around until they came together. Everyone he had met so far had made a speculative stab at the cause but it was too early for an official statement. He searched carefully for the right words, addressing his message to Reggie Cameron with instructions for it to be transmitted immediately to the broker Brian Levine – who, he knew, at 10 a.m. British time would be sitting within sight of a facsimile machine – and the company's principal lawyer Jeremy Skipton. Confirming the date and time of the crash, he described how the old jet appeared to make a normal approach in very strong winds, under the control of the captain, and suddenly plunged, not stalled, a wing impacting with the ground, consuming, as the fuel in it exploded, the cockpit, the crew and the logbook records. The bodies in the cockpit would be so badly mutilated that he expected the Japanese to call on the specialist skills of a recognised American expert. Was it wind shear, the sudden downdrafts and volatile surface winds so feared by pilots? The aerodrome charts for Haneda which Alex had brought with him certainly warned of that particular danger, but so far there had been no mention of it from official sources as reported in the stack of press releases and newspaper cuttings Yoshi Kanagawa had given him.

Copying from the day's notes he tapped out the names of the American pilot, Edward Kidderby, the first officer and the engineer, both Japanese, and the Taiwanese load-master. There were no fatalities on the ground and collateral damage was relatively minimal: obviously the runway and its approaches, and also a flattened observation hut, hangars sprayed with flying debris and a bus and an empty fuel tanker totally destroyed. It could have been worse, much worse, Alex didn't write, reminded of Lockerbie and carbonised bodies among grotesquely distorted pieces of aeroplane. He was thinking of the lawyer when he wrote that environmental damage was not yet quantifiable but there might be a problem with damage to the soil and possibly the underground watercourses from seeping aviation fuel.

He had heard from Tabata, the NNC aide, that the cockpit voice recorder had been transcribed and would be analysed formally tomorrow, Thursday, by civil aviation experts at the Ministry of Transport after the American experts had finished at the site. Alex would not be there. Under the convention of the International Civil Aviation Organization, specifically Annex 13, the state where the accident occurs shall carry out the investigation while giving access to approved authorities from the country of registration and the manufacturers of the airframe and engines. Tabata understood that the FAA was sending two people and the National Transportation Safety Board six. The airframe makers, McDonnell Douglas, were sending one specialist, as were the engine makers' US partners, General Electric. They had already arrived in Japan or were in the sky, closing on the Japanese islands. The insurance sector was not considered pertinent to the search for the cause, more of a nuisance in fact; and, as he expected, Alex had not been invited to contribute to the discussion on the cockpit voice recorder. There was no sign yet of anyone from the Florida owners, he told London.

Once the official investigation was completed – a process that might take a year or more if the cause of the crash was elusive and they decided to put the aeroplane together piece by piece – the wreckage, parts and all, belonged to the insurers Alex represented. He told his London audience, Cameron and his surveyors, the brokers and the lawyers, that his first impression classified the aircraft as a write-off, with only a small, unspecified number of parts that might be salvaged and reused safely. He made a qualified stab at the wreck's scrap value. He ended by praising NN Air for gaining him access to the crash site and hoped their cooperative attitude would continue when he attempted to reconstruct the lost logbooks from the internal records of the operator and studied the current and historical maintenance and medical records.

A private fax could not be supplied to his room – the hotel staff had apologised – so he stood by the machine in the business centre as his long message was transmitted.

With Yuriko Shimada at his shoulder, close enough for him to pick up a faint, misty flowery scent, Alex had been speaking to NN Air's chief Japanese pilot and ranking engineer. He looked hopefully for the surviving foreign pilots, the four Americans and two Australians, but they were all on operational duty around Asia. The deal with South Miami Aviation provided six hulls as part of the 'dry lease' package. The aircrew had been hired separately by NN Air. The Japanese captain had a scratchy command of English. He was probably tired and stressed but he made Alex wonder how he coped on a busy night in a storm over Hong Kong. Asking Miyamoto's aide to prepare him an office for the next day and secure the cooperation of the staff when he requested all manner of records, he excused himself, skirting the chunks of rice and suspicious slivers of colourful raw fish and shellfish, unable to summon the skills of hand and concentration to raise the delicate morsels, dip them in soya sauce and lift them on short sticks without collapsing the rice. He picked up a canapé of cold roast beef and nibbled at it as he drifted with his diluted drink into a corridor lined with elaborately framed photographs. A corporate hall of fame, he supposed.

'You must be tired, Mr Bolton,' Yuriko said gently. She had followed him like an imperial wife, a few steps behind.

'You're right,' he breathed, stopping in front of a black and white print. He squeezed his temples while his eyes were drawn to the blurry image of two men in three-piece suits posing with self-conscious pride beside a ship's propellor the height of the taller, a slight Caucasian with a thick moustache which obscured his upper lip and curled upwards at the tips. The plaque inscription on the frame identified them in English script as R. Jonsson and S. Miyamoto, the place Nagasaki, the date, 8 November 1934. He brought his face close to the old photograph.

'Our founder,' Yuriko said over Alex's shoulder.

He turned, puzzled. The name on the plaque triggered a recollection of a recent piece of extraneous detail. It was the person's name inscribed in the Japanese writing on the old document attached to the wartime diaries. He gestured at the photograph. 'You mean that foreigner set up Nippon Nagasaki?'

She smiled indulgently. 'No, no. The Japanese gentleman, Mr Shinichi Miyamoto, the father of our current president.'

Alex looked at the cloudy portrait again, closely, with tired eyes. He saw the resemblance in the large squarish head, the broad shoulders and short legs. 'Who's the *gaijin*?'

The vulgar word for foreigner did not please her, and she answered coldly. 'He was Swedish, an engineer who helped Mr Miyamoto develop new marine technology when he began his business.'

He must have made a remarkable contribution, Alex thought as they moved on, to get his picture in the NNC honours gallery and his name remembered in an important-looking document issued by Alex's own Japanese company of the day. But he didn't want a complicated distraction, particularly in the first days of the 'hot' phase of the crash investigation. The old piece of paper and the diaries of the late prisoner-of-war had not left his briefcase, let alone the folder they came in. But something snagged his curiosity. 'I might have something for your records,' he told Yuriko. 'Let me show you.' They passed through the boardroom, where the gathering was breaking up. The president of NN Air had been roused and was nodding languidly as his supreme chief, Hiroshi

Miyamoto, addressed a morose circle of airline staff. 'It's an old legal document of some sort,' Alex said on the move. 'Issued by a company we used to have in Japan. It's mostly in Japanese and I don't have a translation, but it does mention a certain Roland Jonsson and a Miyamoto in English writing.'

In a small reception room where the visitors had left their cases Alex unlocked his, delving into a pocket and extracting the diaries and their fragile front sheet. He guided Yuriko's eyes to the English writing. She smiled thinly and took the pages from him, turning her back as she moved them into the best light. Alex yawned, unaware of the short-lived change of expresssion on her face and relieved to see Yoshi Kanagawa at the door. Collapsing the short antenna on his mobile telephone the Japanese broker declared, 'I'm off. Why don't you get some rest too? It's going to be a long day tomorrow. The same NNC driver will take you to your hotel and pick you up at seven thirty. I'll be in the lobby. Is that too early?'

'That's perfect,' Alex said.

'Good. They're going to start clearing the wreckage around noon tomorrow. The McDonnell guy's working down there now, under floodlights. The FAA and the transportation safety people are on the way to Haneda at this moment.'

Alex turned sluggishly towards the Japanese woman who seemed absorbed behind the wad of papers. 'Interesting, aren't they? The odd mixture of English and Japanese in the letter. And the old diary.' He held out a hand.

She was reluctant to return them. 'Very much. I'm sure my president will be delighted.' She finally released them.

'What happened to the Swede, Jonsson?' he asked casually, securing his chart case. 'He's not still alive is he?'

Her eyes jumped in surprise. 'Oh no. And I think it's pronounced "yonson." Mr Jonsson was sadly killed in the atomic bomb explosion at Nagasaki.'

Leaving the room, Alex did a brief round of farewells, shadowed by Miyamoto's personal assistant. 'I'll show you

41

to the garage,' Yuriko said without hesitation. 'I understand there are a number of journalists outside the main entrance. Your car will leave from the basement level into the street at the back of the building and avoid them.' She was silent as they waited for the executive floor lift, a glass-panelled capsule with an open view as it dropped to the marble floor of the atrium. When the doors closed she said, 'I'm sure Mr Miyamoto would be most interested in the document you have taken the trouble to bring to Japan.' She glanced optimistically at Alex's broad briefcase standing between them. 'Would you kindly allow me to study it again?'

'Sure. No problem.' It would have been simple to stoop down and open the case, retrieve the slim folder and fulfil an obligation, thus ridding himself in an instant of a minor irritation, and return to a more pressing agenda. He didn't, remembering that the timid archivist had asked him to show it at their company's Tokyo office. It was time he called BUI's Far East man, Richard Ingleby, anyway. 'I'll let my people here see it first, if you don't mind. Then we can get together again and have a closer look at it.' They were side by side: she had not missed his choice of words and smiled inwardly at some implication or other.

'Somebody's working later than us,' Alex said amiably as they passed a floor where they could see people working deep inside fully lit open-plan offices.

Yuriko looked out. 'NN Air's offices. They have part of the third floor of our building. I'm afraid there's much for them to do.' They reached the ground floor. 'We have to change to a service elevator here or take the steps to the garage.' They crossed the buffed marble, passing the deserted reception desk, their eyes catching a clutch of uniformed security guards milling near the main doors. A pair of disembodied faces pressing forward as they peered inside made grotesque masks against the rain-beaded glass. Perhaps it was fatigue, or a play of light where the fierce illumination

42

in the building met the deep black of the night, but Alex thought he caught that same flash of colour he had seen in the pack of journalists at Haneda airport.

The garage two floors below was lined with lagged piping and split into bays, the atmosphere heavy with stale exhaust fumes. Yuriko spoke to the company driver, occasionally gesturing with her head at the important visitor slumped gratefully in the back of the Toyota. 'Until tomorrow then,' she said finally to Alex, extending a hand. 'Please rest well.'

There was a car ahead of them and they followed it up to the final ramp where an automatic arm barred the exit. It crawled forward while the driver fumbled for a pass card. Leaving the gate and an unmanned booth, the Toyota slowed again as the car in front eased into the road. Alex's eyelids were heavy and when he perceived a thumping noise on a window it registered as part of the hallucinatory prelude to sleep. Then a man's voice roused him. It was the driver who, in the same outburst, was urging the car ahead to clear the way while aiming words and hand gestures at a figure splayed against his car, outside the passenger door on Bolton's side. A bright, red baseball cap on a grimacing, excited face moved with the car's momentum. When Alex found the electric switch, an instinctive reaction, and the window slid down into the door he was nose to nose with a woman, her face shadowed out by the peak of the cap, her eyes obscured by streaks of rainwater on the lenses of her wide, rimless eyeglasses. Straps on denim dungarees flapped loose on her shoulders as she stooped. 'You're the guy from London, right? Working on the Haneda crash.' The voice was deep, demanding, thoroughly American, but the piece of face not masked by the oversized headgear was angular, olive textured, thoroughly Oriental. 'I've got to talk to you.'

So much for the flash of crimson, he thought, looking disdainfully at the cap. A journalist, a mobile one. The car ahead had gone, and Alex's driver was following instructions

43

not to stop for anyone, edging towards the road while trying not to hurt the woman pegged to the side. Her forearm was actually lying on the sill, the hand inside, covering the window control. Alex clawed it away. 'No comment to make,' he spluttered, aiming a firm but controlled push at the face in the window gap. The car had angled into the road, the window was rising.

'We've got to talk,' the woman was insisting. A small card tumbled into the car. She broke away from the car, stumbling into a sideways trot and calling after it. Alex looked straight ahead. 'The pilot of the plane was—'

The window clamped shut, drowning her last words. 'What?' Alex swore and stabbed at the pannel of buttons which controlled the light, window and seat angle, but the car had picked up speed and the woman was shrinking in the driver's mirror. Alex twisted in his seat. The car was slowing again before the corner to a wider road. The NNC chauffeur was satisfied with the result and said something in Japanese to his passenger as he reached for the car telephone.

'Bloody reporters,' Alex returned, which seemed to match the driver's sentiments. He was drunk with exhaustion, but something had stung him and he raised the card that had fallen into his lap and searched hopelessly for the rear passenger light. He gave up, regretting the impulsive reaction that had clipped off the woman's words, and when he turned and peered through the demisted window the figure in the red baseball cap was a distant dwarf waving forlornly into the rain. Two figures were closing in on her and as the car turned into the main road there was a sharp stab of light from a dark recess of the doorway.

Tabata entered with a series of jabbing bows and apologetic hisses, a stack of paper clutched to his chest. The president of NNC was in deep and close conversation with his female personal assistant and ignored his aide's arrival.

'Is this all?' Miyamoto said finally, tapping the soft, beige folder and then flipping through the contents indifferently. He fixed Tabata with an intense glare. Yuriko Shimada slipped quietly over to the window. They had moved to his rosewood-panelled office when the cleaners and waiters had fallen on the ashtrays and scattered plates and glasses in the boardroom. Yuriko was distracted, as if she was mesmerised by brake lights flashing in parallel lanes on traffic slowing for the Kudan-shita bend of the Imperial Palace's outer moat. She turned, hearing Tabata suck in air noisily, a self-effacing sign, full of uncertainty and ragged nerves. He avoided the president's eyes. 'They are the preliminary submissions we are making to the FAA. Copies will be sent to South Miami Aviation, the Japanese Ministry of Transport, the Civil Aviation Authority.' He reached into his memory through his own fatigue. 'And the other agencies as required.'

It was five minutes to midnight when Miyamoto dismissed Tabata, waiting until he reached the door before turning him with a cold, unequivocal decree. 'Make sure the *gaijin* from London sees only what is appropriate for him to make a positive decision. Nothing more.'

Yuriko was standing close to the president's broad, polished desk, a Gucci handbag over a shoulder, rummaging among the contents of a slender, brown leather briefcase. Miyamoto had been pacing the room, thinking aloud. She sensed him approach, then behind her, and shuddered as his grip on the hem of her skirt tightened, his knuckles bruising into her thighs as he jerked the taut fabric up to her waist. His hands smoothed over her legs, spread them and rose to fill her crotch. His breathing was rapid, hot on her neck, and his heartbeat thumped against her back. 'And your role, lovely Yuriko,' he uttered through clenched teeth, 'is to keep the *gaijin* happy until he leaves Japan. And until he gives you that stupid bit of old paper.' His short, stubby fingers were probing, hurting her. 'I'm sure you know how.'

3 March, 1942

We spent yesterday on Japanese destroyer. Got three biscuits each and some water to last all day. At midnight we transferred to the Dutch hospital ship Op Ten Noort *which was captured off Surabaya. Slept on old canvas on deck but it rained all night. Today Jim and I found we had slept outside Bosun's cabin. It was empty so we helped ourselves to 50 Capstan cigarettes and some soap. I found a small notebook and a pencil and was able to start a diary. At 0830 hrs a Jap destroyer came alongside and delivered more survivors from* Exeter, *including Captain Gordon. They had been in the water for twenty-seven hours. I'm glad for the Captain because his order to abandon ship saved most of the crew. We had no water until 1500 hrs when a minesweeper came alongside and filled our ship's tanks. They also brought the day's food: one rice ball each and a tin of meat between ten men. The rice was brown and dirty. At night we got a biscuit.*

8 March

Been a POW for a week. I wonder if Kath knows. I

hope she does and does not give up the house. She always said she would if anything happened to me. We hear we are heading for Makassar in the Celebes, a Dutch island. Japs would not let us hold Sunday Service and Andy got slapped for answering back. Anyhow, CPO Ted Newman said a few words and led us in singing 'Holy Father in thy mercy hear our anxious prayer. Keep our loved ones now far distant 'neath thy care.' Felt homesick for the first time. Food as always: coffee and biscuit for breakfast, rice and a little meat for dinner, coffee and biscuit for supper. It rained for nearly an hour today and I managed to have my first bath for a week.

10 March

Berthed alongside Makassar dock at 1400 hrs without eating. Stood in sun for an hour with no shoes and few clothes while Japs counted us. They shouted at us in Japanese and when we could not understand they set about us with rifle butts or fists. The Dutch have destroyed the warehouses and there's rubbish and glass everywhere. The town's covered with Jap flags and the natives bow to the soldiers. It took an hour to march to the camp and we saw decomposed bodies in the ditches. The camp's an old Dutch army barracks and we were put five to a room. I went for a walk and found a pile of clothes outside the dormitory. I managed to get three pairs of shorts, two singlets, a pink pyjama suit and a pair of socks. A change of clothes at last. At 1800 we got three biscuits to last until midday next day. I heard they got the Houston too.

15 March

A fortnight since Exeter was sunk. There must be 2,000 of us here. A lot of Dutch, then British and Americans. Yanks from the Houston among them. A lot of lads laid up with dysentery. It must thrive in the latrines, which *get blocked and overflow. The sores and things are awful. The mosquitoes play merry hell with us, then flies settle on the bites and the sore gets septic. Japs won't give us any medical supplies. Had two rice balls yesterday but couldn't get any baccy until I paid nearly three shillings for a two-ounce roll. I also borrowed 20 rupees and managed to change ten of them into Dutch money, which is still being used. The Dutch native soldiers get things passed through the fence to them and they sell for a big profit.*

18 March

Couldn't write yesterday. We had to turn out and watch the beheading of two Dutchmen who had been recaptured after escaping. A lot of lads were sick. Then we had a lecture and were told to obey the rules. An American who had thumped a guard was wrapped in barbed wire and dragged around the compound. Then he was hung from a tree and bayoneted. Got my first slap from a Jap today. I didn't see him and didn't bow in time. The captain thinks we lost 150 men on the Exeter *but some more are alive in prison in the town. We had over 700 on board. Went foraging and found enough fag ends for a smoke. We had to cut the grass with our hands as we are not allowed knives. The guards dish out stick at the smallest excuse. We got our first issue of soap and a few other things. Jeff got a towel and I got a toothbrush. We also got lavatory paper, which makes very good cig paper when cut up. I sold some clothes and bought baccy. I paid 2s 8d for a one and a half ounce roll which cost 2d outside the camp.*

The grille emitted warm, dry, recycled air and as with most modern hotels the windows were permanently sealed against the real atmosphere. Shortly after 5.30 on the morning of his second day in Tokyo Alex woke with a grunt from a stuffed nose and time-zone lag and ordered an all-frills western fry-up breakfast from room service, his appetite vigorous after a day of sandwiches on the run and the snacks at Nippon Nagasaki Corporation's head office when he was really too tired to enjoy them. The hour would also let him talk to London before bedtime on the night of the previous day. He showered quickly, shaved and, wearing the hotel's towelled gown, sat at the table in the narrow lounge of his mini-suite, his papers spread around him. Cameron was at home and he had been drinking.

'How's it going?' the technical director of the aviation division asked, as if he had been waiting for the call.

'Fairly well. Sorry to keep you up late.' Alex grinned. 'Thought I'd check in.'

There was a pause. 'Didn't you get today's fax?' Cameron said.

Alex glanced at the bedside table, at the sheaf of papers propped against a lamp. 'I suppose I passed out last night. It was a bloody long day. I went straight to the site from Narita. I got Emma's runner on the plane before the working session last night with Nippon Nagasaki.' He ran his eyes over the new message. 'Crew info. Great. Anything I should know before I get back to the case?'

Reggie Cameron's voice was thick. 'The broker saw the fax you sent me. It looks straightforward.'

'I guess it is. I'll shadow the FAA and the transportation safety board guys. They've been around since last night. I'm going for a last visit to Haneda this morning before they start clearing up later today. Apart from a few fried eels I didn't see anything particularly lethal down there.'

'Did they recover the logbooks?'

'I haven't heard, but I doubt it,' Bolton said. 'The cockpit was a write-off. And the crew I'm afraid. They're going to need one of the American specialists to make anything from

49

the autopsies. That'll take time. I hope NN Air's records are up to date and in good order. I won't get anything out of the yanks or the Japanese. I had trouble enough getting near the wreckage.'

'Keep at it,' Cameron urged. 'But read the fax we sent tonight. The senior pilots they hired were not spring chickens. The youngest was fifty-two.'

'That includes Ed Kidderby?' Alex asked, shuffling his papers. 'The captain of NINA three two eight.' When he lifted a clip of pages a business card dropped onto the glass tabletop.

'He was fifty-six,' Cameron was saying. 'Usual history. US Air Force, commercial airlines. Seems to have been at every airline that went bust. National, Eastern, Pan Am. Jobbed around South America for a while. Didn't stay anywhere long. Had three prolonged bouts in hospital. Double pneumonia, traffic accident and a viral problem of some sort. Lucky to get picked up by NN Air. They must have been in a hurry to get started.'

Alex held the card between his fingertips and twisted it over: Japanese on one side, English on the reverse. Phyl Wakai, journalist, it read simply, with an address. Phyl? The face at the car window was a woman's. An Oriental woman had shoved the card through the window and shouted something about the pilot killed at Haneda. But she *was* a journalist, and an air-crash in a major capital made for big copy, its newsworthiness driven by the dramatic magnitude of the disaster as well as an appeal, in its gruesome awfulness, to the dark, macabre side of the human psyche. Reporters gathered like sharks to feed off it, and were to be avoided. Lawyers, investigators, insurance underwriters, owners and operators wanted to know the cause of the crash and then who to blame, and not necessarily in that order, and a careless quote from Alex, the man with the key to the safe, could be used by one side or another. The woman who had waited in the rain with the others was smart to second-guess his departure tactics and tenacious enough to risk injury to get his attention. And when she had it for a few confused seconds she didn't even ask a question: she wanted to tell him something. 'I'm still here, Reggie,' he apologised. 'I'll have a really close look at Kidderby.' The red message light began to flash silently on the console by the bed. 'I'll talk to you later, tomorrow your time. I should have something by then.'

'Mr James Sanguillen of . . .' The front clerk struggled. '*Souse* Miami Aviation.' He was relieved when Alex repeated the name and said he understood.

'*Firu san, Firu san!*' the Japanese boy insisted, tugging at the hem of the sheet. He was Daisuke, aged ten, the youngest son of the Buddhist priest at the Juenji Temple in Toritsu Daigaku where Phyllis Wakai rented a weathered wooden house among the trees between the back wall of the temple cemetery and the quiet, narrow neighbourhood road. Daisuke seized any excuse to look in on the *gaijin* woman who looked like a Japanese and when he heard her telephone go unanswered as he left home for his primary school he opened the unlocked door, shook off his shoes in the entrance and picked it up. '*Moshi, moshi.*' Hearing a foreign language he said effortlessly, '*Pureese* wait,' before spreading the paper-covered sliding doors to the room where the foreign Japanese slept. '*Denwa da yo!*' he told the lump under the futon loudly. '*Gaijin san desu.* Bye, bye.' He gathered her red baseball cap and tossed it onto the mattress as he left.

The morning light seemed to perplex her, making her dizzy. She crawled to the corridor and juggled the handset 'Do you know the fucking time in Tokyo?' she said thickly. She heard a hiss of interference. 'It might be five in the fucking afternoon in New York but here it's . . .' She looked around desolately for help, which remained elusive. 'Here in

Tokyo it's the middle of the fucking night!' She was slumped against the wall. 'Look,' she said mellowing. 'I'll have the story by Thursday. Fax it to you for the weekend.'

Alex was sitting with Yoshi Kanagawa in the back of NNC Toyota Celsior, creeping in heavy traffic towards Haneda Airport on an elevated road which twisted claustrophobically at rooftop level, stacking precariously where different routes crossed. A firm swing of his arm would have carried the cellular phone Yoshi had lent him into the office windows alongside the course of the road. Stalled again, Alex was amused when the broker told him they were on the Tokyo city high-speed tollroad. Ignoring the driver's offer to use the car telephone, Alex had tapped out Phyl Wakai's number on Yoshi's mobile. The tirade of vulgarity on the line popped his eyes.

'It's actually past eight and it's a beautiful morning out here. Is that Phyl, Phyl Wakai?' He knew there would be a pause while she gathered herself.

'Could be. Who is this?' The voice was rough and suspicious.

'You threw yourself at my car last night. Could have got injured.'

'Oh, you. The English guy. And what do you mean, could have? I did get injured. Those fucking fascist guards your friends at Nippon Nagasaki employ shoved me around. I guess the driver tipped them off.'

Alex glimpsed the slicked hair on the back of the driver's head, remembering the call he had made as they left the basement garage under NNCs headquarters. 'You journalists are a nuisance, but I'm sorry if you're hurt.'

'I stuck around. Wanted another look at your buddy Miyamoto but he didn't show. Too busy fucking that drop-dead-gorgeous so-called assistant, I guess.'

'Those people are not friends of mine,' Alex said, irritated. Studded with freighters, Tokyo Bay was visible beyond the warehouses and factories at Toshiba and the aeroplanes, which seemed to hang immobile in the distant haze, brought his real task back into focus. Yuriko Shimada's face flashed across his mind before he continued. 'I'm here for a particular reason and you seem to know what it is. And I'm short of time. You said you wanted to talk.'

'Easy now, Mr Bolton.' She had stood, now awake and energised, and trailed the telephone a few steps to the compact kitchen where she lit the gas under a kettle. The cotton belt had slipped loose during the night, and her ruffled *yukata* kimono hung open on her lithe body. 'Sure. I know your name. It wasn't difficult. You were the first *gaijin* they let onto the crash site. Wasn't hard to find out who you were. No wonder Miyamoto's crawling up your ass. You're the guy with the loot.'

The hat, he told himself, the flash of red among the bobbing crowns of black hair, the hyperactive Miss Something-or-other in her baseball cap trying to barge through the press pack towards him. He saw no reason to explain that the insurance money would not go to Nippon Nagasaki Air but to the actual owners of the aeroplanes, to the company of the man Alex called before the journalist. As the operator, NN Air were simply cooperating as expected. 'Just get to the point Ms Waka—'

'Phyl. Call me Phyl. Short for Phyllis. Can't stand it. Can you imagine parents calling—?'

'Phyl.' He let her hear his exasperation. 'I'm two minutes away from Haneda. That's all you've got. You wanted to talk, remember?'

'I need more time,' she said urgently.

'No can do,' Alex said flatly. He saw the sliproad to the airport ahead and caught the eyes of the driver in the rear-view mirror. 'I assume you have access to the press conferences and the official spokespeople. They're your source for everything. I have no authority or desire to talk to the news media on or off the record.'

'Oh for fuck's sake Alec. Can I call you Alec?'

'No. It's Alex.'

'I'm a journalist, Alex. Freelance. I write in the local market and string for some Stateside journals. But I'm writing a book on the side. We all are. Political corruption, how to do business here, how to get laid here, you know, the Japan-like-it-is kind of crap.'

'You've got thirty seconds,' Alex interrupted.

'I'm writing about Nippon Nagasaki, the conglomerate, warts and all. It's a great story. That's why I'm not number one popular person at the Miyamoto glass château in Marunouchi.'

'What's this got to do with the pilot? You said something about him last night.' The line crackled with interference, swamping her reply. 'What did you say Phyl?'

'I said we should meet and talk it over.'

The area in front of the crash command centre was still thick with broadcasting vehicles, their staff and equipment: mobile satellite dishes and massive cameras mounted on trolleys and trucks; and microphone booms stretched and swung in frantic competitive desperation at the approach of an official. Alex's telephone was swamped by the power of the generators and the massed electronic wizardry. He clicked off gratefully and gave the small handset to Yoshi. He had heard enough from Phyl Wakai and it wasn't his fault the line had become inoperable.

James Sanguillen did not have the look of a man who had just walked around the scattered remains of his company's twenty-million-dollar investment. He was standing on the fringe of a group of Americans and Japanese who surrounded the half-buried corpse of an engine which was stripped of its cowling, exposing twisted, blackened entrails of cables and fuel lines. Voices lifted as the roar of jet engines carried across the airfield, drowning out the interpreters who struggled with the demands of the foreign newcomers and the fatigued disposition of the Japanese side. The rain had dispersed to the north-west, leaving patchy, thin clouds and a gusty surface wind, which had cleared the haze and slapped at Sanguillen's pleated trousers as he walked towards the other foreigner who did not seem to be belong to an official party. He was around the same height and age as Bolton but his Latin features were sharp, his eyebrows ample, almost meeting. Arriving at his central Tokyo hotel from Miami after two stops and twenty hours, he had first checked there was a message for him giving the Tokyo hotel of the surveyor from British Underwriters International before sending his carefully picked clothes for pressing.

Alex gave the representative of South Miami Aviation a card and an unofficial, expert briefing on the crash of the DC-8-71 aircraft they had leased to NN Air of Japan. He talked precisely and economically, as to a manager rather than a technician. Cranes, trailers and lorries, and bands of workers and supervisors were deploying around the site as they spoke, waiting for the order to clear the debris. Sanguillen's head turned to take in these preparations as Alex indicated the disposition of each piece of the aircraft.

'So we're looking at a massive power failure somewhere along the line,' Sanguillen said, turning his head against a draught of air, dense with kerosene fumes. 'Caused a stall.'

'Unlikely,' Alex said carefully. He raised an arm to the distance. 'It came down steeply, very fast; the tip of the port wing probably hit first. The explosion's not left much to salvage. A stall would have made for a flatter impact. The plane would have broken up, obviously, but not disintegrated to the extent it did. We should get a better idea when they've decoded the flight data recorder. They've got the technology in Japan and they can work on the tapes with the people from your transport safety board. The cockpit voice recorder's being made public later today by the Ministry of Transport. I should get a transcript, or even better a copy of the recording.'

The English-language newspaper hanging on Alex's door that morning had reported triumphantly the recovery of the 'black' boxes and the imminent publication of the data. He had long stopped bothering to explain that worldwide regulations demanded that the recorders be painted in vivid colours to enable searchers to find them easily among blackened, burned wreckage. The recording boxes taken from the tail of the stricken four-engined jet at Haneda were painted in the usual fluorescent flame-orange.

'Poor guys,' the American said. His voice was flat and unmoved, and it had taken something in Alex's explanation to remind him of the fate of the crew and the loadmaster.

'Are you a pilot yourself, Mr Sanguillen?' They had reached the temporary control centre and took a pair of collapsible seats away from the general bustle under the cavernous shelters. Alex brushed off a splash of rainwater which had dripped free from a top corner connection in the canvas awning.

'No way. I'm in finance and legal. I'm here to see there'll be no complications with the claim at this point. We dry-leased, as you know. We're the loss payee in the insurance they fixed up with your guys.'

'Were you satisfied with NN Air's standards? Like maintenance, pilot hiring?'

'We've not had much trouble so far,' Sanguillen declared. 'They were late with quarterly lease payments a couple of times but nothing serious.' He threw an arrogant, self-assured smirk. 'We got them to take out a Breach of Warranty endorsement. We're covered for whatever they got up to. They're not playing rough, are they? That guy Miyamoto's a real hard ass.'

Alex saw Tabata break out of the compound of tables,

look towards him and raise the hand with the mobile telephone. Returning to Sanguillen he said, 'No, they've been very cooperative. I'm going over there this afternoon to look at the records on crew, the plane, the actual flight details, cargo, whatever. I represent the people who insured the plane so I'm obliged to look at every angle.' He thought Sanguillen's face darkened but he had turned to take the telephone from the harassed NNC man. 'Bolton.'

'Hi again. It's Phyl.'

'Why the hell are you calling me here?' Alex groaned. He threw a pleading look at the other man and stood, turning his back.

'I've just arrived. I'm outside. Do you want to come and meet me? Bring me a cup of coffee maybe. Just look for the red cap.'

'I'm going to cut you off, Phyl.'

'I bet my friends out here – gotta be around twenty, thirty of them, with their cameras and microphones – I bet they'd like to know how important Mister Alex Bolton is to this incident. The guy with the power to fuck up Miyamoto and his airline. Maybe they ought to try and get you at the Grand Kanto Hotel, room seven three six, isn't it'

'Don't be foolish,' Alex said, feeling the heat rising on the back of his neck and straining to keep his anger private. He moved to a corner, his free hand cupping his ear against the rumble of a 747's opened throttle. He said, 'I have no official responsibilities with regard to the investigation here and I don't want to see my name in the newspapers or hear it on the television. Stay close to the Japanese Ministry of Transport and the American National Transportation Safety Board. They'll tell you what caused the crash.'

'C'mon Alex. I told you this morning, I'm writing about Miyamoto and that pile of shit he calls a multinational conglomerate. The crash is just symptomatic of the mess he's in.'

'Can't help you, Phyl,' Alex said, mustering a clenched-teeth-friendly tone. 'Perhaps when I've finished up here we can—'

'I knew the pilot, Ed Kidderby,' Phyllis said tonelessly. Alex gripped the handset in two hands. 'Are you there, *gaijin san*? Have I lost you again?'

Alex spoke cautiously. A piece of bait had been cast onto the water; it was floating towards him. 'So what? He lived in Tokyo, didn't he? Would have had lots of friends.'

'Ed Kidderby was sick. Very sick. Did your friend Miyamoto tell you that?'

Yuriko Shimada made it clear to the NN Air staff on the third floor at Group head office that she, the president's personal assistant, had been assigned to ensure Bolton *san* from British Underwriters International was supplied with the data relevant to his deliberations and any request to see him should be channelled through her office. She had prepared him a small corner meeting room overlooking the brackish moat and treetopped wall of the Imperial Palace and had angled the shutters to soften the glare from a clear sky where it blinded the television, tuned in silence to NHK. The government channel had been transmitting the periodic press conferences, called to satisfy the intense public interest about the spectacular air crash at Haneda. She gave him the room key he had demanded and showed him how to activate the record function on the TV-video, offering to translate anything he taped. Folders of documents were stacked at one end of the table, beside the multi-plug electrical fixture installed to take a telephone, Bolton's laptop and a call button. She presented him to a Maruta *san*, section chief in charge of documentation and licences, who had been ordered to find and present whatever else the Englishman requested, and set out a tray of sandwiches and coffee before leaving. At the door she remembered something and turned. Hands clasped behind his head, Alex was rocking on the tubular-framed chair while his computer loaded.

'I must apologise for the unpleasant incident last night,' Yuriko declared. 'I understand you were attacked by a journalist.'

Alex shrugged. 'It was a strange way of getting my attention but I can't say she attacked me.'

She activated the red no-admittance button. 'It won't happen again, Mr Bolton. We know who she is. She has caused too much trouble to my company already.'

Yuriko left while he was still trying to interpret the nuances in her comments. Was it a failure in her English, a semantic slip? Or were the words an accurate manifestation of NNC's sentiments towards the scattily persistent journalist? He huffed once and chewed on a ballpen as he returned to his task.

The diligence of the Japanese investigators would make his work easier, smoother if not necessarily simpler, and eventually the cause of the crash of NINA 328 would emerge. Of course, the wreckage was within the airport perimeter, making it easier to protect than in the jungle or on an exposed mountainside, and he knew he would not arrive to find it ravaged and pillaged by predators or disturbed prematurely by ill-prepared rescuers. There were regular official press updates and if Yoshi Kanagawa or NNC's Tabata were not around there would be a helpful official from one entity or another willing to attempt a translation. His checklist appeared on the screen, twenty-five points to guide him, concentrate his mind when the pressure threatened to confuse and divert him. They were not peculiar to Bolton and not much different from the work-aid list of priorities carried by official investigators. Many of the questions had been answered with his visits to the site and the Transport Ministry statements: damage to the aircraft, deaths and injuries and the pathological data; the fact that the wind strength at the time was severe; the airport, its special features and navigational aids; wreckage and impact information, the history of the last flight and the status of the flight recorders yet to be decoded and interpreted.

He started with the cargo. Apart from a ton of live eels, the manifest supplied to him by NN Air declared that their aeroplane was carrying other live seafood, a consignment of tinned and bottled foodstuffs, semi-processed electronic components and thirty-two canisters of industrial chemicals. He fed a summary into the laptop. Reading from notes and playing back his dictaphone recordings he tapped patiently into the machine, saving his input to the computer's memory frequently, and fuelling his immersion in the task with cups of strong coffee served every half-hour by an emissary from Yuriko Shimada. He wrote the chemical's name in bold script. He knew that somewhere among the columns of figures and the pages of fact and qualified conjecture lay the key to the cause of the DC-8-71's semi-controlled flight into the ground at Haneda. There was nothing sinister in a planeload of fish, he thought with a smile, but the toxicity of the chemicals and the current whereabouts and condition of the canisters needed to be ascertained.

He raised the blinds, noticing how early darkness fell on Tokyo, and left the room, studiously locking it. The visit to the lavatory took him across the open office floor where eyes followed him out and turned away when he passed them on his way back. He took in the nervous activity, the stacked desks and intense conversations, and if it wasn't fear that was palpable it was an unmistakeable overhanging sense of trepidation.

Maruta had crooked his head and hissed painfully when Alex presented his next demands, and the surveyor was only mildly surprised to be told after a long delay while the search progressed that the DC-8's certificates of airworthiness and registration, presumed destroyed in the crash, had not been retained by NN Air in copy form. Another task for London, Alex thought, bringing up a draft fax message on his screen. Reggie Cameron and the team had already opened a working line with the FAA in Oklahoma City and in typing his request for them to make a title search he asked also for a schedule giving a full history of the four CFM-56 engines. The maintenance records for the aircraft, in the form of folded computer printouts and a collection of loosely bound spreadsheets, now made a small mountain on the table. Where were the journey logs?

Fresh coffee arrived before Maruta returned with an armful of boxes. The make and registration number of the cargo jet were stencilled on each of them. Every time an aircraft flies the log is completed by the crew, recording the date, journey times, fuel lifts and any faults that will need rectification. These records are in the form of carbonised sheets, one page being removed on departure and retained by the ground crew as a permanent record in the event of loss. Alex found that call sign NINA 328's journey log file was two and a half weeks behind. The records were gathered at their Narita airport office, Maruta explained, and after examination by the chief engineer were sent to Tokyo, usually once a month. He accepted Alex's insistence that a courier be sent to Narita to fetch all the latest records on NINA 328 to him. Alex flipped through another file before adding to a note and giving it to Maruta. 'And he can bring the up-to-date weight and balance certificates at the same time.'

He was on his guard when, with the help of Maruta and a gloomy engineer, he tried to make sense of the records of maintenance performed. The SBs, the service bulletins issued by the manufacturers, seemed to have been incorporated in the records but he would have to check that the mandatory safety modifications ordered by the makers and the authorities from time to time had been implemented.

The repair of persistent faults, the performance of correct maintenance and the incorporation of urgent safety modifications according to the service bulletins were stipulations of the insurance policy as well as legal requirements. Failure to comply might seriously jeopardise the insurance payout, especially if they were determined to be causal to the loss. Alex would not let himself be drawn to premature conclusions, or to clues that begged for a gut response, but the disorderly, almost haphazard way NN Air maintained their fleet records sounded an alarm, which, if it wasn't screeching, hinted at a slipshod corporate attitude; and it might by extension have infected the practical operation of the aircraft. When the two men had gone, he stood, strolled to the window and stretched. He looked to the empty, darkening skies for inspiration, finally sighing in despair when he returned to the mass of loose papers and rough-edged files, his sense of detachment deepening. NN Air were supposed to be helping him by proving they ran their airline by the strict rules of the Federal Aviation Administration of the US and the Japanese civil aviation authorities and followed the stringent maintenance directives of the airframe and engine makers. He knew he would prise nothing from the American investigators, especially the National Transportation Safety Board. They were notoriously reticent when dealing with insurers in the national jurisdictions of other countries. He ran a thumb down a thick block of uneven sheets. There was much to do: he left the mechanics of flight and continued the fax he had started to Reggie Cameron. He requested the certificates-of-title check through the FAA, provided him with a progress report and expressed his intention to stay in Tokyo beyond the weekend. He drank more coffee and made a start on the crew records, starting with their licences to fly.

A native of San Diego, California, fifty-six-year-old Edward James Kidderby had been flying for thirty-three years, twenty as a flight captain. His rating to fly Boeing 747s had expired long ago and, as a pilot with NN Air since the mixed fleet of six aircraft was leased from South Miami Aviation, he had flown the three converted DC-8s. There had been three on the flight deck when NINA 328 came down. The first officer, Tsuji, had been a married man of forty-two with three children; the engineer, Nakanishi, forty-five and divorced. Copies of Edward Kidderby's ATP, his air transport pilot's licence, and Tsuji's commercial pilot's licence were enclosed in the individual files along with their medical records and details of the regular revalidations required by the FAA. The neatest file contained the engineer's: Nakanishi's flight engineer's licence and the annual medical validations were in sequential order among his other service documents. If the parting words of Phyllis Wakai had not hung over him all afternoon like a cloak he might not have given the tedious batch of medical certificates the attention he did, and it annoyed him to have to sort through a heap of disordered certificates and attribute them himself. Kidderby's pilot's licence demanded six-monthly medicals by FAA-approved doctors and because he was over forty they would have to include a strenuous heart examination supported by comprehensive X-rays and scans. Alex checked back again, assuming they were out of sequence like many of the technical documents he had been perusing, before giving up. According to the records Kidderby, the American pilot, had been due a full medical in January. The next would have been scheduled for July, two months away. The most recent medical report, for January this year, was not in the files. Alex typed this into the laptop. He finished his message and leaned back in the chair with the batch of reports, each several pages long and, apart from the romanised script for the hospital's address and the certifying doctor's name, detailed entirely in Japanese. He assumed that a translation would have accompanied the submission to the FAA, but no copy had been retained in the file, he noted with irritation.

When Yuriko made her next dutiful visit Alex had restacked the documents and built a neat stockade from his briefcase, cameras, recording equipment and notebooks around them. 'Please make sure the cleaners leave this room alone tonight,' he said, easing stiff shoulders into his jacket. 'And I might have to come back tonight. Would you please tell security not to bar the doors if they see a *gaijin* around ten.'

She smiled weakly in reply and moved to the table, clattering the coffee cup and a plate as she gathered them. 'Are you not joining Mr Miyamoto and Mr Sanguillen for dinner?'

He had taken the envelope from his case and had eased the gossamer-thin letter off the staple, its attachment to the diaries only tenuous after so many years. Was she surprised or disappointed, Alex wondered, folding the discoloured old document along its natural creases and sliding it carefully into a smaller envelope. 'I spoke to both of them today. If they think I've given them reasonable cause to be optimistic they can talk as owner and operator and maybe think about a replacement for the DC-8.'

'Is there anything *I* can do for you tonight?' Yuriko said. She was standing by the door, holding the crockery on a lacquered tray. Waves of hair spilled over her cheeks and her lips were parted as if she was about to answer her own question.

Alex locked the door behind them. For an instant he saw Cathy, remembering her smile and the posed erotic pouts she teased him with. It was exactly a month since she had moved out of his house. 'Two things,' he said, his throat dry. He showed her one of his business cards with some handwriting on it. 'Put me in a taxi to this place.' She handed the tray to a uniformed office girl who was still in attendance on the clerks and managers staying late as a gesture of loyalty to the demoralised company, and moved to his side. 'Our car is at your disposal,' she said with a touch of insistence. 'Tokyo taxi drivers are not very kind to foreigners who don't speak Japanese.'

'I've got to try it on my own sometime,' he said. She turned sideways and moved against him, cupping the hand that held the card, the tips of her livid-pink, polished fingernails shivering the hairs on the back of his wrist. '*Roppongi no kosaten*,' she read in Japanese. 'The main intersection at Roppongi.' She released the card and turned away, unsmiling. 'I'm sure you'll have a better time there than with my president.'

'I'm not going there to have fun,' he said sharply, pocketing the card and following her to the lifts.

'Be careful with the automatic door on the taxi and don't give a tip,' she advised, and then, when they reached the lobby, said, 'There was something else you wanted me to do.'

'Of course, and thanks,' Alex said, remembering. 'I've been going through the pilots' documentation, certifications and whatever, and I think one of the medical reports for the pilot Ed Kidderby is missing. I suppose it's got misplaced in the other files. It should be dated about January or February this year and I need it to complete the profile.'

He had not gone very far along the broad road between the Imperial Palace and the Marunouchi business district before he was regretting the decision to leave his tools and notes in the NNC building. But he didn't have time to take them to the hotel before his seven-thirty meeting with Phyllis Wakai, he rationalised – he was already ten minutes late, and he could pick them up later if he wished. If his first evening yesterday in Tokyo had been not exceptional there would be nothing unusual about working in one of the modern office blocks at ten in the evening. And it was not the threat of exposure that had made him agree to meet the pushy journalist – he had avoided the media successfully at other sites – nor the fact that she knew Ed Kidderby. She had hooked Bolton with the throwaway line about the pilot's poor health and had refused to elaborate unless they met. Now he'd found there was a gap in the captain's medical records. A vital, statutory report was missing, probably an oversight, a misfiling, but an unwelcome coincidence nevertheless.

The crossing was beneath the metropolitan expressway he had taken that morning on the way to the airport and he remembered it only because Yoshi had said that Roppongi was *the* night scene in Tokyo, especially for young Japanese women and *gaijin*. He had noticed that neons hung like banners on every building and stand-up advertising signs intruded across the pavements. Now they were lit in an explosion of colours that splashed the roads in broken mosaic confusion. Good-looking women, local and foreign, and men in dinner jackets paraded near their venues, vying good-naturedly for customers with fliers and business cards. It was a weekday and still early and they were trying hard to attract the sparse bands of dark-suited salarymen and predatory male expatriates. Bands of young girls sheathed in silver and black sleeveless mini-outfits swarmed in front of the Almond coffee shop while they waited for friends before moving on to the cavernous discos.

He saw the red cap as soon as he left the taxi and then, as he approached her, his own reflection in her half-tinted wide eyeglasses. If Phyllis Wakai had anything else in her wardrobe beyond baggy knee-length denim dungarees and white T-shirts it was not on show tonight. There was no complaint from her about his tardiness as she steered him purposefully towards Tokyo Tower, the bizarrely accurate copy of the Eiffel, and then into a narrower street of bars and restaurants and finally into an alley of cellar stairways and shadowy doorways. She was about to lead him down a set of rusted iron steps with a loose handrail when she turned towards him, lifting her head and seeming to squint behind the glasses and the protruding peak of the baseball cap. 'Are you gay, Alex?'

'What?'

'If you're gay we can go somewhere else later. I just wanted you to see this place first. Ed used to come here.'

'What makes you think I'm gay?' Alex said, his voice high-pitched with indignation as he followed the tuft of hair bulging out of the back of the red cap.

'I hear a lot of you British guys are gay,' she said, disappearing through a heavy door with a metal plaque at head height.

Easy-listening music soothed from unseen speakers and cigarette smoke spiralled gently in funnels of soft light. A piano stood idle and most of the plain, square tables and counter stools were unoccupied. Apart from two young Japanese women, the dozen or so drinkers were all foreign and the nearest raised an arm in greeting when he saw Phyllis. The place was called Tulip but gave the theme only passing attention with a long floral painting above the mirror behind the bar. It was a private sort of place, not casually stumbled across. The barman was Japanese and made a serious face as he mixed a cocktail in front of an expanse of mirror decorated in one corner with photographs and postcards. A svelte blonde waitress in black Velcro leggings and a matching halter top smiled at the newcomers as she jigged with a tray of drinks to a corner booth. 'Hi, Phyl,' she called in a broad, nasal Australian accent.

'Hi, Sharon.' Phyllis led him to a table near the piano. 'What do you want Alex? Beer? Something else?'

'Beer would be fine.'

Phyllis caught Sharon's arm on her return with an empty tray. 'A couple of cold Malts, please, Sharon.'

'Okay, Phyl,' the waitress responded. She was about to

67

move off, then dipped backwards. 'When's the funeral?
Know yet?'

Phyllis touched the peak of her cap. 'Can't say.' She
looked at Alex. 'Depends on the crash investigation.' Alone
with him, she said, 'The *gaijin* pilots from NN Air and some
other Asian airlines come here when they've got a few days
in Tokyo.' She took in the bar with a toss of her head. 'The
rest are Aussie expats and *gaijin* journalists.'

'Are you a *gaijin* or a Japanese?' Alex asked casually.

She snapped open a tasselled shoulder bag and tossed a
cigarette packet onto the table. 'I'm a *sansei*.'

He felt stupid. 'A what?'

'A third-generation Japanese American. My grandparents
were Japanese, from the south, Okayama Prefecture, and
went to California just before they banned immigrants from
Japan. Being "Japs" they were considered a threat when war
broke out and locked up in concentration camps. My parents
were *nisei*, second-generation Americans. They were both
born in the camp outside San Francisco during the war.' She
shook a cigarette from the packet. 'Have you got a light?'

There was no book of matches in the ashtray. 'I don't
smoke,' he said weakly.

'Well fuck it then,' she groaned, and snapped the
cigarette.

'What are you doing here, in Japan?'

'I told you. I'm a journalist and a wannabe writer. I pay
the bills by writing about the latest volcanic eruption on
Kyushu or the sex lives of three-hundred-and-fifty-pound
sumo wrestlers for the *Grand Rapids Enquirer* and anyone
else who'll buy the crap. When I'm not doing that I'm
writing a book. I want it to be the definitive exposure of
corporate Japan, like the stuff that's been done on Nomura
and Sony, except I'm covering the real corrupt ass end of the
Japanese miracle. And Nippon Nagasaki Corporation is just
as close as you can get to the sewer. That's why I got through

to you. Maybe you can give me the inside story on the crash – another example of Miyamoto's mismanagement – and I can tell you what I know about the pilot.'

'Look, Phyllis.'

'Phyl.'

'Look, Phyl. I've got four, perhaps five, days in Tokyo at the most. I'm an engineer, more or less, not an investigator for the Federal Aviation Administration or the British equivalent, the Civil Aviation Authority. If I say anything at all it'll be completely off the record. You understand, off the record?'

The cap nodded. 'So talk to me Alex. What are you doing here? Off the record.'

He waited while Sharon poured the beers into chilled glasses and then leaned across the table. 'I check things out for the people who've insured the plane and they pay out when I'm satisfied the conditions of the policy have been met. What I do is confidential between me and the underwriters.'

'But you'll pay up eventually, won't you?'

'Not necessarily,' Alex said firmly.

'C'mon. The goddamn plane just crashed, didn't it?'

Alex took a long drag on the beer. 'It's like a car, Phyl. If you don't maintain it it'll break down. In the case of an aeroplane, it's a legal requirement to have the aircraft maintained properly and regularly and evidence it with documentation which has to be lodged with the regulatory authorities. Ed Kidderby's plane was owned by an American company and so came under the jurisdiction of the FAA in the States.' He spread his hands. 'The insurance policy on the aircraft was basically like any other. If you fail to turn your alarm on when you leave the house or keep it operable, the insurance company's going to question any claim you make.'

'So why all this creeping around in a Miyamoto car with

your head in a bag,' Phyllis asked, a scowl breaking across her face. 'They're not the owners, you told me. They won't get the money.'

He took another sip from the glass before replying. 'NN Air operate the aeroplane through a lease with the American owners and all the obligations I've just described fall on them. So I've got to meet their pilots and engineers and their controllers and managers, go through all their records, make sure they've followed the conditions of the insurance. I happen to be dealing directly with the president of the parent company. They're in the same building and Miyamoto runs all his subsidiaries from the front, or so I'm told.'

'He's a crook,' the journalist said, taking her drink casually, as if she had commented on the weather.

'Phyl,' he persisted. 'I'm not a policeman. I'm a bloody engineer. I don't intend to let emotion get in the way. You talk to me for a change. You blackmailed your way to seeing me and I agreed because you hinted the American pilot might have been ill.'

She scoffed, pressing her point by thumping the tulip-shaped beer glass onto the table. The barman looked up and smiled warily. 'Ill? He was a walking intensive-care patient.'

Bolton knew Kidderby's three stays in hospital had been serious enough to rate a mention in FAA records. He had also seen his medical certificates, clean but for the usual aches and pains common to a fifty-plus man, and recalled the gap in the sequence. If there was a recent problem it wouldn't reveal itself in the autopsy unless the condition of the body allowed. Yoshi Kanagawa had it from a source near to the Transport Ministry's investigation team that the impact from the near-vertical dive and the explosion it set off destroyed the vital organs of everyone on board except the loadmaster, who had been sitting with his cargo and expelled from the aircraft in various, but forensically viable, pieces. Cause of death for the three flight crew would probably be phrased as trauma from severe injuries. Not much else they could say.

'Tell me about it,' Alex said.

Phyllis drew a pattern lazily on the frosty glass. 'He had a girlfriend, Makiko Nakamura. She'd be here now but she's with her family. In mourning, I guess. They're all divorced, the *gaijin* pilots. Got families Stateside or in Australia, but here they look after young bar hostesses, or whatever.' She snuffled and toyed with another cigarette. 'They're good guys, good pilots, I hear, but hell, they're the wrong side of forty-five. Ed was way over fifty, worked hard to pay his alimony, send money to a couple of kids still in college and keep Makiko in designer dresses.' She touched her lips to the glass but did not drink. 'He got real sick in here once.'

'When was that?' Alex asked, calculating that the pilot's next official medical would have been in about two months if they followed the six-month sequence properly. He had seen nothing in the records to indicate a chronic, serious condition, but the last certificate was missing. It was beginning to stink.

'Five, six weeks ago. He'd just flown in from LA.'

'Was he drunk?'

'Don't recall so. He looked pretty ill when he came in. Pale, a bit bloated. He had a soda, I think, and then had trouble breathing.'

'Did he go to hospital?'

Phyllis shrugged. 'No. He refused. Makiko took him home.'

'Did he fly soon afterwards?' Alex asked.

'No idea, but I saw him again a couple of weeks later. He seemed okay.'

Alex had listened incredulously, and his next question was delivered with quiet urgency. 'Was that the only time he'd been taken ill? As far as you know.'

'Absolutely not,' she drawled. 'Makiko told me he'd been

71

having chest pains on and off for a year. He passed it off as indigestion.'

'Sounds to me like he was a walking time bomb,' Alex said, mostly to himself. 'Would you say he drank a lot?'

Phyllis sighed. 'I can't deny he liked a few. Heavy stuff too. The Austrialians keep to beer. Ed was a whisky man.'

Alex asked for another round of drinks and a book of matches. While Phyllis looked round to greet a new party in a low sympathetic voice – they had obviously known the dead pilot as well – Alex was in the cockpit, the "office", of an old, converted DC-8 approaching the end of a four-hour flight. He was tired, stressed and annoyed by the diversion to Haneda. He'd probably have to wait on board after landing until clearance came and then fly up to Narita to have the plane in place for its turnaround. He'd have booze in his bloodstream and a racing heart as the plane bucked and bounced in the turbulence. Did the seizure building inside him become so unbearable that he slipped out of the shoulder harness to give himself the mobility to reach the pain, massage the tortured muscle? He was a mile from the airport threshold, low, the wheels down, when the final spasm seared across his chest, paralysing his left arm and throwing him involuntarily forward, over the throttle, carried by the agony to the left, forcing the plane into a steep, leftward roll. Buckled into full restraining harness, and critically close to the landing, the first officer and the engineer had zero possibility of reaching Kidderby, let alone shifting his dead weight and regaining control of the aircraft. Was this the scenario?

'That's really all,' Phyllis was saying, examining the business end of a cigarette.

'How does it all fit in the articles you're writing about Miyamoto and his company?' Alex asked, striking a match for her.

She took a long drag and stubbed the cigarette out. 'I

didn't smoke till I came to Japan,' she confessed. 'But everybody does. It's like a requirement of residence. Anyway, I'm not writing articles, I'm doing a book. That's why you don't have to worry about a crap quote.' She twisted the peak of the baseball cap. 'The genre's changed from the seventies when we all praised Japan Incorporated and the economic miracle. Since then a few wheels have come off and now we're writing about the hidden realities: the absolute political corruption, corporate bribery and cartels and the integration of organised crime into mainstream business. I guess I chose Nippon Nagasaki Corporation because it's a flagship company and there's evidence it's involved in all of these.'

'That's a lot for a neutral like me to swallow,' Alex said, unconvinced.

'There are other attractions for an investigative journalist. It's a one-man show with a very charismatic president. He's also the classic son of the founder, but most of all NNC is a prime example of a corporate monster that might just have pushed itself too far.'

'How far do you mean?' Alex asked.

'NNC and its subsidiaries and affiliates roll up sales of almost two hundred billion dollars a year, mostly from marine engineering and its transport and distribution services. That was how the company started, in the thirties. Miyamoto runs everythings from Nippon Nagasaki Corporation, a vehicle he uses for his own non-core things like general trading, real estate and the leisure business. In the crazy asset-driven feeding frenzy of the eighties he put all his spare cash and anything he could borrow or drain from other group companies into real estate and the stock market. He even put half a billion dollars into Hawaiian hotels in 1987.'

'I don't see a problem with that,' Alex said flatly.

The face behind the glasses and the semicircle of cap

beamed with a writer's zeal. 'The Oahu assets are on the market at two hundred million dollars and there are no takers at more than fifty per cent discount. Miyamoto's operation needs a massive cash infusion if he's going to service his debt, and that's one reason why his airline's got worn-out pilots and crappy airplanes that don't get serviced properly.'

'Did Ed Kidderby talk to you about NN Air?' Alex asked, his mind racing ahead, to an airline in trouble, short of money, scrimping on aircraft maintenance, pilot training perhaps, their health monitoring almost certainly, and other non-productive expenses.

She finished her beer. 'I didn't know him that well. I know his girlfriend better because I drink in her bar occasionally. That's how I met Ed. He put some money up front to help her open it.' She shrugged. 'He was an easygoing guy. Said a few times he was taking shit from the airline but he needed the money and flying was the only thing he knew.'

'What sort of problems was he having? Do you remember?'

She thought for a moment and spoke sadly. 'Things like being on call all the time. Taking three hours to get to Narita and then expected to fly down to Sydney at a moment's notice.' She rubbed the corners of her eyes behind the glasses.

'I'm beginning to see,' Alex said, wiping a thread of froth from his upper lip with the back of his hand. 'I'd like to meet his girlfriend. Should we grab something to eat while you tell me more?'

'Miyamoto's group's got forty-two wholly owned subsidiaries, including of course NN Air, and maybe sixty or seventy more interconnected affiliates. Some of them are classified legally as vehicles for trading, but some are really tax-efficient parking places for the money he and the rest of

Japan were raising in the eighties. Banks threw money around and it was very, very cheap.' They had taken the last two stools at an oval counter behind which a pair of cooks in *happi* coats and knotted headbands of towelling grilled and served skewered *yakitori* chicken in a dozen different ways. The air was rich with the pungently sweet *teriyaki* sauce they used to coat the chunks of breast, leg, liver and crispy skin. 'He also mortgaged a lot of land to buy shares, art, condominiums and the piece of Hawaii.'

'And those assets are worth much less now than when they were purchased and the borrowers can't find the cash to repay the banks.'

'Right,' she mumbled, finishing a ball of grilled minced chicken. 'But the banks are in the same shape, or maybe worse, than their customers. It's a fact that about three-quarters of all outstanding bank lending's for real estate and a lot of it's non-performing: bad loans they're going to have to provide reserves for. That's going to be tough because the banks' capital bases are fucked up. They're holding billions of yen's worth of securities that are worth a lot less than they used to be since the stock market imploded.'

'Didn't I hear you call Hiroshi Miyamoto a crook?' Alex remarked.

She gave an ironic snort and waved for another round of draught beer. 'Your friend Hiroshi couldn't resist the temptations of the eighties and came out hitting for the fence when he should have been restructuring his business according to economic realities. Like he wanted some big jets to paint his logo on. So, and if I read you right on the technicalities, he leases a package of old planes from some Florida money-laundering operation disguised as a legit operation. Sorry, Ed, old friend. Nothing personal.'

'It still doesn't make him a crook,' Alex pressed, chewing into a piece of gizzard and noting her harsh remarks about South Miami Aviation.

'You have to understand how Japan's organised crime works,' Phyllis said. 'You know, the *yakuza*. We're not talking about prostitution and backstreet gambling. That's for the boneheads with perms and tattoos. The big syndicates have put their resources into real estate, the stock market, golf courses and politics and this naturally brings them in touch with people like Miyamoto, the single-minded entrepreneur with an eye for any opportunity to increase his net worth. He might not be a crook by profession but I'll guarantee he's one by association.'

Alex sniffed appreciatively. 'Does your research predate NNC's current problems?'

'Sure. It's a great story. An individual, Hiroshi's father Shinichi, built a successful empire out of a small marine engineering workshop down in Nagasaki, Kyushu, in the thirties.'

Alex fingered the envelope in the inside pocket of his jacket. She had been frank with him and very helpful. It was the moment to reciprocate. 'Did you come across a man called Jonsson while you were doing your research? I believe he was Swedish.'

She sucked the froth from her beer. 'Jonsson, Jonsson.' She crooked her head, her mind in fast reverse towards the early chapters. 'Yeah, I think so. I'd have to check my database but wasn't he a partner or something of Miyamoto senior?'

'Something like that. He was an engineer. There's a photograph of him with Miyamoto senior in the head office. Dated 1934 if I recall.' He tipped the sheet of paper delicately out of its covers. 'Can you read Japanese?' he asked, unsure whether he was being impertinent.

She wiped her hands and took the paper from him with a smile. 'Mom and Dad sent me to Japan seven years ago. To find my roots, I guess. I went to college here and just stayed on.' She ran her eyes along the horizontal rows. Many of the tiny, complex ideographs had degenerated with age, the primitive print faded, leaving them blurred, often inseparable. 'I can handle two thousand of the goddam characters, the number you need for everyday life, but these are a challenge.'

'That's our old Japanese operation,' Alex said, explaining the heading and the logo and how the letter came to him attached to a long tract of wartime diary notes. 'You see there, where it says "Jonsson Nagasaki" and "Nippon Nagasaki Kogyo" in English writing.'

Phyllis was puzzled. 'Yeah. Interesting,' she droned. 'NNC was called Nippon Nagasaki Kogyo until around 1970 I think. Nagasaki's the town on Kyushu, you know, the southern island. Kogyo just means "industries". Miyamoto split off the marine engineering division and kept the old base company as his flagship. He got rid of Kogyo and stuck "Corporation" after "NN". I never came across a firm called Jonsson Nagasaki though.'

'Can you read the text? Get an idea what it means?'

She shook her head. 'Apart from the print, a lot of the *kanji*, the characters I mean, are old-style, pre-war stuff.'

'How do you mean, "old-style"?' Alex asked.

'They had more strokes. You see this one?' She pointed at a hieroglyphic, then drew it in the air. 'They've been making the characters easier to write since the war. You can do this one with seven pen strokes now. Jesus! Look at it then. Thirteen, fourteen strokes. They've even simplified the number characters as well. The date and numbers in here are the old-fashioned types.'

While she read, he watched a serious chef deftly manipulating and turning a spread of chicken kebabs over the charcoal grill. 'Sorry, Alex,' she said finally. 'Apart from the problem of the faded print and the old characters I can't get the sense of it. It's some kind of formal document.' Her voice was trailing. 'I guess it's about a name change or something.'

He took it from her carefully. 'Don't worry. I'll give it to Miyamoto for his records. That was the intention anyway.'

She adjusted her cap and twisted in the stool. 'Don't give it to him yet, please. I'd like to show it to an old American friend of mine. He was an accountant here before and after the war. Retired now, of course, and well into his eighties, but he's still fit and he's a bit of a historian. He learned his Japanese at school in the twenties. Why don't you come with me? He lives by the sea.'

It had turned eleven when the taxi reached his hotel. It was only a short ride from Roppongi. He could have walked, but realised he was totally disorientated and he wasn't helped by an absence of street name signs. How do people get around? he thought. He was smiling when he entered the hotel, the deserted lobby mellow in the subdued evening glimmer from the lights studding the low ceiling like scattered stars. The staff at the reception desk bowed as he approached.

'There's a visitor for you in the Samurai Bar, Mr Bolton,' a smart, crisply uniformed desk clerk said as he handed over the room key and an envelope of messages. 'Please turn left at the top of the escalator.'

Alex was too surprised to ask who it was as he turned away, opening the hotel's envelope on the stairway. The messages from London were happily short, mostly charts and statistics, and a narrative from Emma Healey on office activities surrounding the crash of the NN Air DC-8. Following a corridor hosting a choice of restaurants, he prepared himself mentally for a carefully expressed entreaty from Yoshi Kanagawa for the expeditious release of the insurance money. Or even James Sanguillen himself. Patience, gentlemen, he breathed. A couple of points to clear up first.

It was an intimate place: soft lighting, lots of black leather on deep seats and swivel wing chairs along a bar where foreign business travellers sat drowsily with a nightcap or two and flushed Japanese senior managers pressed drinks and cigarettes on young female companions. Nothing overawed or escaped the immaculately groomed bar director and when he saw the bewildered *gaijin* in the doorway he guided him towards a far corner. Through the half light and the hanging cigarette smoke Alex saw a shimmer of silky stocking on crossed legs. The knees shifted as he approached, revealing the hem of a short tangerine skirt and a sliver of black silk blouse under the matching jacket. Her face was concealed behind the document she was reading in the cone of light from the conch-shaped fitting above her head. When she shifted he saw a span of glossed fingernails rise above the paper and graze an errant wisp of hair from her temple. 'Miss Shimada,' he said uncertainly. He sat across from her, wondering when she had changed out of her professional power clothes.

A waiter was already stooping obsequiously. She spoke to him in Japanese and then to Alex. 'I'm having another Campari. Would you like something?'

Disappointed faces turned back to the bar, to confront themselves in the mirror and reflect on another fading fantasy.

Alex ordered a brandy. 'I didn't expect to see you here.'

She smiled and unravelled her legs. 'I think you said you might return to our offices. I waited for you until ten fifteen and then came here.'

'I'm sorry to have troubled you. My dinner dragged on. Is there a problem?'

'No, not at all,' she said. 'My president told me to make sure you saw this.' She handed him the papers she had been reading when he arrived. 'It was issued this evening. The original's in Japanese, of course. This is the translation for the foreign investigators.'

It was a transcription from the cockpit voice recorder, three minutes of dialogue and sound interpretation. He'd have to hear the tape to get a real feel for those last few moments but it was a start. The drinks were served as he skimmed the three-way cockpit conversation.

'The official discussions will be held at the Ministry of Transport at nine tomorrow morning,' Yuriko explained. 'A press conference is scheduled for midday, or shortly afterwards. I understand you will not be attending the meeting.'

'That's correct.' He read as he spoke. It was only a slight hope, anyway, but Yoshi Kanagawa had telephoned earlier in the day to confirm he had not been invited to the joint session between the Japanese and the visiting American investigators to analyse the crew's final conversation. Without looking up he said, 'I'm going to need a copy of the recording. They'll reproduce it on cassette.' Yuriko wrote in a pocket diary. 'Did you find the missing medical certificate?' Alex asked.

'It should be waiting for you tomorrow. May I ask what time we can expect you?'

'I'm seeing the manager of my firm's Tokyo operation at eight thirty. I should be with you an hour or so later. Can I have the car at eight fifteen, please?'

'Of course.' Closing her notebook, she gestured at the untouched bulb of brandy. 'Please.'

He folded the papers and thought about leaving the drink untouched. He wanted the solitude of his room, to read, and read again, the chilling, final conversation from the cockpit of the DC-8-71 – words that brought Ed Kidderby and his Japanese crew back to life. Then he'd fax it to Reggie Cameron with the technical data he had accumulated during the day. He was even more keen to hear the recording itself, to pick up the changes in voice patterns and the extraneous sounds intruding into the cockpit as the aeroplane's hydraulic systems operated the mechanical parts.

'Do you have a light, Mr Bolton?' Yuriko's hand extended across the table, a cigarette trapped in her talon-like fingers.

'What? Oh, right.' He fumbled in his jacket pocket for the book of matches he had gathered up in Phyllis Wakai's bar. It had a tulip motif on the flap. She drew his hand towards her and when the cigarette was lit blew gratefully towards the ceiling after the first deep drag. When she lowered her head Alex was sipping his brandy, and she caught his eyes snagged admiringly on the taut swell of her silk top. 'You look tired, Mr Bolton. Should I order you a *shiatsu* massage, or get you a sleeping pill perhaps?'

He returned her smile. 'I appreciate your concern,' he heard himself saying, 'but I don't think I'll need help dropping off.'

Phyllis stumbled in the haste to kick off her trainers and get to the telephone. 'Bill? It's Phyl. How are you doing?' The warped front door was open enough to admit a thin curtain of moonlight into the dark, narrow hallway. She squinted at her watch. 'Did I wake you?'

'Of course you didn't.' It was an old man's voice, raspy, patient but firm enough to hide the fact that he had been dozing, seduced into sleep as he faced the Pacific Ocean in a rocking chair, a book open on his lap. He spoke as if to a wayward daughter. 'I was hoping you'd call. I've done a lot of digging for your Nippon Nagasaki background.'

'That's why I called,' she said, her eyes dancing with enthusiasm. 'I've just met an English guy with a legal document of some sort which mentions them.'

'What is it?' Bill Littleton said.

'I can't really make sense of it,' she confessed. 'It's pretty old, the *kanji* are complicated and the printing's faded. I want you to see it.'

'Sure. How old is it?'

Phyllis tapped her forehead. 'It's got to be pre-war. The paper's falling apart and it talks about Nippon Nagasaki and Shinichi Miyamoto.'

'How did this guy get it?'

'It came to his insurance company from a law firm. It was attached to the diaries of a British prisoner-of-war.'

'A POW?' Littleton was silent for a moment. 'Do you think it's significant?'

'I don't know, Bill. I'll try and get him down to Hayama on Saturday with the letter and the diaries. He's pretty tied up with the Haneda crash at the moment.'

Alex sat on the bed near the pillow, his tie loosened. Leaving Yuriko Shimada in the hotel lobby he had stopped at reception to fax the text of the cockpit voice recording to his London office. He peeled off the second sock as he came to the end of his conversation with Emma Harley while the team were still there. Late in the afternoon, London time, there had been an aviation incident in the Middle East and while Emma coped with Alex's output Reggie Cameron was forming a response team in the conference room. 'I'll courier you a cassette as soon as I get one here, hopefully by tomorrow afternoon. I've got NNC's office working on it. I wasn't invited to the meeting with the FAA and air safety team, naturally.'

'Great,' Emma encouraged. 'Any problems I can help you with?'

'No thanks. It's under control.' He heard the tempered knocking, barely. 'I've got a feeling tomorrow's the key day. Bye, Emma, I've got a visitor. I'll be in touch before you go home.' Barefoot, and tightening his belt, he shuffled to the door.

Yuriko Shimada was leaning on the jamb, the collar of her tangerine jacket clutched over a shoulder. She looked only mildly embarrassed. 'I'm sorry to disturb you,' she claimed, propelling herself into the room before he could frame a response. 'I forgot to ask you for the old letter you kindly offered to show me again. Perhaps I could take it to Miyamoto *san*. My president would be very disappointed if I didn't return with it.'

25 March, 1942

We are just beginning to show the effects of three weeks of semi-starvation and also of the rice diet and the bad sanitary arrangements. We are swarming with flies and there's lots of dysentery among the prisoners. Some of us, including me, are having blackouts when standing or walking. A senior Exeter *officer has taken over the conduct of the British prisoners. He's trying to get us three meals a day and the beatings stopped. Chris and I noticed the galley throws away a lot of good green stuff with the rubbish so we collected it and cleaned it to make vegetable stew with half our rice ration. We do this every day while Jeff and Phil do the fag-end patrol three times a day. We found a tin of rice this morning. It was alive with weevils but it gave us about 4lbs of rice after washing.*

2 April

Japs are organising work parties outside the camp. Jeff, Phil, Eric and Jim went and came back with precious baccy. I went to fill in air-raid shelters at the school. Heard that 74 officers and ratings from the

Exeter *are in the town prison. A month as a prisoner now. I hope the Admiralty do not announce the sinking of the* Exeter *until they know we are safe. Lt. Com. R. K. Hudson told us we are having some new guards and some native police to look after us. I hope they are better than the last lot. He also told us our Captain, himself, the Gunnery Officer (Lt. Com. Twist) and the Torpedo Officer and some ratings are leaving us soon.*

3 April

Friday. We got a loaf of bread each yesterday and a tin of fish between 5 men for breakfast. I am in the Galley working party and am in charge of 10 hands. This means we shall have our stomachs full today. I get on well with the Jap in the Galley. It's Good Friday today, nearly forgot it.

6 April

I've got dysentery bad. Went to the head seven times on Saturday morning alone. Jeff and Dean got it first but I was worst. I was scared because five people died of some disease last week. I spent two days going between the head and the bunk until they decided to send me to the Dutch hospital ship. Put to bed straight away. Stomach's still bad but doesn't the tea taste good? First since leaving the Exeter. *I hope to God I am not a prisoner this time next year. I wonder if Kath knows yet and if the children are well.*

12 April

Feeling much better thanks to the Dutch nurses and doctors. The stomach pains are not as sharp. We get tea all day long and twice we had boiled potatoes and greens mashed together and sometimes a small piece of chicken. My diet has been toast and tea. They let me have a cigarette. A yank from the Houston *came on board on Thursday and said one of their naval pilots had just arrived and told them Japs had broadcast an*

account of the sinking of the Exeter, *the* Encounter *and*
Pope *and had list of survivors. I hope it gets back to
Kath. She does worry. I know she's all right for money
for at least 13 weeks after the ship sunk. At least she
will know I am safe.*

15 April

*The dysentery's cleared up but I can't walk. I have
tried to walk but I have foot rot and it started to turn
septic. Had a long yarn with Sister Van-den-Burg.
She's 31 and lived in England for a while. She's about
the same height as Kath and has the same kind of hair.
It's nine o'clock at night here, that would make it three
p.m. at home. I wonder what Kath's doing now. Been
married 13½ years. Best thing I ever did, but it's a
good job one cannot look into the future at times
because if I could have I could certainly have saved
Kath the way she must be feeling now.*

22 April

*I could not get any paper for days but Sister Van-den-
Berg got me some sheets which were used only on one
side. She had heard that her brother had been killed
fighting in Java. She has my deepest sympathy. The feet
are slowly getting better, though they swell when I
stand up. Been on the ship two weeks but I'm going
back to the camp. Bought some butter to take back. It
will give the lads a treat. Heard that the Russians have
landed paratroops at Danzig. Good luck to them if they
have. Heard yesterday they were fighting on German
soil and that Fortresses had bombed 12 miles from
Nagasaki. I will copy down all the news I get. Reg
Riggs gave me a ham and onion sandwich today as
goodbye present.*

Richard Ingleby carried his Englishness in a three-piece suit
and would wear it well into June, when the seasonal rains

arrived and enveloped Japan in a four-week dripping blanket of twenty-four-hour murkiness. It was also demonstrated in his determination to learn no Japanese beyond the rudimentary needs for the taxi and the bar. His five years in Japan running the Far East insurance operation for British Underwriters International had been an intoxication of expatriate wealth accumulation and long, happy separations from his family. His senior Japanese director was an extrovert and competent recruit from the domestic insurance industry and he managed a staff of eighty-six with great energy, producing profits that satisfied London and ensured Ingleby stayed in favour at a time when foreign firms were reappraising the need to keep an expatriate in the world's most expensive city. If head office bothered to put together the components of Ingleby's package; his salary, bonuses, home leave, entertainment, living expenses and school fees they would find he was costing them close to five hundred thousand pounds a year.

'So that's where we are, Richard,' Alex said, pouring another cup of tea. 'I'm not happy about the quality of the records at NN Air so I'm staying around until I'm satisfied they've met all the conditions of the insurance.'

Press reports suggest a sudden downdraught of air,' Ingleby said, nodding thoughtfully behind his long rosewood desk with its slim, empty document trays and redundant computer monitor and keyboard. He was in his late thirties but the swath of baldness between the two ridges of hair trimmed well above his ears gave him an older, maturer appearance. 'It was the fiercest wind I can remember, outside of a typhoon.'

Alex frowned. 'It was certainly forced into the ground but there was a very experienced crew on board. Kidderby took the controls for the final approach so he knew what he was doing.'

Ingleby touched a cup to his lips and indicated a stack of

newspapers. 'They don't paint a very attractive picture of the pilot chappie.'

'Edward Kidderby?' Alex murmured.

'That's him. They talk about high-living *gaijins*, possibly a drink problem.' He had leaned over his desk, a conspiratorial ring in his voice, as if he were offering a new, vital piece of information.

'I read it myself,' Alex said, 'but it's too early to say.' Drink was a great leveller. He was thinking of Phyllis Wakai's revelations in the Tulip bar and how easy it was for the armchair investigators to cope with the image of a drunken pilot steering an old jet recklessly through the windstorm. 'We won't know until they get a Stateside expert here to do the autopsies. The condition of the cockpit bodies is beyond the skills of your usual forensic pathologist. And anyway, a few millilitres of alcohol in his blood won't mean he was pissed.'

'What is it you chaps say about the forbidden period?' Ingleby asked with a grim smile.

'Twelve hours from bottle to throttle,' Alex said mirthlessly, gathering up the transcript of the cockpit voice recorder. 'Look Richard, I might need your help when I get hold of a copy the actual recording. I'm not going to get any from the official side.'

'Any time. I hope I can see you tonight at least,' Ingleby said genuinely. 'Or the weekend perhaps. Jan's away in the UK. Half term and all that. I'm sure we can cope, find somewhere for a slurp or two.'

Alex grinned. 'I'll play it by ear if you don't mind, Richard. I want to keep sharp. There are going to be announcements and comments flying around and some are going to come from me.' Thinking of Phyl Wakai's offer he said, 'I might try and get out of Tokyo for a couple of hours tomorrow but I'll stay on the end of a phone.' He picked one of the loose envelopes he was forced to carry until he regained possession of his chart case and slid it towards Ingleby. 'Almost forgot. Take a look.' In the early hours of the day, in his suite, faced with a smouldering, almost irresistible onslaught, he had come close to telling Yuriko Shimada that the Jonsson letter was still in his briefcase in the room he was allocated at NNC but remembered in time that she had been there when he separated it from the diaries and stuck it in his pocket. After she had measured up his suite and refreshed herself in the bathroom, he reminded her convincingly that he was duty-bound to show the original document to his Tokyo office, as a forerunner of his company had issued it in the first place, even though it was over half a century ago. BUI was his first point of call on his Friday schedule. Soon afterwards he was sure he would be in a position to present it formally to NNC's President Miyamoto as a gesture of goodwill and support. She had cast away her jacket in exuberant relief and was testing the bounce of the bed when the telephone rang. It was London, and it sobered him. He dragged himself from the edge of the sensuous gorge Yuriko was digging around him, shrugging his disappointment as he encouraged her departure, promising himself that she would be his reward when the NN Air job was successfully completed.

Ingleby's secretary returned, sucking air in the now familiar expression that said there was a problem. Alex saw that the faint mauve print had copied patchily, uselessly. 'Sorry, Richard, but I'll have to keep the original for a while. You can have another look if you want and then we'll give it to Miyamoto. He's keen to put it in his company's history book. Do you have anything like it, say sixty, seventy years old, in your archives?'

Ingleby leaned back, spinning a ballpen thoughtfully. 'Doubt it. I haven't seen anything before fifty-five, when we really got going here again. Most of our pre-war documentation was destroyed in the fire-bombings, like everybody else's. I can see why Miyamoto wants it. They're absolutely fanatical here about their corporate histories.'

Alex flicked his sleeve. 'It's almost ten.' He stood to leave, gathering up the envelopes. One contained the two batches of photographs he had taken at the crash site, developed through the hotel, independent of any party involved in the NN Air incident. The video tape could await his return to England before he viewed it. 'I've got to get back to the real world, Richard. I'll try and brief you later today.'

A telephone was activated as soon as the important *gaijin* passed through the automatic doors with his packages and Yuriko Shimada was waiting by the third-floor lift bank. She walked him to his temporary sanctuary, reeling off messages, updating him on the official investigation and issuing an open invitation from the president for the evening if he should be at a loss. It was as if the previous night had not happened, as if she had not emerged from his bathroom with her lips glossed to perfection, her hair brushed to a fine silky sheen. In a room still sweet with her seductive afterglow, he had put down the telephone to London and read the transcript of the cockpit voice recorder again, slowly, word by word, line by line. It was past midnight, and when there was nothing in that first exciting and moving scan to revive his jaded concentration, even after a second and third reading, he had abandoned it to an easy and needed sleep.

Now, halfway through his third day in Tokyo, he knew he had the jet lag beaten. He felt sharper, his mind attentive, alert at last to the fascinations of a new city as he was driven through the tidy, buzzing streets of the capital. He twisted the window blinds in his NNC office against the glare and made space among the stacks of records on the table for the flying charts and landing data for Haneda Airport. He poured a fresh coffee and spread the two photocopied sheets of the transcript. In the lifeless, toneless words Captain Edward Kidderby came over as a serious man: there was no obvious deviation from standard procedures as the crew guided the DC-8-71 in very strong winds towards the airport and none of the flippancy or wisecracking Alex had sometimes heard from experienced pilots moments before a tape cut out, signalling an inexplicable impact with terrain. When the strength of the wind exceeded the limit stipulated by his first officer's pilot rating, he demonstrated awareness and firm professionalism when he took immediate control of the aircraft. Alex selected the procedures chart for a landing on Haneda's runway twenty-two, as the Tower had instructed, and traced NINA 328's approach against it. Then he studied the aerodrome charts and the important footnotes and warnings boxed in a corner. Besides advising pilots that boats with masts up to a hundred feet tall cross approach paths and ordering them not to overfly the Kawasaki Petroleum Complex, it warned of the possibility of downdraughts on all approaches. He circled the notation with yellow marker pen and at this point guessed that the odds were on the plane being brought down by fierce winds and not mechanical breakdown.

Or was it human error? The press had tracked down a real or imagined drink problem and he himself had learned the pilot had a troubled heart. Did Kidderby misunderstand an instruction? In his first exchange with Haneda Approach Kidderby, who had done most of the talking with the airport, had asked the air traffic controller to repeat the heading and runway. He remembered an entry in an airline briefing which described seasonal weather patterns wherever aircraft flew and highlighted significant local problems, like poor communications or radar peculiarities. Taking the stapled, photocopied sheets from his briefcase, he nodded ruefully when he reread the short item on Japan. Japanese controllers, it warned, have a pronounced accent and a tendency to talk too quickly. He flipped the pages: there was no similar entry for any other country in the world. Was Ed Kidderby a victim of local language deficiences? Alex read through the transcipt sequence yet again. Apart from the captain's proper request for confirmation of an instruction, there was nothing in the dialogues to suggest a misinterpretation by the Japanese and American crew.

Alex was aching to hear the actual voice recording: to catch the nuances, sense the edginess as the wind buffeted the jet and assess the degree of crew compatibility as manifested in their voices. The two local nationals no doubt pronounced their specialised workshop English distinctly, as they had to, and Kidderby wouldn't have any problems with it, but their last coherent words would have been a torrent of frenzied, unintelligible Japanese. It was natural: they saw the imminence of their own deaths. Alex assumed Kidderby's last screams were drowned out by his two cockpit colleagues and rendered inseparable in the recording. Until he heard the tape, bringing the voices back to life with the inflections and tones that might point to a changed state of mind, he wasn't able to read anything behind the flat, proper exchanges preceding the panic.

If Phyllis Wakai had not led him to the cellar bar in Roppongi and peered through those enormous glasses as she told him sombrely that Ed Kidderby was covering up a heart condition he might have passed over the annotation the transcriber made when the captain spoke to his first officer for the last time. There was a pause when the captain told him he was taking control of the aircraft from him. There was another pause in Kidderby's last communication with his crew and five times they were audible and recorded as 'er'. And a word, 'fine' had been repeated. The fastidious writer wouldn't have revealed the gaps if they hadn't been long enough to be significant, Alex knew. What had Kidderby seen, or heard, while he was speaking? Why did he check himself in mid-sentence? Or what had he felt? An explosion? Every word, every pause and gap was important now.

And what did the first officer mean when he said 'not again' before his last outburst? Denial was the first reaction in an emergency, disbelief that it was about to cause the unthinkable, the downing of plane. What didn't he want to happen 'again'? Did he shout? Why did he change to Japanese? The working language of the cockpit is English.

Alex returned to the table and jotted some open questions on a pad. He was wondering whether Yuriko Shimada had obtained the cassette, the real record of the last few minutes of NINA 328, when she came in with the clerk Maruta, who dropped a folder showily onto the table and left.

'The journey logs you wanted,' she said flatly. 'They arrived from Narita last night.'

'Thanks,' Alex answered. He looked up. 'Did you find Captain Kidderby's last medical report?'

Yuriko smiled defensively 'We have investigated all possible places but cannot find it. I hope it's not significant.'

'It's incredibly significant,' Alex came back. 'It'd be a serious violation of his pilot's licence to fly if he didn't have a full medical by an authorised doctor every six months and according to the records I went over yesterday he was due his last one in January this year.' Riled, he squared a stack of pages. 'I've heard he may have had some health problems.'

Yuriko's head turned slowly towards him. 'Heard from . . .?'

Something caught his eye in a different file. 'A woman he lived with,' he said lazily, distracted. 'Or someone he knew well.' He looked up. 'I'd like to interview her if we can't get everything sorted out here. That's why I need the up-to-date medical certificates.'

'We understand that point, Mr Bolton,' she agreed. 'And I discussed it with the president before you arrived today.'

'With Miyamoto *san*?'

She almost scowled. 'No, of course not. With Mr Kaneko, president of NN Air. You met him the other night in the boardroom. Mr Kaneko believes some of his foreign pilots preferred to arrange their own medical examinations.'

One of the few faces Alex retrieved easily from a strained memory bank was the weary figure of the airline's chief representative, slumped in a corner armchair and snoring contentedly. 'Where does Mr Kaneko think Captain Kidderby had his last medical and what does he think he did with the certificate? The reports I saw yesterday had the address of a clinic in Nagasaki. Isn't that the spiritual home of your company?'

Yuriko ignored the jibe. 'We expect to find the certificate when we have to sadly clear Captain Kidderby's apartment.' She made a futile sort of motion towards the folders and their spilled contents. 'The airline does not have a large staff, Mr Bolton. This can lead to a certain amount of delay in maintaining the relevant records.'

'You should ask them to try harder,' he said harshly. 'I hear his Japanese girlfriend was worried about his health. He might have had some heart problems the airline didn't know about. Worth following up.' She opened her mouth to speak but Alex remembered the other matter. 'You said you might be able to get me a tape of the cockpit voice recording.'

'Did I?'

'You did. You might ask your boss, your group president this time, Mr Miyamoto, to pull a few strings at the Transport Ministry. I'm not going to be able to get anywhere on my own. I'm the lowest of the low where this investigation is concerned. They'll give me nothing.'

The long afternoon looked like stretching into a late evening, and when Yuriko Shimada left he returned to the documentation, to the load and trim manifests and the carbonised maintenance sheets he had ordered be brought from NN Air's operations centre at Narita. The likelihood of an engine malfunction was receding in his conjectures but he had to eliminate it professionally. The manufacturer of the CFM-56 engines would have called for a hot-section overhaul, where the turbine shafts and discs are removed from the main body of the engine in order to inspect its hottest and most vulnerable part, after three thousand five hundred cycles. He had already worked out that since conversion the DC-8 had been flown over twenty-seven thousand five hundred hours and from sample reports estimated that the engines were started and shut down four times on every trip. He figured that if the aircraft was flying the extremities of Asia it might average four hours' flight between these so-called start and shut-down cycles, making a post-conversion total of around seven thousand cycles in the last eleven years. He plunged into the maintenance records and after calling for Maruta's help discovered that the first hot-section overhaul of the engines was carried out six years earlier. The next was therefore due, but hadn't yet been built into the flying schedules. The CFM-56 engine, while retaining a unique serial number, was modular in construction and over its life parts and modules could be changed during the general maintenance or the repair process. Apart from a few examples of repairs required after engine failures or bird ingestion the maintenance records for NINA 328 showed no deep-seated, chronic, mechanical faults that might point to recurring deficiencies. The aircraft's last maintenance check, couriered from Taipei after a journey that had taken it through four engine cycles to Kuala Lumpur and Sydney before the final outstation in Taiwan, revealed nothing superficially unusual.

He stood and stretched, letting his professional suspicions run free in a mind needled by Yuriko's dismissive reaction to the captain's missing medical certificate. He paced the confines of the room, exercising stiff legs, while he balanced the binder holding the computer-generated medical records. Apart from the heading and a doctor's name, thankfully in English script, he would need help to read and understand the comments in Japanese set against the columns of numerical readouts. There were the overall health summaries to translate as well.

He was nodding ruefully as he flipped the pages when his investigation collapsed. Through the glass panel in the door he saw a group of people filling his vision, bearing down on the meeting room. The men he did not recognise wore conspicuous identity badges, like those he had seen at the Haneda crash site, and he guessed who they were and what their purpose was. The gap he needed to fill was in his hands, and with no time for niceties or explanations he tugged one of Kidderby's medical reports from the binder, and it was folded among his private notes and papers when the door opened.

A feeble knock on the door revealed the president of NN Air, Kaneko, stooped, embarrassed, his broad hairless crown gleaming with sweat. Behind him Alex saw Yuriko Shinada with at least six solemn-looking men around her. On the back fringe of the group Yoshi Kanagawa's face peered apologetically. Yuriko gave him a desperate, almost theatrical sigh. 'These gentlemen are from the Aircraft Accident Investigation Committee of the Minstry of Transport.' One of them held up an identification badge and eased himself into the room. Yuriko followed. 'Group President Miyamoto has agreed to their request to examine the records of NN Air as a matter of urgency. I'm afraid they must take them away.'

'I only need a few more hours with them,' Alex pleaded. Maruta was already separating and repacking the folders and boxes, classifying them for the officials. The table was soon cleared. The airline's president said something to Yuriko.

'Mr Kaneko requests your understanding and cooperation,

Mr Bolton,' she declared like a liturgy. 'He apologises for the inconvenience.'

Alex shrugged. 'Sure.' They had walked into the open office where more documentation was being gathered by harried staff. 'Please thank Mr Kaneko for his concern.' He left them, bristling, returning alone to the room and the table, clear but for his notes and recording equipment. Why did people talk to him in stern, rigid phrases? Everyone seemed to have the same expression for a given situation, as if it were rehearsed. He asked Yoshi Kanagawa about it when the broker came in and closed the door.

'We try not to offend,' Yoshi explained. 'Keep the harmony of the group, all that crap.'

'So how do I know what's going on? What people really want.' He started to pack his chart case.

Yoshi grinned. 'You have to work it out for yourself from what we don't say.' He balanced Alex's compact video camera and took a pretend sweep of the room with it. Then he said, 'Look, if I say to you, "would you like a beer?" and you don't want one, you can't say "no, thank you."'

Alex looked up from sorting his papers. 'Why not? You've got a word for "no" because it's in the phrase book I bought.'

Yoshi made a friendly, patronising face. 'Yes, but you don't use it. It's too direct, too offensive. You say "it's difficult" or "I'm fine". Just keep away from the N-word.'

Alex chuckled, his head rocking. He almost missed the buff envelope holding the flimsy piece of paper with its old-fashioned Japanese writing. It was trapped behind the bulk of the briefcase. He assured himself the letter was in place and tracked inside his case for the thicker folder containing the wartime diaries. He had stored it in a side pocket, he remembered, after detaching the letter from the diary papers stapled to it. There were over thirty pages of single-spaced typing, he guessed, flipping them. He promised himself that once he had reached a conclusion on the air crash he would go beyond the strange note, with the bizarre mention of the Japanese firm he happened to be in, and read the diaries, perhaps on the aeroplane home. He had the typed sheets and the letter in his hands as he looked around instinctively for a stapler or a clip of some sort. But it wasn't right: something pressed his think-again button. The sifting of a million fragments for a hair-breadth fracture in a part the size of a needle had given him his own kind of touch sensitivity and the precision of a surgeon, and when his thumb brushed the thread of metal securing the pages, hard but as thin as fuse wire, he knew it was not in order. He brought it close and touched it again. It was smooth, unblemished. And new. The staple that had held the pages of the diaries and the document together twenty-four hours earlier had a slight dent at each end and it was rough to the touch. It was a very old staple, completely browned with rust. He rubbed the new aluminium clip, then stowed the papers in the case, his movements sluggish, slowed by incomprehension and a creeping sense of wariness.

'How about a beer?' Yoshi said. 'It's half past six and we'll be the first to leave.'

'What? Oh, sure.' Alex woke up with a laugh. 'Since I can't say "no" in Japan I'll say "yes".' He handed the other man his Nikon. 'Let's go to my hotel. I don't want to leave my gear around here over the weekend.'

'The guy from South Miami Aviation's been on to me twice today,' Yoshi said, as they waited by the kerb for a taxi. 'Sanguillen. He's finally got the message that the reason *you* can't talk to him is because you're trying to clear up the mess and get him his money. So he's bugging me.'

A green and white chequered taxi pulled over, its hazard lights flashing. It was tight in the back, with the cases and equipment.

'I hadn't finished with the records the ministry hauled

off,' Alex said. 'There are a few curly bits I want to straighten out before I make a recommendation to the insurance syndicate but I might have enough by Monday to keep Sanguillen calm.'

'Are you staying in the city over the weekend? If you want I can arrange a short trip somewhere. Help you relax.' Alex smiled to himself. Yuriko had used the same words. Everyone wanted to help him relax, in their different ways.

Then he thought about Phyllis Wakai and the visit she had planned to a place somewhere south of Yokohama to meet a real vintage old-Japan hand. They were drifting in heavy traffic on a wide avenue housing the government ministries whose lights blazed into the evening. Normal for bureaucrats, Yoshi explained.

The little cubes with the patterned numbers were no longer made of ivory but the plastic imitation tiles clattered and clacked like the real thing, slammed together by the four players when they shuffled them and built the walls at the start of a new round. It was close to midnight but two tables in the Fukuoka air-conditioned cellar club were still in business, the young *yakuza* around them playing mah-jongg boisterously, half drunk, shrouded in cigarette smoke, ignoring the girls who waited with bored attentiveness until they were summoned with a gruff scowl. At a table backing a wall, with a clear view of the glass-fronted door to the stairway, Kazuo Kamei was already a clear leader as they reached the late stages of their session: none of his three companions had a positive sheet after six rounds. With his clear, pale olive skin, neat salaryman's haircut and trimly-cut suit, he looked out of place around the punched-permed hair, the pocked, scarred faces and the tattoos showing beneath unbuttoned, creased shirts. He was running a moderately high-scoring hand, with an average chance of winning, when he saw a figure descend the stairs and give a note to the

99

nearest girl through a half-opened door. She was still a
teenager, her hair crimped and dyed auburn, too much rouge
on her thin lips, and she swayed across the room on high,
sharp heels to Kamei's table, happy to play the messenger,
eager to impress the senior man. Discarding a white dragon
pai with a flick of a finger and concentrating on the game, he
lifted her sham-leather skirt with his free hand and cupped
her buttocks as he drew her against his shoulder. He flipped
the lip of the envelope and disengaged from her reluctantly.

'Fuck off,' he said, without looking up at the girl. The
other three fell silent, as they knew they had to while Kamei
read the short, handwritten note and slipped the green train
ticket into his jacket pocket. He swore again, this time
silently, to himself.

Across Fukuoka City, in the basement storeroom of a
Hakata cabaret, Wataru Hinohara wiped the cutting edge of
his short-sword on the jacket of the Chinese gangster they
had handcuffed and gagged. The cut he had inflicted on his
face drew a neat curtain of blood while the elasticated waistband they had used to gag his protests and keep his moans to
a throaty growl was already soaked since Hinohara had
delivered an opening kick to the man's mouth. The booming
beat from the disco somewhere above and the wails from a
row of nearby karaoke cubicles served to muffle the noise
they made; even the clatter from the collapse of a stack of
crates, which spilled and smashed the empty beer bottles in
them when the prisoner put up an arrogant front and was
punished for it with a volley of fists to his stomach and
kidneys.

Hinohara had discovered the power of his brute strength in
his early adulthood when, at twenty, the killing of a man from
a rival gang had put him in prison, charged with
manslaughter, for five years. He was exceptionally strong and
had not yet learned how far he could go, how much hurt he
could inflict before pulling back. He came out of prison to the

usual raucous party of welcome at a local hotel, a hero to the three hundred punks in the gang. The *oyabun* chief believed in him but forced him to understand the self-control techniques of karate and sent him to Hawaii to learn to shoot effectively, before giving him his own patch of *pachinko* pinball parlours and massage salons to manage. Now he had caught a scout from a Shanghai gang working out of Tokyo who'd been spotted once too often on Hinohara's turf, cruising the cabarets and *soapland* rub-down dives to evaluate the possibilities of business expansion in the Kyushu capital.

'This is Okudaira-gumi territory,' he bellowed at the broken face on the floor, his own rough skin flowing with sweat. 'You understand that, you Chinese piece of shit, Fukuoka is ours.' The crippled man doubled and rolled instinctively to avoid a kick that never came, shards of glass crackling under him. The three Okudaira *yakuza* bawled in delight, one of them swivelling to deliver a swing-back kick to the groin when the muscles of the Chinese relaxed.

Another crop-headed man, a colourful shirt hanging over his jeans, appeared at the head of the short flight of stairs that led to an alley where he had been on watch. He was clutching a mobile telephone. He smirked once at the writhing figure on the floor and motioned to Hinohara, who sheathed the sword and wiped his hands before taking the call in a corner. He nodded, smiling weakly and grunting as he accepted the orders arriving over the line. When he had finished he handed the telephone back to the guard and growled, making a triumphant fist.

'It's a few days in Tokyo for me, lads. First train out of Hakata tomorrow.' He looked long at his watch. 'I mean later today. You'll have to survive without me.'

They were making envious noises when one of them nudged the Chinese with a pointed shoe. 'What do we do with this? In the bay as usual? Or scattered?'

'*Baka!*' Hinohara scowled. 'Don't be a fool. He's got to

101

take the message back to the Chinese scum in Tokyo. Hands off Fukuoka! Dump him in the fucking station lavatory.'

Yoshi Kanagawa was good company, his competent English enriched by an exaggerated American drawl and a spread of idioms, all slightly out of context. They had finished a couple of beers in the Samurai Bar and Yoshi introduced Alex to *tempura,* sitting at a counter in a hotel restaurant which smelled of new pine as the chef dipped prawns, fillets of small white fish and leaves like nettles in a delicate batter in front of them. By ten thirty Alex was alone, stretched on his bed. He looked listlessly at the depressing batch of photographs he had taken at the site, his task still unresolved and his suspicions about the health of the chief pilot shouting for attention, but he was distracted by the diaries that lay next to him, their pages now joined with a new staple. Anyone could have entered the conference room where he had left his unlocked briefcase and photocopied the diary pages while he was eating with the journalist and fending off Yuriko Shimada. Why? Or was he wrong about the staple?

He was stooped at the mini-bar when a reception clerk telephoned, apologising for the lateness of the hour but informing him that a package had been delivered for him. When the light knock came he half expected to find Yuriko propped against the door frame, one leg crossed over the other, her pink-tipped fingers dangling a pair of long-stemmed clinking wineglasses. He smiled at the young bellhop who brought him the paperback sized padded envelope. Inside he found a cassette tape. The compliments slip with it was blank apart from the vivid green NN Air logo drawn inside the contours of an aeroplane's tail. The tape was too large for his dictation machine and he felt disinclined to instigate a midnight hunt in the hotel.

He called Reggie Cameron in London, explaining that he

was now working blind following a sweep of NN Air's records by the official investigators, but was leaning towards human error rather than mechanical failure or abnormal meteorological conditions. The cockpit voice recorder might yield something and he promised to call Cameron at home at a decent time on Saturday after he'd found a machine to run it on. He completed his preliminary report on his laptop and had it faxed to Cameron. Returning to his room, he stripped and showered and went to bed with a brandy and the wartime diaries of an old POW called Tom Humphrey.

<u>24 April 1942</u>
*Got back to the camp today after two weeks in the
hospital ship. Given egg, rice and soup for supper.
Dysentery everywhere. Three more Dutchmen died on
Thursday and an Englishman yesterday. Bro Buff has
been put on danger list. A lot of people have bad septic
sores on their hands and feet. They are awful to look at.
The Camp gets only so much medical supply every day
and the Dutch get treated first. There's nothing left by
the time the English and the Yanks get through.*
<u>29 April</u>
*No working parties today. Jap emperor's birthday. Had
another stunt in which we all had to face the sun and
keep silent for a minute. Not issued any rice today but
we were given soya beans and cucumbers for dinner
and meat, potatoes and spinach for supper. It was quite
a change from rice and everyone enjoyed it.*
<u>3 May</u>
*Brenda's birthday today and no card from Daddy. Poor
kiddie. I trust I will be in a position to send one next
year. She's nine years old. I bet she's growing into a*

fine girl. Went with working party to clear out a burnt warehouse on the docks. It kept my mind off home. It held some tinned milk, some of which was good, and I was allowed to drink it with my dinner. I hid 4 tins in my clothes and got them into camp. They will last me several days. It's the first milk since leaving the Jap destroyer which picked me up on March 1.

8 May
No work parties today so spent the day washing clothes and doing odd jobs. Started a garden with another chap called Hassell. We have got 4 rows of Beans, 2 rows of Onions, 5 Marrows, 3 Tomato plants and 3 Water Melon Plants. Opened a tin of milk. Boy, was it good.

12 May
Inside working party today, in charge of refuse cart. Took it to the dump outside the camp and was allowed to buy some bananas, or peesang as the natives call them. Managed to smuggle some into camp. It was Pat's birthday on 9 May. Again not a card from Dad. Doesn't seem 12 years since she was born.

16 May
Made some cheese with the milk that had started to go bad. It might be fit to eat in a week's time. Inside working today, with the cart again. Bought 40 packets of cig paper and resold them, making a Golden profit. Have got a very bad sore on my left leg that will not heal.

24 May
Empire Day today. Leg is not getting better and I have got an abscess on my left buttock. The Dutch have been stopped from going on outside work parties. Japs say they have been receiving news from the natives. Heard that one was beaten to death. Made another 50 cents selling cig paper.

28 May

Jap sentry showed me photo of the Exeter *being sunk. They came from a book like our* War Weekly *at home. 1st Lieut told us tonight that the Japs had not sent any list of the POW names from the Island to Japan yet but said the Captain's still trying to get it sent home. I hope so, as after next week Kath's money will stop. From now on I shall write down all the news that I hear under the heading Today's Buzz. So here goes for today. Allied troops landed on Java. A Jap destroyer in harbour with a large hole in her bows.*

30 May

Today's Buzz. 100,000 Yankee troops landed in England. Japan had biggest air raid since she entered the war on Tokio and Yokohama. Russia still advancing slowly. Local – saw three planes this afternoon. Don't know who they belong to. Hope they were Yanks. It's been 13 weeks since Exeter *sunk.*

1 June

Don't feel so good today. Can't sit down and I can hardly walk. Today's Buzz. 1 Jap cruiser sunk off Makassar. Japs expecting attack on this island. 1500 British planes carried out attack on the Ruhr. Germany asked for peace. Yanks reported to have landed on the north of this island (Celebes). Hard to believe really.

9 June

I could not write these last few days. The pain's been awful. Doc finally cut the abscess out of my backside this morning. I am writing this lying on my stomach and already feel better. There's not been much food this week. The soups are thin and the rice is dirty. I got slapped on Tuesday for getting my number wrong at roll-call. Tenko they call it. I was delirious with pain at the time from my abscess and bad leg. Buzzes today: naval battle off Midway, today's results; Japs lost 2

carriers, 3 battleships, 4 cruisers and 7 small
warships, Germans launched attack against Karkov,
British forces made a hit and run raid on channel
ports, 4 big towns in Germany bombed out.
11 June
Feeling brand new today. Can sit down fairly well on a
cushion but my leg and feet are not much better. The
Japs beat up a Dutchman who had received a letter
from his wife and she had to witness it. After that they
destroyed her home. Buzz today: Germany invaded
England. America has given Japan the last offer of
peace terms and if she does not accept, Yanks say they
will bomb Japan until it is flat. Buzz from outside
working party – that Jap troops have been moved to
the north of the island.

The roofs on a row of immaculately polished executive cars
parked inside the hotel grounds, facing the fake earthern-
style wall bordering the road, reflected the brilliance of the
sun. They were all plain, black company vehicles except for
a squat British Mini with a smiling whale painted on its sky-
blue roof and a pair of large five-toed footprints stencilled on
the two side doors. Bored chauffeurs lounged in groups or
wiped their cars with long-handled feather dusters. Alex
watched from his window, coffee cup in his hand, as he
waited for Phyllis Wakai. He checked the delicate old
document, folded along its original sharp crease, and the
fading pages of the diaries, both now held together with a
gentle, plastic bulldog clip. He packed them into a hotel
envelope with the cassette of the cockpit voice recording. A
call came from reception and he found Phyl in the lobby,
clad as usual in her baggy dungerees, white T-shirt and the
red baseball cap, her rimless, smokily opaque glasses
masking her face like a pair of goggles. She bowed from the
waist when he approached. 'Learn the customs, *gaijin san,*'

107

she smiled as she looked up. She bounced jauntily on her sneakers as she led him to the strip of parking space in front of the main entrance. 'I managed to find a place out here. Saved me from the underground garage.'

His face sagged when they stopped at the Mini. Alex was dressed plainly. He had not expected much time away from the investigation and he was wearing the only casual clothes he had brought: slacks, chequered cotton shirt and a blazer. The whale's grin seemed to widen when Alex opened the door below its mouth. He threw it a mean scowl as he eased his six-foot frame into the low-slung car.

'Like it, huh?' she asked, throwing him a cheerful glance. 'We've about three, three and a half hours to go, if we're lucky. It's only thirty miles or but it's wall-to-wall buildings and cars and the roads wind a bit.' She turned on to the Toranomon slip road, her arms almost embracing the oversized steering wheel.

Alex felt trapped. 'We could have taken a train, couldn't we?'

'C'mon Alex. This is more fun. And it gives us a lot of time to talk.' She picked up the Daini Keihin Tokyo–Yokohama road at Shinagawa. It was broad, but the pressure of traffic kept them at a crawl and the grey, urban cityscape was even more claustrophobic. Old and modern buildings were at all angles to each other and separated by the narrowest of alleys. Occasionally there were gaps where clusters of trees hiding a Buddhist temple or a Shinto shrine broke the dullness, or the forecourt of a train station carved a plaza for a taxi rank or bus stop. The urban railways they crossed were part of a vast web whose strands cut through the city, brushing between houses and buildings; the roads were overcrowded arteries where cars, hardly any of them more than two or three years old, Alex guessed, made an endless gently flowing stream, nudged along by lorries decorated with lights and chrome and harassed by nippy utility vans and motorcycles. The streets

Phyllis followed were universally narrow, with plain painted lines marking off nominal pavements; encroached by vending machines, pillars and poles, and straddled endlessly by wires and cables.

'Want to try?' she asked cheerfully as they approached the Ohashi Bridge to cross the Tama River. The river was wide with sandy islands and deep troughs as it neared its end a few kilometres away in Tokyo Bay. The banks were even wider, accommodating a dusty, flat golf range on one side of the water and an area of baseball diamonds and soccer pitches on the other. 'We drive on the same side of the road as you guys, right?'

An aeroplane, low and silent in the distance over Haneda, reminded Alex of his mission. The voice recording of NINA 328's last minutes was in his jacket pocket and he had slid it mentally into Phyl's car cassette player a dozen times. But he wanted to listen to it alone first: she had known the pilot and he wasn't sure how she would react emotionally while she was driving. And she was a journalist, and he still wasn't sure about her.

'Right. And no thanks. I'll just enjoy the concrete scenery.'

'Look at that,' Phyllis said. 'Your friends.' They had stopped for a red light and Alex followed her eyes to the refrigerated lorry in the parallel lane. On its side was a bold pentagon whose white interior held three roman letters: two fused green N's followed by a hyphen and a bold T. She said, 'All the component companies of the Nippon Nagasaki group have the same basic logo. Trading, marine engineering, transportation like this truck, insurance, you name it. It's the two N's plus a little something else to identify the business. That one's obviously "transportation". The airline adds the word "Air" to its planes, as you know. All group workers have a miniature logo on a badge on their jackets. You must have seen them.'

Alex nodded, grateful for the piece of Japanalia. He *had* wondered why all the dark-suited men around Marunouchi, NNC or otherwise, had a little sphere in their lapels.

'His name's William Littleton,' Phyl said when they were in a steady crawl within the industrial city of Kawasaki, heading for Yokohama. 'He's eighty-four, eighty-five I guess. There are still a few of these guys left. Some women as well. They came here like pioneers in the first decades of the century and a lot of them stayed on. There's an American in Osaka who was repatriated back home after Pearl Harbor, fought the Japanese, got captured in the Philippines, came back here as a prisoner and ended up in a camp two miles away from his old house.'

Alex remembered the POW's diaries. He had read the close print as far as the day in 1942 when the English sailor and other survivors of *HMS Exeter* had settled in to a camp on the Celebes with hundreds of Dutch and American prisoners of war. 'Amazing. Was your friend interned here when war started?'

'Yes, but not for long. I think the secret police thought he was a spy or something. He did a bit of journalism for an English-language newspaper in the thirties but he was actually an accountant. They let him go finally on one of the repatriation ships.'

'Did he join the forces as well?'

'Because his Japanese was absolutely fluent they put him in intelligence and when the war ended he came back with the occupation forces. Worked at the war crimes trials and then went back to his old work in accountancy.'

'You seem to know him well,' Alex said. They were in a jam, close to the ramp leading to a stretch of motorway which by-passed central Yokohama. A group of schoolgirls in sailor uniforms giggled at the car's decorations and peered inside.

'When you're in journalism and you've been here a while

110

it's worth getting to know guys like Bill Littleton. They're like living history.' She glared from under the cap at the back of a car that cut in sharply. 'Dickhead! But Bill's special. He's kind of adopted me. Says he knew relatives of my grandparents who came from Okayama prefecture, down in the south of Honshu.'

'You think he can figure out what my letter means?'

Phyllis adjusted the red cap. 'I think so. At least the language. His parents came to Japan as missionaries and they sent him to the local schools. He learned all that old shit, you know, those out-of-date characters and all. I know he still reads and writes Japanese because he earns a few yen from translations. He's also been helping me with my research on the Nippon Nagasaki group, like the early days, where most of the documentation and records are only in Japanese. He's going to love your bit of paper.'

Kamei elbowed his dozing companion when the *Nozomi* super express shuddered gently, the brakes engaging as it slowed through Shinagawa. High from the beating he had inflicted on the Shanghai mobster twelve hours earlier, Hinohara went on to visit a sauna bath-house under his gang's protection, calling a dating agency as he soaked. The twenty-year-old university student they sent stripped to the *muzak* out of her high-school sailor uniform while he received a rub-down from a blind masseuse. When they were alone, she played her fingers over the patterns of the garish tattoos on his belly and thighs until he was aroused and then blew him. Tired but content, he had made the bullet train with minutes to spare, breakfasting on beer and seaweed rolls and sleeping for most of the three hours since passing through Hiroshima.

He yawned loudly as they left the train at Tokyo Station, following Kamei in the bustle of people heading for the steps leading down to the exits. Suddenly Kamei turned round and they jostled against the flow towards a stairway nearer the back of the train. A woman dressed for business with a briefcase and rolled newspaper paused at the head of the steps, casually sweeping the destination signs hung above the platforms. As the two men approached she moved towards them, her eyes still inquisitively distracted, slowing only to drop the newspaper in a litter bin. Kamei caught her eyes as she passed and moved to the bin. There was nothing unusual in a suited salaryman exchanging his own newspaper for another or for a discarded weekly magazine and Kamei picked up the last deposit, casually checking the title and walking away. On the steps, Hinohara at his side, he funnelled the newspaper and tapped it against the heel of his hand, in time with the rhythm of the descent. By the last step the locker key inside it had slipped into his hand.

It was smoother than Phyllis had imagined. The weather was turning, discouraging the Saturday trippers from a day on the Shonan beaches. She turned onto the Yokohama–Yokosuka road, which split the Miura Peninsula along its spine, and then onto a new stretch of road which met the sea between Zushi and Hayama. They stopped to eat when the forested hillsides gave way to a village that straddled a narrow road twisting between vegetable plots and farmhouses surrounded by small rice paddies. The sea they had glimpsed often as a short flash of iridescence appeared when they rounded a bend at the foot of sharp hill, and they ate fat, deep-fried prawns on rice in a simple café overlooking a harbour.

Half an hour later, frustrated by buses and lorries on the narrow road, they reached the little resort on the west side of the boot-shaped peninsula. Hayama, Phyllis explained, where the Imperial family kept a summer bolt-hole, was an upmarket area of quiet hillside villas and holiday apartments around the marina. Bill Littleton's two-storey weathered old house was on a short spur of land between the sea and the rising road, almost hidden by the canopy of trees whose roots had broken through the rocky break on the ocean side. Phyllis said it was over seventy years old, which was quite rare in Japan because wooden houses were usually reconstructed after forty or so. She thought that Littleton's parents had built it on leased land and as Hayama grew, attracting the wealthy, Bill, who still paid a derisory ground rent, had resisted efforts by the landowner's descendants to dislodge him.

There was no response to her call so she let them in, chiding Alex when he strode up from the hallway step without taking his shoes off. He rapped his head on the low beam to the main rooms and learned quickly that he should move around a Japanese house in a permanent stoop. The side of the house facing the bay was open, the windows and rain doors drawn aside, and even the breeze filtering through the insect mesh made little impact on the musty odour of damp, weather-scarred wood. The main room was on two levels, separated by a single step. The lower room was made into a study. On plain floorboards, it was packed with books, some on shelves, others in tidy heaps on the floor. William Littleton worked with his back to the sea at a lacquer-topped desk. His eyes would be on a faded *sumie* ink scroll in an alcove. The elaborately written ranking of wrestlers from a long-ago sumo tournament was framed on another wall. The larger area was covered with tatami reed matting, flanked with more book shelves and a television in a corner and centred with a knee-high table on four stubby legs. Photographs filled a patch of wall in a monochromed personal history of a lifetime in Japan. Some were simple portraits with no background, others views of village streets where the women still wore kimonos.

'There's Bill,' Phyllis said. She had pulled the insect mesh apart and stood on the veranda, overlooking the wide beach which dipped unevenly to the shoreline. A string of yachts furrowed a lazy sea in the far distance while windsurfers strained against a stiff breeze closer in. Alex joined her and followed the direction of her arm to where a bare-chested, wiry, tanned figure in khaki shorts was talking to a Japanese couple at the water's edge.

'Bill! Bill, we're here!'

Littleton waved back, bowed away from the Japanese and jogged barefoot up the coarse sand towards his house, a bunch of lumpy seaweed in his hand. He had strands of silver hair brushed back over a speckled, raw-red scalp and leathered, taut skin on a slender face. Sinewy arms swung easily against his chest, which was a mat of dark grey curls. He did not look eighty-five as he skipped up the short stepladder to the veranda and embraced Phyllis. His age was in his voice – a gravelly, lazy, slightly strained way of speaking – and in the heavy, layered eyelids. He shook hands with Alex and led them to his kitchen, where he dropped the seaweed into a strainer and boiled a pan of water. 'Sake?' There was nothing else on offer. They squatted around the low table and Littleton poured the warmed rice wine into ceramic thimbles as Phyllis described the circumstances of her meeting with the English insurance investigator.

'A terrible thing,' Litteton drawled. 'Thank God it wasn't a passenger plane.'

'Do you share Phyl's negative attitude towards Nippon Nagasaki?' Alex asked.

Littleton shifted on his cushion, as if preparing to make a well-practised speech without notes. 'The multi-layered Japanese conglomerates are much the same and I'm sure you've come across them in Britain. Mitsubishi this, Mitsubishi that. They're usually made up of a bank, a big general trading arm, a high-tech enterprise, a chemical, heavy industrial producer, even a department store chain. You're looking at more than a hundred companies linked by interlocking shareholdings and sharing a commonality of purpose and support, if you will. You can guarantee that if you visit a Mitsui group company, everything in that building has been produced by a Mitsui company or a member of its *zaibatsu*. The elevators, the desks, the steel, the ferro-concrete and the goddamn cars that carry the bigshots around.'

Phyllis touched Bill's arm and said to Alex, 'We call them *keiretsu* nowadays. A group of related companies. *Zaibatsu* has some old connotations.' Alex leaned back on his hands, his legs and back beginning to ache.

The old man was relishing the occasion. 'They lead the economy from the front. They're the guys who roam the globe, buying raw materials, building factories and selling their production. Always have done. They ran the economy for the military before and during the war, bought up everything that went bankrupt or came on the market and, when the big bad generals had been hanged, rose from the ashes after the US occupation forces tried and failed to break them up. Mitsubishi, Mitsui, Sumitomo, and the others.'

'Seems to me Miyamoto and his kind have done a great job for Japan,' Alex said.

Littleton cleared his throat. 'NNC don't fit into the traditional *zaibatsu* mold. They don't have a couple of centuries of history, like Mitsui, for example. They're relative newcomers, somewhat like Toyota and Matsushita, firms that came to fame after the war as specialists, not as general traders.' He tapped the solid cover of a thick Japanese reference book. 'It was founded in Nagasaki, hence the name, between the wars. Kyushu was the heart of Japan's massive shipbuilding industry so it was natural that marine engineers and the technology they had to offer gravitated to the southern island. The demand for ships up to and through the Second World War was of course the greatest spur to NNC's prosperity. They've never looked back.'

'I've seen a photograph of a *gaijin* with NNC's founder, Shinichi Miyamoto. Was that common?'

Littleton puffed. 'There were thousands of foreigners in Japan before the war. Like me. Engineers, lawyers, journalists, teachers. The Japanese needed their skills. Don't forget that for two and half centuries, until the overthrow of the shogun generals who ran the country, it was forbidden on pain of death to enter or leave Japan. The new order had a lot of catching up to do.' He smiled ruefully. 'When the military fanatics got back in control and went looking for an empire, the foreigners were expelled again.'

Alex's face showed a trace of impatience. 'Phyl's saying that my clients at NNC and Miyamoto don't follow the rules. That they're, what? Criminals?'

Littleton smiled at Phyllis, as if apologising for having to explain yet again to a dumb Westerner how Japan worked. He let her fill his sake cup. 'I don't want to bore you with the Japan Incorporated stuff,' he said to Alex. 'Just let me say that Japan is essentially a conservative country where the deeply held belief that its people are absolutely superior to all other countries embraces ninety-five per cent of the population.' The old man's head shook. 'It doesn't mean they're all fascists and want to take over the world. It means that all the components within this hundred-and-twenty-five-million-person society, from the trade unions, the multinationals and Japan's notoriously corrupt politicians to the folks in the corner shop, share unwritten common beliefs. And common objectives, if you will. And there will be interaction between these groups, even if on the surface they seem to be opposites.'

'Even between gangsters and businessmen?' Alex asked suspiciously.

'And politicians,' Littleton declared. 'The crime syndicates – the Japanese call them *boryokudan,* "violence groups" – are organised like any other corporate institution and their services are on offer to anyone who'll pay for them. It would be very unusual if a Japanese company didn't have contacts with the *yakuza* in one form or another.'

Alex shook his head at revelations he had not come across in the Japan briefings he had attended over the years.

'Show Bill the letter,' Phyllis said softly.

He slid the old document carefully from its envelope and laid it on the table. 'The foreigner in the photograph in NNC's boardroom is a Swede called Jonsson. My guide pronounced it like "yonson". Anyway, his name's mentioned in this piece of paper which was issued by our former operation in Japan. I'm just interested in knowing what it is before I give it to Miyamoto for his company records.' He raised his eyebrows to Phyllis. 'And she wants to know whether it's relevant to her research.'

The old man put his elbows on the table and pitched his vision at the appropriate distance to read the letters without touching the fragile paper. He emitted a low, long groan from the throat. 'The main fold line cuts right through a line of characters.' He raised himself from the floor. 'I'll need some time,' he said, lifting the letter gingerly by a corner. 'With the dictionaries and magnifying glass in my study. Why don't you guys take a walk on the beach or something.'

Phyllis steadied herself against his arm on the slippery stepladder, then jumped the last gap onto the beach. The pebbles crunched under their feet.

'How much of NNC's early years did you cover when you started researching your book, Phyl?' Alex asked.

'Getting hold of any kind of reliable information is really tough in this country. Miyamoto's office were really kind to me when I first got in touch. They thought I was going to write another book glorifying Shinichi Miyamoto's part in the Japanese miracle.'

'So they stopped cooperating with you?'

'When they realised I wanted the real story, not the gloss, they got a little rough with me. Threw me physically out of their building one time and threatened me with lawsuits unless I repeated the official version. That's why they shoved me around and photographed me when I jumped your car the other night. They know me well.' They reached the water's edge, where the shingle gave way to dark grey volcanic sand. 'The problem with searching for the truth is that Japanese companies like to create their own myths, especially the *zaibatsu* who drove the war machine. Then there's a shortage of real evidence. A massive amount of documentation disappeared in the 1923 earthquake, which destroyed Tokyo and Yokohama, and even more from allied bombing in the war. The wood burned and the brick buildings collapsed, destroying records, documents, stock certificates, everything that wasn't in solid safes. There wasn't much left of Tokyo after the fire-bombings in March 1945.' She emitted an ironic grunt. 'A lot of companies erased their wartime sins by burning their own records and claiming they were destroyed by the incendiaries.'

'Is that what happened to NNC's old records? They were lost in the air-raids.'

Phyllis scooped a flat stone and sent it skimming into a limply breaking wave. 'I guess so. My opening chapter's going to be short. The marine engineering works and ship repair yards in Nagasaki suffered a little damage but they weren't destroyed. The B-29s went after the Mitsubishi dockyards and the armaments factories closer to the city. But Nippon Nagasaki's old Tokyo headquarters, where the records were kept, was completely flattened. Left in a pile of ashes, like everything else.'

'It doesn't seem that defeat did them much damage in the long run,' Alex said. 'Like Japan itself.' They had reached the sea wall protecting the marina and turned back, into a high, bright sun.

Phyllis explained how defeat had indeed been kind to Nippon Nagasaki KK, as it was known at the outbreak of war, and to the Miyamoto family, who still held large blocks

118

of shares in NNC and the main group companies. Her writer's façade of impartiality was beginning to crack; her voice barely hiding the scorn she felt for her subject. She told Alex how the ships the founder Shinichi Miyamoto purchased cheaply from distressed customers had been sunk but the land and factory capacity, and the skilled workforce, stayed largely intact. More significantly for the Miyamotos' prosperity, she said, jabbing the air with a finger, the wrath of General Douglas MacArthur's occupation forces fell on the giant *zaibatsu*; Mitsubishi, Mitsui, Yasuda and the other seven family holding companies that controlled three-quarters of Japanese industry, finance and commerce at the start of the Second World War. Long before it ended they had been identified by the Allies as the locomotive driving Japan's devastating imperial ambitions.

The occupiers broke them up as well as they could but since the Japanese claimed most of their records had been destroyed by the Allies themselves it was impossible to unravel the family shareholdings completely. The house of Miyamoto was lesser fry, deemed to have done no worse than any other patriotic company when ordered to direct production towards the war effort. The Nippon Nagasaki factories came to life again, repairing vessels, restoring engines and turbines and supplying equipment for the surviving coastal shipping fleet. Through growth and acquisition, opportunism and a rich mixture of skill and ruthlessness, Shinichi Miyamoto built a multi-billion-dollar empire around marine engineering and a nationwide transport network and over time took share interests in companies with no obvious allegiance to their big-brother, re-emerged *zaibatsu*. Around Nippon Nagasaki Corporation were subsidiaries or affiliates in finance, commerce and industry where employees proudly wore the five-sided green logo. Hiroshi Miyamoto, son of the founder, ran the conglomerate from his position as president of NNC.

'And it was Hiroshi who decided to move into air transport,' Alex guessed.

'Right. He already had a fleet of container ships and the second biggest land transport network in Japan and completed the circle with air cargo when he set up NN Air six years ago.'

'Phyl!' Littleton was waving from his veranda, beckoning them back, and when they were closer he urged them to hurry. They found him sitting at the work desk in his study, two thick, well-used books opened around a notepad and an Anglepoise lamp craned low over the faded, dark purple printing.

Phyllis put a hand on his shoulder. 'Have you figured it out, Bill? They could tell he was quietly pleased with himself. He was rubbing the heels of his hands together.

'The subject's not that complicated,' he said, his hands skimming over the paper. 'I came across a few like this in the thirties. 'See these characters in this headline, Phyl?'

She leaned over the desk, Alex on the other side. 'Something about "change",' she ventured.

'Right. It translates as "amendment to company registration". It's actually a legal document.'

Alex pointed to the extravagant logo of his old Japanese operation at the head of the page. 'We're in insurance, not law. I don't see how the company could issue something like this.'

Littleton turned his long weathered face upwards, his eyes lively with knowledge. 'No, no, they could. Foreign insurance firms were really big here after the First World War. American and British mostly. The Japanese were only just starting to understand what insurance was, so the *gaijin* firms had an open market. When their foreign clients wanted a tie-up, or some kind of contract with the Japanese, they had to act as quasi-legal entities. There weren't many foreign lawyers around at the time as I recall.' He directed them to a cluster of four faint reddish circles and a similarly vermillion-coloured square, each of them containing a blurred jumble of lines. 'These are *hanko*,' he said for Alex's benefit. 'Seals, chops, whatever you want to call them. They're carved with individual Japanese characters and act in the same way as a signature. They have the same legal force. At the time this was drawn up they were the only way to legalise a document.'

'Still are, mostly,' Phyllis told Alex.

'So who put them here?'

Littleton's face creased. 'They're not too clear, are they Phyl? I'm pretty certain this larger one's your old company, Alex. The others are going to belong to the two companies specified in the document and I'm fairly sure the square one belongs to the government agency that authorised, or notarised, the deal it talks about.'

'Can you make out the deal?' Alex said, both entralled by the unravelling story and mystified as to how meaning could derive from these bizarre jumblings of penstrokes.

'That's a fairly simple job,' Littleton declared proudly, without boasting. 'It's really only a document of recognition. That's a Japanese concept. There's probably a more detailed contract somewhere with the finer points more explicitly laid out. This simple page could be copied easily and carried around, attached to licences, whatever, to prove that the company's name has been legally changed.'

'How do you mean *changed*?' It was Alex.

Littleton brought his hands together triumphantly. 'Let's sit at the table. Have a coffee if you like.'

'I can take a hint,' Phyllis intoned with mock annoyance.

Alex would have preferred to stand but the other two were sitting with straight backs around the sawn-off table, Littleton's reference books and notes besides them. The sky over the bay was streaked with heavy clouds and Littleton had responded to the coolness by changing into trousers and a buttoned jersey. He served Phyllis's coffee with a dish of spongy *manju* bean-paste cakes and tore a page from his notebook. 'I did a very rough translation while you were on the beach.'

J o n s s o n Nagasaki KK
N i p p o n Nagaski KK
To acknowledge and recognize changed circumstances concerning the above companies in relation to the nationalization statutes dated the fourth day of the fourth month of the thirteenth year of Showa:
1. Henceforth, Jonsson Nagasaki KK will be legally named Nippon Nagasaki KK.
2. In consideration of mutually agreeable compensation, 30% of the issued shares of the former Jonsson Nagasaki KK, now legally known as Nippon Nagasaki KK, have been re-registered in the name of Shinichi Miyamoto.
Dated: Month 5, Showa 13

'Month five is May, of course,' Littleton explained. 'The year is 1938, thirteenth year of the reign of Emperor Showa. You know him better as Hirohito.'

Alex passed the translation to Phyllis. 'What's KK mean?' he asked Littleton. 'I see it everywhere.'

'Kabushiki Kaisha. Like our "incorporated", your "limited company".'

'Right,' the Englishman remembered. He gave himself a tap on his forehead to wake his thinking processes. Eyes closed, he addressed the table. 'I'm missing something here. 'What we now call Nippon Nagasaki Corporation used to be Nippon Nagasaki KK, right?'

'That's my understanding,' Littleton said.

'And before that, according to this piece of paper, it was Jonsson Nagasaki KK.'

'That's how I read it.'

122

Phyllis agreed with a vigorous nod. 'It ties up.' Squinting at the old paper she said, 'Does it say why they changed the name from Jonsson Nagasaki to Nippon?'

'No,' Littleton said. 'But I think I can tell you. You've got to remember that by 1938, the thirteenth year of Showa, the year this document was drawn up, Japan was already an outright totalitarian state and only military men became prime ministers.' He laid a hand on a thick reference book. 'The big blow came in March when the military government pushed through the National Mobilisation Law. It gave them absolute control over labour and wages, all economic resources, production and prices. Oh, and it also suppressed undesirable meetings and publications.' He shook his head as old memories surged forward. 'They'd been building up to it for a decade. Military drill and education became compulsory from 1926 – the year Hirohito became emperor, as it happens. I remember our school. I was fourteen at the time and my father took me out the following year because of the drills and indoctrination. The secret police, the *kempeitai*, monitored lessons and behaviour and followed all foreigners. Nothing could stop the rise of the military and anyone who tried was assassinated.' He looked up at the ceiling; he was droning on wistfully. 'Korea was already a Japanese colony and they wanted China. They occupied Manchuria in 'thirty-one and Shanghai in 'thirty-two and in July 'thirty-seven decided the moment was right to provoke the right incident. There was an exchange of gunfire at the Marco Polo Bridge and that was enough of an excuse for the wholesale invasion of China by the Japanese.'

Alex broke in. 'I still don't see—'

Littleton raised a hand. 'I'm coming to it.' He drained his coffee cup. 'Xenophobia was a powerful force used by the military. Of course, the Americans brought a lot of it on themselves with their own racism and blatantly anti-Japanese laws. Anyway, the military governments here passed a series of edicts to remove foreign influence and Japanise Japan, if you will. Companies wholly owned by foreigners had to take on a Japanese partner by selling them shares.' He lifted the old document. 'Like this. Another edict banned the use of foreign words, like "baseball" for example, and they had to invent a lot of new Japanese words to replace all the things they had borrowed from the West. So whoever owned Jonsson Nagasaki in 1938 sold thirty per cent of it to Shinichi Miyamoto and changed its name to Nippon Nagasaki Kabushiki Kaisha. As you know they now put themselves about as Nippon Nagasaki Corporation.'

Alex cut in with a raised arm. 'Since it was first called Jonsson Nagasaki do we assume this Swedish guy actually owned what we now call Nippon Nagasaki Corporation?'

'I guess so,' Littleton uttered.

Phyllis released a long whoop.

Alex dragged himself to his feet and rubbed life into aching legs. 'Are you sure you've got it right, Bill?'

The old man looked slighted. He fumbled with the document but quickly let it go. 'I am,' he said confidently. 'Once I'd deciphered the complicated characters the meaning was pretty clear.'

Alex turned from the windows. 'It doesn't make sense. You just said, "whoever owned Jonsson Nagasaki in 1938 sold thirty per cent of it to Shinichi Miyamoto." According to NNC's head office, Shinichi Miyamoto's the founder. *He* owned the company in 1938.'

'And that's the official line,' Phyllis added. 'It's in all their company literature.'

Alex thought for a moment and said, 'They told me the man in the photograph on the boardroom wall, Roland Jonsson, was just an engineer.'

'Was there a date on the picture?' Phyllis asked.

Alex dropped sideways onto the cushion, his legs stretched in front on him. 'Sometime in 1934 if I remember right.'

'Four years before the letter,' she said.

Littleton looked at it again and smiled ruefully. 'I might be wrong – there are a few characters distorted by the crease – but I figure from this that Shinichi wasn't the owner of Jonsson Nagasaki when it was written. It's most likely it was owned, as well as founded, by this guy Jonsson. I guess one of the *hanko* seals at the bottom belongs to him but you'll need a real expert to decipher them. What's certain is that it became Nippon Nagasaki in 1938 and a Japanese, namely Shinichi Miyamoto, got a thirty-per-cent piece of it.'

'Why did Yuriko Shimada tell me her boss's father was the founder of the company?' Alex protested.

'I told you,' Phyllis chided. 'It's the official line. It's in their history.'

'Do you know what happened to Jonsson?' Littleton asked.

'They told me he died in the atomic bombing of Nagasaki in August, forty-five.'

The old man twisted on his cushion. 'So I guess he had time to work out another deal which gave full control of the company to Shinichi Miyamoto.'

But the obvious was really too preposterous; and it was written on three bewildered faces. Alex tried to rationalise for all of them. 'But if there wasn't another sale of shares, and if this document's genuine, Roland Jonsson, or his heir, is still the owner of seventy per cent of Nippon Nagasaki Corporation.' While they paused, their senses in denial, the growing squall in the bay sent a gust towards the house, stirring a set of wind-chimes on the veranda.

'Tell me again Alex,' Littleton said finally. 'Where did you get hold of this document?'

Alex told him once more how it came to light with the papers of a prisoner-of-war.

'Fascinating,' Littleton said genuinely. 'Can I see them? The diaries.'

'Sure. I'll leave them with you if you like.' They were trapped under one of the reference books. 'I've only managed the first few pages. I've been tied up with the crash as you can imagine.' He frowned, brushing ruffled hair from his eyes. 'I don't understand why Jonsson had to die in Nagasaki. I would have thought he'd have been repatriated when war broke out.'

The old man's face brightened. 'You're forgetting Jonsson was Swedish, the citizen of a neutral country. He'd still enjoy relative freedom of movement if he chose to stay here.'

'So you think he carried on working for Nippon Nagasaki during the war?'

Littleton shrugged. 'I can't begin to imagine. He had the right to stay, or work if his loyalties allowed him.' He folded the letter gently. 'According to this he actually *owned* the company. Why should he leave?'

Alex stood up again, glancing at his watch. 'I ought to be getting back to my real job in Tokyo, Phyl. This letter's a distraction I didn't want.' He turned to Littleton. 'I'll take it back with me but please hang on to the diaries if you want. I just don't have time to go through them.'

Littleton accepted gratefully.

Alex remembered the tape. 'Before I go, Bill, have you got a cassette recorder I could use for a couple of minutes?'

'Sure.' He levered himself to his feet.

'I've got one in the car,' Phyllis said brightly, springing up.

'I need to be alone with it,' Alex said

'Well, screw you,' she said, hands on hips.

Littleton led Alex to the kitchen and produced a portable radio-cassette player for him. Then he joined Phyllis by her car. She was wiping sandy deposits off the windscreen. 'Thanks, Bill,' she called. 'Appreciate it.'

'It could add a little spice to your book,' he returned.

She brushed dust off her dungerees and tossed her head

towards the house. 'He won't let me look after the letter and now that his curiosity's been satisfied he wants to get back to his goddamn air crash.'

'I can understand that,' Littleton said, patting the grinning whale.

She looked pensive, straightening the red cap and gazing out to the ocean. 'I guess there must have been another contract somewhere.' She turned to Littleton. 'You know, selling the rest of Nippon Nagasaki to the Miyamotos. I'll have to check into it.'

'Maybe. But I think it's a long shot. Just remember that a colossal amount of legal documentation was lost in the fire-bombings and the post-war chaos.'

Alex joined them, his face sombre. 'Thanks for your time, Bill. I enjoyed the history lesson.'

'So did you fuck her?'

'What?' Alex's mind drifted away from the three-minute tape. The clarity had pleased him and he would sit and listen to it in the peace of the hotel. Now he was back in the nineteen thirties, in streets patrolled by the *kempeitai* secret police, with seventy million foreigner-hating Japanese mobilised for a world war that was inevitable. He was thinking of the Swede Roland Jonsson, an entrepreneur with skills to offer an emerging nation, battling against the *tsunami* of nationalism to protect his investment and struggling with an ethical dilemma as the company he had founded geared up to support the war effort. Phyllis was steering the Mini in an endless belt of polished, sparkling cars snaking across the Tama River into metropolitan Tokyo.

'Yuriko Shimada,' Phyllis said irritably, throwing him a sidewards glance. 'Did you make it with her or not? I guess you did.'

'Do you ever give up, Phyllis?'

'Phyl. No. Not when I smell a problem with my book.

I'm going to have to work on this Jonsson angle. I had him down as an engineer, not the goddamn owner of the whole frigging show.'

'He *was* just an engineer. He must have sold the rest of the company to Miyamto senior at some stage.'

She settled her glasses more comfortably. 'Look, Alex, I won't publish anything till you've gone, okay? I know how important your job is here. I won't embarrass you.'

'That's very kind of you, Phyl.'

She released an ironic grunt and scowled at the driver of a four-wheel-drive Pajero in the parallel lane. 'There's something you're not telling me, right? What has Miyamoto done to you?'

'Forget it, Phyl,' he said, thinking suddenly of the diaries and his belief that someone at NNC had copied them; and of Yuriko's desperate efforts to get hold of the Jonsson letter.

'C'mon Alex.' She slapped the steering wheel. 'I might look like a squeaky-clean Japanese butterfly under this hat . . .'

'If I could actually see you under that bloody hat and those goggles I might be able to decide whether you're squeaky-clean or not.'

'You need me, Alex,' she said, unmoved by his rudeness. 'Japan's a nightmare for a virgin *gaijin* like you. The locals laugh at foreign presidents, prime ministers and insurance loss adjusters. They'll tell you what you want to hear and then do whatever's in their own interests. Look at Japan's trade balance. They'll agree to open the markets here and then manage to delay implementation for ever.'

'Drop me at my hotel please.'

'Do you know how long it took to get New Zealand apples into this country? Twenty goddamn years after import liberalisation.'

'I'll call you before I leave,' Alex said blandly.

Traffic was thinner once they were in Meguro ward and it was a good ten minutes before Phyllis spoke again. 'Can I use your mobile, please? I promised to call Makiko.'

'Makiko?'

'Makiko Nakamura. Ed Kidderby's girlfriend. You said you wanted to talk to her about his health.'

He'd forgotten Phyllis was the go-between. He dialled a number for her on Yoshi Kanagawa's telephone.

'She's pretty cut up about her pilot,' she said, taking the slim handset. 'I promised to call her today.'

By the time the long conversation in Japanese had finished they were deep into the business heart of Tokyo, approaching Kamiyacho. Phyllis sighed when she returned the handset. 'She wants to talk to you about him.' She engaged second gear with a savage grind. 'Can you spare her a few minutes, like tomorrow morning? Early?'

9 October, 1942

It's Friday. Finally got my diary back. The Japs confiscated it in June and beat me up for having it. Don't know why they didn't destroy it. So I have some gaps to fill in between June 11th and today. We get the usual rice and veg but there's been some fish and meat. I've put on some weight because I worked in the galley every other afternoon. When food was short I had to steal it. Everyone's doing it. Deaths were down to two or three a day. Dysentery and beriberi take people because they can't get treated. One of the lads was beaten to death in August for hitting a guard. About a month ago the English prisoners were put to work on the road round Maros airport. We get a bit of extra food and as the road goes through native farms we get a bit of arrowroot which we bake in the fire and at night cut into chips and fry it in oil. I've also made some jam with it. The Japs told me yesterday that I've been detailed with 200 others to go to some place in Japan. Reg Riggs, Jim Bishop Phillips and Frank Willsmore are also going. They say we're off to a shipyard. I hope not.

12 October
Passed the Jap medical on Sunday, worse luck, and got issued with 2 green army coats, 2 pairs of trousers, 2 flannelled blankets, 2 singlets, 2 prs of shorts and pr of rubber shoes. First issue of clothes since capture March. Today they took us to the football field and taught us Jap orders for right and left turn, attention, stand at ease, on and off caps, to salute and bow Jap fashion. We did some PT as they want us to arrive in Japan fit.

13 October
Well, Kath, we got spliced 14 years ago today and this is the first time that I have not sent you a card or something. Never mind, sweetheart, every day will be a Sunday bye and bye and I won't forget you. You have been a good wife and I do not regret marrying you. I hope that you have had a happy day today and that you and I will be able to spend our next together and also many more.

15 October
Left Makassar for Japan at 1900 yesterday on the Jap ship *Asama Maru* belonging to the NYK Line. We have a mine-layer for escort. We are quartered in no. 2 hold. The Dutch are in the 3rd Class cabins. They seem to get the best of everything. The first night was red hot. There's no ventilation. We try to sleep on pallets over the cargo of bauxite and we're covered in dust by the morning. Lots of the lads were seasick and couldn't make it to the latrines. Did I say latrines? There are two small huts slung over the stern. You climb in and straddle a pair of planks. The line at dawn was long and a lot of people couldn't wait.

17 October
Allowed on deck for half an hour again. It's a big ship. Must be about 1,000 of us, about 200 British, and a couple of thousand Jap marines. We're covered in

131

sweat and dust but there's no fresh water to wash in. When you're wet with sweat and wash in sea water it causes prickly heat. Our escort left us today and we proceeded alone.

19 October

35 yrs old today. This time last year I did not think that I would be a Prisoner of War and spend my birthday in a cargo hold of a Jap ship. A friend gave me two rolls of good tobacco as a present so it was like a year ago when I was in Bombay and a year before that in Plymouth. I wish to God I was there now. I would know how Kath and the children are. It is 11 months since she posted the last letter I received.

20 October

It's getting colder. The further north we get the more we're going to feel it. We have no thick clothing. Hope we get some in Japan. Hard wind blowing top sides but the ship has hardly any motion. You can sit on the planks over the stern and wait for a dip and get your backside wiped. Most of the Dutch are sick and cannot eat. We don't mind. We eat their share as well as ours. The Dutch were never hungry in Makassar. They had plenty of money and got round the guards to let them buy extra food. Supper and dinner are the same every day: rice and a stew of beetroot, onions and potatoes. There's some bad diseases going round. A soldier from Newcastle died from diphtheria today.

22 October

Big scare today. A large number of wooden battens fell and made a devil of a noise. We all thought we had been torpedoed. Riggs restored order quickly. After we tidied up I realised I had been sleeping near a colony of rats. Everyone's got a bad cough. It's very cold and as we don't have warm clothes we stay in the hold all the time.

24 October

Arrived in Nagasaki yesterday but stayed on board all day. Disembarked today at 1000 and lined up on shore. I think we're on an island. A Jap officer spoke to us in very good English. He said he was in charge of our camp and if we did not obey orders and work hard we would be punished. We would be executed if we tried to escape. We marched to the camp where we were put in 56 men to a room. In the room are 4 rows of bunks, 2 a side, and 5 tables laid out with utensils which comprise one shallow dish, one basin and a pair of chopsticks. Each bunk had three blankets and a pillow. We were given a meal at 6 o'clock of rice, fish, beans and tea and at 9 o'clock the daily routine was read to us. It is: 0500 Turn Out. 0510 Rub Down. 0520 Roll Call. 0600 Breakfast. 0620 Roll Call for Work. 0730 Start Work. 1200 Lunch. 1230 Resume Work. 1700 Leave Work. 1730 Fall in and march back to camp. 1900 Supper. 2030 Roll Call. 2100 Turn in, or Sleep as the Japs say. Well, by this routine we won't have time to wash. Then we each got a number and were told to learn it in Japanese and other words. I am ichi hachi yon, 184.

28 October

Puraded today to get work instructions. I am to be a stage builder or rigger in the dockyards. The Naval Officer in charge told us we would be punished if we did not work hard but we would get presents if we did. The job was to last 2 to 5 years. The civilian head said when it was over we would be sent back to our wives and children. He spoke in Japanese and the translator made it sound like he would give us a new wife and kids. We've had four days of rice, barley soup, a bit of pickled fish or shrimp. We had our photographs taken in groups of 16 and were made to sign a form which stated we solemnly declared not to try and escape. If we

133

tried the punishment was death. We filled in another form with parents details, date of birth, etc. and the address where we wanted it sent. I put Padstow. I wondered if Kath knows I'm alive. A dozen civilians came in yesterday. Rumour has it they were captured, fighting on Wake Island. They've been in a rough camp somewhere and were not in very good shape.
30 October
Japs are mustering all our gear today. They're going to take away all our writing materials, knives, extra blankets and soft pillows. I will try and hide my diary.

It was early Saturday evening, the light already dimming, when Phyllis Wakai left him in front of the Grand Kanto Hotel with an arrangement to meet him there at ten the following day. He had listened to the tape on a borrowed hotel player and again with the transcript propped against the sauce bottle that came with his room-service hamburger supper. The break from three days of adrenalin-driven tension, his instincts acute to the conflicting interests and machinations and pressures from the parties, was welcome and needed. It had helped clear his mind, opening it up to receive and accept the remarkable interpretation from Bill Littleton and fertilising the wild, unreal suspicion that the people he was trying to help had, for reasons he could not fathom, secretly copied a prisoner-of-war's fifty-five-year-old diary and were anxious to possess the crumpled page of Japanese script stapled to it. He should have thanked Phyllis Wakai, he told himself, before sorting a heap of telephone messages and faxes into priority levels. Perhaps even invited her to hear the tape. He needed somebody neutral, trustworthy, not the broker Yoshi Kanagawa, certainly not Yuriko Shimada or anyone from NN Air, just somebody to listen to the last, tragic words uttered by the Japanese first officer in his own language. 'Not again', the translation read.

'I called her again last night,' Phyllis said, when they were back in the extravagantly painted Mini on a clear, cool Sunday morning. 'Confirmed we were coming to see her.' The roads were clear of heavy vehicles and the taxi and chauffeur fleets and their progress towards Shinagawa was smooth, letting Alex see how hardwearing plants and shrubs had been packed into every possible gap between buildings and shops, on garage forecourts and on the narrowest of balconies. There was no graffiti and the only litter he saw from his ground-level position in the Mini was scrap paper trapped behind the concrete pillars supporting the elevated expressways. Phyllis threw him a glance. 'You okay, Alex? You look beat.'

'I had to talk to people in England last night. They're not easy to get on a Saturday. Then send a few faxes. I didn't get through with them till late.'

'Alex,' she said, without looking over. There was a plea in her voice. 'You've got to let me have a piece of this story. I've kept my mouth shut so far, haven't I?'

'I haven't told you anything worth using.'

Her hands jumped off the wheel. 'Look what I'm doing for you! I'm the one who told you Ed Kidderby was sick. Your girlfriend at NNC didn't tell you, did she? She'll take off her pants for you and get you whimpering for more exotic pleasures but if you step out of line she'll show you a different kind of oriental delight.'

'I brought you in on that old bit of paper,' Alex said. 'Could be useful for your research. You might get some real dirt on the Miyamotos.'

She drove in silence through a string of traffic lights where the Sakurada road narrowed on its approach to Takanawa, gunning the engine in frustration whenever they changed against her.

'Tell me something about the woman we're going to see, Kidderby's girlfriend. Mack . . .?'

135

'Makiko. Makiko Nakamura.' She turned into a narrow road bordered by plane and gingko trees and then into a short drive which led to a block of flats. 'She used to be a hostess around the big Tokyo cabarets. You know. Holding the hands of drunken salarymen, laughing at their jokes, mother substitute kind of stuff. Easy money and you might get lucky and meet a company president like Miyamoto and he'd set you up somewhere. She's about forty now. Got her own little "snack" place in Akasaka, runs some girls of her own. She met Bill when he came to Japan to fly for NN Air about six years ago. They really got on well. I think I told you he put some money into her club.'

The building was coated with terracotta brown tiling and raised on columns to provide a few precious parking places below it. Phyllis let Alex out and lined the car close to a border wall. She had no handbag and instead kept her keys, journalist's notebook and pens in the pouch at the front of her dungarees.

'Does this cabaret line means she was a prostitute?' Alex asked, holding open the door to a lobby lined with mail boxes.

'Hell no,' she answered, the red hat swinging. 'They've got bars for everything here. You must have seen a few when I took you to Roppongi. Some are just pick-up joints, you know, a drink and then off to a love hotel round the corner.' They were waiting for the lift. 'Most are like Makiko's snack, just drinking places with a few tables and chairs and some karaoke equipment and a few hostesses. Clientele tends to be regular.'

Alex had noticed just how Tokyo changed at night. It was the intensity of the neons, clamped like beacons to every spare bit of space on the buildings, and the way they floodlit the lurid concentrations of bars, restaurants and discos into a sort of artificial daytime.

'Fourth floor, please,' Phyllis commanded when the lift

arrived. 'Makiko's place is in Asakusa. Upmarket entertainment district. She's got a few faithful patrons and she had Ed Kidderby as a friend.'

'Did they live together?' They were in hallway, a door at each end.

She rang a bell. 'No, no. The airline paid his rent on an apartment and of course he was away a lot flying. And the Japanese don't like people who aren't married living together.'

'What the hell does it matter?'

'Where is she?' Phyllis pressed harder, persistently. 'She knew we were coming.' Turning to Alex she said, 'Guess I hit a nerve there somewhere, *gaijin san*.'

'The door's open,' Alex said. It was heavy, needing firm pressure. The last person leaving or entering had let it close with its own momentum but it had not locked.

'Makiko *san*,' Phyllis called, a tentative foot in the entrance. 'Maki *chan*.' She slipped out of her trainers. 'What a bother!'

Alex followed her, barefoot and cautiously stooped, through an archway into a living room where a couch, a pair of armchairs and television-video set and coffee table cluttered it, leaving them to trip sideways as they looked for the woman. The compact kitchen doubled as a dining room and the table was laid out to eat. The odour of coffee lingered and a piece of buttered toast lay against the lip of a plate, teethmarks visible around the edges of a missing corner. 'What's that smell?' Alex asked, sniffing. 'Not the coffee.' It was pungent: a sharp, rich perfume.

They passed an opened bedroom door. Phyllis leaned inside. The double bed was unmade and scattered with a collection of furry creatures. Her voice was tentative, the face behind the cap and glasses twisted with bewilderment. 'Makiko *san*?'

'She's not in the bathroom,' Alex said.

The scent came from the adjoining room, measured out in the standard six-and-a-half tatami size, where the flower-patterned curtain on the single window was drawn apart. The space behind the sliding wall doors would reveal mattresses and blankets to make up the futons for overnight visitors. On an inlaid shelf was a simple *butsudan*, the small wood-panelled cabinet, containing an image of Buddha between a miniature pair of family mortuary tablets. To one side, with a slender vase holding two white flowers, was a framed photograph of Edward Kidderby, smiling in his captain's uniform. Makiko Nakamura had offered the spirits of her ancestors and now her lover a bowl of rice and a cup of sake. The stick of incense, the source of the odour, had burned down, a centimetre or so still smoldering in a bed of grey ashes.

Phyllis stood before the altar-piece and lit another slender stick of incense, wafting out the flame with her hand and setting it upright in the ashes. She tapped a tiny bronze bell to summon the spirits and brought her hands together as she dipped her head in a few seconds of silent reverence. Then she touched the remains of the incense stick. 'She was here forty, fifty minutes ago,' she guessed. 'These things last about that long.'

'What is it?' Alex said, peering closely at the arrangement of miniatures.

'A Buddhist altar. Keeps people in touch with their ancestors. Most families have one. Makiko's parents are dead so she's technically head of the family.' She looked round helplessly, hands on hips. 'But where is she?'

Alex led them back to the kitchen and dipped a finger in half a cup of black coffee. 'Still just warm.' But Phyllis was not behind him. He found a door, hidden by a cabinet. It was open, and he looked out onto a fire-escape landing which connected to the iron staircase clamped to the rear wall of the building.

'Alex! Come here.' The short, urgent command echoed through the flat and he found himself hurrying to Makiko Nakamura's bedroom. 'Look at this.' She was holding up a short-sleeved, mauve, cotton nightdress. 'It was on the floor.' It probably reached her knees, Alex imagined, with the few tiny buttons at the open neck probably left undone. But it had been ripped to the waist, as if two firm hands had gripped the vee of the neckline and torn it apart like a scrap of waste paper. Phyllis's face pleaded for an explanation.

'How did she do that?' he said.

Phyllis drew the dress to her face, her eyes squeezed, watering behind her glasses. Alex took the torn dress from her. 'Come on Phyl. Let's talk to the neighbours. There's bound to be an explanation. Maybe there's a caretaker or something. I can't speak Japanese.'

'This is ridiculous.' She was shaking her head. 'Where's she gone?'

'Could be anything. Popped out to buy something, like you said.'

She threw the shredded nightdress on the bed and bawled at him. 'How did that happen, for fuck's sake?'

The flat on the same floor was unoccupied. From cracked-open doors they heard hisses and apologies but no one had seen Makiko Nakamura that morning, let alone in the last hour. A woman in the flat above Makiko's explained with some embarrassment that her downstairs neighbour's working hours were the opposite to most of the tenants and Nakamura *san* was rarely seen during the day. The caretaker, someone else told them, did not work in their block on Sundays. Back in the flat, Phyllis called a mutual friend while Alex searched again, producing an address diary, which she used to find the numbers for Makiko's chief barman and some of the young women who worked in her bar. They stayed for two hours before Phyllis decided to call the police. 'Not from here,' she said, stuffing notes and her ballpen into her pouch.

'She might not be missing,' Alex protested, following her out of the building. 'The police are not going to search for her right away.'

'I'll leave the thought with them,' she said jerking the Mini alive. 'And tell them about the nightdress.' A curtain in a flat overlooking the driveway parted gingerly, the eyes behind it following the absurdly painted little car as it left.

'Impossible to park in his damn city,' she cursed, minutes later, half blocking an entrance in a side street. 'Look after the car and play the dumb *gaijin* if a cop stops to talk you.'

'That won't be hard,' he called after her.

Ten minutes later she returned. 'Why didn't you call from her apartment?' Alex asked, as they headed towards central Tokyo.

'There's a ritual for everything in this country, Alex, and after the tea ceremony and a Noh play the police have the longest and most boring. If we turn up at a police box and declare somebody we know's gone missing we're there for three or four hours, making statements, giving descriptions, naming friends and coming up with our own explanations. It'd be like we were somehow involved in the disappearance, as if we were suspects in a crime yet to be revealed.' She let him think while she negotiated the Ichinohashi intersection. 'And of course we're *gaijins*. Even me. They'd split us up, bring in interpreters for you and we'd be making statements which they could use against us.'

'You're exaggerating, surely.'

'No way. There's not much of an underclass here. Look around. The kids all dress the same, look the same and are well fed and the streets here are pretty safe. The cops do their bit to keep the violent *yakuza* element under control but they don't change their methods much when they deal with the rest of us. They get desperate for convictions and go for the easiest suspect. With no juries to worry about they just beat the shit out of you till you confess.'

Roppongi was deserted, the debris from a Saturday night in the bars and restaurants packed into small hills of see-through grey rubbish bags. 'The big problem in Japan is the real crooks get away with it,' Phyllis said bitterly. 'Japanese politicians are totally corrupt but since bribery's part of the system, and everyone's involved, it goes on. They get their funds from people like Miyamoto at NNC and the underworld syndicates. The bureaucrats, especially the Ministry of Finance and the guys at Trade and Industry, actually run the country and they get great retirement jobs in business. It's a great, unstoppable Ferris wheel of money and patronage.'

'It seems to work,' Alex said. They had reached the back road approaching the Grand Kanto Hotel. 'So did you leave your name with the police?'

'No. I hung up when they got a bit heavy. I gave them Makiko's address and phone number and asked them to make a precautionary visit. They don't need me any more. They'll make some general enquiries but they won't put out a formal missing-person notice for forty-eight hours at least.'

Alex thought about the whale on the roof, the next best thing to trailing a piece of string from Makiko Nakamura's apartment to Phyllis's house, wherever it was. She drew up to the hotel entrance. 'So what now, *gaijin san*?' Alex thought he heard her voice catch. She managed a flicker of a smile. 'I've hardly known you five minutes and I've lost Ed Kidderby and now his girlfriend.'

'You pursued me, remember?' he shot back, unkindly.

'Frigging Brit!' She straightened the red cap with a rough two-handed jerk; but he hadn't heard her. 'Are you okay, Alex?'

He was staring through the windscreen, remembering something he had said to Yuriko Shimada. Something about Ed Kidderby's girlfriend and his health. He turned his head sharply. 'Yes, of course. I just thought of something when you put Kidderby and Makiko together.' He hauled himself out of the car.

'What are you talking about?' she called, leaning across the passenger seat. 'Talk to me Alex, goddamnit!'

The doorman, in a gold and grey suit and top hat, rocked on his heels in the hotel's elaborate entrance and watched them. Then a black saloon drew up and he opened the door to let James Sanguillen out and guide him to the foyer. If Alex hadn't spent days in and out of Nippon Nagasaki cars he might have overlooked the shield-like logo containing the green letters on the upper part of the front passenger door. The driver caught his eye but quickly checked himself. Alex watched Sanguillen disappear and let a chain of priorities click into place before leaning into Phyllis's car. 'I surrender. I need your help.'

'Now you're talking, *gaijin san*.' She gave a low yelp, and a hand left the wheel and pulled his face down, rasping it against the rim of her cap as she attempted a kiss.

He freed himself, catching her wide smile. 'I've got a few things to do first. Tell you what: come round tonight and we'll talk some more about Hiroshi Miyamoto and Nippon Nagasaki. If you can face it, I'd also like you to listen to the cockpit voice recording. It might be a bit traumatic.'

'I can cope, but it'll leave you absolutely obligated to me. It's called *giri* and you have to repay it sometime. Sooner rather than later.'

'How about starting with another dinner?'

'You got it.'

He noticed how her grin faded quickly. 'Phyl,' he said cautiously. 'Can I make a small suggestion, and please don't take it personally?'

'No problem, Alex.'

'I'm sure your friend's going to turn up, probably misheard the time or whatever. But if there *is* a problem out there I'm a bit worried how you sort of telegraph your identity around this city. You know, the cap, the dungaree uniform and the big glasses.' He tapped the roof. 'And this bloody whale. Might be wise to lower the profile a peg or two, don't you think?'

He found James Sanguillen backed by a bamboo screen in a corner of the lobby coffee shop. The American rose and stretched out his hand. He had not dressed down for Sunday: his grey, lightweight suit was newly pressed and his shirt, a pink silk Brooks button-down, hardly rippled over his trim waist. His broad smile revealed even, worked-on teeth but no warmth.

Alex apologised for his late arrival.

'No problem, Mr Bolton,' the American said stiffly. 'I'm just glad we're close to resolving this unfortunate matter while I'm here. I'm leaving tonight actually. Coffee?'

Alex looked puzzled. He had sent a preliminary report by fax to Reggie Cameron late on Friday night after a couple of drinks with Yoshi Kanagawa, Phyllis's revelations about the dangerously unstable health of the pilot, Edward Kidderby, deep in his thoughts as he wrote. They'd had all of Saturday to mull it over, as no doubt they were planning to meet over the weekend, and it seemed to have set off a chain of vital messages. He had been very guarded in the way he had laid the known facts before his chief. He confirmed what documents he had managed to check before the Japanese official investigators moved in to NN Air's offices and expropriated them. The unceremonious removal was an ominous sign, like the missing medical report that made him unable to state categorically that the pilot's health condition was not potentially a causal factor in the crash. The condition of the bodies meant that the results of the post-mortem would be delayed while an American specialist was flown to Tokyo, and Alex saw this as a reason to anticipate the wishes of the underwriters and stay on site a little longer. What he was able to do meanwhile, and pending an official determination, was confirm the absence of any war-loss implications that might prejudice the claim.

Sanguillen struck a pose of amicable menace. It told Alex that the American had heard about the negative aspects of his situation report, with the implication that it might delay or impede the payout to South Miami Aviation. How did he hear? When? Alex had insisted on watching the hotel staff dispatch the fax and retrieved the original as soon as it left the machine. The leak must have been in London. His message, part or all of it, in written or oral form, would have gone from Cameron at BUI to the brokers Matthias, Montague & Broome, who would have updated the underwriters, reminding them of the exact amount of their liability but advising them that the claim was not resolved and they would be informed when it was. Sanguillen's uncompromisingly hard face showed that news of some sort had circled the globe, via Miami, Alex supposed, reaching the executive in Tokyo.

'I want to thank you,' Sanguillen said drily

Alex shuddered, hoping it didn't show. What had he missed? There were constant announcements from the Ministry of Transport and hastily-called press conferences, but he had checked that nothing significant had happened while he was in Hayama with Phyllis Wakai. He fumbled. 'I haven't completed my assessment yet but I can't see any reason to deny the principal liability at this stage,' he said, mindful of unresolved issues and now angry at himself for having been away from Tokyo when important announcements were being made.

Sanguillen waited, his attention taken by the waitress who arrived with their coffee, and content to relish the other man's discomfort. She wore a pale lilac kimono embroided along its length with wispy purple irises and caught Alex's eyes before stepping back with a slight bow. Then the American pierced Alex with his own dark, expressionless eyes. 'There was a special press conference this morning. I believe you were away sightseeing or something.' The pause that followed was an instant, but enough for Sanguillen to enjoy with a blank face the other man bristle. 'The chief Japanese investigator announced that the cause of the our airplane's crash was wind-shear. Of course, it's subject to conclusive analysis of the flight data recordings and publication of other findings.'

Alex sipped his coffee, needing the moment to gather his thoughts and prepare to recover a little self-respect. But he still wouldn't be drawn into speculation on the cause of the DC-8 crash or open up about his suspicions on the pilot's physical condition. He had no proof. 'At the very least it may explain why the aircraft dropped out of the sky the way it did,' he said cautiously.

'But I gather from your tone you're not satisfied with the official explanation,' Sanguillen said. He leaned forward and steepled his hands. 'Perhaps you're in possession of some information the rest of us are not.'

Alex turned away as another spasm of discomfort jolted him. Yes, he had something: a stolen medical report. His weak smile said he was trying find a way back to normality. 'I'm afraid I'm not. The Japanese investigators came for NN Air's records when I was going through them. Nothing I could do about it. I've got no natural right to look at them first.'

Sanguillen frowned. 'Does that mean they suspect malpractice of some sort? The announcement today suggests they have reached a conclusion.'

'Not necessarily,' Alex said. 'The Japanese are as thorough as they come; there are no barriers they can't cross. If NN Air had resisted the Ministry of Transport's probings in any way it could be construed as deliberate obstruction.' He let the

American absorb that little aside as they sipped from the blue and white porcelain cups. 'Has Miyamoto's operation ever given you cause to doubt their ability to conform to the conditions of the lease? I'm asking you frankly.'

Sanguillen sighed audibly and took a leather three-tube cigar holder from his suit jacket. 'It hardly matters now,' he concluded, making a show of sniffing the No. 3 Romeo y Julieta before clipping a wedge out of the rounded end. He stressed his point while singeing the tip with the flame of his lighter. 'My company's got a hundred and twenty aircraft leased out around the world,' he drawled. 'A lot of our thirty-year-old 707s and DC-8s are landing on airfields in Africa where the fire service is a couple of fucking buckets at the end of the runway.' He drew hard on the Havana. 'You don't have to be a genius, Mr Bolton, to assume that what we hold dearest is the protection of our assets and our people are paid extremely well to make sure we're covered for every little oversight by our clients.'

Alex had brought the summary slip the broker had given him on the way to Heathrow Airport and two days later the bulky policy itself had been couriered to his hotel in Tokyo. Sanguillen was correct: South Miami Aviation had taken every legal precaution to protect their interests. NN Air had taken out insurance on their six-plane fleet when they dry-leased it from them, naming the Florida company as loss payee and agreeing to their stringent Breach of Warranty endorsements, which meant the owners got paid even if NN Air were found to have committed violations of the policy. That was why James Sanguillen sank back in the comfort of the deep sofa chair, his face breaking easily into smiles between short draws on his cigar. He would get paid even if Yuriko Shimada and her pet dog had been at the controls of NINA 328 when it crashed. Well, maybe. Alex suspected NN Air of negligence, but the main evidence, in the logbooks and the pilot's body, had been destroyed in the cockpit's disintegration, and if there were clues in the airline's disordered records they were now in the hands of the official investigators. He remembered something Sanguillen had said at the Haneda crash site. 'The airline missed a few lease payments, didn't they?'

Sanguillen smiled thinly. 'We had to remind them a couple of times. You know how these guys run on tight cash flows. When the money arrives it comes from all over the place, in odd amounts from different accounts. It's not unusual in this business. NN Air's our biggest single client and we're talking a million five hundred a month.'

'Will they come to you for a replacement plane?' Alex asked.

'We're already talking,' Sanguillen grinned, beckoning for the bill. 'I trust that you'll now bring yourself to move your side of the situation forward – I'm sure you'll wish to do so, particularly after the announcement from the Transport Ministry this morning – and expedite the payment to us under the loss-payee clause according to the provisions of NN Air's insurance policy with your company.'

Alex was looking for an evasive reply but Sanguillen was already on his feet, making stabbing motions with the cigar as he made to leave. 'My company lawyer's taking my place in Tokyo today. I can assure you, Mr Bolton, he's not as patient as I am.'

He picked up his key and two messages from Yuriko Shimada, timed at two hours apart, requesting a call-back to her flat. He screwed up the slips of paper before he reached his room. Reggie Cameron's Saturday message was in the safety deposit box in his room where he had left it before he went to meet Phyllis Wakai. The three pages gave him a corporate profile of South Miami Aviation, detailing the fleet it owned and the destinations of the dry- and wet-leased aircraft. It was loosely coded, personal names and companies described by initials Alex would recognise without compromising the security he demanded. The company's capital was held in various nominee names but the writer alluded to 'Hispanic' interests in the ownership. He was faxing from the office, Cameron mentioned, requesting that his on-site surveyor defer any enquiries or comments until at least nine in the morning on Sunday, London time. Alex glanced at the bedside clock: his boss had another ten minutes in bed if he elected to call him. But he didn't. He checked that the Jonsson letter was in the safe, regretting for a moment he had left the diaries with Bill Littleton, and under the fax he found the medical certificate he had lifted from Ed Kidderby's records before the documents were taken away from him. He had it under his desk lamp when the telephone rang. 'I've just walked in,' he lied to Yuriko Shimada.

'I'm very happy to find you in the hotel. May I take a little of your time?'

'Go ahead,' Alex said cheerfully, hearing the relief in her voice.

'I mean, can I visit you there?'

The memory of stretched fabric and the outline of legs as she kneaded the bed flashed by him. A call and an excuse to Phyllis could make it a reality again. He shook his head to clear it. 'Unless it's really urgent I'd prefer to catch up with you tomorrow. I've got a report to write, a few people to talk to.'

She uttered a few words of disappointment and then delivered an invitation. 'My president has asked me to thank you for your cooperation in resolving this sad incident and wishes to do so personally at a dinner of special appreciation tomorrow, Monday evening.'

Someone else happy to buy the wind-shear conclusion, Alex sighed. 'That's very kind of him. Will I see you there?'

'Of course,' she said brightly. 'Can I speak frankly, Mr Bolton?'

'Alex, please. And be as frank as you want.'

She uttered his name tentatively. 'Alex. Mr Miyamoto may give you a small gift, something to show the appreciation of the Nippon Nagasaki group, especially NN Air, for your assistance.' Alex was ahead of her but let her stumble along. 'In Japan we have many customs, which foreigners sometimes cannot understand.'

'Like all this bowing and sucking air,' Alex interrupted.

Her chuckle was flat and quickly faded. 'It is quite common to show reciprocity for a kindness, however small. It is sometimes a big nuisance for us to have to calculate the value of a gift and return one for about half its value.'

'I'll bring a bottle for the host,' Alex said.

The quip floated past her – she hadn't heard him. Framing her words carefully, she said, 'May I suggest that it would be an important and sincere gesture if you gave Mr Miyamoto the historical document in your possession? It refers to our company at the time of its foundation and would be a valuable addition to our records.'

Alex wondered if she was reading from a script. There was a hint of desperate insistence in her voice, a finality, a trace of a warning. Had Yuriko Shimada herself searched through his papers while he used NNC's offices and ordered the copying of the diaries? What on earth could scare a multi-billion-dollar conglomerate in a wad of desperate scribblings by a starved and beaten prisoner-of-war more than half a century ago? 'It shouldn't be a problem,' he heard himself saying. 'But please make Mr Miyamoto aware that I haven't submitted my final report yet.'

There was a brief, eloquent pause. 'I'm sure it's only a question of time.'

'I hope so. When and where please? Tomorrow night.'

He wanted to return to the medical certificate and the faxes but Phyl Wakai was probably already in the lobby. He allowed himself a quick shower and returned to a shirt, tie and blazer. The vast lobby was always crowded, but few people seemed to be residents. The hotel was host to endless weddings, corporate parties and daytime seminars and the uniformity of height and hair colour of visitors and guests made it a task to pick out an individual unless you were up close or able to approach from the front. He walked slowly down the stairway, alongside an upward-moving escalator, into the centre of the lobby. He was cheered not to see a red baseball cap standing out among the elegance. He was a head taller than all but the scattering of Westerners and moved against the flow of people, hoping to be seen by the journalist.

The reception desk stretched the length of the lobby and when he turned past a granite column he saw her there, back towards him; not Phyl but Yuriko Shimada, talking to a male clerk, her right foot upturned, resting on the tip of a stiletto shoe. She must have been in the hotel when she telephoned him. Her hair was longer than he remembered, but the curves of her body were unmistakeable, and she flaunted them in a powder-blue moulded dress which ended above her knees. A black satin jacket squared her shoulders and hung just above her waist. He backed behind the column and looked for Phyllis and a route unseen out of the hotel, but Miyamoto's personal assistant was soon in his sights again, outstanding among a group of women in black wedding kimonos, her head turned away, sweeping the faces on the other side of the lobby. He was rooted, immobile, when, slowly, she swivelled towards him.

'Alex! Over here,' she called, smiling warmly. She was clutching the tangled chain of her shoulder bag as he approached. 'What's the matter? Seen a ghost?'

He looked stupidly over towards the deserted reception desk and back to the figure in pale blue – and the face of Phyllis Wakai.

'I was calling your room,' she said.

'I didn't recognize you, Phyl,' he said, steering her by the elbow towards the row of lifts. He dwelled on her taut, smooth skin and her Japanese features, the broad mouth and slightly downturned lips touched with pale pink lipstick. 'You look a little different. What happened to the glasses?'

'Contact lenses. I'm off duty.' A lift attendant bowed them in. 'Anyway, you told me to change clothes. Where are we going? I thought you're supposed to fill me up with drink before you try and get me into your room.'

He grinned. 'I want you to listen to a cockpit voice recording. And have a look at the Japanese on a piece of paper I happened to have stolen.'

'You're learning the Japanese way, *gaijin san*,' she breathed. 'And starting to trust me, huh?'

Inserting the card key, he said, 'I forgot to thank you for taking me to see Bill Littleton yesterday. Cleared up one of the mysteries I brought with me.'

'I think we turned up more problems than we solved,' she said, looking approvingly around the two-room suite while Alex set up the borrowed tape player on the coffee table. She stopped by the desk. 'Is this the report you "borrowed" from the airline?'

Alex had retrieved the tape from the closet safe. 'Right. Let's take it out with us tonight. I want you to listen to this first.' Sitting at the low table he said, 'Has Ed Kidderby's girlfriend appeared yet?'

She joined him and slumped onto the couch, her face swept with misgivings. 'Not a sign. I called everyone I could think of.' She took a cigarette from her bag but only thought of lighting it. Looking up she said, 'Do you mind if we drop in at her bar tonight? Take a look. Maybe they've heard from her.'

'Sure.' He slid the last voice recording from NINA 328

into the player. 'You're going to hear Kidderby's voice and two others. You'll also hear some screaming. If you can't handle it I understand.' She moved her head, almost imperceptibly, and finally lit the cigarette.

'Good,' he said gently, handing her the transcript of the last exchange in the cockpit.

'I've seen this, or parts of it, in the Japanese press,' she said, her eyes skimming the pages.

'It's a matter of public record. Some official investigators release it, others don't.' He tapped the cassette. 'Follow the conversation with the text first. It's only a few minutes. Don't worry about the technical language.'

He leaned back in the chair, hands clasped behind his head, watching her while she listened. He tried to imagine what it was like to hear the voice of someone you knew who was now dead. He didn't mean to stare, but if it wasn't for the same loose easy drawl in her speech he'd swear the tall Japanese-American woman across from him wasn't the shapeless, hyperactive journalist street fighter who'd pestered him into submission. He soon realised that behind the glasses, which coloured according to the light, he hadn't seen properly the deep, darkly oval eyes or under the baseball cap the hair that now shimmered free across her shoulders. Or the clear, pale-olive skin on a generous body. At the end of the sequence, she looked up and caught his eyes. She smiled sadly, stabbing out the half-smoked cigarette. 'What a terrible moment for them. Poor Ed.'

'Exactly. There was lot of tension there. You can almost touch it.'

'Why did Ed have to take over the plane?' she asked.

'The co-pilot was doing fine but conditions were deteriorating very rapidly and he wasn't authorised to fly in such strong winds. You can hear the Tower telling them winds were gusting up to forty knots at one stage, putting it way outside the co-pilot's permitted flying limit. And winds of that severity could have meant there was fierce turbulence around. I checked with the pilots' records at NN Air: Kidderby was absolutely right to take over. I wonder if he thought of aborting the landing and going somewhere else.' He leaned forward and pressed the rewind button. 'Did you detect anything in his voice, anything different from normal?'

She sighed. 'Not really. I never heard him use his business voice. And there's a lot of noise on the tape.'

'Listen again, please. Ed was doing the talking to Haneda airport but you hear early on how he may have started to feel something because he asks the controller to repeat an instruction. You can actually hear him hestitate before he speaks. It could have been from pain or some perceived danger, or simply a language problem, of course.' They listened to the entire recording again, then Alex played with the stop-start button until he was able to isolate and run the same short tract effortlessly. 'Someone in the tower at Haneda gives them the wind conditions on final approach. There's a pause and then one of the Japanese crew – it doesn't say whether it's the first officer or the engineer – suddenly speaks in Japanese. The translation says it means "not again".'

'That's right,' Phyllis agreed. 'But he uses only one word in Japanese, "*mata*".'

'Would you listen again, please?' His face pinched, and he brought a thumb and forefinger together, almost touching. 'I've imagined Kidderby's ill and getting worse so I'm looking for anything, any minuscule hint, that he's suffering. Okay? I've put it back to where he tells the first officer he's going to take over the plane. Listen for the pause after he says the first "I'll". It's a good four and half seconds before he repeats it.' He indicated the moment on the transcript. 'Then listen for his co-pilot's reply. "If you're okay". What is he asking? Is it "if you don't mind"? Or "are you ill"?' He made a circle on the paper. 'And then a few seconds later, listen to Ed Kidderby's last words, where he acknowledges Haneda Tower. He says "that's err . . . fine" and then repeats "fine", as if he's not sure.' Three more times Alex played and rewound the tape, each time trying to modulate out the static with the limited functions on the portable player. He looked up at Phyllis hopefully after the third round. 'Can you get any feeling at all for the meaning? The translator obviously can't.'

'There's only one word, Alex,' she complained. *"Mata"*. Or "not again" in English.'

'Can't you tell what kind of "again" it is?'

'How do you mean, what kind of "again"?'

Alex scratched his scalp. 'Is it a "don't do it again" sort of "again"? Like if he were asking the pilot not to apply power again or not to make some other adjustment again. Or is it a complaint kind of "not again"? You know, like "you haven't crashed the car again?" A question, an accusation. And don't forget. it was the guy's last intelligible word on earth. He knew he was going to die so he said it in his own language. What was his message?'

Phyllis started the tape segment, listened and replayed it from the beginning. Alex went to the mini-bar and gestured to her as he dropped to a knee.

'Beer, please,' she mouthed. He fixed himself a gin and tonic and took the drinks to the table. Her face had brightened. 'Since you defined the options it's a little clearer.' She took a long drag on her beer. 'Thanks, I needed that,' she said, picking up the second page of the transcript. She puckered her lips. 'It's definitely an interrogative "not again?"' she concluded. 'And he's definitely not asking Kidderby or whoever to desist from doing something once more.'

'How can you be so sure?' Alex pressed.

'"*Mata*" means "again" in Japanese but it doesn't mean

"once more". You'd say "*moo ichido*" for that.'

Alex watched her keenly. 'So how would you assess the situation on the tape when the Japanese says "*mata*"?'

Phyllis opened her palms defensively. 'Hold on, *gaijin san*. Don't pin the cause of the crash on how I interpret one goddamn word.' She caught his nod and smile of apology. 'Okay. It's like the guy's saying, "What? Not again surely?" As if he's noticed an old mechanical problem's reappeared and it's going to cause them to crash.'

They were sitting with their elbows on the table, close to the cassette player, watching it as if it were a fortune-teller's ball with a perverse play function to the past. They listened again to the unidentified Japanese crewmember's last coherent outburst, then a few seconds of pause before the shouts, followed by the screams and the urgent mechanical warning message as the aeroplane plunged to the ground. Alex was nodding ruefully. 'I think you're right.' He rewound the tape to Ed Kidderby's last words with his crew. 'So what do you make of the long pause and the repeat of "fine"?'

'You tell me,' she said, throwing out her hands expansively.

Alex raised the glass to his mouth, then groaned as he put it down untouched. He was absolutely certain he knew what caused the crash of NINA 328 and knowing that it could have been avoided filled him with anger.

'You okay, Alex?'

'What? Oh sure.' He jabbed the recorder; the tape popped out. 'The meaning of "not again" baffled me until you just cleared it up,' Alex said, almost sadly. The Japanese guy's reaction is absolutely normal in a serious crisis situation. He's trying to refuse to believe it, deny there's a problem.' The gin and tonic tasted more bitter than usual. His words were disjointed, precise, as if he were giving evidence. 'Kidderby's having trouble understanding the Tower. There are pauses between his words with his crew. One of them even asks him if he's okay. And then an unneeded repetition in a forced, probably unintentional, remark. Why? Because he's having a fatal heart attack, the power of which in a few seconds is going to impel him forward over the controls. My guess is he slipped out of the shoulder harness to try and jiggle the pain out of his left side or try and massage it away. He's only got the belt round his waist to restrain him now and it wasn't enough. The plane's already very low and it dips sharply forward and rolls to the left. The co-pilot's strapped into full safety harness of course and can't even reach Kidderby. There simply isn't time for him to get out of the straps, pull him off the controls and take over. The engineer's probably moved from his normal place at the side of the cockpit to the central seat between the pilots to monitor the landing but he's strapped in as well. And even if they could reach him, their captain's a big man and he's already dead weight, and the plane's already too low and in a plunging roll. It's too late. There's just enough time for one of them to guess aloud, quite correctly, that Kidderby is having another one of his heart spasms, and it's about to kill all of them.'

'When this is all over, Phyl, I'll give you enough material to show that NN Air, and by extension its parent under Hiroshi Miyamoto, have broken eight or nine US Federal and Japanese laws and various international agreements.' They were in a basement restaurant, sitting at a square of *teppan* hotplates served by a pair of morosely efficient chefs in colourful towelled headbands. Large, live prawns, soaked in sweet sake, danced into the air when they hit the fire-hot steel. Alex winced.

Phyllis leaned across and dabbed a splash of sauce from his chin. The transparent sliver of raw *hirame* flounder, soaked in horseradish-spiced soya, had dripped as he bundled it, clamped between his chopsticks, into his mouth. 'Are you going to tell the crash investigators what you know?'

'They should be able to work it out for themselves. I represent the insurers, the people who have to fork out twenty million dollars this week.'

She brandished the chopsticks and looked puzzled. 'So who's going to pay the piper on this one?'

Alex slipped off his jacket while Phyllis negotiated with their designated chef on the preparation of the chunks of Kobe beef he had chopped for them.

'It's going to be NN Air,' Alex said. 'If I'm right. When they dry-leased the six aeroplanes from South Miami Aviation and insured them through the London market they took on a whole bunch of obligations. The insurers will pay the owners for their loss but if we can prove the operator's been negligent, deliberately or otherwise, they are going to look at it as a serious act and might think about cancelling the cover they give under the existing policy.'

Phyllis rolled her eyes and grasped his wrist. 'You're losing me again Alex. Dry what?'

'Sorry Phyl. NN Air's contract's for the aircraft only. They hired the crews themselves. That's called a dry lease. If the crew had come with the planes it'd be a "wet-lease" contract.'

'Got it,' she declared. Perplexed, she rippled her cheeks. 'But how can they be negligent about Ed Kidderby?'

Alex shrugged. 'If they didn't ensure that he had his regular six-monthly medical checkups or if they submitted false reports to the civil aviation authorities.' He took the report he had kept from the Japanese investigators from his jacket. 'It would be a major violation of Japanese rules if they were not conducting full examinations of the aircrew or accepted certificates from the pilots which were not real statements of their health condition.'

'What would happen to the airline if they were bending the rules or cheating?' Phyllis asked.

'They could lose their operating licence, the whole fleet could be grounded, and they'd get hit with heavy fines and the possibility of imprisonment for the executives.'

Phyllis ran her eyes uneasily over the two sheets. 'And you think Ed was covering up his heart problems? So he could carry on flying?'

'I'm almost certain. The certificate for the check he should have had in January's not in the files. Ed and the other foreign pilots were over-the-hill, non-complaining types, lucky to still be flying. It's probable the airline took advantage of them and colluded with them. It would let Miyamoto cut corners, save money by ignoring safety and health procedures and keep a cheap flying staff.'

She seized his arm, swirling the beer in his glass. 'You've got to let me use this, Alex, when it's all over.'

He scooped up a small heap of steaming bean sprouts and pushed them tentatively into his mouth. 'In good time, Phyl. I don't have any real evidence yet. Maybe you can help me.' He touched the medical report covering her knees. 'There aren't any translations in the files. The only thing I understand is the name of the clinic and the doctor.'

She ate while she read. 'There's nothing in the Japanese comments about a major problem.' She hummed. 'Says he was overweight, cholesterol a touch on the high side.'

Alex cut in. 'What about medicines, blood-pressure control drugs? He must have been taking something.'

She finished the last cube of steak and dabbed her lips. 'I can't see anything about medication.' She shrugged, indicating a series of vividly bordered spaces. 'I can't figure out some of the technical medical terms in the text but there's nothing entered in these red "care" boxes.'

'So it's a dead end,' Alex concluded. 'I still want to know why the last report's missing.'

'Not quite a dead end,' Phyllis said.

'How do you mean?'

'The hospital's in Nagasaki.'

Alex sneered. 'I noticed that. Everyone I meet here seems to come from Nagasaki.'

'Not just Nagasaki, Alex. The clinic's in Yanagi, the same district as Miyamoto's local headquarters and his engineering factories. Oh, and the family estate.'

Alex murmured, 'He must own the place. And the people in it.'

'What are you going to do? Do you want me call the Nagasaki clinic for you?'

Alex sipped, thinking. 'Not yet, Phyl, thanks. I really ought to talk to the Americans.'

'Why *are* the Americans involved?' she asked intensely.

'The planes are owned by the outfit in Florida and that makes them US-registered, putting them under the jurisdiction of American regulations. They're tough. That's why the FAA and National Transportation Safety Board are here. According to international agreement, the country of registration has the right to participate in the investigation with the officials where the crash happened.'

'Do you think they'll work out what happened? You know, about Ed's heart?'

'Eventually. They didn't have you to tip them off about his health like I did. They'll play it by the book, absolutely methodically. They'll look at the obvious, external factors like the weather – and it was horrendously windy that day – the condition of the plane, air-traffic control instructions before the crash. They'll be going through NN Air's files, like I was doing, and they'll be well into the maintenance logs of the DC-8 by now, probably the aircrew records as well.'

'It didn't take *you* long to figure out Ed's records weren't in order.'

'It would have taken longer without you.' He turned to her. 'I'd just arrived here and I had to concentrate on the physical mess at Haneda. You pointed me to the pilot's medical problem and it gave me something to zero in on when I got to NN Air's records.' He gave an ironic scoff. 'I expect Yuriko's found a way to explain the missing certificate to our friends from the States.'

Her smile was a forlorn one; she swiped at an errant thread of hair. 'So Ed's the person to blame for the crash.'

He touched her wrist. 'Don't think like that. Ed Kidderby was a good guy. He just wanted to keep flying. If he'd worked for a big airline they'd have their own doctors; and if it was a scrupulous airline without in-house medical facilities they'd make sure the required health checks got done at a reputable clinic. Ed Kidderby worked for neither, and took up the offer to use NNC's friendly, captive doctors. The other pilots must have known he wasn't fit enough to fly but they'd been hired by Miyamoto's airline as well. It wasn't it their interests to denounce one of the senior officers.'

'Can I have a whisky, *gaijin san*?' she said. 'A *mizuwari*,' she ordered, anticipating his agreement. 'Why did he risk it? He must have known he was sick.'

'He was desperate to work. He'd be paying alimony and support to his family at home and he needed to fund a few investments in Japan and elsewhere in Asia. You told me yourself he'd put up the capital for his girlfriend's bar.' He had brought them back brutally to the missing woman.

'Where does Makiko fit into this?' Phyllis demanded to know. 'Why has she gone away?'

Alex fiddled with the redundant chopsticks. 'It's not easy to see,' he said wearily. 'She knew how sick he was. That's obvious. Maybe she's just taken her grief off somewhere.'

Phyllis turned on him. 'I don't think you mean that, Alex. She had a business to run for chrissake. I know there's something you're not telling me. It's about Makiko, isn't it?'

'I don't know, Phyl. It's too absurd to believe.'

'Just tell me,' she insisted.

His face carried a deep frown. 'I think I told Yuriko Shimada about Makiko.'

'What?' The animated din from other diners around the table broke for a instant as they looked across at the outburst. 'You did what? I don't get it.'

'It must have been Friday. You'd taken me on Thursday night to that bar in Roppongi where Kidderby used to drink and told me Makiko was worried about his health.' He shrugged. 'I asked Yuriko to find the medical certificate missing from the sequence and she asked if it was important. I said it was, even more so since I'd heard from Ed's girlfriend that he had a heart problem.'

Phyllis fell into thought, sipping the whisky torpidly.

'I don't know what to read into it,' Alex said.

'I think it's time you tried, *gaijin san*,' she declared, swivelling out of the chair. 'It's getting scary.'

She had picked the *teppan yaki* place in Akasaka because it was a few minutes' walk from Makiko Nakamura's bar in a building decorated in neons and filled with restaurants and drinking salons. They walked silently past a sand-plastered wall broken by a slatted wooden porchway which led through a dense garden of dwarf pines and plum trees to one of the old discreet *ryotei* entertainment houses so beloved of politicians and their big business friends. 'That's the kind place you'll find Hiroshi Miyamoto,' Phyllis said, struggling to match Alex's urgent stride. 'Kissing political ass. Or rather buying it.' She outpaced him to a corner and suddenly stepped across to block him. Holding her waist lightly, he twisted forward and followed her gaze to a black and white police car parked in front of the brightly lit building. A few people with spare time hung around it. 'Makiko's place is on the second floor.'

'Then let's go and visit her,' Alex said.

She held him back. 'I don't want to walk in if the police are talking to her staff. If they're on Makiko's case they're going to know a tall *gaijin* and an odd-looking Japanese with a foreign accent were looking for her this morning. It's not worth getting involved, Alex. I told you that already.' She slipped from his grip. 'Wait out of sight while I find out where the police are.'

She returned within a minute. 'Walk away casually,' she commanded. 'They're in her bar. Get us a cab and let's go over to my place. I want to show you my files on Miyamoto and his evil empire.'

A vivid, pitted moon crowned the apex of the tiled temple roof, its pale light streaking the forest of mortuary columns in the graveyard and the grove of bamboo around it. A gate opened from the road onto the precious plot of land studded with conifers and cherry trees. 'I pay my rent to the priest,' Phyllis said, leading Alex over cracked stones to the weathered wooden house with a smaller second floor attached to it like a turret. 'And teach his kids a bit of English.' Kicking off her shoes inside the doorway, she said, 'It's a little cramped, I guess, but make yourself at home – and watch your head.'

He did not have to be told. The beams were low, the rooms small, covered with *tatami* matting and decorated with travel posters. The furniture was chipboard and minimally functional: a desk for a word-processor and a rattan chair, simple bookshelves and a plain dining table in the kitchen. Scattered beanbag cushions suggested Phyllis sat wherever she left her books and notes, in small piles around the house. He passed a room which smelled of fresh reed matting. A futon, thick with soft down, was laid out in the centre; the empty dungarees spread across a hanger on the knob of a sliding cupboard made him smile.

'Bring a chair from the kitchen,' she said, drawing up to the desk and booting the computer. 'There's beer in the refrigerator if you want it.'

He declined the drink and watched her work the mouse through the directories, then the chapters, of the still unnamed book. 'Jonsson, Jonsson,' she muttered with a hard 'j', chewing on a fingertip. She tapped again and revealed a reference file. 'I was under the impression Shinichi Miyamoto started the company and I just didn't zero in on any others, especially a foreigner. There's not much, but take a look.'

'"Roland Jonson, Swedish engineer",' Alex read over her shoulder, '"adviser to Nippon Nagasaki Kogyo, 1930". You got his name wrong,' he said. 'An "s" missing. "Introduced latest turbine technology. Invaluable contribution to marine division of Nippon Nagasaki Kogyo". You can say that again,' he told her. 'If Bill Littleton's translation's right, Jonsson started the company and still owns the bloody thing.'

She rolled the page forward. 'I've got nothing else on him.'

'You can say he died in the Nagasaki atom bomb. When was it exactly?'

'August ninth, 1945.' She tapped it on the keyboard. 'Not exactly a full biography, is it?'

'I'll ask Miyamoto about him tomorrow. I'm invited to dinner. But don't you have a source in Nippon Nagasaki?'

Phyllis made a tortured face. 'I got most of my general background material on the company from them before they realised what kind of book I was writing. Now I'm absolutely blacklisted from any of their group companies and now they intimidate me whenever they can, particularly if I talk to people like you. They'll certainly stop me finding a Japanese publisher and if it comes out abroad they'll use their influence to make sure it's never sold here.'

'Why should they do that?' Alex wanted to know.

She clicked into another file. 'It's all about skeletons in Miyamoto's cupboards and the peculiar problem the Japanese have when it comes to remembering a case of corruption or a scandal for more than a week.'

Alex's yawn ended in a smile.

Phyllis brushed at a strand of hair. 'I reckon you've had enough lecturing on Japan from me and Bill.'

'Give me one more session before I call it a day.'

'Okay,' she enthused, tugging the hem of her short skirt and wriggling until she was comfortable. 'The great bubble boom of the eighties – that's what the Japanese call it by the way – burst at the end of the decade. A whole Mount Fuji of shit exploded, splashing down on literally millions of people. Real-estate values collapsed, lenders went bust, the big banks had billions of dollars' worth of uncollectable loans out to the *yakuza* and other low life and some came close to bankruptcy. Just about all members of the Diet were found to be corrupt, taking bribes in exchange for their influence, and the *yakuza* syndicates had fingers in every kind of illegal business and more and more in legitimate. Look at this. One of Hiroshi Miyamoto's skeletons.' A new file appeared, reproducing a letter. 'Two years ago a really pissed-off aide of Miyamoto's sent a letter to the three main daily newspapers. He'd listed a hundred and eighty members of the Diet, that's the parliament here, who'd received around thirty billion yen in cash or shares from Miyamoto. He didn't discriminate among the political parties. He gave to the government and the opposition.'

'Hang on. Thirty billion.' He made a quick calculation. 'That's about two hundred million pounds.'

'Right. Three hundred million bucks.'

'Why isn't Miyamoto inside? In prison?'

She gave him a wide smile and tossed her head. 'You're

beautiful, *gaijin san*,' she said with loud sigh. 'I think I'll dedicate my book to you.'

'You haven't answered my question,' Alex said, puzzled.

She looked at the screen, and the bullet points drawing attention to her bold letters. 'The newspapers sat on the letter. You have to understand that they rely on the official briefings their journalists get as members of the press clubs attached to the police, the ministries and important government agencies. If they write anything critical they'll be excluded and their newspapers won't get the copy. Needless to say, foreigners are not invited to join these jolly little gatherings. Since the letter from the Nippon Nagasaki guy and its allegations hadn't come from an official source the newspapers exercised self-censorship, thus killing the story. There's nothing intrepid about the media here, Alex, unless they all do the exposing together.'

'But *you* know about the letter, don't you?' Alex remarked.

'Sure. When he got nowhere locally the guy sent it to the foreign press here in Tokyo and it got a bit of cover abroad. The Japanese scandal of the month sort of thing. Problem is, hardly a week goes by without another cabinet minister declaring the Nanking massacre never happened or found to have forgotten to declare a few billion yen's worth of campaign contributions. As we speak there are two former cabinet ministers awaiting trial for their involvement in gangster-related golf club membership scams.' She scoffed. 'Anyway, it wasn't in the country's interest to indict half the Diet for taking money from the president of Nippon Nagasaki Corporation and so story just faded away.'

'So why did you pursue the accusations against him?' Alex asked.

'I'd just started researching my book on NNC when the story broke. I tracked the informant down and got in touch through an intermediary.'

A dog's bark broke the silence, causing Alex to jump. 'And?' he said, hooked.

'A couple of days before we agreed to meet he died in an automobile accident.'

Alex shook off his blazer. 'I think I'll have that beer now.'

'Bring me one too,' Phyllis said, closing down the computer. The room had glowed from the screen; now it was the tepid spray of moonlight shaping Phyllis's silhouette as she pulled the windows together and shivered when a trapped draught of cool air enveloped her. He found her in the hallway, cradling the telephone, listening hopelessly to a hostess at Makiko Nakamura's bar. She turned at the hiss when Alex snapped the tags on the tins.

'I was right,' she said, seizing the tin of Sapporo Dry desperately. 'The police were there tonight, responding informally to my call about Makiko, but she won't be considered officially missing for another forty-eight hours.'

Alex joined her on a heap of cushions bunched against the wall. 'She'll turn up,' he said, convincing neither of them.

She looked at him, her eyes spiritless, shadowed from fatigue. 'Can we get back to Jonsson?' she slurred. 'Take my mind off Makiko.'

'Not tonight,' he said.

She sighed, stifling a yawn, and nodded thoughtfully. 'Okay. Maybe later.' He caught the beer can as her grip on it loosened. She was leaning against him, her face flat against his chest, her hair smooth on his face. She was mumbling something. He lowered his head and brought hers closer with a hand: they were slipping down the wall, onto a bed of cushions. Her arm reached across him and he felt the softness of her body moulding to him.

'Please, please, Alex,' she breathed. 'Don't give Miyamoto the old Jonsson letter tomorrow.'

七

<u>*2 January, 1943*</u>
*TODAY I GOT MY DIARY BACK. I managed to steal it
and as it is a day off work I will try and fill in gaps.
Since 31st October 1942 I've been working in the No. 2
Shipbuilding Yard. I've been slapped for not working
hard enough. So have Jim Bishop, Phil, Reg Riggs and
Mahoney. We try to drag out the work as much as we
can. Conditions are dangerous. Open fires, sparks
flying and no safety equipment. The Japs that work with
us shout at us in Japanese and get wild if we cannot
understand them. Each party has an interpreter. Ours
cannot speak English. He's fairly old and crippled and
at first I felt sorry for him. After working with him I
don't. Once he tried to bully and push me about but I
had a large staging iron in my hand and I made him
understand that he would feel what it was made of if he
did not lay off. He was better afterwards. Most of the
guards are former soldiers who were wounded and sent
home. We give them nicknames. One's called Liver
Face because he lost most of his face from a grenade in
China.*

Everything's carried by hand, mostly by what we call Yo-Yo, a pole with a basket slung in the centre and two men or women carry it on their shoulders. By the way there are a lot of women working in the dockyards, collecting scrap.

During November I managed to stay in Camp for 16 days through having no boots. I didn't mind at all. Jim Bishop had flu from 11 to 21 November. Reg had 4 days in with a bad stomach and got a job as Camp Cook, so we get a bit of extra food like burnt rice, baked yams and now and again some salt. The menu never changes, day in day out: rice, barley broth with a few carrots or turnips and some tiny fish, like sardines. A 20 lb slab of meat turns up now and again but doesn't go far among 1,000 men. Flip's the Jap mess sergeant, Liver Face is his number two. They are brutal with us and don't mind us seeing them steal our rations.

Two Americans were caught trying to liberate the Red Cross parcels the camp received. They were beaten and locked up in the punishment cages. One of them won't last long. The Japs just keep the parcels themselves. We get little tins to take our rice and veg to work in. They don't hold much of either but it does not matter because we only get half an hour for lunch. Sometimes we manage to warm up the tins but if we are caught it means a beating from the Guards. There isn't really much to eat. The Japs promise a lot but we get nothing. They promised us 10 sen per day pay but we never get it. For work clothes we have a shirt and long pants made of sacking. In Camp we wear a Jap Army suit. We have no underwear. We have an overcoat but can't wear it outside the Camp. Lice are a bloody nuisance. They live in the clothes and we can never get rid of them. We can bath once a week. Hardly a bath. It's a pipe with holes in it and we all parade under it for a few seconds.

Tobacco's getting short. Jim, Phil, Spike and I have nearly finished what we brought with us from Makassar. It's hard to keep it safe because petty thieving is everywhere. We can only smoke at certain times anyway.

I think I've caught up with Camp life and will finish with Christmas. I hear the Camp Commandant is a Catholic and that there are a lot of Christians in Nagasaki. On Xmas Eve we were allowed to sing Carols. We worked a full day in the dockyard as the Japs do not keep up Christmas but on Xmas Day a Jap padre conducted a service. The Japs had promised us a special treat with our Christmas dinner and it turned out we all got an apple each.

4 January

Back to work after Jap New Year holidays. It snowed hard all night. It's very cold. It's impossible to keep warm. We try to skive round the riveter's fire but the guards knock us around. There's a pneumonia outbreak in the Camp and it's carrying off people every day. Frank Willsmore S.B.P.O. was injured in the eye from blasting.

16 February

A really nasty head civilian supervisor came round the dockyard. He knocked Terry over for smirking and kicked him unconscious. A Jap Navy guard we call The Kid doles out punishments for him with a baseball bat. I trapped my left hand and will be in camp for a few days. Getting short of paper so will not be writing daily. Frank's getting worse. Dr told us he was bleeding in the upper part of his bowels.

2 March

Another accident to my left hand. Few more days off work. Jim Bishop has been told to rest for three days so Spike is the only one of the gang working. Two men died this week. They took their bodies across to Nagasaki for cremation. Flip and his mess corporal are holding back our food. Thirteen Dutch-Indonesians accused of stealing rice balls were beaten up by Flip and other guards. They screamed all night.

18 March

The guards in the dockyard are getting a bit rougher, mostly the young ones. We know when the Japs have lost a sea battle because they take it out on us. The Kid likes to kick you behind the knees. Food supplies low. Your rations get cut in half if you're sick — no work, no food rule — and on rest days, the Japs call it 'yasumi' and it's every eighth day, we get 400 grams instead of the usual 630. Dutch commanding officer got slapped around for asking for release of Red Cross parcels. We got nothing. Our ribs stick out a bit but at least it's getting warmer.

23 May

Dutch officer of the week told me there are 12 men in hospital, 14 in the sickroom, 50 sick in own bed and 52 sick but not in bed. One death today. Our room, 5, was punished after evening muster for not bringing back rice boxes in time. Made to stand to attention for two hours. 13 lads fainted.

25 May

Paper still a problem but I stole scraps in the dockyard. Yeoman of Signals Phillips was killed in the dockyard in April. He was replaced in our room by a civilian. Johnson's not very friendly. I was detailed by Lt. Cmdr. Chubb to act as duty N.C.O. This means I will be working in Camp every eight weeks.

19 June

Frank Willsmore now permanently sick. Never recovered from a beating he got for messing up his number at roll-call when he was delirious. We now

*have a bath-house instead of the pipe so we can wash
every few weeks. It's Jap style and we are supposed to
wash before getting into the tub. Even so, it's like
getting into mud if you're number eight hundred in the
line. The dead are washed in it before they are
cremated. No sign of new clothes though. Mine are
alive with lice. If it's not lice at you, it's mosquitos and
bloody huge cockroaches. It's all getting hard to take.*

'And after the break we go back to Tokyo and the crash of
that Japanese cargo airplane a week ago.'

Alex dabbed at a fleck of blood and cursed. He had been
shaving the line of his jaw, only half attentive to the sound of
the television piped into the bathroom. Wrapped in a hotel
gown and clutching a hand-towel to his face, he moved
smartly to the room in time to catch the last tract of CNN
self-publicity changing to the gates of the Japanese Ministry
of Transport, a backdrop for a disembodied voice identified
by the caption as Leon Calkin, the channel's senior Tokyo
correspondent.

'It's Monday morning here in the capital of Japan.
Officials of the civil aviation bureau of the Transport
Ministry, who have been working in this building behind me
all weekend, have again reiterated their contention that
mechanical failure has been discounted as a possible cause
of the crash last Tuesday of the twenty-five-year-old DC-8-
71 cargo airplane at Haneda airport, Tokyo. The US-
registered airplane was operated by NN Air of Japan.' He
checked his notes. 'In a statement issued yesterday, the
Aircraft Accident Investigation Committee said it is possible
the plane was downed during its final approach by wind-
shear, a sudden, lethal downdraft of turbulent air. This
assessment may change, of course, as flight data recordings
are analysed and other factors are taken into acount.'

You can bet on it, Alex told the screen, packing the

171

cassette and his papers into the chart case.

'You don't share the common view,' Richard Ingleby droned. He had left his suite to take coffee with Alex and the aviation insurance broker Yoshi Kanagawa, who had arrived before him and taken a quiet corner in British Underwriters International's Kudan-shita offices. Alex turned from the window, where he had been watching a tourist bus disgorge another group of country visitors, about to be awed by the scale of the Imperial Palace walls and the massive wooden gateways. Yoshi was patrolling the open-plan floor, scowling into his cellular telephone and alternately slapping his forehead in frustration.

'He's trying to get me a line to an FAA official or someone from the National Transportation Safety Board,' Alex explained. 'I need to talk to them about Ed Kidderby's health. And to answer you, no, I don't go along with it. It's actually a very plausible theory and there's actually a warning in the pilots' manuals about wind-shear around Haneda.'

Ingleby poured himself a coffee. 'So where's the problem? It's going to look to NN Air like you're doing everything you can to deny their claim.'

'The approach to the airport was normal,' Alex declared. 'The crew was aware of the danger from the high winds and there was no flippancy, no silly banter between them in the last minutes. I think Ed Kidderby was in rough physical shape but he sounds to me like an old pro.' He raised his eyebrows to Yoshi, who was circling the desk and trying to catch his attention. 'And wind-shear is usually associated with the presence of thunderstorms and there weren't any within a hundred miles of Haneda last Tuesday.'

'I don't understand,' Ingleby confessed.

'The shear's caused by the change in wind speed and direction and this is most likely around a low-pressure storm system. Wind-shear-related accidents to date have all been in areas of thunderstorm activity.'

Ingleby's voice pitched high. 'So you think it was the pilot. You think he collapsed or something?'

'Right. His heart packed up probably. And the plane was too low for the crew to rectify the dive when Kidderby collapsed over the controls.'

Ingleby took it in for a moment. 'We'll still have to pay out to that Miami firm,' he said finally, his voice an annoying know-all whine.

Alex made sure Yoshi was out of earshot. He didn't want the broker exciting the insurers with the possibility that the claim was going to be denied. He stood sideways on to the Tokyo director. 'I'm almost certain Ed Kidderby had a serious heart condition which he and his employers at NN Air conspired to hide.'

'What makes you so sure?' Ingleby asked, hardly hiding his scepticism.

Alex knew he was on soft ground. 'I hear he liked to have a drink or three too many. He was stressed out and he may have suffered one or more mild heart attacks this year.'

'My wife thinks *I* drink too much,' Ingleby huffed. 'The ticker flutters a bit sometimes but the tests I've had show it's not in bad shape.' He leaned forward, fiddling with the cuffs of his jacket. 'You can't make a case on hearsay. You'll need forensic evidence.'

'Given the way the cockpit took the brunt of the impact explosion there might not be enough viable tissue left to reveal a chronic problem,' Alex said. 'At least the Japanese realise how tough the problem is and are bringing in one of the two top US specialists to conduct the autopsy. I want to stay in Japan until he arrives, at least try and get a feel for his preliminary findings. If I'm right about Kidderby's longstanding dodgy heart NN Air might be in breach of the conditions of the insurance on their fleet.'

'Proof?' Ingleby asked. 'Apart from hearsay.'

'There was a medical certificate missing from Kidderby's

records. The airline knew about it before the Japanese investigators came for the files.' Alex's face creased. 'I expect Miyamoto's aide, Yuriko Shimada, will make sure a misfiled certificate will find its way back into the right place, along with the proper apologies from the airline.'

'It would be your word against theirs if push came to shove.'

Alex thought about another coffee but slid the cup away. 'NN Air are not big enough to have their own medical facilities. They'd send their crews to designated clinics or the pilots might arrange their own checks. I know where Kidderby went and I'm fairly sure who sent him there. It's a hospital down in Nagasaki. Home of the Miyamoto empire. I'd need to look at the old certificates again with a good, neutral translator, see if there's a pattern. I was too wrapped up confirming the tests had been done as required to examine the actual contents of the reports.'

Stretched back on a chair, thumbs tucked into the pockets of his waistcoat, Ingleby took up a pensive posture. 'You might not get a crack at the records until the American and local civil aviation characters have finished with them. That's going to take time and long before you see them the lessors are going to want their money. I don't want to be negative, Alex, but you've got to come up with some real evidence, demonstrate beyond reasonable doubt that the pilot's heart problem caused the crash. And soon. If you don't find anything in the next three or four days you'll have to put up or shut up.'

Alex thought about Makiko Nakamura. Ed Kidderby's doctor might have been inveigled into giving him a favourable prognosis twice a year, but the woman Alex had never met was his only reliable lead as he searched for the facts he needed to reconstruct Kidderby's last tortured six months. 'His Japanese girlfriend can testify to several blackouts in the last year which he obviously kept quiet from everyone else.'

'You've met her?' Ingleby said incredulously.

'Not exactly. Look. It's a long story, Richard, and I can't go into it here.' Yoshi approached them, collapsing his mobile angrily. 'Any luck?' Alex asked hopefully.

'Nothing. Can't get to first base with those awful bureaucrats. I asked them at least to pass your name on the Americans. They said they knew who you were but they asked for your cooperation at this hectic time.'

Alex snorted. 'Which means?'

'Which means "back off, go away, we don't want to talk to you".' A call came in on his mobile and he turned away with a grim, apologetic smile.

'I'll leave you to it,' Richard Ingleby said, as the telephone on Alex's desk rang. 'Shout if you need anything.'

Alex waved limply at the departing figure and dragged the telephone console closer. Yoshi Kanagawa was losing his precious Japanese cool and his voice was rising to a level that turned heads at the nearest desks.

'Hi, *gaijin san*,' the familiar throaty voice said. 'You can't have your evil way with an innocent maiden and just walk away.' The usual brashness, the tone of impudent confidence, was missing from the quip but it still forced a much-needed smile from him.

'If I had my evil way with you last night, Phyl, I can't say it was memorable.'

'Pig!' she chided. 'Thanks anyway for seeing me to the futon. I was really wiped out. And thanks for locking the house as well. I don't normally do it.'

Her voice thinned, almost to a whisper. 'Alex, I've got a problem. Can you come over?' Yoshi Kanagawa was approaching the desk, jabbing a finger at the cellular phone and mouthing something.

'Hold on Phyl,' Alex said, irritated. 'What's up, Yoshi?'

'We've got some real problems here Alex.'

'Everybody's got problems all of a sudden.' His elbow

was pegged to the desk when he spoke to Phyllis. 'I'm tied up right now. I can't get away. Is it about Makiko? Has she turned up?' All he heard in the interval was her breathing.

'I haven't heard from her or about her,' she said, her voice strained. 'I'm scared, Alex. Please come over. Take a cab to the Juenji Temple. I'll meet you in front of my house.'

The clock was running out. He raked his hair, tugged by the urgency in his mission and the plea from Phyllis. Finally he brandished the telephone at the broker. 'This sounds pretty serious too, Yoshi. Be a good chap and put me in a taxi to this place.' He tore off a message slip and scooped his own mobile. 'I won't be long. A couple of hours, no more. What's *your* problem?'

The Japanese broker trailed him across the open office. 'The Haneda Airport authorities are submitting formal demands for the removal and disposal of contaminated earth.'

Alex rolled his eyes on the move. 'Tell them to get in the queue.'

They were in a crowded lift. 'They will, right behind Tokyo Water, who want the insurers to pay for the examination and possible restitution of the water table from pollution caused by the kerosene seepage and any collateral damage to pipes caused by the explosion.'

'Put them through to me here later, not at Nippon Nagasaki Corporation, or I'll see them this afternoon,' Alex said as they spilled into the building's reception hall. 'I could be in Japan till Christmas at this rate.'

Yoshi flagged down a taxi and spoke to the driver. 'Should be about four thousand yen,' he said to Alex. 'Maybe twenty minutes away if you're lucky with the traffic.'

Alex was about to swing his body into the rear seat when he looked up at Yoshi. 'I want to know sometime how Yuriko Shimada fits in here.'

Tapping a Seven Stars gratefully out of its packet, the Japanese gave a derisive snort. 'She's as tough as they come and when she speaks you know it's like her boss Miyamoto talking.' He sucked on the cigarette and made a wry, cynical smile. 'It can't be long before she uses her personal skills to help you reach a positive decision.'

'If she hasn't already,' Alex said, unsmiling, as the automatic door slapped shut.

The broad glasses had returned to dominate her face, and the rich, dusky hair was tucked back under the red baseball cap, but the floppy dungarees had been replaced by scuffed blue-grey jeans. A collarless jacket was pulled in against the fresh breeze, which threatened to drag in the rain clouds Alex had seen drifting in from the south-east. Her mouth was drawn in a sour scowl when she slid in beside him and spoke sharply to the driver. Directed by Phyllis they drove without speaking a short distance along a narrow, nameless busy road of small shops to an even narrower passage between houses sheltering behind low walls. She stopped the taxi and was strangely wary as they walked to a junction, which became a bridge crossing a drainage culvert, its sides stepped in concrete. On the other side of the bridge they turned along the road bordering the canal, passing people who had stepped from their cramped homes into the sunshine to trade theories on this disturbance to their orderly and quiet lives.

When they turned a bend she took his hand to slow him and kept it there, her grip tightening. The crowd on both sides of the culvert had thickened, surrounding the police cars and a red utility van from the fire services, which blocked the narrow junctions by the next bridge. They watched while uniformed police and men in caps and overalls moved below them, some patrolling beside the shallow channel of water, others perched awkwardly on the flagstone-paved banks. The police looked confused and bemused by the incident, and the pair with clipboards were

177

close to finishing their meticulous measurements without reaching a rational explanation. The flat lip of Phyllis's cap seared his chin when her head spun and crushed against his chest. The water was not deep at this time in May; but in a month's time, when the prolonged rain of the *tsuyu* season washed the country incessantly, it would fill the floor and rise against the concrete walls. Stirred by the firemen's rubber boots the water sloshed and lapped against cracked windows, just deep enough to cover the dented and gouged roof. The smug whale was under water for the first time in its life. When the Mini had been shunted through the corrugated metal barrier it had slewed momentarily on the uneven slope before rolling onto its back, rasping the roof and finally drowning the whale as it hit the water. The exhaust piping and chassis lay exposed, like the armoured belly of a reptile, and tracks of oil from the torn sump seeped erratically over the upturned body. The noise from the crash had brought the closest residents into the quiet backwater streets at about four, perhaps four fifteen, in the morning, they told the police enthusiastically.

Phyllis started to sob desolately into his shirt. A man on the opposite side of the canal nudged another and gestured towards her.

'They must have done it after I left,' Alex said. 'I remember seeing your car clearly in the moonlight. We call them joyriders. Another British export.'

She mumbled without looking up. 'Bullshit. They were *waiting* for you to go. They weren't joyriders.'

Alex felt helpless, half his mind, his mental concentration, still hung on a twenty-million-dollar decision he had to make within sixty hours. Feeling the heaving body against him he knew that his mission and hers had somehow converged, melted together in a way he was trying desperately to comprehend. They were half concealed by a sturdy metal telegraph pole. 'Do they know it's your car?' he managed.

Her head turned against him, towards the activity around the wreckage of the Mini. 'I don't think so. Not yet anyway. Daisuke, the little son of the priest at the temple, told me about it. He'd followed a police car on his cycle and came back and woke me before he went to school. Said they'd found my car in the river thing, the drainage canal, whatever. Poor kid was so happy I wasn't in it. I ran over here but I didn't feel like talking to the police. I still don't. I need time to think.' She left the warm refuge of his body. 'Let's get out of here.'

They moved into the sunlight, then quickly into the shadow cast by a wall. 'They'll find out sometime,' Alex said, his eyes drawn to the pathetic, upended corpse of the compact little car. An elderly woman on the other side of the culvert caught Alex's eye. Her head was turned to one side but an arm was pointed in their direction.

'Let them work it out for themselves,' Phyllis said harshly, moving away. They retraced the route along the canal and back towards the main road. Her hand had moved to his arm and stayed clenched to it. Alex pulled up when they passed under the awning of a *sakaya* liquor shop.

'Who did it, Phyl?'

'Isn't it obvious, for chrissake?' She pulled free and looked around helplessly.

Alex was behind her. 'It can't be Miyamoto.'

She spun, the corners of her mouth trembling. 'For fuck's sake, Alex, I told you last night that the poor guy who might have given me the inside story on Miyamoto died, was killed I should say, before I could meet him. And where's Ed Kidderby's girlfriend, Makiko? You told that monster woman, Yuriko, about her, didn't you? Now it's my turn. They've known I've been talking to you since they slapped me around their garage last week and they don't like it.'

He took her shoulders. He didn't need a cassette recording to remind him that Yuriko Shimada had said

179

something about interfering journalists and he shuddered at
the memory of it. If he'd got it right she'd tried to assure him
that the problem of nuisance journalists was being
addressed. Her exact words escaped him. A woman in a drab
dress, the wife of the drink shop owner, wiped her hands on
a cloth and watched the strange couple suspiciously. 'These
things don't happen, surely Phyl,' Alex insisted. 'Not in
Japan.'

'Bullshit, Alex. You'll find out how the cover-ups work
and the statistics get massaged if you stay in Japan much
longer.'

They had set off again, and it was minutes before Phyllis
broke the silence, throwing up her arms when she had the
words properly sharpened. 'We're talking murder, Alex.' She
seized the lapel of his suit jacket. 'Don't you get it? Murder.
Corporate killing. And I've just had my first warning.'

They walked to the road from which Phyllis's house was
a short distance away. There were no police cars or their
bicycles on the street or in the forecourt of the temple but it
wouldn't be long before someone remembered the little car
with the painted whale and footprints and the unusual
Japanese-looking woman who drove it.

'Come into town with me, Phyl,' Alex suggested, glancing
at his watch. 'I don't want you stay here, or anywhere, on
your own.' They were in the *tatami*-matted living room of
her house. He had made her a coffee, which she sipped
cheerlessly. She was slumped in a cushion, her hands
clasped around the red cap, searching for answers, when the
words she wanted to hear came from him again. She looked
up, her face widening. 'You can shadow me if you like,' he
said, pulling her to her feet. 'I've got a meeting or two this
afternoon.'

'And the big dinner tonight with Miyamoto.' The
bitterness in her voice was not for him. She gathered a
notepad, camera and the diskettes backing up her unfinished

book and research material on Nippon Nagasaki Corporation. 'Just in case,' she said, flourishing the disks.

Alex's borrowed cellular telephone purred soon into their taxi journey. It turned into a long conversation, Alex scratching jerky notes onto the back of an envelope, occasionally throwing a frustrated scowl out of the car window. They were already passing the edges of Shimbashi, the gates to Hibiya Park appearing on their left, when he finally snapped the mobile off.

Phyllis spoke to the driver and then to Alex. 'I'll get out at the next intersection. The Foreign Correspondents' Club's over there, between the grey building and railtracks.'

'Will you be all right? You're welcome to stay around my company's offices.'

She drew her bag to her and hitched it over a shoulder as the taxi slowed by the kerb. She leaned over and kissed his cheek. 'I'm feeling a little better, thanks to you. I'll be fine. I'll stay in the club, make some calls, work in the library, whatever. I'll call you later.'

'What are going to do tonight?' Alex said. 'Are you going back to your house? I've got this showdown dinner with Miyamoto which I can't really get out of.'

The driver had the emergency lights blinking and he looked round at his passengers impatiently. Traffic headed for Otemachi in three solid lanes and he was slowing the flow.

She eased herself from the taxi and then leaned back inside. 'I'll probably go to the Tulip bar in Roppongi – you know, the place I took you to first to talk about Ed Kidderby. If I can't get you by phone later today, maybe you can catch me there later. Can you find it?'

Alex said he could – he had kept a book of matches – and watched the red cap shrink through the rear window. The taxi moved forward in a frustrating block between traffic lights, and Yoshi was waiting on the pavement, his head swivelling expectantly between the two directions of traffic. They had ten minutes to get to the Transport Ministry. 'I agreed to meet them on neutral ground,' Yoshi said, dropping a packet of sandwiches in Alex's lap. 'These okay? I said you hadn't got time to go to Haneda and City Hall and Tokyo Water so I got them to arrange to borrow a room in the Civil Aviation Bureau of the Ministry. They're all pretty keen to get you alone before you leave so they fixed it for two.'

'Let's get it over with,' Alex muttered. 'But I'd have preferred to get back to finding what brought down NINA three two eight.' He was thinking aloud and it was a mistake. He didn't want anyone, least of all the man representing the broking company that had sold the insurance deal around London in the first place, to get the notion that a payout on the claim was not to be a foregone conclusion.

Yoshi's narrow eyes flashed sideways. 'I thought we're talking wind-shear,' he said in his fluent American.

Alex backpedalled. 'It looks that way, but I want to see the analysis of the flight data recordings. It should throw up any mechanical breakdown in the basic functions which might have caused or contributed to the crash.' He tore the plastic wrapper and eyed a creamy tuna sandwich unenthusiastically.

'But it won't affect the payout, will it?' Yoshi insisted. 'There are no war loss implications, are there?'

'No there aren't,' Alex confirmed, biting into the bread.

'So what are you saying? You got a problem with the claim?'

'I didn't get through all the documentation, as you know.'

'Sorry.'

'Do you think we can find the Americans in the ministry?' he asked abruptly. 'The FAA guys especially.' They were in a broad avenue with wide pavements and a border of forlorn trees. Kasumigaseki. The heart of administrative Japan.

Yoshi exchanged some Japanese with the driver, then turned to Alex. 'Can't say. They've removed the wreckage to a hangar on a Japan Air Self-Defense Force base outside Tokyo. They could be there.'

Alex crunched the empty plastic container and dabbed his mouth with his knuckles. 'If the first stage of the official investigation's over then I guess British Underwriters International are now the proud owners of a few million pieces of junk.'

It turned into a long afternoon in a badly ventilated room near a service lift, leaving no one any better or worse off. By the end of it Alex had received business cards from representatives of the airport management, the local municipal district, the suppliers of fresh water and various subsidiary organisations whose functions he quickly forgot. Each delegation brought three or four people, although only one from each petitioning group actually spoke, and insisted on separate interviews. In expressing their regret at the tragedy, they wanted to give Bolton *san*, as representative of the insurance syndicate covering all liabilities in respect of damage, an informal indication of the claims they were planning to bring against it for damage to infrastructure, fixed structures, underground cables and pipes and the environment. The amount demanded was still to be assessed, but Bolton *san*'s understanding and cooperation was respectfully requested.

The evening was already purple-dark when Yoshi Kanagawa put him into a taxi in front of the Ministry of Transport. 'Don't say I didn't warn you about Yuriko Shimada,' the Japanese broker smirked. The frustrating, wasted afternoon had stressed him, but Alex threw him a smile and a wave. In the hotel he found a batch of messages, including a tetchy fax from Reggie Cameron suggesting he send a report, which somehow mirrored the pronouncements from the Japanese civil aviation investigation team. There was nothing from Phyllis. He had half an hour to shower, revive his spirits with a stiff gin from the mini-bar and generate some enthusiasm for a dinner with the great leader of Nippon Nagasaki Corporation before the car came for him. Thinking how an evening with Phyl Wakai, without the dungarees and the damned cap, was a better option, he called the Foreign Correspondents' Club. She didn't answer when they paged her. He found the book of matches, with its tulip design, traced a mental route to the cellar bar in Roppongi and believed he could find it later. The Grand Kanto's customer services manager personally delivered the package he had requested them to prepare and wrap when he'd left the hotel early that morning. No, Alex did not want to open and examine it because it was already formally gift-wrapped and the recipient's name written in beautiful caligraphic style. And yes, the cost should be added to his account.

Alex was lost. The same NNC chauffeur who had met him at Narita and driven him during his first days in Tokyo had collected him from the Grand Kanto Hotel and muttered a destination that meant nothing. They had driven in silence for half an hour, leaving the part of Tokyo familiar to him and crossing a forest of ultra-modern high-rise buildings he had seen from far off but did not know was the seat of Tokyo's metropolitan government. Passing signs in roman writing for Shinjuku, then Ikebukuro, both night-time playgrounds lit up fiercely with neons, they stopped finally on the edge of another entertainment quarter by a stuccoed wall topped with steepled terracotta tiles. It reminded Alex of the discreetly understated, exclusive eating place they had passed in Akasaka when they tried to visit Makiko Nakamura's bar. Phyllis had said it was beyond the budget of all but politicians and company presidents. He was met at the latticed porch by an elderly woman in a dark kimono who bowed and led him wordlessly through the garden to the weathered wooden *ryotei* house. Subdued lighting, hidden in low clusters of young bamboo and a grove of white birch, washed over a short wooden bridge which crossed a kidney-shaped pond surrounded by azaleas and trimmed box trees. Light pooled around a lantern in the water, attracting the koi carp to roll and flip against its stone legs.

Yuriko Shimada and Miyamoto's more taciturn aide Tabata were waiting in an anteroom. Her short, pale-lilac dress, shot-silk jacket, hunched at the shoulders, and generous make-up contrasted bizarrely with the simple austerity of the room. Alex took Tabata's pinched smile and awkward bow as a greeting. His role, it turned out, was to keep quiet unless Hiroshi Miyamoto needed prompting about a date or a piece of information that eluded him and to make an occasional note or light the president's cigarette. Yuriko's greeting was less restrained and she turned her knees towards him after he joined her on the couch. He knew she had looked long at the squarish, gift-wrapped slim package he had brought with him and now leaned against the glass-topped table and saw her eyes drift to it more than once as they sipped whisky and made small talk. He felt uncharacteristically vulnerable, sitting somewhere in Tokyo, lost and linguistically illiterate, with people he believed were duplicitous, and if Phyllis was to be believed, ruthless and casually violent to the point of being murderous. Distracted from a complicated and unfinished task, he felt an urge to throw up his hands and walk out. But, of course, they had his shoes.

Hiroshi Miyamoto arrived with a flourish, an obsequious, heavy woman with black, heavily lacquered hair at his side with a whisky-water on a tray. He apologised for his lateness and suggested they go straight in to eat. They followed him, shuffling behind the kimonoed woman along a narrow corridor whose bare floorboards smelled of polish and

185

squeaked under their slippered feet. Muffled male voices and sudden belly-laugh outbursts behind sliding doors signalled the presence of another harmony-enhancing party of business giants and the bureaucrats in their pockets. The moody tones of a *shakuhachi* flute drifted from another low hallway.

Except for the air-conditioning unit above the sliding door, the *tatami* room was as simple as a monk's cell: rough, sandy-textured walls, one recessed into a *tokonoma* as Alex had seen in Bill Littleton's seaside house. The alcove was hung with a fragile-looking *kakemono* depicting clusters of deep-purple irises on a misty-dawn background. Cracked with age, the scroll would soon be replaced by another, its subject reflecting the change from spring to summer. One side of the room, behind a *shoji* screen, a window-door could be drawn aside to reveal a small courtyard of evenly spread gravel crossed with a path of cracked stones coated with moss. The low dark-wood table, surrounded with cushions and back-supports, was laid out with dishes, delicate sake cups and bowls for sauces and rice and, at each guest place, a set of chopsticks laid on an ivory fish-shaped rest.

Alex had not seen the youthful-looking president of NN Corporation since they had met over the corpse of NINA 328 at Haneda Airport on his hectic first day in Tokyo and at a late working session in the company's head office the same evening. It wasn't a great start, he had mused later. Alex had bawled him out for lighting a cigarette near kerosene-soaked earth and it had made them both tense with apprehension and suspicion. He had wondered whether Miyamoto himself had sent Yuriko Shimada to make the claim decision more bearable for the lonely Englishman but could not remember at what point he had realised that the creased old Jonsson letter, yellowing away for more than half a century in an English attic, was the real objective of her bungled seduction. It was probably at the weekend, when Phyllis

Wakai had recalled the fate of one honest NNC man who had tried to denounce Hiroshi Miyamoto's corruption, and now he, the assessor from London, could be a few short sentences away from restoring a murderer's financial wellbeing to the tune of twenty million dollars.

Legs in the pit below the table, they settled on the cushions, leaning comfortably against the backrests. Alex accepted Miyamoto's invitation to remove his jacket; Tabata kept his appearance intact. Where pure Japanese etiquette should have placed Alex alone, facing his three hosts across the low table, he found himself inevitably next to Yuriko, her face breaking into a shared smile of embarrassment as he recounted every gaffe he had made in manners since arriving in Tokyo. They shared toast after toast of warmed sake, chatting amiably while the motherly serving ladies came and went, kneeling at the table with a parade of morsels on delicate blue and white porcelain. Yuriko tried to translate the species of fish, struggling with the raw slivers of almost transparent *hirame* and *tai*, settling finally on flounder and sea bream, and describe the *miso* sauce basting a fillet of grilled yellowtail. She explained the tiny mushrooms and other ingredients floating in a clear soup and cajoled him to drink it from the bowl like a native. There were cubes of tofu in a soya and shallot sauce, bowls of steaming rice and multi-coloured root-vegetable pickles. And there were more thimbles of sake, and each time Yuriko raised the fragile flower-patterned beaker and turned to fill his cup her hand brushed against his, her loose hair settling on his shoulder. She was generating heat, and it made him shudder.

Tabata said nothing, his contribution being to nod at each inane quip with a dull smile fixed on his flushed face. Miyamoto's English improved, in fluency if not accuracy, as the sake flowed and he smoked between all ten courses. There was a moment – Alex thought it might have been when the green *ocha* tea was served – that seemed to signal

187

the end of the frivolous part of the evening. Yuriko had followed Miyamoto to the toilets and when they returned there was no more banter and, apart from a gentle correction to her translation, no more English from the president. Alex ignored Tabata in their absence, angry at himself for letting go and at one point telling himself that these were nice guys after all. He had tried to shake the fuzz out of his head before they returned.

Miyamoto slurped his tea and lit another cigarette. When he spoke it was in short bursts of Japanese to Yuriko, sometimes sideways to Tabata, and when he reached the business point of the evening it came gradually, through casual questions about Alex's work, the crashes he had investigated, the dangers he had encountered. Alex missed the moment when Tabata reached for a notebook. He saw Miyamoto through a haze of smoke and wondered if his hosts had really been matching him drink for drink. The strength of the rice wine surprised him, as strong as sherry, he guessed, and it had loosened his tongue while dulling his reactions.

'And were all of these incidents as easy to resolve as ours?' Yuriko translated, another flask of sake poised over his cup.

'I heard something on the television,' Alex said lamely.

Extending his hands, one stacked over the other, Miyamoto mimed a downward rush of air on his aeroplane.

'Wind-shear,' Alex said. 'I interpret the Transport Ministry's announcement as an interim statement of belief pending analysis of the flight data recordings and elimination of all other possibilities.'

Yuriko anticipated her chief's response. 'What other possibilities?'

Alex shrugged. They were obvious. 'Mechanical failure, pilot error.'

Miyamoto erupted with a staccato outburst.

188

'There is no evidence that the pilot made a mistake,' Yuriko said, her eyes almost closed as she searched for the appropriate words in English. 'Our aeroplane was affected by a sudden – how can I say? – push of wind.'

Then the alcohol made its move. For two hours it had lifted him onto a euphoric platform of tranquillity, where he believed he had reached a level of professional agreement with his hosts and they were celebrating their mutual understanding together. But Yuriko Shimada, Miyamoto's exotic, ruthless mouthpiece, had worked on him throughout the dinner, smiling at every stupid story, touching his skin whenever she topped up his sake cup and hinting with every bloody movement of her body against his that their evening didn't have to end when the party finished. Any resolve he had made to keep control had been eliminated. His defences had turned out to be as fragile as the paper on a *shoji* screen. 'It wasn't Ed Kidderby's error that downed the plane,' he blurted clumsily. 'He was sick. His heart. He collapsed over the controls and forced the plane down accidently. And I believe there are people who knew how bad he was.' Images flashed behind his eyes like a tape on fast-forward: missing medical records, hands searching in his briefcase for an ancient diary, a strange old letter, a torn nightdress, Yuriko's body stretched on his bed, a battered, upturned car and Phyllis's face, a picture of fear, ranting about the murderers around him. He let out a huge sigh. I'm pissed, he admitted to himself.

Tabata was making notes, his brow beaded with sweat. Miyamoto held an unlit cigarette near his mouth as Yuriko stretched her translation. He nodded, grunting gently at each point she made. Finally she turned to Alex. 'Mr Miyamoto spoke to Mr Sanguillen of South Miami Aviation yesterday, before he left for Florida. Mr Miyamoto received the impression that the matter was resolved satisfactorily and you were going to recommend that the insurers meet their

189

financial liability. He apologises if there has been a misunderstanding.'

Alex reciprocated with his own anodyne expression of compromise. He needed a little more time, he told Miyamoto, but he was sure the result would satisfy all parties. The president of Nippon Nagasaki Corporation did not wait for a translation. He smiled icily and nodded the sign to his aides. He raised his elbows and levered himself to his feet. The evening was over. At the low, ornate entrance to the *ryotei*, watched with lowered heads by the senior women of the house, Yuriko reminded Alex that the purpose of the dinner was to express the president's appreciation for his cooperation and produced a large, square box, formally wrapped and decorated for an important recipient. Joviality of a superficial kind had returned and Miyamoto presented the gift with a broad smile and a firm handshake.

'I hope you like it,' Yuriko said. 'I chose it for you. It's a very special kind of vase.'

He knew he'd lost face. Phyllis had warned him not to raise his voice, not to give them the psychological edge by appearing to lose control, and getting drunk wasn't a good excuse. He wondered if Yuriko had translated the bit where he implied the airline probably knew about Kidderby's condition. They were standing above him, watching him totter and overbalance as tried to slip his shoes on and talk at the same time. The NNC car was waiting to take him to his hotel. Then, his head clearing when a draught of air caught him, he remembered his part in the ritual; Yuriko looked relieved she did not have to remind him. 'In there,' he said, indicating a corner room. 'I almost forgot my gift for you.'

One of the kimonoed women shuffled away to fetch the package. Alex held it out to Miyamoto. 'The hotel got it framed for me.'

'I open it,' Miyamoto beamed.

'Please,' Alex said tentatively.

Miyamoto opened the package without tearing the elaborate wrapping and tugged the grooved walnut frame free. The glass cover made up most of its weight and the reflections on it from overhead lights blurred the old writing, leaving it almost invisible. Miyamoto shadowed it with his body and read the text silently, his head nodding as another piece in the history of his company reluctantly revealed itself.

'They found a printer specialising in these old documents,' Alex said, 'who even had some old paper.'

Tabata had been dismissed; Yuriko paced the bridge in the garden, a cellular telephone pegged to an ear. Hiroshi Miyamoto had taken the framed letter to the room where they had dined. The long table had been cleared, leaving only a new pot of tea and two bowls, and the windows drawn aside to refresh the air. He stood in the space, facing the gravelled dry garden, and read the letter again and once more until he had extracted every nuance from the text. Yuriko entered, silent, barefoot, but he sensed she was there and spoke without turning. 'Did you talk to them?'

'Yes I did,' she murmured. 'The situation is in hand.'

He turned slowly, his eyes bloodshot, the corners of his mouth quivering. He sank to his knees on the *tatami* and raised the frame above him. His knuckles were white, his voice a feral growl. 'It's a fucking copy. The *gaijin* gave me a copy.' He brought the letter down against the corner of the table, the sharp tip shattering the glass and frame and ripping the letter apart.

Alex dozed in the back of the Nissan, the window opened a finger's length to let the air wash over and revive him. He had seen enough of NNC and its staff and dismissed the chauffeur appreciatively in the hotel forecourt. He left his bulky gift unopened with the concierge and thanked the same customer duty manager for finding somewhere to copy the Jonsson letter and get it framed, all during a single day. Try that in England, he had thought. Had Miyamoto realised it was only a copy, he wondered in the taxi to Roppongi. And did it matter? If anyone deserved the old document it was Phyllis. Her case against the Miyamoto group was taking shape and he was beginning to share her feelings about their business ethics. He was convinced their cover-up of Ed Kidderby's serious medical problems was just a reflection of Miyamoto's casual concern for regulations, and if Phyllis was right, it was an attitude shared by Japan's business movers and tolerated by a government that took the credit for their successes and a bureaucracy that retired into fat jobs with them. But surely not murder?

It was midnight made noon by the neons and the headlights of the cruising taxis. Did Tokyo ever sleep? Not even on a Monday night? Alex took his bearings from the Almond coffee shop and after two mistakes he put down to drink-induced confusion he turned into the alley street where he recognised the railings protecting the stairway to the cellar bar. He had somehow expected it to be half empty, like the time when Phyllis had shown him where Ed Kidderby used to drink with his *gaijin* pilot friends. But then it had been early, and now the place was packed, mostly with Caucasians and young Japanese women. Air-conditioners stirred the dusty, smoke-filled air and the back-beat from sixties songs jogged drowsy heads along the bar. He sidled across the room, peering into booths and at the tables in the darker corners. Phyllis wasn't there. He propped himself against a pillar where a stairway led to the toilets. A tray of ice-cold beers passed before him and he thought about a drink. He exhaled deeply; his legs were weakening. The waitress he remembered as the Australian Sharon had an arm over a seated customer and when Phyllis failed to appear from the basement he elbowed a passage towards the table.

'Sharon?' He touched a bare shoulder. 'I'm looking for Phyl Wakai,' he said economically over the din. 'She said she'd be here.'

Sharon jumped, flinching at the familiar brusque drunk's jab against her skin.

'Sorry,' Alex slurred. 'I'm Alex Bolton. I was here with Phyl last week.'

'Yeah, right' she said pleasantly, when his face registered. Balancing a tray of empty glasses and bottles, she led him through the swaying drinkers to the bar, like a boxer avoiding punches. 'You look ratted,' she exclaimed pleasantly, shouting a new order to a barman.

'It's a tough city,' he grunted. 'No prisoners taken. Has Phyl been here tonight?'

Sharon barked something to the barman in Japanese. Alex heard his own name. The man did not look up. Beer hissed from the row of bottles he was opening as he spoke. Sharon filled the tray. 'She called around eight, eight thirty. Said to tell you she'll call you tomorrow.'

'She probably decided to go back home,' Alex said, rubbing his neck. 'When I've slept this off I might drop by and surprise her. Anyway, thanks, Sharon. Any news of Ed Kidderby's girlfriend?'

She hoisted the drinks. 'Makiko? No. We're all getting pretty worried.' She had caught the lazy slurred edge in his voice. 'Take it easy out, Alex. You don't look too neat tonight.'

He thanked her with a soft pat on her arm. 'It's been a rough sort of day.'

3 January, 1944

A welcome rest on big Jap holidays. We lost two lads in December from pneumonia and the civilian in our room has been very ill with it. Some more Yanks arrived in October and their commander became the Camp senior officer. We turned out in the cold and watched three men get a beating for stealing. The Japs released some Red Cross parcels for Christmas but they kept most of the food tins. Got a bit extra fish during the holidays but daily rations have been cut to 750 grams for workers, 530 for sick and light workers and 390 grams for unperforming officers.

10 February

Still very cold but no new snow. There's no more charcoal for the stoves. New Jap three stars sergeant arrived in Camp. Christened Bo Ko Go because he had Camp working parties digging Air Raid Shelter. That's the Jap name for them. Bo Ko Go has taken dislike to some of Duty N.C.Os. Five have been sent back to dockyard. I had a run in with him about sick men in Camp working. He solved the problem by knocking me

down with a bamboo pole, but I seem to have won a
point with him as he leaves me alone.

2 March

Two years since the Exeter went down and I was taken
prisoner. Got the first issue of cakes and cigarettes
yesterday but the food always the same. Dirty rice,
boiled barley with a few scraps of meat or fish and
sometimes some sweet beans or bread. I can't keep my
stomach settled though. There is a new Camp
commander but he never appears. Bo Ko Go runs the
Camp day to day.

29 April

Paraded today for Jap emperor's birthday but then
went to the dockyards. Men are still beaten up for
trivial offences such as wearing caps inside rooms,
knocking over boxes of sand in passageways or not
bowing low enough to the Japs. Spike Mahoney and I
were beaten for not working hard enough. Only got six
with a baseball bat. I also received twelve strokes from
Flip and Napoleon for heating up my rice for Dinner.
The only way to get a hot meal.

19 May

Getting hard to write. We are made to work hard on the
ships. The civilian we call Cyclops has been here all
week. We had to watch out. The younger guards are
getting worse. They enjoy knocking us around. We
wonder if the Japs are losing the war. The older men
who were wounded in action are easier to get on with.
One shipyard guard is very kind. Got me out of a
couple of beatings.

7 June

Major Horrigan is in bad trouble. He's charged with
running a daily news bulletin. Someone's been stealing
Jap newspapers from the dockyards and bringing them
into the Camp. Somebody who can read the writing

translates them and they circulate the news. Beethoven made him kneel for three hours, then beat him and had him locked in the guardhouse. The cell's just about big enough for a normal man but he's well over six foot. There must be a spy in the Camp and we think he is Dutch.

15 June
Major Horrigan released from cells. Very ill. Put in hospital.

10 August
A company of Aussies arrived in Camp in July. They were in tropical clothes and in really rough shape. Worse than us. They had worked for the Japs in Burma and came here in a convoy that was attacked. Two of the ships were torpedoed by allied submarines on the way.

1 September
There's an outbreak of dysentery. Also some malaria and beriberi. Not surprising. Food's getting shorter. A bit of whale meat now and then but it's already rotten. I am fine except for another septic ulcer and problems with the hand I hurt in the dockyards. I can't use it very well. Dr thinks the lads from Burma brought the tropical diseases with them. Ten have died so far since July. It's too hot to sleep and anyway the lice won't let us.

27 December
The Japs had a big cleanout in September. I handed in my diary voluntarily and escaped a beating. When I was working in the store-room last week I found it. Took it back and filched a bit of spare paper. A few things to catch up with. The Japs are getting harder on us. We have been making air-raid shelters as well as the dockyard work. I saw Yank bombers go over in early December. Johnson's not very well again. He

lacks military discipline and does not have any friends in the Camp. Bo Ko Go picks on him so he is in hospital again and only allowed half rations.

Christmas was miserable. No extra food. A gang of Yanks fought some Dutch over stealing but we all got punished when the Japs took away the smoking times for two days.

<u>*30 December*</u>

Christmas finally came. We had first issue of one complete US Red Cross Parcel per man. It had some corned beef, chewing gum, cigarettes, soap, chocolate, condensed milk and jam.

Reggie Cameron put the thickness in the voice down to the lateness of the hour in Tokyo. He reckoned if it was five past five in London on a drizzly Monday afternoon – and he was thinking of packing his briefcase because he was feeling ill – Alex Bolton was calling him at just after one on Tuesday morning in Japan. He listened tolerantly to the reasons why his surveyor had not returned his calls or answered the day's fax messages but he was not satisfied. 'I'm with you all the way Alex, but you've got to get to the FAA boys or the Japanese and convince them the captain was sick. The windshear argument's looking very persuasive as we stand at the moment.'

'They've got to take the cockpit voice recording apart.' Alex was sitting on the bed, the drink souring inside him. He was enunciating slowly, timing his words with the throbs from his head.

'The chairman got a couriered letter this afternoon from South Miami Aviation,' Cameron said flatly. 'I'm sure you can guess what it says, but I'll tell you anyway. "Our attorneys see no legal reason." he paraphrased, "why British Underwriters International should not discharge its liabilities with regard to" blah, blah.'

'Put them off for a few days,' Alex said.

'It's going to be a mite hard, Alex. There are no war loss implications. Insurers pay out on less clear claims than this and we're expected to follow suit with the DC-8.'

'Look, Reggie, If NN Air were derelict in their legal requirement to keep their pilots healthy they're more than likely to be negligent in other areas. I just want the regulators to know this.'

'Aren't you taking all this a touch personally?' Cameron said.

He'd hit a nerve end. 'Why do you say that?' The chameleon swings of Hiroshi Miyamoto during the evening were still clear through the boozy haze in his head.

Cameron cleared his throat. 'The person in Tokyo who briefed his chief executive officer by fax in Miami alleged you're not giving his company's claim your full and proper attention.'

'What?' Alex rose slowly from the bed.

'It's not ambiguous. Let me read you a piece from the letter to the chairman.' He coughed again. It was clear to Alex his chief had been keeping it close, waiting for the moment to quote it. 'Blah, blah, "while our senior executive had made a considerable effort to make himself available at the scene of this unfortunate accident your representative there was conspicuously absent at crucial times." Unquote.'

Sanguillen. Alex cursed under his breath. The American must have contacted Florida before he left Japan. 'I saw him again on Sunday afternoon. He didn't give me the impression he was bothered because he couldn't contact me earlier.'

'So what happened? What took you away from the action?'

Reggie Cameron was showing his patrician tolerance to the full. If it had been Alex talking to a junior out there in Tokyo he would have demanded to know why the fuck he

198

wasn't besieging the Japanese civil aviation bureau or slipping notes into the hotel rooms of the American federal investigators. 'It wasn't entirely unconnected with NN Air,' Alex tried lamely. 'I was sort of distracted away from Tokyo on Saturday by that old bit of paper that came out of company archives. You remember? It mentioned Nippon Nagasaki. The president of NN Corporation, Miyamoto he's called, is so anxious to get hold of it he tried some non-professional Oriental methods.'

'I trust you resisted,' Cameron remarked humourlessly. Racked with fever, he swallowed painfully and wiped a ridge of sweat from his brow.

'It wasn't difficult,' Alex lied. 'Anyway, I came across an expert in these things and had him look at it. He happens to live outside Tokyo.'

'Did it take all weekend?'

Alex felt the heat rise in him. 'On Sunday morning, I was following up a lead on Edward Kidderby's bad heart. That's how I missed the ministry statement on the wind-shear theory and pissed Sanguillen off because I wasn't around for him.'

'Sanguillen?'

'The guy from South Miami Aviation. I think I told you he was here in a fax.'

'So you've got what you wanted? Proof the captain had a heart attack and forced the plane down.'

'I'm trying to prove he was sick enough to have died at the controls,' Alex said, grimacing, his mouth dry. He could almost hear Reggie Cameron's sigh.

'I gather you haven't got any evidence yet, Alex.'

'There's a witness. Kidderby's longstanding girlfriend. The problem is I can't find her at the moment. When I do —'

'Okay, Alex, I understand,' Cameron said curtly. 'Get some rest. You sound as though you need it more than I do. And please, no more surprises, and let's get this settled in the next thirty-six hours and get you back here. I don't want to have to move unilaterally from this end.'

He overslept, forgetting to ask for a hotel wake-up call or to set his own travel clock, and was jolted from a shallow, dream-ridden half night of sleep by the breakfast service. He didn't remember filling in the order form, let alone hanging it on the door handle. He called Yoshi Kanagawa on his mobile while he sipped a second cup of bitter coffee and the news from the broker went some way to easing the spasmodic thumping in his skull. The whereabouts of the pair of engineers from the airframe and engine manufacturers was unimportant. Alex wanted wanted someone, anyone, from the National Transportation Safety Board. 'There are six of them for chrissake, Yoshi. Just get me to one of them with the voice recording. Or one of the two button-down shirts from the Federal Aviation Administration.'

'There's a strategy meeting today, this afternoon,' Yoshi enthused. 'I got the word from one of the Japanese underwriters.'

'Time?' He heard the familiar noisy sucking of air.

'Probably late afternoon. It's kind of open-ended.'

'Place?'

'Maybe the Ministry.'

'That's a lot of maybes, Yoshi.'

'Keep close to your mobile. I'll see you at nine in any case.'

The low purr of the room telephone was almost smothered by the television. It brought him from his chart case, as he was preparing to leave. The woman's voice was flat and precise, as if the speaker was reading a message. 'Are you Mr Bolton?'

He failed to put a face to the voice. 'Yes, it's . . . You are . . .?'

'This is Makiko Nakamura.'

'Makiko . . .'

'Nakamura.'

Alex's face twisted. The telephone was pressed to his ear as he lowered the volume on the television with the remote control.

'You know me?' The voice was soft and strained, the accent heavy.

'Of course. Phyllis Wakai told me about you and Ed Kidderby.'

'That is good. I must speak to you about him. It is very important.'

And he wanted to talk to her. To ask about her two empty days, a torn nightdress, but first of all the real story about the health of the NN Air pilot she was so close to. The calm urgency in her voice warned him that the agenda was hers. 'I can meet you any time,' he said quietly.

'Please come to Wakai *san*'s house at eleven this morning. *Wakarimasu ka*?'

'Yes, I understand,' he said, recognising the familar question. 'Where is Phyllis? Is she safe?'

'Yes. Please do not worry. She will meet us at her house.' She hung up as gently as she could, it seemed to Alex, without seeming rude.

The meeting with representatives from the small Japanese insurance syndicate to which Yoshi Kanagawa had sold two million dollars' worth of liability on the hull of NINA 328 was an interminable exchange of rhetorical banter, hissed excuses and restrained demands. The Japanese side were under pressure from the airline and their own internal controllers, Yoshi had warned him. A claim had been made, a clear call on the insurers, it seemed to everyone, and they wanted to settle the liability, remove the uncertainty hanging over their financial resources and get on with their business. Would the surveyor from London, the assessor with the power, please authorise the claim or deny it? What was the problem? They were all aware that the guarded official statements from the Transport Ministry had not even hinted at the possibility of pilot error, and, although the examination of flight data recordings and the tangible remains of the aircraft and their history of maintenance and care was going to be a careful, prolonged process, no evidence had arisen so far to indicate that a mechanical malfunction or a procedural error by the crew had contributed materially to the crash at Haneda. By midday tomorrow, Wednesday, Alex told the group, Reggie Cameron's deadline hanging round his neck like a lead weight, he would announce his own conclusions.

He gathered his papers labouredly and glanced at his watch again, wondering if the reclusive woman waiting for him at the temple house knew, or could even guess, that twenty million dollars and his reputation might depend on the accuracy of her recollections. When Phyllis had taken him to the Roppongi basement bar and told him how concerned Makiko was about Ed Kidderby's health it amounted to no more than hearsay. But until they found the doctor who had examined him, and prised out the truth about the contents of the pilot's medical certificates, Makiko was the only person who could testify to his recent history of heart attacks, fainting and heavy drinking. He slumped with relief when Yoshi led the underwriters out, engulfed by an uncommon feeling of insecurity and a strange uncertainty at what might happen if Makiko Nakamura failed to produce the goods.

The broker was annoyed to lose him again at the critical moment in the case and sniffed his annoyance, guessing correctly he was meeting the woman called Wakai again, and forcing a muttered apology from the figure hurrying from the office.

He was almost ready to venture onto the Tokyo underground, riding it to Shibuya, and then overground on the Toyoko Line. Five stations later it would have left him close to Phyllis's temple as it brushed between houses on its way to Yokohama, but it would have made him late. He stopped a taxi and pronounced impeccably the familiar temple and its district to a wary driver. He was becoming used to the labyrinth of the city, how it was ringed with arterial roads and spoked with broad roads which drained and filled the capital and converged around Tokyo Bay. The taxi driver was grateful to be directed in the last stage of the journey by the *gaijin* and drew up before the temple's ornate gateway. Phyllis had previously brought him directly to her house through the gate leading from the quiet side street but he was keen to see where she had parked the Mini before it was taken the day before. The rain that he had forecast had come and gone in the night, slicking the mossy edges of the paving stones on the forecourt and reviving a cushion of vermilion *tsutsuji* azaleas flowing over a miniature cliff formation of rocks. It had also washed the dust off the temple roof tiles, freeing the glaze to sparkle in the sun. Her car wasn't there: he assumed it was still under repair in a garage somewhere or in a police pound. He skirted a vividly bronze maple tree whose roots had cracked the old concrete block wall separating the temple precinct from the small forest of tomb columns and funerary tablets. Beyond the cemetery, through the bamboo groves, he could see the roof of the house Phyllis rented from the chief priest.

He peered sheepishly into the temple, glimpsing the gilded statues of Buddha, the elaborate darkwood carvings, the worn side of a huge drum and the decorated artefacts of the sect. The air inside was cool and still rich with incense long extinguished. The door to the priest's house next to the temple was drawn aside and a barefoot girl of about three stood on the step, clutching a pink cloth to her cheek. He passed too close to her and smiled as she ducked inside. He sensed she was watching him cross the cemetery, following him towards the old house where the Japanese *gaijin* woman lived. Thinking of Phyllis, and wondering why she hadn't called to reassure him she was safe, he slapped his jacket pocket. He swore silently. He had left the mobile telephone in the BUI offices, on top of the chartcase in a locked room. A short flight of slippery steps brought him to the front door. Somewhere inside, the bell responded to his calls. He knocked tamely when no one answered, then harder and more persistently. His watch read eight minutes past eleven.

He ran the short conversation with Makiko Nakamura through his mind. She *had* said eleven and had declared that Phyllis would be there. He turned the aluminium knob and tugged. He expected the door to open because Phyllis said she rarely locked it. Warped, it resisted once. 'Phyl? Are you in?' He shook off his shoes instinctively. 'Nakamura *san*? It's Alex Bolton.' Phyllis kept that silly red cap of hers on a shoe stand in the entrance. It wasn't there. He couldn't imagine her going out on business without it and she'd been wearing it when he had dropped her in Marunouchi yesterday. Growing irritation niggled him. He could have used the time, a precious chunk of his last thirty-six hours, to hound the American investigators, demand they hear the cockpit voice recording again after listening to his suspicions about the real state of the pilot's health. If he had to do it without Makiko Nakamura, so be it, but he had to get them to listen to the tape. He thought of ringing Yoshi from the telephone in the narrow hallway and then leaving, but he was drawn to the connecting rooms where Phyllis worked, relaxed and ate.

The two mugs looked like the ones they had drunk from yesterday and they stood where they had left them, upturned on a washing board by the kitchen sink. The islands of cushions on the *tatami* floor of the living room lay carelessly unplumped. He called out again unconvincingly, running a hand over the surface of the cold computer in the corner where Phyllis worked, surrounded by books and papers. The room at the back of the house where he knew she slept was empty, the folds of a futon bulging from a half-opened cupboard. A dull creak somewhere reminded him there was a second floor, stacked on top with its own layer of overlapping roof tiles, but smaller than the ground surface and typical of the Japanese houses he had noticed.

'Phyl. Nakamura *san*,' he called uneasily, his socks sliding on the narrow, steep bare wooden stairs. The place looked abandoned. There seemed to be three rooms; a space, like a large cupboard, at the head of the stairs, used as a store-room, corners of boxes and suitcases visible through a crack in the door, and a western-style lavatory at the end of the hallway. The *fusuma* doors to the other room were drawn a hand's width apart. Framed in the space Alex saw a window, and through it bunches of dark green and leathery leaves on a camphor tree, which left the room in a pale half-light. Unaired, it had a musty, slightly fetid odour, like an open drain. It was undecorated, the size of six *tatami* mats, and was probably kept for overnight visitors. His eyes fell on a futon mattress, where Phyllis Wakai lay on her side, asleep under its generous covers. He smiled a sigh of relief and slipped quietly inside. Her face was buried deep in a soft pillow, her hair covering her profile and spilling over the hem of the padded quilt. He glanced at his watch, and there was a touch of annoyance when he spoke. 'Phyl. It's Alex. Shouldn't we be seeing Makiko?' If she stirred it was too gloomy for him to detect the movement. He dropped to his knees to press his knuckles playfully into the body beneath the eiderdown. The fabric was damp to his touch, and kneading it seemed to release an unpleasant smell. 'Phyl, what's going on?' he said stupidly, flinching at the odour. His head jerked round at a dull, sharp thump. The front door to the house had been opened and then jammed shut on its warped frame. He returned to the futon, folding the cover back, exposing a bare shoulder. The skin was cold to his light touch and she did not stir or even flinch when he eased her body over. Her head slumped lifelessly, a blackened tongue ballooning from her mouth, wedged in a corner. The movement parted unruly trails of hair streaking her face, lifeless eyes bulging through them in empty disbelief. Alex froze, Phyllis's name forming uselessly on his lips. Slowly, his eyes settled on the blood spotting his knuckles. Her neck was ringed with a blue-black welt and the force of whatever had been used to strangle her had ruptured the skin. At some point in the killing, her body had voided, but Alex did not notice the smell any more, or hear the scream behind him.

Phyllis stood between the sliding doors, her hands clasped to her ears, as if unable bear to hear herself shriek. 'Makiko *san*! What's happened, Alex? What have you done?'

He tried to stand but his legs gave way from shock, fear and now relief. He turned slowly, focusing on a blur of red. The baseball cap. 'I thought it was you,' he howled, senses numbed, his fingers spread pleadingly towards the body. She slid to her knees beside him, an arm smothering him, the free hand reaching out to the corpse. They screamed unanswerable questions and spat delirious outbursts, clutched together in shared hysteria, before settling against the door, hearts racing, bodies suffused with sweat.

'She called me. Told me to meet her here.'

'She couldn't have.'

'At the hotel. Said you'd meet us here. At eleven.'

'She didn't know where you were staying.'

'Where were you?'

'Bill Littleton's. In Hayama. Spoke to him last night. Invited me to stay down there with him. Said he'd got something for me. About the diaries.'

Alex held her, his fingers biting into her back. 'I thought you were dead. I thought it was you.'

They clutched each other desperately and levered themselves to their feet. 'Makiko *san*, *do shitan desu ka*?

Phyllis was muttering, staring at the lifeless form of her friend as they staggered backwards through the doorway. She slumped at the foot of the stairway, followed by Alex. Time, like reality, was suspended, irrelevant. They didn't know how long they sat there, or how long the doorbell had been ringing. Alex made to move but Phyllis found her composure first. She stepped unsteadily into the kitchen and gingerly spread the blinds on the side window.

A short, old, slightly stooped woman in a conical straw hat stood in the porch, her legs ballooned in baggy trousers. She kept the graveyard clean, picking up rubbish and burning leaves and the visitors' faded flowers. Her leathered face was pinched into a fixed apologetic wince, displaying a single gold tooth in the corner exposed to Phyllis. She pressed again and thought about trying the door. Phyllis started to heave, tasting the bitter acidy vomit churning inside her. The woman wouldn't go. Phyllis was breathing deeply, holding down the surge. Finally she left, unable to satisfy her nosiness about the strange noises, perhaps a muffled scream, her snow-hole eyes too confused to catch the sudden change in the window blind as she turned away. Phyllis ran from the kitchen, clutching her mouth as she passed Alex on her way to the lavatory. That triggered his nausea and he reached the kitchen sink in time.

Settled, he washed away the mess and found Phyllis curled on the cushions, holding her knees, her eyes vacant. 'What's the police emergency number?' he said thickly.

'One one zero.' She was drained, but managed to raise an arm. 'Sit down, Alex.'

He hardly heard her: he had reached the corridor.

'Alex!,' It was a desperate command, short of power but calm and effective. 'Please get me some water, then sit down and talk to me.'

He thought about it, another element in the chaotic swirl of twisted realities and what-ifs flooding his mind. He hooked the telephone back on its base, wondering where he was and what he was doing there. He carried two glasses of water from the tap and dropped beside her.

She sipped cautiously. 'I thought you had a stronger stomach. Don't you see dead bodies all the time?'

'Depends on the state of the site and how soon I get there. It's odd but it's hard to see air-crash victims as former humans. The crash and the explosions don't leave much that's recognizable. Not like — '

Phyllis shivered and stopped his ramblings with a hand. 'Let's get out of here first. Then we talk this over.' She sprang up, spilling water over the *tatami*.

'Call the police first,' Alex insisted. 'Get an ambulance for the poor woman at least.'

She was stuffing a shoulder bag with things from the drawers of her desk. She turned on him. 'Whoever killed her and set you up to be here will make sure she's found, preferably with you and me in attendance.' He levered himself reluctantly to his feet. 'C'mon Alex. We can't help her by sitting on our ass.'

They left quietly by the roadside gate and separated, Alex following fifty metres behind her as they walked to Toritsu Daigaku station. She handed him a ticket without speaking, and they stood apart on the short train ride to Nakameguro where they changed to the underground system, following the same pretence as they travelled to Hibiya, surfacing near the Imperial Hotel. A corner of the vast lobby coffee shop gave them the anonymity they couldn't get easily in most places, where the presence of a white foreigner still merited a slot in the memory bank of the waiter or the sales assistant. Neither felt hungry, and waved away the solicitous waiter with the snack menu.

Her eyes were reddened, the rims raw behind her broad glasses. She had stuffed the baseball cap into a subway rubbish bin and shaken her hair loose from the clip. 'Run it past me again, Alex. We've got to get the story right.'

'Like I said, a woman came on the phone, about eight, eight fifteen this morning. Said she was Makiko Nakamura and had to talk to me about Ed Kidderby. I said great, any time, anywhere, and she told me to be at your house at eleven. I asked about you. I was getting worried. I'd called that foreign press club place and you weren't there and you didn't call me last night. Anyway, she said you'd be at the house as well.'

Phyllis gripped the corners of the table and craned forward. 'Weren't you suspicious? I hadn't talked to Makiko since Saturday night, when I told her we were going to visit her on Sunday. I don't remember telling her which hotel you were staying in.'

'If she was so desperate to talk to me she could have tracked me down through NN Air.' He was flaying around for an explanation. 'So it could have been Makiko on the phone. I don't think she was killed much before I reached your place. She'd have plenty of time to get there before me.' He remembered thinking it was Phyllis on the floor, how he'd bit his tongue as he brushed the woman's hair aside, touching the soft clots of blood around her throat, horrified at the stains on his fingers. 'She hadn't been dead very long.'

Phyllis rolled her eyes at the ceiling. 'She would have called *me* first,' she said emphatically. 'And they wouldn't have brought her into the house in daylight.' She shook her head sadly. 'They came at night, got in through the gate from the road. Absolute cover guaranteed. They guessed I wouldn't be there, not after what they did to my car yesterday, but if I had been . . .' She drew a finger across her throat. 'But you, my *gaijin san*, walked right into the trap.' Her head dropped. Her coffee, thick and creamy as the Japanese like it, was tasteless to her. 'Do you think it was Yuriko Shimada on the phone?'

209

He shrugged. 'If it was her she was doing a good job disguising her voice. The caller's English wasn't very fluent.'

'It doesn't matter. They wouldn't have any problem finding a woman to read the script.'

Alex clamped his temple between his fingers. 'Phyl. What's going on? 'Who are "they" you keeping talking about?'

Her hands flew. 'Can't you see? It's them. The people who want me off their backs but most of all want you off the case.'

Nippon Nagasaki Corporation. NN Air. For the first time since arriving in Japan he'd gone for more than fifteen minutes without talking, thinking or hearing about Miyamoto and his damn business empire and now he was back as if he had never been away. 'Look Phyl. Miyamoto doesn't even stand to get the insurance. It goes to the owners of the plane in Florida.'

Phyllis checked the closest tables were unoccupied. 'For fuck's sake Alex,' she hissed. 'We're not talking about fifty million bucks here.'

'Nearer twenty,' he corrected gently.

'Whatever.' She thumped the table. 'It's the letter you brought with you. Don't you understand?' Three suited businessmen took the table next to them. 'Let's walk,' she commanded, gathering her unopened cigarette packet.

They crossed the road and entered Hibiya Park through the flower-shop gate. The breeze had freshened, and when it dragged a cloud across the sun Phyllis drew her jacket tighter. She led him from the gravelled enclave, past the fountain and the flower beds around the lawn, to a path skirting the pond of a Japanese garden. The office workers had finished their box lunches and left the park to the tourists, amateur painters and a vagrant or two dragging their bags. They were alone in this leafy, placid corner. She gripped his arm with two hands;

he was half pulling her as she slowed to choose her words for emphasis, reluctantly forced to relegate Makiko Nakamura in his chaos of priorities.

'Bill Littleton got me at the Press Club and I must have left before you tried to get me. He said he'd spent the last two days totally absorbed by what he'd read in the Jonsson letter and the diaries and would I like to go down and see him again. I needed somewhere to sleep last night, anyway. I didn't feel much like going home so I called the Tulip in Roppongi and left you a message and then took a train down to Hayama.' They stopped, absently watching a pair of ducks snapping between the water-lily leaves. 'Not that I slept much. We went over the diaries together till four. He took me to Zushi Station about nine, had the diaries copied for himself, and here I am. I called your office and that Japanese guy, Yoshi, thought you were going to meet me so I went straight over to my place.'

Alex held her protectively. 'You said Bill had something to tell you. About the letter and the diaries.'

'Yeah. The letter really got to him. He's certain it's authentic, that Roland Jonsson sold thirty percent of Jonsson Nagasaki to Shinichi Miyamoto, but what's really exciting is the possibility it was never superseded by another deal which sold the remaining seventy per cent of it to him. If it's still valid Jonsson's heirs are the principal shareholders in a multi-billion-dollar Japanese conglomerate.' She tugged his arm. 'Can you imagine that?'

Alex allowed himself a rueful smile. 'Fifty years is a long time, and the rest of his immediate family might have died in the Nagasaki bomb with him.'

'We're going to look into it,' she enthused. 'Check with the Swedish Embassy. Being neutral, they stayed open here during the war. So anyway, Bill went through his own records, called some old friends, scholars, Japanese businessmen and what not.' They had begun to stroll again.

'Most people knew, like I did, that Nippon Nagasaki Corporation started out as a kind of joint venture using foreign expertise, technology, but nobody can imagine it not being a pure Japanese company now.'

'Isn't there a strong chance the records on the rest of the share sale were destroyed in the Tokyo fire bombings? You said it was a major problem after the war to sort out who owned what.'

'Sure. But then why is Hiroshi Miyamoto trying so hard to get hold of your letter?' Her grip tightened. 'You didn't give it to him last night, did you? Tell me you didn't. Please.'

'I gave him a copy,' he said, a thin smirk on his face. Phyllis held him back again, her head moving in a languorous swing. He saw it as well, even before her eyes had filled with tears. 'I'm trying not to believe it. I can't believe it. We're saying that when Miyamoto found I'd given him a copy of the old letter he went and ordered Makiko Nakamura killed?'

'Damn right he did,' Phyllis said, in a frantic half sob. 'He asked you politely for it, sent his poisonous mistress for it and when you served up a real slap in the face last night he'd had enough. You were holding up the crash insurance payout but, far more significantly, Alex, you hung onto the bomb that might destroy him. So how could he get to you?' When he shrugged, she said, 'He could start by neutralising you.'

Alex wafted the dust off a bench with the envelope that held the wartime diaries Phyllis had returned to him. He answered her question as she steadied herself and dropped beside him. 'Apart from the doctors he kept in his pocket, Miyamoto knew Ed Kidderby's girlfriend was the only person who really knew the truth about his heart attacks. It would hurt him all ways up if there was no payout for the crash, and on top of it the insurers might hit him with claims for negligence. All because I told I that bitch about Makiko.' His voice drifted away to a slur, his head slumped back in surrender.

Phyllis finished for him. 'So he had her kidnapped on Sunday, kept her alive until he knew which way you'd swing on the claim and, more important, whether you'd give him the piece of paper which could take away his empire and probably put him in jail. When you gave him a piece of shit he declared war on you.'

'I killed her,' Alex said flatly. 'I told Yuriko about her.'

Phyllis pressed closer. 'You did nothing wrong.' The vivid memory of an NNC man she'd never met, who had also tried to denounce Hiroshi Miyamoto's corruption and had died for it, flashed across her consciousness. 'You just didn't believe that Japan's corporate movers are not afraid to do a little shaking.'

They sat silently until the sky clouded over and it was too cool to be comfortable. 'Let's go to my hotel,' Alex said firmly, slapping his knees. 'Get things moving on Makiko. And then I've really got to talk to the office, maybe give Bill Littleton a call.'

She had to skip to keep up with him. 'That reminds me,' she said, as they stood on Hibiya-dori, competing for a taxi. 'Did I tell you what else Bill found?'

'About the letter still being legally valid? Yeah.'

Her face brightened, softening the sadness. 'No, not that. About Shinichi Miyamoto, Hiroshi's father, Jonsson's partner in the early days.'

'No. What about him?'

'He might still be alive. Bill can't find a date of death in any of his reference books.'

Passing in front of the Transport Ministry, the taxi slowed where lanes merged. Alex's eyes raked the windows, his thoughts straying again from the swollen face of Makiko Nakamura to her sick lover, the pilot of NINA 328. Behind the blinds, perhaps, was an expert from one of the US investigation agencies with the intuition and the temperment to listen to the preposterous speculation of the insurance

213

assessor from London. The key was in the cockpit voice recording, but its interpretation was disputable unless the state of the captain's health was understood by the listener and insinuated into the sequence. He knew that the forensic evidence was going to be crucial but the longer it took the American expert to announce his findings the more likely it was that the body was too severely damaged to make them conclusive. In less than a minute they were turning at the Toranomon crossing. His eyes were closed but he was seeing behind the lids the screaming, petrified face of Makiko Nakamura.

Phyllis kept herself in view, shuffling around his hotel room, chewing on a cuticle, waiting her turn for the telephone. She had tuned the television low to a news channel.

'Are you going to call the police?' Alex asked, relinquishing his place.

'No. Bill Littleton. He might want to come to Nagasaki with me.'

Alex splayed his hands on the table. 'Phyl. We've got to report the murder. The longer we leave it the more we get implicated.'

She replaced the telephone and clamped two hands over it. 'The only way I can help Makiko now is to open up Miyamoto's empire for the prosecutors, prove to them that corruption's not something he's just discovered. It looks like his father cheated Roland Jonsson out of his company and his son has bought up half the Diet's politicians, killing an honest employee of his in the process and now an innocent woman.'

'There's been a murder in your house,' he said, stifling a strong need to shout. 'You can't say you didn't notice you had a body upstairs. The best way to help the poor woman is to get the police in. Then go after Miyamoto.'

'The second floor's a store-room, and a place for my

visitors to sleep,' she intoned. 'I sometimes go for days without going up there. I could be in the house now and not find Makiko.'

He slapped the table. 'But *I* found her,' he insisted. 'We're involved in a murder.'

'Did anyone see you?' she said blandly.

His head slumped back and he blew at the ceiling. 'The taxi driver, but he dropped me on the other side, by the temple gate.' He saw a young child cuddling a piece of cloth, watching him cross the courtyard. 'I don't think I was seen going into your place, unless — '

'So you've got time to talk to the US federal investigators before your deadline tomorrow.' She tipped a cigarette from the packet and tapped it on the table. 'I suggest you use it. Once the police get us, that's it.'

'How do you mean?' Alex glared. 'We don't have a motive for murder. We're trying to help her.'

Phyllis sighed. She flipped the unlit cigarette aside and walked to the window, hands thrust into the pockets of her jeans. The top of a solitary umbrella jogged along the road above the hotel perimeter wall. Turning, she said, 'I don't want to lecture you, Alex, but the legal process here is not quite as mindful of justice as yours might be.'

'You're confusing me again, Phyl.' He brushed his jacket with the back of a hand and slipped into it. 'I've got to try and get to the Americans. They're in a hotel.' He read from a piece of paper. 'The New Otani. Let's meet up and sort this out later.'

She put herself between him and the door. 'We didn't find a stranger, Alex. We found a woman I knew and who you were desperate to talk to. That gives them at least one, maybe two, reasons to hold us if we hand ourselves over.'

'What do you mean "hold us"? They can question us, that's all.'

'I'm talking the Tokyo Detention House,' she said,

savagely determined. 'A prison in real terms. That's where they'd keep us. Hours of questioning in a dirty room and if they see the slightest possibility of a motive the detention notice would be as open-ended as they needed. We could be locked up for weeks. And forget your Western rights to have a lawyer or keep silent.'

'We don't have a motive.' He clipped a pen into a pocket. 'I'd never even met her.'

She made a clucking sound. 'She's promised you some information which would save your professional ass and when you meet her, in a quiet house, nicely hidden in the trees, she demands money. A lot of it. You get mad, you've no other way of proving her guy was a sick, drunken pilot, and so you attacked her. I believe you said you'd had a few drinks too many last night.'

'Bullshit, Phyl, and you know it.'

'So what were you doing at her apartment on Sunday morning. You broke in, tore her night-dress off her and forced her into hiding.'

'Is this how you journalists invent stories?' he scoffed.

'Got an alibi? I have. I was with Bill Littleton on Monday night. I'm going to the Swedish Embassy now and tonight I'll make myself pretty visible in a hotel near Tokyo Station and tomorrow I'll take the seven ten bullet train to Hakata and then a local to Nagasaki. If nobody saw me there with you today or yesterday I can say I haven't been near my house for three days. What about you? Where were you last night? What time did you get back to the hotel. About one? Was it three? How drunk were you? Oh really? So you were full of sake when Makiko laughed at you and told you to come back with some more money.' She stood over him as he dialled the combination on the closet safe. 'So I'm exaggerating. Just ask yourself why the Japanese police have a ninety-five-per-cent clear-up rate for murder.'

'Because they're good?' Alex said humourlessly.

'Because they don't worry about reasonable doubt and burden of proof and other little Western idiosyncracies. If there's only one suspect he must be guilty.'

'The jury won't be fooled, surely,' he said, sifting through envelopes holding his money, tickets, passport and a small stack of papers.

'They gave up juries fifty years ago,' Phyllis declared, angry rather than smug. 'You go before three judges, and local wisdom says that if you get that far you're assumed to be guilty. Oh, and they prefer you to make a confession. It shows a little remorse. If they like you they'll give you a life sentence. If they don't, they'll have you hanged.'

Alex looked up. 'I suspect a touch of exaggeration, Phyllis. I want to know who's going to look after the poor woman in your house? The people who set me up won't. That'd look a bit suspicious.'

'You're right. They wanted you call the police right away.' She thought for a moment. 'I'll call the temple later today, tell the priest I think I left a light on upstairs. Would he check please? I'll tell him I'm calling from a train so he can't get back to me.'

Alex slammed the door to the safe. 'Shit! I can't find the Jonsson letter.'

Phyllis sprang on him. 'What? Don't talk like that, Alex.'

He leaned against the wall and massaged his temples, flailing blindly through the mist drawn across his mind by shock and a lingering hangover. He talked himself through the sequence of events. 'I gave it to the client services manager when I left the hotel in the morning. I came back about six, six fifteen, took a shower before the Miyamoto dinner. Then the chap brought the framed copy to my room.'

'It's not here,' Phyllis declared, finishing her own eager rummage in the safety deposit box.

'Don't panic,' he said, patting the air. 'I think I asked him to put it into the hotel safe. I'll check on the way out.'

'I hope so. It'll be secure there.' At the door she remembered. 'Can I take the diaries with me to Nagasaki?'

'Why are you going there, Phyl? You've got nothing to go on.' They were in the lift.

'Don't know really. Nose around, try to talk to some people close to the Miyamotos, maybe take some pictures around their estate.'

Outside the hotel, in the greying, late-afternoon light, she held out a hand, which he took as a formal gesture of farewell in the spirit of shared conspiracy, but ended up in his arms. 'I will call the police about Makiko, Alex. Just give me a couple more hours.'

Yoshi Kanagawa hid his anger behind a mask of Japanese indifference. He had been trying to contact Alex for four hours, beginning sixty minutes after the Englishman had left his Tokyo office to visit a girlfriend. That didn't bother him: Alex's job involved secrecy and discretion. But what drove a bus through Yoshi's façade of composure was finding out he had been calling the telephone lying on a briefcase in an empty office. 'Sorry,' Alex had apologised economically, gathering the mobile and the case. 'I called as soon as I could.'

Built on a rise, in the grounds of a former samurai lord, the upper floors of the Hotel New Otani's tower and annexe commanded a spectacularly detached view of the sprawl of modern Tokyo. The lobby shone with the usual Asian ambience of busy efficiency and genuine warmth from the staff. Yoshi engaged in a drawn-out conversation with a receptionist while Alex looked around for a familiar face. He had met a handful of the people from the Federal Aviation Administration and the National Transportation Safety Board at previous incidents he had attended where the doomed aircraft was US-registered. They were secretive and reticent by order and had little time for an unofficial foreign insurance investigator, so their encounters had rarely passed beyond a polite greeting. Nevertheless, he had kept some names in his files and there was a small chance he might get lucky with one of the eight making up the contingent. The Japanese Civilian Aviation Bureau had politely refused his request for a meeting, claiming it would not be appropriate until the official results of their investigations were completed. Alex knew the process could take years, unless they all signed off on the wind-shear explanation, which seemed likely.

Seeing Yoshi making little headway, Alex noticed that a broad-leafed rubber plant had masked a sign board at one end of the long glass entrance and he walked over to it. He passed an elegant young woman with lustrous hair who reminded him of Phyllis without the cap and dungarees, and without effort the next image that crossed his mind was also female. The corpse of Makiko Nakamura. Indifferently, he scanned the stack of handwritten tablets announcing the day's wedding parties, receptions and conferences. They were all in Japanese script except two in roman which told him McDonald's franchise-holders were gathering in the *Tachibana* room and Sony Distributors Asia somewhere else. He knew the US aviation boys wouldn't advertise: if they were meeting in the hotel it was in secret, perhaps in a guest suite. Yoshi's persistence had brought out a manager with a carnation in his buttonhole from an interior office and then another man appeared from a corner of the lobby. Bearing an identification badge on his lapel, he wore a two-way radio visible on his belt and a carried a larger-model cellular telephone. After a short conversation, Yoshi backed away, shaking his head and shrugging, and joined Alex. 'They'd only say there's a room booked by the Japanese Civil Aviation Bureau for a private meeting.'

'Do you reckon it's the Americans?' Alex pressed.

Yoshi crooked his head and hissed. 'Our people wouldn't meet in a luxury hotel. It's got to be a cover for the FAA.'

Alex looked over the other's shoulder. 'Go back over to the desk and catch their eye,' he ordered. 'Just distract them for a second then walk out of the hotel. I'll follow the chap with the phone.'

A scattering of people helped unwittingly to screen him and as the man ignored the lift Alex followed him casually from a stairway to a mezzanine floor and along bright, thickly carpeted corridors to a parade of rooms named for Japanese flowers. The security guard, or whatever he was, vacillated in front of the Sakura room. Alex passed him and turning a corner for cover rummaged in his briefcase for the identity badge he had been issued with at the Haneda accident site. The stiff envelope containing his deposition, the dispassionate statement of his suppositions and assumptions concerning the crash of NINA 328, was already in his jacket pocket. A sharp corner pressed into an armpit, just enough to remind him it was there, ready to leave in a final desperate plea should they elect to throw him out without a hearing. He steeled himself with a deep breath. He needed a few feet between the door and the guard, and once he was in the room it would be hard for them to expel him without a spot of unseemly commotion. He chose the moment that a maid, pushing a rattling trolley of cleaning materials, distracted the guard to slip out of cover.

The door was unlocked, the room empty. He had seconds to take it all in, to decide whether the briefcases by the chairs belonged to a delegation of American aviation experts or to the sub-committee of a Japanese convention, and what was the purpose of the high-tech recording equipment and the meaning of the lines and annotations on the charts suspended on an easel? The conference table was spread with papers and set with water glasses for eight or nine people. The smokers had sat at one end, traces of their habit still heavy in the dry air. A clock suggested they had taken an early dinner and the state of the room that they intended to continue after it.

'Excuse me,' the Japanese said from behind, his English uncertain. Alex turned and bought time by calmly indicating his ID badge. The Japanese was flustered. He did not want the embarrassment of mistakenly suggesting this foreigner was not from among the group whose privacy he had been protecting for three hours. He was a clerk with the Japanese Civil Aviation Bureau: he didn't like speaking English and he wasn't too fond of foreigners, especially when they all looked the same.

'Where is everyone?' Alex asked, an eye on a flip chart. Thin falling lines had been drawn with a blue felt pen and at stages along them numbers had been plotted in red. Altitudes? Flap settings? Wind speeds? He backed towards the furthest corner.

'Private dinner,' the young functionary managed, his suspicions rising. 'They come back later.' His eyes narrowed and he fidgeted with a button on his intercom radio.

The loose pages Alex glimpsed were typed and the front of the notepads handwritten. Everything catching his eye was in English. He reached the head of the table, by the flip-charts and where the chairman would sit, and bingo, there it was. A batch of photographs, all glossy with newness and enlarged. The top picture was enough: it was similar to one he himself had taken at Haneda a week earlier: the front view of a blackened engine, fan blades twisted in its gaping mouth. He mouthed an apology, raising a hand in surrender and ostentatiously finger-tipping the letter from his jacket. He had addressed it URGENT FAA/NTSB URGENT. He propped it against a water glass in front of the chairman's photographs and let himself be escorted from the room.

He stretched on the bed with a drink and called Nippon Nagasaki Corporation, on the direct line into the office of the president's secretariat, knowing that at seven thirty there was no chance it would be unoccupied. Yes, it *was* a wonderful dinner last night and no, he *didn't* want to talk to the president of NN Air, he told Tabata: he wanted to talk to Hiroshi Miyamoto, the NNC group president. Yoshi had left after a drink together in the Samurai Bar and they had shaken hands with a finality Alex found strange. True, the case from the Japanese broker's standpoint was almost over: severe weather conditions most probably brought down the aeroplane and he could tell the insurers in Japan they were about to be billed for their share of the claim on NINA 328 and bring joy to his contacts in NN Air, not to mention South Miami Aviation, the beneficiary of twenty million dollars. It remained for Alex to put the group president on notice that the pilot's heart condition, and the possibility that medical evidence confirming it was deliberately withheld from the investigators – or altered or forged – would be noted in his final report, notwithstanding Alex's decision to recommend that the underwriting syndicate pay the claim made by NN Air. He spoke down the empty line and clucked in frustration. Finally, Tabata returned and chose his words with restraint and caution. 'I am afraid Mr Miyamoto is not able to speak to you.'

'Put Miss Shimada on,' Alex demanded. He heard the familar sucking in of air.

'Miss Shimada is with the president and the board of directors.'

'Get a message to one of them, please. It's very important.' Another pause brought him to close to eruption.

'My president and executive directors have gone to Nagasaki,' Tabata said finally and reluctantly. 'For a regional board meeting. Nagasaki is — '

'I know about Nagasaki,' Alex interrupted, hanging up.

Pouring another gin and tonic, he ordered a steak dinner from room service and set up his laptop computer. The payoff memorandum to Reggie Cameron, with its message for the brokerage house of Matthias, Montague & Broome, their parent company, the insurance syndicate manager and by extension to the syndicate in total, was three-quarters drafted. It needed only his conclusions and recommendations. He saw no cause, he wrote reluctantly, why we should deny the claim but circumstances may arise whereby the insurers may wish to consider cancellation of further cover for offences under the Japanese and US federal aviation rules. He drained his glass as the printer purred out the message. The drink played on his fatigue, driving him to a dulled state of confused euphoria: the relief at a situation resolved tempered by something still to be done. He took the note to the hotel's business centre and stood by it as it was faxed, and when he returned to his room the trolley with his dinner was trundling along the corridor.

He ate silently, hardly seeing the technical notes on the table as he drank too quickly of the indifferent California red Sauvignon for which they were charging forty pounds a bottle. Eight quid in Guildford, he told himself aloud. He did not finish the slab of marbled Kobe beef, garnished elaborately with a soya-shallot sauce, and heaped the leftovers under the silvered dome before pushing the wagonette into the hallway.

He took a punishing shower, the water pummelling him like blunt darts, forcing his breath out in bursts and taking with it the image of Makiko Nakamura. She soon returned in the stillness of the suite. Head on the bedboard, he turned on the television and surfed the channels, passing baseball games and quiz shows and thinking about CNN but settling on the lighter, local English-language channel and an action film it was playing. Emma Healey called at a point when his consciousness was drifting on the edges of hallucinatory oblivion.

'Reggie's off sick today,' she explained. 'Got your fax, Alex. Are you all right?'

'Me? Yeah.'

'So you've signed off on the NN Air claim?'

'I don't seem to have a choice,' he said bitterly. 'I can't hold back the payout but I want my reservations to go on the record. I gave Reggie a full account this morning.' The film had ended and after a commercial a stone-faced American and a Japanese anchorwoman were presenting the local news in English for the expatriate community. He phased out the sound with the remote.

'I think Reggie wants you back here,' Emma said flatly.

Alex saw in his mind the letter he had left with the American investigators. 'I need a couple more days. Clear up some loose ends. See what the autopsy comes up with.'

'I'm not sure — '

'I know South Miami Aviation's complained about me,' he said testily. 'They were out of order. I was not taking the weekend off to screw around. There are things here that don't add up and I want to stay around until they do.'

'So what do I tell him?' Emma asked in the unsympathetic voice she used when she put herself in Reggie Cameron's place. When there was no response she said, 'Are you there, Alex?'

He had flung his legs over the side of the bed, the telephone dangling limply. On the television he saw the image of a familiar carved roof between the pillars of a gateway and the figure of a man speaking silently into a microphone. 'Hold the line Emma,' he said, throwing the words at the telephone and juggling the remote control. Hurried, he first changed the channel accidently before finding JCTV again. They had actually plugged into a live broadcast from a local Tokyo channel and the newsreader was overtalking the commentary in English.

'. . . were called to the house in south-east metropolitan Tokyo by an anonymous telephone call at six forty this afternoon. The call led police to a body later identified as Makiko Nakamura, the proprietress of an Akasaka bar. A police investigation has been initiated but they say it is premature to speculate on a motive for the strangling. They are keen to interview the American woman who rents the secluded house in the temple grounds. She is believed to be travelling outside Tokyo.'

'What's happening Alex? Somebody with you?'

He was still watching the screen after the story had changed to a minor earthquake in Hokkaido when Emma's insistence finally roused him. He gave the handset a cold, empty look as he lifted it again. 'Fax me before you leave tonight, Emma. Tell me what action you took in response to the one I've just sent you.'

'Okay. And when can I tell Reggie you're coming back?'

His grip on the telephone tightened, as if on the hilt of a knife. 'Soon.'

The Samurai Bar was starting to clear for the night. No one sat at the long bar and the guests seemed to be on their last drinks at the tables. The corner where he had sat with Yuriko Shimada was occupied by a group of Japanese businessmen, heads shrouded in cigarette smoke, still chattering and nodding earnestly as semi-drunks do, however trivial the topic. He dropped onto a stool at the deserted bar and ordered a glass of white wine from the barman called Joji who greeted Alex by name. Like most of the hotel's staff, Joji Yamaguchi was a university graduate and would train in every discipline of the trade. He would work behind the bar for eighteen months and one day he might become the hotel's president. He had never been abroad but his English was impeccable. 'Chablis, Mr Bolton. I hope you enjoy it.'

When the barman had filled a simple table order for a Guinness and a spritzer, Alex asked, 'Have you ever been to Nagasaki, Joji?'

'Yes I have, sir.'

'Recently?'

225

He shook his head with a smile. 'About fifteen years ago, I think. Most Japanese go to Hiroshima or Nagasaki on school trips at the end of their primary education to visit the atomic bomb memorials. My school went to Nagasaki.'

Alex sipped the cold wine; Joji smiled and started to sidle away.

'One more thing, Joji.'

'Yes sir?'

'Were any foreigners, any non-Japanese, killed in the atomic bombings?'

Joji sucked air and thought. 'There were some Korean and Chinese workers among the victims, I think.'

'They were there because they were brought from your colonies and conquests, weren't they?' Alex stated, remembering a piece of Bill Littleton's lecture. 'As forced labourers.'

The barman's face stiffened. 'I believe that was the reason.'

'What about foreign soldiers? British, American, Australian prisoners captured in battle. Were any of them in Nagasaki, do you think?'

'I've no idea, really sir.' A waiter read him the last order for the four businessmen.

'They were there,' Alex persisted, his voice slurred by fatigue and a touch of anger. 'They were forced to work in the factories and shipyards. Didn't you read about the prisoner-of-war camps in your school textbooks?'

The barman calmly arranged four glasses of whisky on a tray and poured from a bottle of soda water. 'There was nothing about those things in my school books, Mr Bolton, so I don't think such a situation actually happened. Can I offer you another glass of wine?'

226

1 January, 1945

Holiday from yard. 0900 Church Service. Music allowed in all rooms. Captain Weefisy, Dutch M.O. beaten by Jap N.C.O. Jap N.C.O. in Galley leaving. Wonder what new one is like Old one about average Jap.

3 January

All men searched on return from Yard. Guards had no luck. 150 sacks of rice stored in Concrete Pill Box by Guardroom.

6 January

0900. Air raid alarm. Workers returned from Yard. 1115 All Clear. Workers back. Only allowed bath every 3rd day. From today 1000 and 1500 smoking periods stopped in Camp.

8 January

American Red Cross overcoats (156) issued. I was unlucky.

13 January

Galley broken into during night. 8 men admitted it and placed in cells.

14 January
Holiday from yard. Men in cells got no food today and spent the night without blanket. Temp. Av. 37F. I am Duty Officer for next week.

22 January
Notice passed around to all rooms re Red Cross. P.O.Ws must understand that they get this by goodwill and pity of Japanese Army and must appreciate this more fully if it is to be continued. We know the Japs are not releasing food or medicines. Cyclops in Yard today and unhappy. He had the Kid beat a riveter called Hampstead for poor work.

23 January
Three men found reading after 'Pipe Down'. Taken to guardroom and beaten.

25 January
312 Red Cross Parcels and 15 cases of comforts arrived in Camp.

26 January
Major Horrigan informed by Japanese that Red Cross food parcels could not be given in full to P.O.W.'s. Coffee, chocolate, gum, raisins, soap, sugar and cigs would not be issued individually and remainder of food sent to galley. Red Cross comforts eked out to Dockyard workers according to list supplied by yard.

27 January
Man reported sick. Jap duty N.C.O. refused to allow him to remain in Camp. Jap N.C.O. then hit him about the body six times. Duty P.O.W. Medical Orderly tried to intervene and was also beaten. After this, the sick man was allowed to stay in Camp.

28 January
Holiday from yard. Good workers receive Red Cross comforts. Speech by Camp commander: must not grumble about food or orders for dividing Red Cross

parcels. 2 men placed in cells, reason unknown.

5 February
1 man injured in dockyard. Rooms 3, 5, 7, 8, 9 and 19 punished for putting cig. butts in dirt boxes. Men allowed to chew gum only in their rooms and only at certain hours.

19 February
Issue of Jap cigs, 60 per man. Rooms 1, 5 and 24 searched. Heard planes but no air raid warning and heard no explosions.

25 February
I was duty officer and saw Bo Ko Go and Dead Pan Joe beat the Yank hunchback with baseball bats. It went on for hours. They aimed for his hump. He was put in the cage. They say he stole a rice-ball.

28 February
The hunchback died in the punishment cage. Our doctor does not think he had been fed for three days.

4 March
Holiday from yard. ½ tin of Red Cross corned beef per man issued. Just over three years a prisoner. Still a long way from home.

7 March
Air raid warning during the night. Camp visited by General in charge of P.O.Ws. ½ tin of meat issued per man. Allowed to write home 40 words. I wrote: 'Dearest Kathleen and Children. Interned in Japan. In the best of health. I trust all are well and everything is same in Padstow. Please tell Flossy and tell her to let mother know. Please send photographs. Love to all. Tom.'

8 March
Saw smoke over dockyards on mainland. Lt. Com. Chubb, Lts. Blain & Jenkins lose camp jobs, i.e. looking after chickens, goats and pigs. All officers to

work making gardens; A.B. Cross & Payne with the animals. Johnson too ill again to work in Yard.

18 March
Holiday from yard. Air-raid alarm, in camp shelters for 1½ hours morning. Another alarm later, 2½ hours in shelter. Jap word to take care is 'TAIHI' and guards have been ordered to take action with rifle butts if men are slow. Lunch and supper served together.

22 March
Army taken over administration of P.O.Ws from the Navy in the dockyard. No smoking for rooms 2–7 because somebody crapped in passageway, also no smoking tomorrow unless man confesses.

23 March
A.B. Sullivan confessed and gets extra work for a week.

26 March
1,416 American Red Cross food parcels arrived in camp. Yesterday issued Jap cigs, 60 per man.

31 March
All men warned by Cyclops to be more submissive at Yard. He kicked a Dutchman who smirked. Returned to Camp after air-raid warning and spent 1½ hours in shelter.

1 April
Getting warmer. Only two deaths this week. No. 1806 caught stealing Red Cross food supplies. Placed in cells after beating by mess guard we call Flip. Whole camp punished by stoppage of food and smoking. 4 parcels missing.

5 April
One man put in cells for stealing rice tins from P.O.Ws at Yard. We are not getting much from the Red Cross parcels. C.O. slapped for complaining. Men with experience of motor driving and mechanics ordered to report.

9 April

A man caught stealing bean paste from store. Camp inspected by officer from Fukuoka. Circular note concerning safety of P.O.Ws outside Camp issued. Air-raid warnings almost every day now. Big dockyards on mainland definitely hit.

15 April

Arch broke left leg, three way fracture. Got the civilian a job in the galley. He is a bit happier to be away from The Kid and Cyclops in the Yard. The Americans given a speech by Jap officers about stealing. They get us all into trouble.

26 April

Air raids in six of last ten days. We see Yank planes crossing coast. Dockyard workers return to Camp and spend a lot of time in shelters.

29 April

Jap emperor's birthday. Holiday from Yard. ½ tablet of soap issued per man. Started work on Camp gardens.

2 May

Air-raid warning. Yard workers return to camp and go to shelters. ½ tin of Red Cross salmon given per man. Rumours of an execution of Yank officer for hitting guard.

5 May

Air-raid warning. All men to shelters. Yard workers have to run a mile back to camp each time we have a warning. Our yard not hit but thick smoke coming from mainland dockyards and town. All ceilings removed today from all rooms, except sick bay.

13 May

Almost had it yesterday. Closest shave since action on the Exeter. I was in the garden with our padre when two yank Lockheed Lightnings strafed the camp. Padre swore like a sailor. It was a holiday from Yard so lot of

231

*men about but thank God nobody killed. At least we
know the Allied forces are getting closer.*

A cleaner draped with electric cable bowed in surprise as he
shuffled past her across the deserted expanse of lobby. If the
demure receptionist was curious when the English guest in
the blazer and casual slacks checked out at 5.40 in the
morning she hid it behind an expression of practised
efficiency. Keeping Yoshi's cellular telephone, he consigned
his suitcase and cameras to the concierge and changed his
chart case for the Jonsson letter in the hotel safe. 'Seoul,
South Korea,' he said randomly when she asked politely
where his destination might be, 'for a short break from
business.' He expected to be back in Tokyo in three days to
pick up his belongings and would advise in good time if he
needed a room. No, that wouldn't be a problem, she had said
and of course any messages that came for him would be held
for his return.

Alex had been woken by a sickeningly chirpy telephonist
at five after another short night of broken sleep – eased only
slightly by the knowledge that Makiko Nakamura had been
found – and had packed a travel bag with a few spare clothes
and the contents of the room's safety deposit box. Although
deceptively light from Tokyo's premature dawn, it was too
early for the breakfast room service or the coffee shop and
after checking out Alex found a solitary, optimistic taxi in
the forecourt rank. Determined to keep his movements as
private as possible he had not asked the receptionist to
scribble his destination on a card for the taxi driver in the
usual way but he was lucky when he showed the elderly
driver in the woollen pullover his railway guide.

'Tokyo Station,' the driver said proudly in English, smiling
broadly. 'Yes.' A few minutes into the short journey, he had
assembled his next communication. 'Tokyo Station very big.
Many, many lines, many doors. Where will you go?'

'The bullet train,' Alex said economically. He heard the familiar sucking of air. 'Very fast train,' he tried. Then he remembered and fumbled in his bag. The cover of his guidebook, like almost every postcard and poster, showed a sleek blue and white blunt-nosed train gliding past the snow-capped volcano cone of Mount Fuji. He held it out for the driver.

'Ah, *Shinkansen*,' he utttered. 'We call it *Shinkansen*.'

Alex was let out at the Yaesu-side entrance, convenient for the high-speed train tracks. Signs in English for the *Shinkansen* tickets led him to a window and another language nightmare resolved by the patience of a clerk already familiar with the problems of the independent *gaijin* traveller.

'Hiroshima?' the clerk said, splitting the syllables helpfully for the foreigner. 'Osaka, Kobe?'

Alex's brain stirred. Phyl was going to Nagasaki but only so far by the bullet train, he remembered. Time, seven something he knew, but which train? The clerk leaned forward and pointed to a massive board suspended from the ceiling. He was about to complain he couldn't read Japanese when the sign revolved to display the same information in English: destinations, departure times and the appropriate platforms. He had somehow expected the fanfared bullet train to leave ceremoniously every hour and was confounded to see a departure every ten to fifteen minutes, even at the start of the day. He recalled the time rather than the destination and against ten minutes past seven he read 'Hakata'. 'One way,' he said, gesturing with a finger, 'to Hakata.'

Phyllis stood out among the clusters of early business travellers heading for Nagoya and Osaka, both accessible on a day-return basis courtesy of the *Shinkansen* fleet. She had drawn her hair up and secured it with a comb, making her look taller, and clutched a bundle of newspapers. Her face barely changed when she saw him, as if she had been expecting him to rise like he did above the lip of the escalator. She kissed him lightly. 'Did you get reserved or free?'

He showed her the green ticket.

'Free,' she read. 'Like mine. There's no problem getting a seat at this time in the morning. Let's take the non-smoking car. We'd suffocate in the other.' They waited between the designated lines with a group of high-school students in stiff-collared uniforms. The endless train arrived, washed and cleaned, for a departure seven minutes later, and they took two seats towards the centre of the carriage. 'This is home for six hours and something,' Phyllis said, letting him store their travel bags overhead.

'You didn't seem very surprised to see me,' Alex declared. She had lifted the elbow-rest and threaded an arm into his.

'We have to keep our emotions under control all the time,' she said, giving him a warm smile, full of sadness. 'It's not easy having Japanese blood.' Alex grinned. She squeezed his arm. 'Did I say something funny?'

'Absolutely not,' he said with a dismissive flourish. 'Just that I remember a conversation one week ago with a woman in a red cap. I'd never met her either but she didn't have her emotions under control.'

'Yeah, yeah,' she drawled, recalling her intemperate outburst when Alex had woken her, graciously taking time to make contact after she had thrown her business card at him as he was being driven away in the NNC car. 'I think you got the American-side personality by mistake.' The shared mellow moment quickly evaporated, the lifeless face of Makiko Nakamura too recent in their memories and constantly intrusive. She said, 'I knew the only way you're going to get at that airline's misdemeanours is to prove there's a doctor in Nagasaki putting his name on phony medical certificates.'

Alex pondered it and sniffed. 'Maybe.' Then, when they were under way, crossing the Ginza between the sleek high-rise offices at Yurakucho, he asked, 'No problems at the hotel? The police want to talk to the American woman who rents the house where the murder took place. That's you.'

She showed no emotion. 'I can get by as a Japanese,' she explained. 'I used a different name and paid in cash. If I were a *gaijin* they'd ask to see my passport.'

'I was surprised to see the temple on television last night.'

'So was I,' she admitted. 'I guess the priest wanted a piece of publicity after he'd called the police.'

Spears of sunlight flared in the carriage when the train glided past the tall, new bay-side buildings. Phyllis showed him short columns on the murder of Makiko Nakamura from the *Asahi* and *Mainichi* dailies but translation lags and the late discovery of the body meant it didn't make Wednesday's English-language *Japan Times*. The first stop, two minutes at Yokohama, came quickly, and the three seats opposite theirs were taken by a harried mother and two pre-school children. Phyllis explained how the frequency of violent crime, the rare use of guns and the incidence of murder were low enough to attract very wide publicity, both constructive and sensational. The emotion and heat generated was multiplied if there was a sex angle or the involvement of *yakuza* gangsters, corruptible, philandering politicians or drug-taking actors. The downmarket mass-circulation magazines, she said, pointing out a spread of them on the trolley with the refreshments which passed along the aisle, would seize on Makiko Nakamura's murder as this week's sensation. Truth and accuracy would be lost in the vagaries and circuitousness of the Japanese language, replaced by speculation, innuendo and inference. There she was, a former bar hostess turned mama-*san*, the mistress of the hard-drinking divorced *gaijin* pilot who had died landing his aeroplane only a week earlier, brutally murdered in the house of another *gaijin*, a *nisei* Japanese no less. And how long would it be before a concerned citizen, coincidently a prominent business leader, remembered that the *gaijin* investigator from England had been tracking the dead woman for reasons not really explained? The story would be on the cover of a hundred weekly magazines when they came out tomorrow and Friday, she told him.

They emerged from a long tunnel, the sea shimmering below them. There was barely any vibration in the carriage, even when it closed on 170 m.p.h. as they skimmed between villages and steep, wooded hillsides studded with hotels, balloons of steam from the volcanic springs rising above them like silent explosions. 'We've got two days at most before we find ourselves assisting the Tokyo Metropolitan Police,' she figured.

When Alex told her Hiroshi Miyamoto and his board, including Yuriko Shimada, had left for Nagasaki before he could deliver a measure of good news concerning their claim, Phyllis was not surprised. She folded back one of her Japanese newspapers to a photograph of the NNC president in a posed picture, probably from the annual company report, with a transport van with the logo prominent. 'He's gone to ground,' she announced, slapping the page with the back of her hand. In the jumble of incomprehensible ideographs, Alex saw a display of small charts and graphs, columns of figures and a pyramid of boxes he took to contain the component companies of the Nippon Nagasaki conglomerate. The page was ruffled, creased from use, and he wondered how long she'd been sitting at Tokyo Station reading the newspapers before he had found her.

She summarised the substance of the article without having to check or translate it. Investigators from the Ministry of Finance's National Tax Administration and other agencies are ready to submit papers to the Tokyo District Prosecutors with a list of charges which include offences against the law on political contributions, serious contraventions of the Commercial Code, including the laws on securities and stock exchange operations, and illegal accounting practices. Ministry of Transport investigators have also impounded operational records and other material from the offices of NN Air as they look for the cause of the crash of the airline's cargo DC-8-71. Although too early to tell, charges may result from their investigations.

'I was there when they came for the records,' Alex said thoughtfully. 'They'll be able to throw in the trashing of various Japanese and US civil aviation laws if I have my way.' Then his eyes narrowed. 'Not forgetting the little matter of murder.'

Phyllis brightened and patted the article. 'The *Asahi* even mentions the case of the NNC employee who died in the so-called accident after he tried to denounce Miyamoto for bribing the Diet. The guy I was trying to contact.'

'That's why Miyamoto's gone into hiding?' Alex offered. 'To get away from things?'

'More or less. He's got a big estate down there in Nagasaki. After all, that's where it all started, with Roland Jonsson and Miyamoto senior. That's where their workshops were, hence the corporate name. With his different group companies, he's probably the biggest local employer and that means he's going to get protection, whatever his shortcomings.' She paraphrased more. 'He's gathering the presidents of the companies he controls and they're going to thrash out a strategy for restructuring and rationalisation. Well, that's what he told the press at Haneda Airport yesterday before he took off for Nagasaki.'

'No doubt neglecting to mention the small problem of a strategy to stay out of prison,' Alex quipped.

The prospect of Miyamoto's humiliation brought some light into their own flight. Phyllis pointed to a sky-field of haze and thin cloud, and they shared a cheery moment of

relief when she said behind it was the famous view of the
twelve-thousand-foot volcano he had assumed came
courtesy of the cost of the ticket. By the third stop, at
Hamamatsu, between the endless drab industrial sprawl on
the ocean side and the glimmer of the lake on theirs, the
carriage was full. Phyllis, in the aisle seat, rested her head
against his shoulder, a hand casually on his thigh. The trolley
returned, reminding him he had eaten nothing since the
unappetising dinner in his hotel room, and he bought soft,
white-bread sandwiches and barley tea for both of them.

'So how come Bill Littleton thinks Miyamoto senior's
still alive?' Alex asked, remembering, and wiping his
fingers.

'He can't be sure,' she said wearily. 'He just couldn't find
a date for his death. You saw how big his library is. Some
real deep Japanese stuff too. He was nosing through his
books, looking for Jonsson and maybe a reference to the old
Nippon Nagasaki shareholding structure. He noticed that the
biographical notes gave Miyamoto senior's birth year as
1906 but he didn't come across a death date.' She cracked
the empty plastic sandwich box with her thumbs. 'Bill's
from the same generation. Of course, he says Miyamoto
might have died in the meantime. His books are pretty old.
But if a powerhouse like Miyamoto had died in the last few
years he'd have noticed. These business guys are Japan's
only heroes.' The train jolted, and she paused for the seconds
it took an oncoming train to flash past. 'There'd have been
huge memorial services in Nagasaki and Tokyo. Still, Bill
admits he could have missed his death. He's got more
interesting things to do than track an old, retired
entrepreneur.' She tipped her head up at the luggage rack.
'He gave me some stuff he'd found on the POW camp. He
hardly slept for three days. He knows Nagasaki well. Spent
some time there after the war and used to visit from to time
since.' She drained the tea and asked, 'Didn't the

photographs you saw in the NNC gallery give Shinichi Miyamoto's dates?'

Alex frowned. 'Only the date the picture was taken, November 1934. I didn't notice much else because I wasn't particularly interested. I was dead on my feet from jet lag and an afternoon at Haneda in the wreckage. I was making a general observation about the *gaijin* in the picture. Yuriko told me Jonsson had died in the Nagasaki atom bomb. She didn't mention Miyamoto. I just assumed he'd died at some stage.'

'So did I,' Phyllis beamed, grasping his shoulder. 'But if we can get to the old fossil we can find out what happened to Jonsson between 1934 and the atomic bombing in 'forty-five. And the company shares.'

Her naïve enthusiasm forced a smile from him. 'If he's not dead he's probably a senile old cabbage with permanent incontinence. He'd be over ninety, Phyl.'

She pouted. 'Bill's not senile, and Miyamoto was only four years older.'

Alex hunched his shoulders. 'Okay. So we get to his bedside and he knows what day it is. Then what? He breaks down and confesses that, yes, when his partner and the principal shareholder in their company died in 1945, he conspired to use the chaos and confusion which followed Japan's defeat to carry on as if the Miyamoto family were the outright owners of Nippon Nagasaki?'

'Right. That's absolutely plausible. As Bill told us, the devastation was a cover for legally dubious, uncontrolled reorganisation by the *zaibatsu*. The occupation forces let them do it. They had more important things to do, like hanging the war criminals and making the country safe for democracy, US style. I'm going to go for it.'

Nagoya, home and modern fief of the Toyota empire, seemed to arrive quickly and they were snaking through the town, past the Chunichi Dragons' baseball stadium into the darker confines of the station. Announcements in Japanese and English had finished and departing passengers were gathering their bags and cases. Alex stood, stretched, then sat with his head against the rest. He spoke to the roof. 'A couple of things occur to me, Phyl,' he declared solemnly, 'before you put your Pullitzer on the trophy shelf.'

'Tell me now, *gaijin san*, because I've spent the prize money ten times over.'

He shared her zeal, but his smile was short-lived. 'First of all, Miyamoto junior's not going to stand around while you interrogate his poor old dad. He won't let you get within ten miles of him.' He motioned her to let him finish. 'Second. If you accuse him of stealing the company, he'll just claim the contract evidencing the legitimate sale of Jonsson's remaining interest was destroyed, like you said, along with everything else in the country in the fire-bombings. That won't be legally disputed. You've got nothing to show that Shinichi Miyamoto intentionally dispossessed Jonsson or actually committed a crime in the process.'

She became quiet, staring blankly through the window as the train drew away. Finally she turned, nodding gently. 'Let's talk about that. Get the diaries out.'

He stood and lowered her travel bag, extracting the manila envelope.

'Where's the Jonsson letter?' she said abruptly.

He tapped his jacket. 'It's okay. It's here.'

'It's all we've got.' She lowered the table and flipped the typed pages, her fingers playing over the faded print.

'I didn't get further than 1942,' Alex admitted.

'I understand. Your crash and everything. Bill read them over the weekend and again on Monday night with me. That's why I only got a couple of hours' sleep.' She hissed like a real Japanese. 'I'm trying to remember what Bill told me. Makiko's murder's kind of wiped my memory clean.'

'Take it slowly,' he suggested, lowering a table. 'Tell me

what you were looking for.'

'For the link between the diaries from the war and the document your old company drew up in 1938.' She flicked the pages as she condensed the long, ragged narrative that brought back in stark simplicity the horrific experiences of the Royal Navy seaman, his heavy cruiser sunk in a fierce sea battle with the Japanese in March 1942, and his rescue and transportation in appalling conditions from the Celebes islands in the tropics to Nagasaki, Japan, for almost three more years in a labour camp as a prisoner of war of the emperor. The Japanese port was the first common element, Phyllis stressed. 'Both men, the prisoner Tom Humphrey and the neutral Swede Roland Jonsson, could have been in Nagasaki at the same time; at least we know they were there once, on August ninth 1945. The POW survived the atomic bombing, the Swede Jonsson died in it, your friends at NNI said.' The diaries were vivid, sometimes humorous, and the inhumanity of Tom Humphrey's experiences – the ever-present threat of death from beatings, injuries, poorly or untreated illnesses and, towards the end, allied bombing; and the vermin-ridden filth of daily living – made their own situation shrink to insignificance. Even the death of Makiko Nakamura was a one-off sad event, she rationalised, and there was nothing to fear because she and Alex were completely innocent. They couldn't even be accused of neglecting her: they couldn't have foreseen that her relationship with a foreign pilot would lead to her murder.

Head on the rest and lulled by the soothing motion of the bullet train, Alex wondered with genuine admiration how the man had kept the notes hidden in the camp, how many risks he had taken to steal paper and something to write with. The archivist in London had said the original diaries were lodged with the Imperial War Museum and he made a mental note to go and see them when this mess was sorted out.

The captives, British, Dutch and Indonesians who stocked

Camp Nagasaki Six when it opened in October 1942, were joined later by two hundred American POWs taken on Java, a contingent of engineers captured while defending Wake Island under arms, a squad of Australian survivors from the Burma railway and the odd Canadian and Norwegian. Among the prisoners was a second-generation *nisei* Japanese-American from Texas called Fujita, who kept his origins secret from his captors until the middle of 1943. At its peak it held around twelve hundred prisoners. They arrived in rags and varying degrees of physical degeneration on the small island of Yanagi-jima in the entrance to Nagasaki harbour. Packed together in wooden sheds and kept alive on a grim diet of rice and barley broth, embellished occasionally with scraps of fish, rotten meat and vegetables, they marched as slaves at dawn to face the dangers in the shipbuilding yards a mile's walk away. There they worked and died as riveters, scaffolders and welders to build ten-thousand-ton ships for the enemy. A sick and exhausted sailor called Phillips from HMS *Exeter* falls asleep on a plank of scaffolding and tumbles sixty-eight feet to his death. Two soldiers are blinded from caulking and grinding without protective goggles. A hunchbacked American civilian called Reed is beaten senseless and dies after spending three days in the punishment cage. He has stolen a rice-ball. An *Exeter* seaman called Bennet has a bucket of sea-water forced down his throat for taking water from the wrong tank. Men die in the camps from pneumonia, encephalitis, colitis, acute enteritis and beriberi, and the results of beatings and starvation. Some just die from a broken spirit.

Phyllis guided his eyes to a cross she had pencilled in the margin of a diary page. 'Look at this, Alex. Bill noticed it.'

He drew the page closer and smoothed it.

'It's May twenty-five, 1943. Tom – that's the British POW, right?'

'That's right. Tom Humphrey.'

'One of Tom's room-mates has been killed in the dockyard near the camp and another guy's been assigned to take his place. Look at the name.'

'"Johnson",' he read, a sceptical groan emerging from his throat when he saw where she was heading. 'It's not Jonsson.'

'I know that but . . .' She turned the pages. 'We're now in 1944, December the twenty-seventh. They've had a fucking awful Christmas. Here. "Johnson's not very well again. He lacks military discipline and does not have any friends in the Camp".'

'So he was a lousy soldier,' Alex said. 'And a loner.'

Phyllis raised her hands to him. 'Okay, I agree.' Folding back a page and pointing, she said, 'But Bill Littleton spotted something else. Third January, same year: ". . . and the civilian in our room's been very ill with it." The civilian again. He caught pneumonia.'

'And?'

'Bill said the camps only held military prisoners. Civilians from enemy countries who were living in Japan when the war started were repatriated or interned in softer conditions.'

'But he *did* write Johnson and not Jonsson. You can't get away from it.'

Her fist clenched, eyes clamped shut, Phyllis searched for an explanation. '*I* got his name wrong at first. Don't you remember? On Sunday night. You had to correct my file because I'd spelled Jonsson wrong. And I wasn't under any pressure. Now put yourself in the POW's position. He only mentions "Johnson" two or three times by name, but if you're a plain seaman, physically and mentally exhausted, and risking your life to scribble down a record for no one's benefit, just simply to keep yourself sane, you're not going to bother with the niceties of spelling. Or the correct pronunciation. I guess it's read as "yonson" in Swedish but in that kind of environment of stress and fear you hear what you want to hear and don't ask twice. Johnson was as close as damn it to Jonsson.'

'I'm absolutely with you, Phyl, but is there anything in the diaries to explain what a Swede, a citizen of a neutral country, was doing in a military labour camp?'

'Fuck it, Alex,' Phyllis groaned helplessly, loud enough to attract a reproving look from the mother across the aisle when one of her children, slumbering across her lap, stirred. She spoke with controlled intensity, close to his ear. 'You told me that you think someone in NNC found the diaries in your briefcase and copied them. That's what's weird about this whole goddamn situation. There's got to be a reason the Jonsson letter came with Tom Humphrey's diaries and for Miyamoto to want them both so badly. We'd better work it out before we get to Nagasaki – we're about six hours away.'

'We should have flown,' Alex said lamely, the diaries folded back over the staple as he read.

'And leave a trail of ticket stubs with our names on them?'

He nodded ruefully and read in silence for a few minutes. 'At least he's only got nine months left in that hell-hole,' he said, running down the entries for 1945.

Phyllis was watching the countryside, her angular chin cupped in a palm. 'They say the only way to survive was to stay close to your comrades. Do everything together, share everything, the food and the pain of the beatings.'

"It doesn't sound like this guy Johnson was a team player,' Alex said, showing her a note of a dockyard beating from a nicknamed guard. 'Maybe Tom was his only friend.' Remembering, he asked, 'Did you find anything in the Swedish Embassy yesterday? You said you were going.'

Her smile was warm, but it told him she had not learned much. 'Guess what. They lost a lot of records in the air-raids.'

'Like everybody else,' Alex said.

'They were evacuated outside Tokyo when the raids got heavy and frequent and took the important stuff with them. Records of Swedish residents who attended formal dinners and national day ceremonies weren't considered important enough and were lost.'

'Another dead end.'

'Not quite. There were a couple of R. Jonssons on the microfilm records of pre-war residents. One deregistered himself when he went back to Stockholm in 1940.'

'The other?' Alex asked.

'It's probably our Roland. Most Swedish citizens here registered with the embassy for security reasons. There were no other obligations on them.'

'No record of what happened to him?'

Phyllis removed her glasses and examined the lenses. 'None at all. If he died in the atom bombing it wasn't recorded at the Swedish Embassy.'

'End of that particular line then.'

'Maybe,' she said, embedding her glasses in the rich hair above her forehead. 'The Swedish guy I spoke to suggests we check the memorial book for the victims of the Nagasaki atom bomb. Jonsson'll be in it if he died on August the ninth, 'forty-five, or even if he died later from the effects of injuries or radiation.' She shifted in her seat. 'Oh, and he gave me the address of the public records office in Sweden. He said I could pay someone to track Jonsson's family, get a few leads to possible survivors.'

'If it ever gets to be a real issue I'll go over there myself,' Alex offered. 'It's only a couple of hours' flying away.'

Phyllis beamed. 'Would you?' She leaned over and kissed him. 'C'mon. Let's go stretch our legs and get a beer from the refreshments car.' Then she remembered something and touched his arm. 'Almost forget. Your clinic. The place you suspect of issuing false medical reports.'

'What about it? It's also in Nagasaki, right?'

'It sure is, but I checked the detail with Bill. It's in Yanagi Town, if you remember from the report you showed me. The site was formerly Yanagi-shima. "Shima" means "island".'

'So?'

'Check the diaries. That's where the old POW camp was. The camp was on Yanagi Island, now Yanagi Town, and the biggest house on the former island belongs to Hiroshi Miyamoto and his family.'

Three carriages back, in a non-reserved smoking section, Wataru Hinohara was beginning to annoy his companion. With a horse-race tabloid spread across the table, he shifted the cigarette across his mouth with his tongue, all the while rubbing his hands together, or steepling his pliant fingers and drawing a crack from the knuckles when he snapped them backwards.

'For fuck's sake keep still,' Kamei said, grinding the words through tight teeth. The long carriage, configured in rows of two and three seats with the aisle between, was full: mostly men, most of them smoking.

Hinohara huffed without looking round and placed the hands that had garrotted Makiko Nakamura under the newspaper, in his lap, cupping his crotch. Killing did that to him. Kamei would hold back on the celebrations: they had not finished by half yet. The mission had gone reasonably well but they had failed to snare the *gaijins* into panicking when they found the body in her house. The guy from the Okudaira syndicate's Tokyo branch did well: the foreigners had confused him by leaving her house separately but he stuck to his task and followed them to the Imperial Hotel. He had to decide smartly which one to stay with when they parted. He made the right choice, and when she eventually finished the day in a Yaesu hotel opposite Tokyo Station it was pretty clear what her intentions were. He'd got to know her well in the twenty-four hours since he had tracked her to the Yurakucho foreign press club after they had trashed the Mini and then followed her comfortably to the home of the old *gaijin* in Hayama.

And it was just as clear where the white *gaijin* was going when he checked out of the Grand Kanto Hotel at six o'clock. Alerted, Kamei and Hinohara were at the station to follow the foreigners separately onto the *Shinkansen* platforms, having anticipated their destinations perfectly. Money wasn't a problem: the key the woman had given them on Saturday opened a locker that held a million yen in expense money. It had also supplied them with a photograph of an older, attractive woman with a *gaijin* in a pilot's uniform and various addresses, including a safe house for the hostage in a Sanya slum tenement. Kamei smiled to himself, thinking of the fun he'd had with Hinohara, taking the stupid little foreign car with the whale on the roof from the temple and dumping it in the drainage channel. He was resting his head, pleasant thoughts of the Japanese-looking *gaijin*'s body and what he would do to it warming him, when Hinohara nudged him, directing his gaze forward with a slight cock of the head.

Phyllis followed Alex through the automatic doors. They steadied themselves on seat edges against the gentle rocking of the train as they walked the length of the carriage. The Fukuoka *yakuza* lowered their eyes to their laps as the foreigners passed. 'Go with them,' Kamei commanded. 'Get us a whisky or something, but don't get too close.'

The cellular telephone in Alex's pocket broke into a muffled purr before they reached the refreshment car and he stopped to answer it between carriages. Two and a half hours had put almost three hundred miles of clear track between him and Tokyo before someone looked around and wondered why the guy from London wasn't around to tidy up the NN Air case.

247

The usual jolly, clipped edge to Richard Ingleby's voice was absent. 'Alex? Where are you?'

'I'm trying to clear up a case before a deadline.'

'That wasn't the question.'

Phyllis had to press beside him to let a stocky, square-faced man pass. A small gent's handbag swung incongrously from a thick, smooth wrist and he hesistated, as if taken by surprise to find the corridor blocked. Phyllis watched him sidle by and shuddered.

'Is there a problem, Richard?' Alex said.

'Not more than usual,' Ingleby answered humourlessly. 'You might like to know the police are asking about you.'

'The police?' He leaned lower as Phyllis turned an ear closer.

'Is there something you're holding back on? About the crash or something?'

The connection was holding uneasily. Alex said, 'I'm down to the last straw and I haven't got a good grip on it. It's the pilot's medical certificates. There's a strong chance they were fabricated, produced to order by a tame doctor. I've got an address and I'm going to take a look.' Hesitantly, he asked, 'What do the police want?'

'They didn't say. Just want to talk to you at this stage. Let me tell them where you are or you can take down the number they left and call them.' The line crackled when a Hikari express boomed past on the up-line. 'What's that noise, Alex? Where the hell are you? The police seem to think you've gone to South Korea.'

Alex cupped his free ear, recalling the off-the-cuff destination he gave when he checked out of the hotel. 'I'll be back with you tomorrow night.'

Phyllis shook her head furiously.

'Make that Friday. Are there any other messages for me?'

'I'm just an answering service, Alex,' Ingleby complained amiably. There was a pause. Ingleby was shifting through his notes, no doubt. 'The hotel tracked you to my office. Apparently they're holding a fax or something for you. From Reggie, your dear old boss, I expect. I suppose that's why he called here when you didn't respond. It was midnight London time. He sounded pretty pissed off because you didn't reply by return.'

'Nothing else?' Alex said blandly.

'Perhaps that broker chap's got something. Whatsisname . . .'

'Yoshi. Yoshi Kanagawa.'

'He's been part of the furniture since you arrived but I've not seen him here this morning.'

'Do me a favour, Richard, please,' Alex said, more as a demand than a request. 'Call him at Matthias, Montague & Broome in Tokyo. I need to know if he's heard from the Americans. I got a message to the FAA team yesterday, told them what I suspected about the medical certificates, and left Yoshi's number as well as my mobile.'

'Oh all right, but I don't see why you can't call him yourself.' Alex heard a loud, theatrical sigh and then, 'Undercover, I suppose. All part of the game. Don't want your calls traced.'

'Something like that,' Alex muttered. 'I'll call you tomorrow.'

'I wonder how the police got on to me.' Alex said when they had settled across a window table in the buffet car with two cold Malts beers and a dish of potato crisps. 'I suppose I was seen at your house.'

'But not recognised, surely.' Phyllis contended. 'The police want to talk to me, obviously, and when they track back and find out I was in Makiko's apartment two days before she was murdered one of the neighbours is going to remember there was a tall *gaijin* with me.'

'They'd work out eventually who I was,' Alex supposed.

'But their job would be lot easier if a concerned citizen

249

phoned them in distress, suggesting casually they might look to have a talk to Alexander Bolton, currently prowling around the Haneda crash scene and living at the Grand Kanto Hotel.'

'The killer,' Alex sniffed. He had not realised until now how easy it was becoming for him to say words like 'killer' and 'murder'.

'Or his paymasters,' Phyllis corrected. 'Whoever planned the abduction and set you up. And you know who they are.'

Too much had happened for him to doubt her, let alone question her. He forced a thin smile. 'And we're heading for their lair.' When they had returned to their seats, Alex said, 'I can't see how the POWs in the Nagasaki camp survived the atomic blast.' The sun had passed over the train and Phyllis drew the curtain apart to give them skipped, hazy views of forested inshore islets pitting the Seto Inland Sea. Passing through the endless spread of modern Hiroshima, an hour from the end of the bullet-train part of their journey, they had stood as Phyllis pointed in the direction of the peace memorial, near the hypocentre of the explosion from the four-ton bomb they called Little Boy, dropped from the B-29 called Enola Gay by its crew on 6 August 1945. Only a single kilogram of uranium 235 in the payload actually fissioned, but it was enough to set off the TNT equivalent of thirteen kilotons of explosive power. In Hiroshima, where sixty per cent of the population lived or worked within a mile of the centre of the explosion, two hundred thousand people died.

'The island in Nagasaki bay was about five, maybe six miles from the hypocentre and I guess the prisoners had a touch of luck,' Phyllis said grimly. 'The bomb on Nagasaki was more powerful than Hiroshima's and the destruction was greater, but the hills around it concentrated the blast and protected a lot of people from the radiation. And the fire-storm was much smaller than Hiroshima's.' She reached for her journalist's pad and the notes she had made at Bill Littleton's seaside home. 'I had to look up the detail to put Roland Jonsson's death in some perspective.'

Once the Americans had recaptured Japanese-held islands in the Marianas, like Saipan and Tinian, in the middle of 1944, mainland Japan finally came within reach of land-based bombers and the war came home to the people in the form of swarms of B-29s with their endless cargoes of high explosives and fire-bombs. A heavy toll fell on southern Japan, with its concentration of munitions factories and shipyards. At 9.50 a.m. on 9 August 1945, seven hours after a laboured, dangerous take-off from Tinian, Charles Sweeney, a twenty-five-year-old major in the US Army Air Force with twelve more men in his crew, was steering the B-29 Superfortress nicknamed Bock's Car above thick cloud towards his primary target: a gigantic arsenal in the city of Kokura on the northern tip of the island of Kyushu. Three days earlier he had flown with Colonel Tibbets in Enola Gay to witness the destruction of Hiroshima, so he knew the plot. Two weather planes ahead of him had reported clear skies over the next target. In the bomb-bay he carried Fat Man, a plutonium device designed to produce an explosion equal to twenty-two kilotons of TNT. Yellow, with black fins, Fat Man was ten and a half feet long, four and a half wide, weighed almost five tons and resembled nothing more than a giant, tapered pineapple. At 8.40 a.m., under strict radio silence and with no escorts, Sweeney had rendezvoused over Yakushima with two more B-29s, one carrying scientific instruments, the other a team of observers including Churchill's representative, Leonard Cheshire.

Thirty thousand feet over Kokura, Bombadier Beahan peered through his Norden MK15 bombsight and spotted through now broken clouds the largest arsenal complex in Japan, but just as the bomb doors were opened fate and irony took over. Blinding smoke from the Yawata steelworks and shipyards, bombed conventionally a day earlier and still burning, drifted across his view, blotting out everything. As bomb aimer, Beahan was now in charge of the aeroplane. He was not a coward, he had already been shot down four times over Europe, and in spite of heavy flak from the most fiercely defended area in the Japanese empire he ordered another pass over the target. Close to the outer limit of its range, Bock's Car had left its base without reserve fuel because of a broken transfer pump and had enough to reach the island of Iwo Jima if it still carried the bomb. Sweeney turned Bock's Car into a tight left turn and headed south with its deadly cargo towards the secondary target, the Mitsubishi dockyards on the outskirts of Nagasaki, a hundred miles away. The Christian city's fate was sealed. The five harbours were home to the greatest concentration of private shipbuilders and repairers in Japan and four other gigantic Mitsubishi war production sites making, among other armaments, a series of A-class, frighteningly lethal torpedoes.

'That's what took Miyamoto and Jonsson there in the first place,' Phyllis remarked. 'With their marine engine business.' Nagasaki is built where the harbour forks to become two parallel valleys with mountain ridges between them and in spite of the attractiveness of the targets its geography made the war facilities operationally difficult to hit. Serious air-raids did not begin there until 1 August 1945, only nine days before the city's total destruction.

The weather planes had reported twenty per cent cloud cover but when Bock's Car arrived over Nagasaki at 10.50 a.m. on 9 August the crew found it closer to seventy. Approaching from the north-east, six miles above the town, Bombadier Captain Beahan squinted into the sights again, discerning in the scudding, thickening clouds the outline of the harbour, the main downtown area and the surrounding mountains, but not the Mitsubishi shipyards to the south. On the B-29's radarscope Nagasaki appeared light blue against the dark blue of the hills. Sweat stung Beahan's eyes. He was instructed to drop the atom bomb visually but decided to release it according to the radar sighting and ordered the bomb doors opened. Then suddenly he saw the city through a yawning hole in the clouds and again took directional control of the aircraft from Sweeney. Two miles north of the intended aiming point he saw a structure familiar from the briefing sessions and yelped. It was the Mitsubishi Arsenal Plant, the secondary target after the shipyards. Beahan's heart was racing as he released Fat Man.

The bomb fell for fifty-three seconds before reacting to barometric pressure, which caused arming and firing switches to close. Responding to the high voltages amassed in the condensers, the detonators around the high-explosive charges erupted, compressing the active material until fission occurred one thousand five hundred feet above Nagasaki, and at 11.02 on the morning of 9 August a third of the city was levelled in a single explosion. It created pressure a hundred and twenty times greater than the strongest typhoon, the blast travelling outwards at nine thousand miles an hour, consuming, blow-torching, everything within a thousand yards of the hypocentre. Heat, blast and radiation would claim about sixty thousand lives and injure a similar number. A hundred and twenty thousand would be homeless.

The B-29 lurched upwards when the bomb left the bay and when Sweeney saw a live cloud of boiling fire shooting upward towards him in violent concentric swirls he turned his plane into the sharpest banking turn, fearful the fierce turbulence and the strain were bound to threaten the airframe. Desperately low on fuel, he lumbered towards the nearest safe landing strip, leaving behind a mushroom cloud, glowing orange with fire, rising sixty thousand feet above Nagasaki. Ninety minutes later, Sweeney was surprised to be still airborne. Two engines had cut out and a third was spluttering when Bock's Car dropped heavily onto the runway at Okinawa, only seven gallons of fuel remaining from the six thousand two hundred and fifty in the tanks at take-off from Tinian.

'I figure from the diaries that Tom's camp, Nagasaki Six, was about five and a half miles from the hypocentre,' Phyllis said.

Alex finished her assumption. 'And if the bomb had exploded over the Mitsubishi shipyards where it was intended, the camp and our diarist wouldn't exist.'

'I guess so.' She turned a page. 'I wish Bill were here. He's got such a rich store of facts to draw on.'

A large man brushed against Alex's shoulder, a mild nudge, not firm enough to distract him. He gave them both a long, thin apologetic smile. Alex did not look up, but Phyllis's eyes followed the man with the dainty handbag as he rocked carelessly along the aisle. 'It's a bit surprising,' Alex was saying to Phyllis, 'that the Americans were so casual in their bombing. They must have known there were POWs in the area.' He tracked back to the entry for 13 May 1945. 'They strafed the camp with fighter bombers.' He gave an ironic snort. 'I assume they weren't aware it held hundreds of American and other allied prisoners.'

'Bill's sure they knew about the prisoners,' she declared. 'But nothing was going to stop the destruction of Japan. It's probable that thousands of allied POWs died when the ships bringing them to Japan were torpedoed by the Americans and more when the railyards and factories in Japan were bombed. The labour camps were built close to the worksites, like Nagasaki Six. The POWs walked to the dockyards. And there were several more camps in and around the city. The closest was Nagasaki Fourteen, about a mile from the explosion. It was destroyed, of course. About seventy men were killed. Four from Nagasaki Six were killed apparently, but it could have been more.'

Leaving the main island of Honshu, the train slowed marginally when it descended to the Kammon Tunnel, the compression of air seizing the carriages as it entered. It was only a short time before they emerged on the island of Kyushu. Passing through Kokura, Phyllis reminded her companion that the air had been thick with smoke and cloud fifty-one years ago, sparing the city the fate of Nagasaki. Soon they were passing a complex of red-and-white-striped smokestacks as they approached Fukuoka City, the bullet train terminus at Hakata Station. The final digital news run, flickering over the automatic doors, gave way to the distance-to-destination countdown, a signal for the passengers on the last leg of the journey to gather their bags and things while a conductor thanked everyone for their patience and announced the connecting lines. They had a twenty-minute wait before a local train would take them on a scenic two-hour winding route to Nagasaki.

The warm southern air was turning humid, the seasonal rain front already passing Okinawa, closing in on Kyushu. Palm fronds on the station forecourt trembled from the blasts of diesel exhaust as the city buses pulled from the bays. A bag on each shoulder, Alex squinted at the light as they left the shade of the entrance. He nudged Phyllis's gaze to the advertisements for different products and services blazing from billboards along the station's perimeter fence. They all bore the fused roman letters of the distinct Nippon Nagasaki logo. Phyllis took an elbow and pressed him towards the nearest set of steps to the steel walkways that straddled the broad junction and the simple roof over the tram stop.

'Let me get my bearings,' he protested.

'Keep going,' she said, her eyes straight ahead. 'I want to try something.'

Leading him briskly to an alley of bars and shops behind

the banks and plain-fronted business hotels opposite the station she sauntered to the tall, glass front and neon invitations of a *pachinko* parlour. The tinny rattle of pea-sized silver ball-bearings being coughed from rows of upright machines resounded into the street. It was late afternoon and the place was two-thirds full, mostly students and older women passing time before going home after shopping. 'Have you ever played Japanese pinball?'

'I don't somehow think this is the moment . . .'

But she was inside, buying a tray of balls to feed into the machine and hopefully into the jaws that generated the winnings. They sat together, unnoticed by the lines of people mesmerised by the noise, the lights and the simple challenge as the little balls danced on tiny nails inside the glass cases. 'Stuff them in there,' she commanded with a finger directed at a hole, using the cover of his profile to watch the movements in the street. 'And look straight ahead.'

Outside the two men had lost their marks when the foreigners surprised them by making a sudden turn off the main road and when they reached the corner they were not in sight. Kamei pressed his face to the smoky-dark window of a coffee shop and Hinohara frightened a cashier girl in a step-down convenience store when he pushed over a stack of plastic baskets as he checked the aisles. 'They're in there,' Kamei mouthed, gesturing with a thumb at the *pachinko* parlour and motioning Hinohara to join him. He had gone ahead of the other *yakuza*, glancing into shop windows before passing the pinball house. The man they knew as Alexander Bolton stood out in the middle of a row, his sharp, pale profile and broad shoulders commanding. He was getting to grips with this unique Japanese pastime, but in that instant Kamei couldn't see the Japanese woman *gaijin*.

'He's just walked by the window,' Phyllis hissed. 'The big guy from the train. He followed us to the restaurant car and then he came by for a closer look. He nudged your arm, remember?'

Alex shrugged and turned to her, the magic of the silver balls spinning inside the case already passed. 'He probably just lives around here.'

'Yeah, sure. Let's go.' The passage to the lavatories led to a staff room and kitchen where a small, middle-aged woman in a white smock drank green tea while she read a weekly magazine. Alex filled the doorway, and like an image from one of the endless rape scenes so popular in the *manga* cartoons the vision of a rampant *gaijin* had become reality and the tea bowl shook in her hands. Phyllis sucked air, dragging out her apology with a succession of stabbing bows. Yes, there was a rear door the woman said, the emergency exit leading to an alley and yes, she would gladly guide them to it in view of the unusual circumstances. Phyllis would not be hurried. She first checked that the man she was convinced was a *yakuza* was not lounging on the corner of the alley where it opened onto the wider street where the front entrance of the pinball parlour was located. Then they dashed in the other direction, slaloming around black plastic rubbish bags and empty beer crates towards the light.

They avoided the broad spaces around the station and the trams trundling by it, instead taking a taxi the short distance along the tongue of the Urakami River, finally turning into a narrower parallel road and stopping at the foot of a flight of steep, uneven steps bordered by clustered dark, wooden houses behind coarse stuccoed walls. Alex stopped to gaze up at the stark shape of a single spherical column with a short, cracked crossbar balanced on top of it.

'We're staying here,' Phyllis said when they reached the head of the steps and stopped in front of a latticed-porch doorway. Alex was standing beside another concrete pillar lying on its side to make a long bench. He looked at the street below and if anyone had followed them he figured they would have time to slip into the alleys and narrow paths that tracked up the hillsides between the houses. Mount Inasa rose sharply behind the buildings across the river, brooding over the city, the radio antenna on its peak streaked with thin cloud. A cable-car seemed motionless, suspended from an invisible thread.

'I came here a couple of years ago,' Phyllis said, shifting to the shade from a branch overhanging the inn's wall, 'when I wanted a touch of atmosphere for my book on Nippon Nagasaki. It's a *ryokan*, a Japanese-style hotel. Bill used to come here after the war to get away from things. It had to be rebuilt after the bombing, of course, but it's been run by the same family for generations.'

'What gives with the statue?' he asked, jerking a thumb upwards.

Phyllis clucked. 'It's not a statue. It's a *torii*, the entrance gate to a Shinto shrine.' She gestured to a corner. 'The path leads to the Sanno shrine.'

'What happened to this one?'

She smiled sadly. 'We're in the zone of total destruction, maybe half a mile from the hypocentre of the atom bomb. It brought down the pillar we're sitting on and they decided to leave the other one and half the cross-piece as a memorial. It's called the One-Legged *Torii*.'

'You said Shinto. Is it like Buddhism?'

'No. It's the native religion of Japan, a kind of primitive nature worship, a focal point for local communities to gather and thank the gods for good fortune if I remember, with lots of gongs and chanting. It goes on in temples, like the place I live near. People here are really pragmatic. They have birth ceremonies at shrines and funerals at temples. Covers most bases.'

'I saw a church on the way here,' Alex said, his voice trailing when he saw the green roof of a taxi draw up below them. It was empty, until a couple appeared and got in.

Phyllis led him along a short path of stones to the inn door, explaining that Christianity had never caught on seriously, except here in Nagasaki and other parts of the island of Kyushu. While it was now trendy to get married in the churches scattered across Japan, in Nagasaki there had been a thriving congregation of real believers since the middle of the sixteenth century when Francis Xavier had landed with his missionaries. In 1600 Japan was unified under the shogun generals and ruled from Edo, present-day Tokyo. Apart from Dutch traders, confined to a small island in Nagasaki harbour, the shoguns sealed Japan to the world for two and a half centuries, banning Christianity and forcing believers to renounce it by trampling on their own precious religious images. Those who refused were crucified. But the survivors were resilient and practised their religion secretly around Nagasaki until the shogun rule was overthrown in 1868. After further persecution by the new emperor-driven military rulers they were allowed to worship again. If Christian belief exists at all among the Japanese it is expressed most purely in Nagasaki.

'So how frigging ironic,' Phyllis cursed bitterly, sliding the doors of the inn apart, 'for Uncle Sam to pick on the only Christian city in Japan and drop its atomic bomb almost exactly on top of the biggest cathedral in Asia.'

The granddaughter of the woman Bill Littleton had known welcomed the *gaijin* and the almost-Japanese woman without change of expression. There was a short bout of air-sucking and gently persuasive words from Phyllis before they were shown to an airy *tatami*-matted room, which opened onto a small Japanese garden garnished with dwarf pines and neatly trimmed shrubs.

'The lady apologises because there's only one room available,' Phyllis said with a grin. 'But don't worry, *gaijin san. Ryokans* are sexless places. Everybody puts on the same coloured *yukata* gowns and there's only one size. We're all one in Japan.' The room smelled of recently laid reed mats and was austerely decorated with a faded wall scroll and a two-stem arrangement of morning-glory flowers in the shallowest of *tokonoma* alcoves. The television on its corner stand seemed out of place. They sat at the low, centre table, a map of Nagasaki and their bits of paper spread between the bowls of green tea brought to them by a maid. Phyllis lifted her broad-framed glasses and traced a long finger over the map, her eyes skipping from it to the dead NN Air pilot's medical certificate.

'I'd like to try and find the clinic before the light goes,' Alex said. 'And before my time runs out.' He thought of making a call to London.

'It's here,' she said confidently, a fingertip over a hammerhead shape on the map. The scale made it about four kilometres between its widest points. One end bulged naturally, the other was squarish, where landfill had created an industrial complex for docks and warehouses.

'The island Tom wrote about? Yanagi-jima.'

'Yeah. Except it's not an island any more. Look.' The map was overwritten in Japanese and large enough in scale to show a block of land joining Yanagi to the mainland. 'I didn't realise where exactly the clinic was when you first showed me the certificate. I just took on board the fact that it was in Nagasaki. Bill pointed out it also happens to be near the Miyamoto family's home base.' She drained the tea bowl. 'Let's go and look for Madame Butterfly.'

Loading one of their travel bags with a camera, binoculars, the mobile telephone, maps and papers, they approached the main road warily, unsure of the *yakuza* they wanted to believe they had imagined. Rush-hour traffic rolled slowly and patiently and the Lucky taxi seemed reluctant to leave the flow to pick up a foreigner. The driver caught Alex's eyes in his rearview mirror whenever he stopped at a light. Was he just being curious or was he logging my face, Alex wondered? Phyllis's paranoia was getting to him.

The inspiration for *Madame Butterfly*'s setting was the home of a late-nineteenth-century British trader called Glover who became a prominent figure in Nagasaki and married a Japanese woman. It stood imperiously on a bluff overlooking the harbour and had been turned into a museum and park. They reached it up a twisting street lined with souvenir shops and three flights of covered escalators. The house and gardens were closing, the departing visitors posing rigidly for the regulation photograph in front of a bed of yellow flowers. Phyllis directed the taxi past the high fence bordering the estate to a viewing deck on a high point between a restaurant and a row of souvenir shops. It was already dark enough for the deck lights of the cargo ships and ferries in the harbour and quays below to sparkle. Across the bay, ringed with giant cranes and gantries, the sprawling docks and workshops of the Mitsubishi shipbuilding and repair yards dug deep into the shoreline. She swept the panorama with a broad sweep of Alex's compact, powerful binoculars, then gave them to him and led his eyes to the tip of a promontory jutting from the headland at the mouth of the harbour. 'Yanagi,' she declared. 'Let me have another look, please.'

He handed her the binoculars and while waiting for another turn imagined a rust-bucket of a ship rolling into the calm waters of the beautiful harbour fifty-five years ago with its cargo of starved, sick prisoners-of-war. Spilling onto the decks into the autumn sunshine – the diaries said it was October – they would have been deceived by the serenity and beauty of the pine-, camphor- and maple-covered mountains surrounding the city of Nagasaki and its bay. But not for long. Prodded with bayonets and kicked to their feet if they stumbled, they were herded into a compound of lice- and rat-infested shacks, given forty-eight hours of rest before beginning the first of many marches to the dockyards. Their ordeal was to last for another two and a half years. Epidemics of untreated disease and the beatings took their toll in the camp, and in the shipyards death and injury stalked the forced labourers, erupting indiscriminately as they confronted dangerous work conditions with simple, primitive tools and no protection from open fires, unguarded scaffolding and caustic materials. Later, death threatened from the skies when American B-29s droned above them in swarms. If that wasn't enough, a pair of 'friendly' American fighter-predators mistook the camp, with its brutalised, stinking near-skeletons in rags, for a legitimate target of opportunity and raked it with cannon fire. And it *wasn't* enough. Alex looked across the water to the Mitsubishi shipyards, about a mile and a half from Yanagi. If Bock's Car's bombadier had managed to find the primary target for Fat Man, Tom Humphrey and seven hundred survivors would have had their misery ended in half a second of hell.

'Take a look,' Phylis said, offering the binoculars. 'We're just about three miles away, about the same distance back the other way to the A-bomb hypocentre.'

He focused on the dark outline of the mound of hills that covered the one-time island. The coastline was ragged, lights in the inlets promising fishing hamlets, and there were more concentrations of light where the uplands had been stripped of trees and foliage to make way for houses and blocks of flats.

'Can you see where they joined it to the mainland? It's the wide strip of land with the rows of lighting. To the right of it you can see where they've reclaimed more land to expand the shipyards.'

'I've got it,' Alex said.

'That's where Nippon Nagasaki have their repair facilities and the warehouses. If it wasn't so dark you could probably make out the logo on the roofs.'

'Where's the family estate?' Alex asked, lowering the glasses.

'On the far side, with a view out to sea. You can't see it from here.'

'And the POW camp?'

Phyllis took another long look through the binoculars. 'It shouldn't be hard to work out. Bill reckons it's down there, near where they built the land bridge. The old Nippon Nagasaki yard was there and the diaries say the prisoners had to walk about a mile to reach it. The only main settlement's a small town on a little bay. The camp's now the community primary school. We can check it out tomorrow.'

'When we look for my doctor.'

'Let's call Bill on your mobile and tell him what we're doing. He made me promise to.'

The old man was agitated, his voice thick with strain and anxiety. 'What's happening, Phyl? You've got yourself into big trouble. Is Alex with you?'

'Yes he is,' she said calmly, knowing what was coming.

'The police are looking for both of you. The press are saying they want to talk to Alex about a murder. Is is true?'

She shivered and moved against the Englishman, shielded from the breeze, which had sharpened. She flinched when she saw over his shoulder a shadow moving across the cone of light from a lamp hidden in the foliage on the wall.

'Are you there, Phyl?' Bill Littleton growled.

Two figures, a young couple, moved into the light, their arms joined. Seeing intruders they giggled and took their loveplay elsewhere.

'Yeah. I'm here.' She told him how Makiko Nakamura was murdered while she was staying in Hayama with him and how Alex had been set up to find the body. He had been close to proving that NN Air had been criminally negligent in their work practices but she was certain it was more than that. It was the diaries that threatened Miyamoto and his empire. That's why she and Alex had opted to buy some time and head for Nagasaki.

'Buy an evening edition paper,' Littleton said grimly. 'They've got Alex hung out to dry with you as his accomplice.'

'I'll take a look. How did they figure it was Alex? I don't think he was seen at my house.'

'An anonymous call to the police, I think.'

She scowled. 'I can guess who it was and I think they followed us to Nagasaki.'

'What? I can't hear you very well and I think I've got a visitor.'

Phyllis heard the wind-chimes from the veranda over the line and imagined her dear old friend there with his beloved view of the ocean. She smiled into the handset.

'Take it easy Bill. I'll call you back in fifteen minutes.'

'You do that,' Bill said firmly. 'I think I've really got something for you. Have the diaries with you when you call. The last part, just before the guys were liberated. Gotta go. Someone's in the house.'

She moved away from Alex and packed the telephone.

'Are you all right?' he asked. She was staring across the harbour.

'It's getting cool,' she said after a pause. 'Let's get back to the inn and work out a strategy.'

An hour of lancing rain had flattened the sea and it made no more than a soothing rustle as it broke over the rough sand on the shoreline. Moonlight dappled a stray cloud, making a furrowed path across the water to the house, and with the rain doors drawn aside it flooded the house and silhouetted the outline of a man in the doorway to the hall. He had something in his hand, probably a mobile phone, Bill thought. 'Sorry, I was on the telephone,' he said in Japanese, closing the window doors behind him. 'I didn't hear you ring. How can I help you?' There were two of them now, and then another man he had not seen. He approached from Bill's study and moved behind him. The old man turned towards the light switch.

'Don't touch it,' one of them ordered in rough Japanese. 'Turn round and kneel on the floor, hands on the table.'

Bill caught the rasp of a southern dialect and the deliberate, rough-edge talk of the punk *yakuza*. Turning his back on them, he had only the briefest of moments to focus his weak old eyes on the intruders. They were all men, wearing loose soft-fabric jackets, and in the patchy half-light he imagined he saw a blade. He heard his heart racing and felt a rush of sweat to his scalp.

'Can you recommend a pleasant hotel or *ryokan* in Kyushu, say in Nagasaki? Somewhere discreet, you know, private? Somewhere a couple on the run can bed down quietly for a while? Keep out of the way?'

'Are you the police?' Bill said. His knees ached on the raw *tatami*. One of the men crossed the room and tugged the telephone cable from its socket. Another swaggered into the study, straddled Bill's swivel chair and made a mocking pretence of reading the diaries of Tom Humphrey before sweeping them onto the floor.

The interrogator let Bill see the telephone dangling from a wrist. His face closed on Bill's ear and his voice hardened, the words slurring from a corner of his mouth. 'We followed the fucking *gaijins* from the moment they left that house of hers in Tokyo.' He smirked. 'After he murdered the bar hostess.' He made a mess of pronouncing 'Bolton', causing the others to snigger. His sour breath made Bill flinch. 'My friends were with them as far as a *pachinko* parlour opposite Nagasaki Station and then they lost them. I wonder where they went. You know Japan better than me, don't you, old man?' Something sharp and cold pressed into the back of

Bill's neck. 'Where would *you* stay if you went for a very short visit to Nagasaki?'

They retraced the route to the inn by tram, standing apart, watching the passengers arrive, looking for a second glance, an odd reaction to the tall *gaijin*. Phyllis might turn a head for her looks, not for her race. The warmth of the southern city at sea level brought the people to the street and kept the shops open late. Entertainment blocks blazed their neons early. Phyllis threw him a glance and they left with half the passengers at the Nagasaki Station stop, bobbing among the knots of commuters and students in their severe, high-collared uniforms. Alex rocked on his heels, watching from a pillar as Phyllis shouldered a path to a newspaper stand where she feigned interest in the headllines of the evening editions of the broadsheets and sensationalist tabloids. FIND THE GAIJINS, inch-high red or blue characters screamed with drama and economy from a selection of newspapers.

'This piece of crap'll tell us what's going on,' she mumbled, a newspaper folded under an arm. They were waiting for the tram for the last short leg to the inn. Darkness had closed quickly and it helped. 'See anything familiar?' she said from behind the opened pages when they were in motion.

He did. Grainy images of the Buddhist temple by her house and the frontage of the building where Makiko ran her bar. There was also a staff-file photograph of Ed Kidderby, which had embellished many newspaper articles after the crash of NINA 328.

'I think we're running out of time,' Phyllis said morosely when they were back within the rough, simply adorned walls of their *ryokan* room. She had called Bill Littleton's number from Alex's cellular phone twice in ten minutes: the line was dead. No engaged tone, just an a definitive cut-off click. The instrument spun across the sheen of the reed matting when she pushed it aside. She was squatting at the low, polished table, the newspaper folded in her lap. They had not ordered dinner, and it was too late for the family to prepare the ritual spread with the proper ceremony. Instead, they called out for a delivery meal of *tonkatsu* deep-fried pork fillet, trimmed with miso soup and pickles, with a plate of raw tuna belly slices for starters. The maid brought them warmed sake, which they chased with chilled Kirin beer. 'Get this.' She paraphrased the violent, vivid article. '"Haneda air-crash. Is there a murder connection? A spokesman for Tokyo Metropolitan Police told journalists at a press conference today, Wednesday, twenty second of May, that, following information from an anonymous source, a Caucasian male was seen at the house in Toritsu Daigaku where the body of Makiko Nakamura, forty years of age, was found. The operator of a high-class snack in Akasaka, Nakamura *san* was brutally strangled sometime late Monday night or early Tuesday but her body was not discovered until later that evening following a request from the American tenant, calling from an unknown location, to the head priest of a nearby temple to inspect the premises. Was Nakamura *san* raped? We will give our readers a full account of the autopsy as soon as the results are made public."'

Phyllis knocked back a thimble of rice wine and let Alex refill it. 'Brace yourself, *gaijin san*,' she said with a deep sigh. 'We star in the next bit.' She cleared her throat. '"Sensational scoop! The murdered woman was the mistress of the pilot who died when the DC-8-71 aeroplane belonging to NN Air, a subsidiary company of the Nippon Nagasaki commercial and industrial group, plunged to the ground at Tokyo International Airport, Haneda, during a period of severe air turbulence. The *gaijin* male seen at the scene of the murder is believed to be the investigator from London representing the insurers of the ill-fated airplane. His name is Alexander Bolton and he has disappeared, perhaps to the

Republic of Korea. The whereabouts of the tenant of the murder house, an American *sansei*, Phyllis Wakai from California, is also unknown, although she is believed to have spent Tuesday at a hotel on the Yaesu side of Tokyo Station.'"

She sniffed angrily and carried on. "'What was the relationship between these four people? Two of them died within seven days of each other. The British man Bolton is reported to have told a waitress in a Roppongi bar in the early hours of Tuesday morning that he intended to go to the house in the temple compound where the murder was committed. It is vital this man be found. Police and immigration officials are checking departure declarations but have so far not found evidence that he left Japan for Korea.'" She tossed the newspaper away. 'Heard enough?'

He needed the food but the taste was bland, even with the treacle-thick sauce and the strong mustard. He let a glob of rice slip from his chopsticks. 'I've got to hand it to the police here. It didn't take them long to find out I told Sharon at the Tulip I might go over to your place. I was drunk. I was talking nonsense.' He managed a chunk of pork trapped in a wedge of chopped cabbage.

'Don't give them too much credit,' Phyllis said bitterly, her elbows on the table. 'They have a lot of help. Miyamoto wants us out of the way. If we hadn't shaken off his hired goons at the *pachinko* parlour we'd be in detention right now.' There was a shout somewhere in the lanes around the shrine. It pierced the wooden walls and made them turn instinctively towards the expanse of window which had been drawn aside to expose the insect meshing. She added, 'We can't hurt Miyamoto if we're fighting the Japanese police system for our lives.'

'Or if we're dead,' Alex heard himself say. 'Look, Phyl, let's get some sleep and try to get out of here at dawn. We know where we're going.'

She gave him a tired smile and rose on stiff legs. 'Best suggestion yet. Would you please try Bill again? If he's cracked the diaries we ought to know what he's found before we drop in on the Miyamotos and your dubious doctor.'

While Phyllis bathed leisurely in the deep Japanese *ofuro*, Alex watched the two maids in plain purple kimonos clear the table, move it to a corner and then lay out the futons they unfolded from the sliding-door cupboards. They turned as one at the door and bowed. '*Oyasumi-nasai*,' they chorused. 'Goodnight,' he guessed, settling in the corner with his telephone and diary pages.

'Your turn,' Phyllis called. She emerged from the bathroom wrapped in a blue-and-white-patterned *yukata*, her skin glistening, her rich hair flying as she rubbed her head vigorously with a towel. 'I'll show you what to do. There's nothing like a Japanese bath to revive the spirits. Not to mention the body.'

The room was steamy. The deep sunken bath refilled, overflowing onto the tiles. 'Did you get through to Bill?' she asked earnestly, directing him to put his clothes in the plastic crate in a narrow antechamber.

'It's strange. The line's dead. Not even engaged.'

'Why has he unplugged the goddamn thing?'

Alex dropped his socks into the basket. 'He said he had a visitor. Maybe he didn't want to be disturbed.'

Phyllis hung the towel and raked her fingernails over her scalp. When she turned to him she was distant, absorbed. Finally she said, remembering, 'He didn't say he had a visitor. He said there was someone in the house. Not the same thing.'

Alex slipped off his shirt, sniffed at it from a distance and tossed it into the basket. He drew a bright smile of relief from Phyllis. 'Not exactly a California tan, *gaijin san*, but not bad muscle definition. Did you get anything from the last part of the diaries?'

He shrugged. 'I'll have another look when my head's clearer. It's incredibly dramatic stuff but I can't see what made Bill think he's solved the bloody puzzle. Eh? What do I do now?'

She had slid the bathroom door open. 'I'm going to try Bill again. He's got to be there.' Turning from the doorway she gave him a big grin. 'Get your pants off and get to work. You've got soap, a little stool and a ladle. Scoop water from the tub, wash yourself and rinse off. Then get in and soak for as long as you like. Leave the water. I might go in again later.'

He found her in the futon, one arm extended across the floor, her fingers still touching the short antenna on the cellular telephone. Strands of damp hair strayed across her sharp, beautiful profile. The strip lighting in the room and the lamp inside a *toro* garden lantern had been extinguished and in the dull natural radiance he grimaced, remembering another Asian body in another mattress bed. Tying the belt loosely around the *yukata* that matched hers in pattern and size he approached her tentatively. His feet were still damp and left an outline on the interwoven matting. She stirred when he dropped to a knee and lifted a trail of hair from her eyes. Relieved, he locked the door to the room and drew a screen across the window-doorway to the garden. A muted honk from a car and a distant rumble from a late train reminded him he was in the heart of a city. Seeing the sleeve of Phyllis's *yukata* he realised the cotton gowns were also for sleeping in. Slipping carefully under the bedding, he discovered there were actually two of the single, spongy futon mattresses and they had been laid out together, the quilted covers overlapping, giving the impression of one. He stared at the ceiling, hands clasped behind his head, the chaos of a week tumbling through his tired mind. In crude terms it had looked like a routine aviation disaster with a better than average chance of a quick, positive assessment,

270

helped as it was by an accessible site, a manageable spread of wreckage, retrieved cockpit and data recorders and a thoroughly reliable local investigatory organisation. And what seemed to him to be insatiably inquisitive media generated a provocative and stimulating output of fact and speculation. The coverlet alongside rippled, releasing a soft fragrance of jasmine and warm body. He looked over at her. He couldn't blame her for the situation they were in: if it hadn't been for Phyllis Wakai he wouldn't have reached the truth about the crude attempt to cover up Ed Kidderby's dire health condition. He turned on his side, his back to her. But she was totally to blame for the warm tingle of his skin and the swelling ache between his legs. He should have been home by now, case over, his report with the lawyers and the underwriters, then perhaps a reflex shot at a reconciliation with Cathy. But he was lying on the straw floor of an old wooden shack wearing a bloody kimono. He was also suspected of a murder, wanted both by the uncompromising police and the tattooed morons from the Japanese underworld who seem to march to the orders of Japanese business tycoons. That wasn't all: at the end of the road, if he made it, he would walk into a right rollocking from Reggie Cameron for deserting the case of NINA 328 and displaying a serious lack of professionalism, perhaps drawing an official reprimand, possibly something more negatively conclusive. He was a player in a game whose rules eluded him, the prey in a deadly hunt. And he was lying next to the most beautiful woman in Nagasaki and he sported a massive hard-on. He forced a silent, ironic sniff and it echoed round his head. He shifted again, intoxicated by her sweet, perfumed aura. He thought of the diaries and it eased him. He was about to abandon a pointless attempt to sleep and get them when—

'Can't you sleep either?' she said thickly. Her bedding susurrated in the darkness.

'Let's try to rest,' he tried.

She shuffled quietly through the covers under the soft down of his futon and moulded her body against his back, an arm over his waist, slipping beneath the single knot of his *yukata*'s waistband. 'We should've done this before, *gaijin san*.'

He rolled over. 'I was getting to like the creature in the red hat when she evaporated.' He felt a playful thump. 'I seem to remember the new model falling asleep on me.' Another jab, then her fingers were under his crumpled gown, raking through the sheen of hair on his chest, moving down between his legs, cupping him, smoothing his shape. He used two hands to loosen the knot on hers, then take her supple breasts and their stiffening tips.

'How long have you been like this?' she breathed.

He nibbled her lips and an earlobe. 'An hour, maybe two,' he mumbled. 'Must have been the hot water. You?'

Her hands were damp against his thighs. 'Hour, maybe ten.' Her voice was a throaty groan and she was still gripping him when she moved a long leg over his waist. 'Just unscare me for a while please, Alex.'

14 May 1945
Two air-raid warnings, all men in Camp to shelters. Issue of Red Cross cigs (3 pkts) and 1 pkt fruit per man except rooms 15, 19 & 20, the men in them getting only 2 pkts of cigs.

27 May
Holiday from Yard. Issued with a small orange. Last week got ¹/₃ tin of Red Cross meat. Held big air-raid exercise yesterday and fire drill. We were warned about saluting better and to be more careful in the dockyard. Japs say accidents are our own fault. Two men received electric burns on Wednesday. One died.

12 June
2 men in cells with no food for having materials for lighters. It was a bad two weeks for deaths but we got 3 more pkts of Jap cigs and some fruit. A man returned to camp on Tuesday after two years in prison for hitting Jap. Yesterday, 859 men leave for camps 9, 21, 26 & 27.

19 June
Issue of soap

3 July

Air-raid warning at dawn. We have two a day and don't go to the shelters now unless aircraft are overhead. Issue of Red Cross chocolate and sweet milk drink.

19 July

Most of us have been ill. Doctor thinks it's from the mosquitoes or the lice. Murphy and Johnson are the worst. I managed to steal some more paper from the empty school on the way to the yard. All the children seem to be out working.

26 July

73 men admitted smoking in dockyard shelter and were punished by Cyclops by being kept in the prone position for ½ hour, enforced by guards with bats. Whole camp forbidden to smoke for two days.

29 July

The guards are very nervous. I got slapped by Napoleon for some reason or another. Spent 25 minutes in the shelters. Swarms of planes went over the town yesterday.

31 July

In shelters today for three hours.

2 August

No soup for breakfast from now on. Cannot get anything to make it with. A Dutchman died in the cells.

6 August

Dockyard workers searched on return to camp. 3 men found with contraband and were made to stand holding the gear in front of them for 1½ hours and then placed in cells without food.

7 August

In air-raid shelters for two hours, like yesterday. Rumours from the guards about a death ray used on Japan.

Wednesday, 9 August
(Evidence presented by me and taken from my diaries)
I was duty officer P.O.W., Non-Commissioned Officer
in Camp Nagasaki Six on the island of Yanagi in the
approaches to the harbour of Nagasaki on the southern
island of Kyushu, Japan.
0700 hrs Dockyard working parties were assembled
and marched to dockyard. Sick men who remained in
camp were detailed for work cleaning camp and
gardening.
1000 hrs Air-raid warning Red. At that time I was in
an air-raid shelter and as I was leaving the shelter I
was facing towards Nagasaki. I saw a flash of intense
brilliance which seemed to blot out the sun. After
which there was complete silence for 10 to 15 seconds.
As the brilliance faded a ripple of warm air struck my
face and upper parts of my body. This increased in
heat and velocity, accumulating in an ear-shattering
roar of a very heavy explosion which shook the camp,
causing window frames and glass to fall. Still looking
towards Nagasaki, I saw a huge ball of orange and
purple smoke which continued to change colour as it
rose into the air. This was followed by three columns of
heavy black smoke which formed a large cloud over
Nagasaki. My impression was that the ammunition
works at Nagasaki had received a direct hit. Damage
to the camp – 15 window frames complete, 134 panes
of glass, two large pinewood doors and the end of the
single-storey building cracked and broken, and the
ceiling of the Sick Bay was sagging and broken.
1300 hrs One man was sent back from the dockyard
with injuries and from him we learned that four others
had been injured by flying debris.
1700 hrs Dockyard parties returned to camp. From
them we learned that half of the town of Nagasaki was

still burning, but nobody could tell us what had caused the explosion. Three steam ferries have capsized off-shore.

10 August
Nagasaki still burning. Supplied 40 kilos of rice to Camp 14 in the town, which was badly damaged by yesterday's explosion. Dockyard working parties sent to yard as usual. PM. Air-raid warning Red: stayed in shelters for three hours. Heard from one of the guards that the bomb yesterday was a new kind of bomb.

11 August
Dockyard workers sent out at 0700 hrs. Sent more rice to Camp 14. A lot of men killed there we hear and we have some missing from here. The Navy guards in the yard beat up eleven men for nothing, an Able Seamen and the civilian from our room were among them. Seven have bad scalp wounds.

12 August
Joined a dockyard gang but there was not much work to do. Everyone else stayed to clean camp; also practise going to shelters. A party sent to Nagasaki to clean up. Johnson has not recovered from injuries but was forced to go.

13 August
No dockyard work today. Japs told us to keep cleaning the camp. Had a long talk with one of the guards. He told me the war was over and the bomb dropped on Nagasaki was an Atomic bomb. As the camp was still under the control of the Japs I decided not to spread the news around in case it was not true.

14 August
I wonder if yesterday's news is true. Japs are very quiet. No dockyard work today but another party sent to Nagasaki to help with the clean-up and I joined them. The civilian must have been transferred to

*another camp with the others because I have not seen
him since Saturday.*

She had slept well but lightly and the muffled metallic click
of a car door closing had the resonance of a gunshot in the
stillness and made her rise on her elbows. Alex had gone, but
her eyes were misty with sleep and she had to roll over and
pat the crumpled covers to make sure. Then he appeared like
a spectre from the bathroom, the prison-camp chronicles
rolled in his grip. He was dressed, the Jonsson letter
disappearing into his jacket pocket after a final check.

'Get your clothes on quick,' he commanded. 'I think
they've found us again.'

She staggered upright, rubbing her eyes. 'What time is it?'

He was filling a travel bag. 'Half-four. I heard car doors.'

'So did I, but— '

'We've come this far. We might as well try and finish it.
Let's not take any chances.' He skimmed a pair of ten
thousand yen notes from his wallet and dropped them onto
the table. 'I also know what Bill came up with in the diaries
and I think I know why Miyamoto probably wished he
hadn't.'

She had pulled on her jeans and was buttoning her blouse.
Hoarse with sleep she said, 'You scared me. Your empty
futon.' Alex went to the doorway of the room and returned
with their shoes. He pulled aside the sliding windows to the
garden. 'I couldn't sleep any more so I sat on the lavatory
seat for an hour with the diaries.'

Phyllis dashed to the bathroom and splashed water onto
her face.

'We'll go out the back, over the wall,' he announced,
holding his voice to a whisper and tugging on a shoe as he
hopped after her. 'Come on, Phyl. Leave the stuff in the
bathroom where it is.'

They both stopped at the sound of deadened, remote

277

rapping on wood. 'It's the main door,' Alex breathed, handing her down onto the gravel from the plank-like veranda skirting the garden on three sides of the inn. The stones crunched and scattered under their feet, their footprints clear and deep where they had trodden and flattened the meticulously raked furrows. A light came on somewhere and thinned the darkness. The trimmed trees and manicured bushes, silhouetted by a pale, pitted half-moon, and an old, thick-stemmed web of wistaria rising against the side of the inn gave them a modest degree of cover while they contemplated a head-high tile-topped earthern wall. Backed against it was an artificial cliff of dark grey volcanic rocks made slippery by the night mist. It offered them a tricky natural springboard. Alex took a short, carefully measured run and sprang upwards, his hands reaching for the tiles on the top of the wall. One of them cracked and gave way as he levered himself over to straddle it and he felt the sting as a shard pierced the skin on the heel of his left hand. He dropped the bag into the cobbled lane beyond the wall and then reached for Phyllis, drawing her up onto the wall to face him. They managed a desperate, shared smile when she took a second to catch her breath.

'Ready?'

She blinked the swiftest of nods and then leaned into his lap before twisting over the wall, letting him ease her down the other side. He followed, landing heavily on bent knees. They heard a puzzled, questioning male voice, breaking the silence from inside the *ryokan*. The wound on his hand stung and it was oozing blood, which was spotting his jacket and trousers. The alley ended where a huge camphor tree and two tall stone lanterns signalled the entrance to the Sanno shrine, forcing them the other way, towards a crossroads splitting the houses on the slope. They slunk along the gutter until ahead, where the road curved upwards, Alex saw light dancing off a wall, as if someone was approaching in a hurry, still out of sight, a flashlight jerking in a hand. He stopped her with an arm and pointed.

'Shit,' Phyllis cursed under her breath. They were standing on a flat bridge which crossed a culvert. Like a winding water chute it guided a shallow mountain stream over a stony bed between the thin concrete slab walls of the packed terraced houses and under the roads to spill into the Urakami River beyond the mainline railway tracks. A thin pipe had been fixed to the wall of the gully and it followed the watercourse like a handrail. A shout, an order, echoed in the stillness. They exchanged a glance. 'Let's go for it,' Phyllis grimaced.

They climbed over the low railing and lowered themselves into the culvert, their heads now below street level. Alex dug out a handkerchief and Phyllis tied it around his left hand. The cut was deeper than he'd thought and blood seeped quickly through the fabric. The water was clear and icy and they flinched when it flooded their shoes. The passage was wide enough for them to stretch their arms and touch the sides but they descended in near-total darkness with a firm grip on the pipe, slipping and sliding on the moss and worn, smooth stones. Apart from the sound of splashing water and a dog whining somewhere in the night there were no other noises. The bed of the drainage channel levelled and deepened before it flowed under another narrow lane. Walls crowded it and there was no way to clamber up onto the concrete slab bridge without going back. 'After you,' Alex said humourlessly, a hand directed at the black gap under the road. Breath held, they monkey-crawled through the short tunnel, unseeing, water soaking to their knees, Alex's head grazing the rough underside of the bridge. They exchanged a quick smile of relief when they emerged, Phyllis swiping at a glob of mud that stuck to her face like a leech, before slip-sliding again down their escape flume. When they reached the next claustrophobic tunnel the watercourse had levelled to little more than a gentle slope and this time they were able to reach the metal guardrails over the gulley and pull themselves onto the road. Dawn was opening up, thinning to a pale purple light, and it was exposing their natural cover. Stooping, they crossed the road, wider than the traffic-free lanes on the hillside and lined with shuttered shops. Phyllis whispered that they were on a level with the foot of the steps leading to the one-legged *torii* gate next to the inn. At the corner with another lane Alex drew Phyllis under the angled awning of a convenience store. Fifty yards away, scarlet and white lights bounced and flashed like strips of neon off the network of cables criss-crossing the street. He leaned out but saw they were reflections from somewhere he could not see, probably the short driveway leading to the shrine steps.

'Police car,' he muttered, breathing rapidly. He took Phyllis's hand and they skipped along the short lane, so narrow the balconies of the shops and restaurants lining both sides almost touched. They passed a small leafy park surrounded by parked motorcycles, approaching stealthily the broad, main city avenue, divided by twin tramlines and running from the railway station along the Urakami Valley. Nagasaki was as quiet as it would ever be: the last revellers had staggered from the Shianbashi entertainment quarter hours earlier and it would be another before the first trams trundled from their sheds. Heavy-duty street lighting flooded the empty roads uselessly and the beacon on the peak of Mount Inasa blinked through the thin mist.

'The police must have the inn sealed off,' Alex guessed as they closed on the corner. 'And we're not far enough away.' He paused and turned to her. 'How do we get to Yanagi?' He eyed a pair of bicycles tethered to the pillar of a porch.

'Let's put some space behind us and then think about,' Phyllis said, crouched, overtaking him, almost at the corner. She tripped past a stand-sign and a rubbish bin and then suddenly checked herself, blocking his body with a sharp swerve. No vehicles had crossed the mouth of the lane since they had been there and the main road was a no-stop-or-park zone. But twenty yards from their corner she had seen the boot of a burgundy red Mercedes E320 parked a few feet behind the same model in black. The inevitable black-tinted windows announced it as the *yakuza*'s favourite vehicle. The lights were on and the driver's door was opened across the pavement, and she could hear the low purr of the engine in the easy stillness. Both cars had crossed the carriageway and parked in contra direction outside a furniture showroom. A lamppost rose like a giant arm and its broad spread of light trapped the figure of a man, bringing his heavy profile to life. He was alone, propped against the dark red Merc, a cigarette in one hand, a telephone in the other, its spiral cord stretching from the car. 'The guy from the train,' Phyllis uttered. 'We gave him the slip in the *pachinko* parlour.'

'What the hell is *he* doing here?' Alex hissed from behind. 'Now we've got the police on one side and the bloody mafia on the other.'

'No idea, *gaijin san,* but I think we're screwed.'

Behind them, where the buildings and houses rose in packed, neat terraces, the first lights from curious locals flecked the fading darkness. Alex ventured a look over Phyllis's shoulder. The *yakuza* had tossed the telephone into the car and was trotting on heavy legs away from it, towards the narrow road that led straight to the steps and to the Sanno inn where the Nagasaki prefectural police were conducting a frustrated investigation into the escape of the two *gaijin* wanted for questioning by their colleagues in the capital. No way was he going to miss the action. He had left the door of his car open, lights on, engine running. Phyllis embraced the steel coating of a telegraph pole and peered again into the main road. Her shoulders sank with relief, while her mind raged against fear and tension as she thrashed for a solution. There were no buses, trams or taxis at ten past five, even on

281

Nagasaki's main drag. If getting arrested wasn't on their agenda, the only alternative was to risk running to the left, towards the station, hugging the contours of the buildings and moving into the quiet, narrow dips and rises of the city as soon as they could. 'Follow me,' she commanded.

Alex felt a tug on his sleeve but he resisted it. He shivered. Part of his body was clammy from exertion while the heavy, soaked trousers and socks numbed his legs and feet. He had stemmed the bleeding in his hand for the moment. His mouth was dry, and he hoped he didn't transmit his fear to Phyllis when he spoke. 'We may as well go in for a pound,' he said, pinching the flesh on her arm as he drew her the other way, towards the two cars. She guessed what he had in mind and her arm locked straight in protest.

'We won't get half a mile without transport,' he insisted. 'Let alone to Miyamoto's base.'

She hesitated for a second before giving him a glazed 'what the fuck' look and together they broke into a stooping run, brushing the walls of a bank and a real-estate office between the corner of the lane and the nearer Mercedes outside the furniture shop. The steering wheel had been adapted for Japan's left-lane driving while its twin in front retained the fashionable left-side Continental format. The engine on the burgundy Merc was still running, the driver's door invitingly open. 'Or in for a yen,' Alex muttered. Pressed in a recess, opposite the open door, they waited for the inevitable shout from nasty tempered *yakuza* or the scream of a police siren, even gunfire. They were múrder suspects, for chrissake. The thought stupidly invaded his mind and for a moment he hesitated. Then, in a firm, controlled voice. 'Get over to the other side and hang on.'

She measured her stride perfectly, grasping the rim above the driver's door and vaulting across the front seats, escaping with a thump to the temple which cracked the frame of her glasses and a knee bruised on the passenger-side window.

282

Alex followed, tossing the bag into the back before he landed heavily in the driver's seat. He had the automatic gear in drive before she was upright and had spun the power-steered wheel into a one-eighty-degree turn. The rim of the open door caught the rear lights of the black Mercedes, smashing its single casing, before the car's momentum forced it shut. The catch of tyre on the tarmac sounded to him like the ultimate scream, the surge of power from the finely tuned engine an echoing roar. A hundred yards, he told himself, teeth gritted, an eye flashing to the rear-view mirror. Give me a free hundred yards. If he could get round the long curve in the road, past the flags and banners outside a garage, before they saw their car was missing, the *yakuza* would have to waste time deciding which way it had gone.

Phyllis straightened her jacket, strangely quiet for a moment. Holding the car level with his bloodied hand, Alex stabbed fingers under his shirt collar at the back, mashing the rim of sweat chilling his skin.

'Slow down,' she erupted. Two police cars, warning lights flaring, sirens stilled, skimmed towards them and quickly disappeared round the curve.

Alex braked, skidding on a tramline, and glanced at the view in the mirror, for the headlights and flashing colours of a suspicious police car or a pissed-off *yakuza* who wanted his car back. When they had cleared the bend and the road in the mirror was clear he shifted in the seat and breathed out noisily.

Phyllis snorted. 'Just add car theft to the list. What's one more felony?' She dragged the seat belt across her body. 'At least we're actually guilty of this one.'

'Can you steal from the *yakuza*?' he asked, not really wanting a reply. They passed Nagasaki Station where Phyllis indicated an illuminated sign. Painted in blue and white for principal roads, it was written in Japanese and roman script. 'Yanagi straight on,' she read. 'On the four nine nine.'

Alex forced a smile. 'Nobody can see through these,' he said, tapping the smoky door window.

Phyllis sniffed. 'That's the good news. The bad news is only the *yakuza* drive with blacked-out windows. Don't have to hang a sign on the car for the cops to track us down. All they need to know from their gangland friends is we're in a red Merc.'

'It didn't take the police long to find us at the hotel, Phyl.' Alex was calmer now. They had passed Dejima, where a desultory taxi prowled optimistically for early business and a pair of cyclists enjoyed the early freedom of the road. The Urakami River had broadened into the harbour when they drove below the slopes of the Glover gardens, where a few hours earlier they had contemplated the tip of Yanagi through binoculars.

'Or the *yakuza*.' She was suddenly thinking of Bill Littleton.

Alex said, 'Do you think the inn people called the police?'

'No,' she said quietly, definitively. 'We're friends of a long-time trusted guest. And we've only really been an item in the news from yesterday, since the police figured we were together. Like I said before, Miyamoto's hired thugs are making sure the police get to us and somehow they found out where we were staying. They even came to watch them take us.'

'So what brought them to the inn so soon?' Alex asked, puzzled.

She lifted the car telephone handset. 'I'm getting kind of worried about Bill.'

'Don't use that,' he told her. 'They'll trace the calls back to the car. Mine's in the bag.'

Solid items clumped together when she lifted the zip-up holdall to the front.

He said, 'I left the spare shirt, underpants and stuff at the

284

inn.'

'I didn't get anything out either.' Her hand came out with the binoculars. 'I've got these, your Nikon, your little recorder, notebook. No telephone.'

'Shit. It was on the floor, probably under the futon.'

'I've got to risk it, Alex,' she said, folding a hand over the telephone handset between the seats. 'Something's wrong. Only Bill knew where I planned to stay in Nagasaki.'

'He won't like being woken at this time in the morning,' Alex chided, hiding his own unease. 'But go ahead please.'

'I won't mind him getting mad at me at the moment,' she said stabbing the buttons. 'I've got to know.' It was light enough for her to read the map, unfolded on her lap, without the interior lamp. They were approaching a fork in the road. The factories and tenements had given way to wooded hillsides, dotted with houses and remote hotels. 'I'd be happier if you took the two three seven,' she said, still listening hopelessly to the dead telephone line. 'Better if we stay off the main road.' He slowed the unfamiliar car and drifted leftwards. 'We hit the coast road again in a couple of miles or so.' Finally she hung up the telephone and sank back into the seat, turning her head away from him. Overpowered and preposterously grand for the narrow, twisting road marked on the map as a class-one route, the deep-red Mercedes was wider than the lane Alex was working hard to stay in. A short tunnel surprised him, and then a sharp turn forced him to hit the brakes, jolting them forward in the belt restraints. When a straight stretch through a village gave him a breather he caught the back of Phyllis's head with a quickly taken glance. He thought she was asleep; but he looked again and the sagged, jabbing head told him she was sobbing. He shifted a bloodied hand tentatively from the wheel and touched her shoulder.

National Highway 237 twisted between thickly wooded peaks sheltering hamlets and sprawling villages. Alex turned off the car's lights and slowed for a narrow stone bridge over a shallow ravine. 'Go right,' Phyllis sniffed. 'Let's take a break.'

He stabbed the brake harshly, seeing ahead a turn-off half hidden by the overhang from the larch and maple trees encroaching to the roadside. Turning into the lane he pulled over after a bend took them out of view of the road they had left. Taking the notebook from the bag he flipped the pages.

The rims of Phyllis's eyes were raw. A slender mauve swelling had formed above her right eye. 'What are you doing?'

'I'm calling Richard Ingleby,' he said, a hand poised over the telephone. 'Our director in Japan. He called me on the bullet train. Remember?' It rang as he was reaching to lift it, as if the caller had been waiting for the moment. They both recoiled, staring at it blankly. Alex glanced at his watch as the buzz droned monotonously. 'It's taken them about seventeen minutes to work out their car's been stolen.'

How could the Fukuoka *yakuza* possibly not reward themselves with a front-row view of the show of police force they had orchestrated? They could have done the job themselves, as soon as word came from the Yokohama boys that the old *gaijin* in Hayama had helpfully suggested his young *sansei* friend might take lodgings at the Sanno inn, in Hamaguchi-cho, central Nagasaki, but their orders were absolutely clear: leave the two foreigners to the police; but make sure they are apprehended by assisting them, like any good citizen, with a call to say that you believed the suspects in the Tokyo Nakamura murder case were hiding in a Nagasaki *ryokan*. The drowsy night shift at local police headquarters opposite City Hall called for help and waited for a squad from the prefectural detective force. It cost them thirty minutes and lost them the suspects. Kamei and his young driver had waited patiently, watching from the dark corners on urban road two zero six while Hinohara was in and out of his red Merc, begging to lead a strike and take the foreigners for the police. After all, the syndicate was only repaying in a small way the favours bestowed on the *yakuza's* Nagasaki chapter by their cooperative, blind-eyed uniformed friends in the prefectural police force. Hinohara had been standing on the pavement, telephone in hand, in touch with a friend who was tuned to a police frequency. He could almost hear the crackle of radios from the patrol cars banked against the steps leading to the One-Legged Shrine and the confused grunts from the officers at the scene. But he had to see the bit where they led the two frigging *gaijin* out of the *ryokan*, handcuffed and horribly pissed off. He tossed his phone into the car and hauled himself through the approach streets, joining Kamei and his junior from the black Mercedes to watch the drama as they sipped coffee from a bright vending machine trapped in an alley beside a shuttered liquor shop. The police finally emerged from the inn, at the head of the steps, muttering into radios and scuttling around like chickens without heads. They had no prisoners; Kamei cursed them and led his band back in frustration to the place where they had left two hundred thousand dollars' worth of customized German cars. The space behind the black car held them in wonderment. They walked around it, looking for the hole that had taken the burgundy Merc. A footsoldier in a black suit and slick-backed hair squatted by the black car's bumper and ran his hand tenderly over the jagged edges of the broken light casing.

Phyllis sprang the boot from inside and left the car when the weak buzzing of the carphone finally stopped. She leaned against the car, removed her Nike shoes and dried her feet on the border of coarse grass. She hadn't had time to leave with her socks. Alex twisted water out of the hems of his trousers from the driver's seat before raising the telephone gingerly and pressing the buttons. It took Ingleby a minute to get to the telephone and swallow the thickness out of his voice. 'Alex? Is that you? What time do you think this is? I know you chaps like to get on with it but half past five's a bit bloody extreme.'

'Sorry Richard, I— '

'At least you've called in. You really are in deep shit, old son. I was trying to get you all evening.'

'I switched the mobile off. I didn't need incoming calls.'

'But the murder . . .' Ingleby pleaded.

'Shut up,' Alex snapped. 'I need you to do something for me.'

'The only thing I can do for you is get you back to Tokyo to talk to the bloody Japanese detective who decided to camp in our building all yesterday afternoon. I expect he'll be there when I get in this morning.' His voice was coarse but his brain was beginning to engage. 'Oh, and news of the murder of that bar-girl has reached London, right into British Underwriters International to be precise. As you haven't had the courtesy to get in touch with him I am hereby transmitting Reggie's demand for your immediate return. Unless you give yourself— '

'Shut the fuck up, will you Richard? Do this for me now and you might prevent another murder.' The line went quiet. 'Got a pen?'

'This is ridiculous,' Ingleby was muttering. 'Go ahead but I shouldn't— '

'Wake your secretary, or your Japanese manager, and get one of them to call the local police in Hayama. That's — '

'You don't have to spell it,' the other man broke in. 'I've been there.'

Alex read and repeated Bill Littleton's address and gave him the number of the dead line, demanding a call to the telephone exchange to have it checked. Then the police. 'You can tell them you've heard from me and Miss Wakai although you don't know where we are. That ought to get their attention. In case you and the police haven't worked it out yet, I'm with the American woman who rents the house where Ed Kidderby's girlfriend was killed.'

'That was the speculation on the news last night,' Ingleby said gravely. 'I guessed you weren't alone when I talked to you on the phone yesterday. By the way, where are you?'

Phyllis slipped back beside Alex and seeing he was still occupied began examining the contents of the pockets and crevices in the car and pressing buttons on the monitor of the car navigation system, which broke the sleek line of the dashboard. 'You'll know in a second. First tell the police that Mr Littleton's a very old man and he may have had a serious accident. Could even be dead. I want a car sent over to his house now.'

It wasn't too early for a touch of sarcasm from the man in Tokyo. 'Is that all?'

'No, it isn't,' Alex shot back. 'When I finally sit down under the swinging light I want to talk to them about another murder.'

'You mean the pilot's girlfriend, Naka something or other.'

'No. I'm talking about a murder a long time ago. Like fifty years ago.'

Phyllis had snapped open the leather-covered-padded, glove compartment and was rummaging inside it but her head suddenly whipped sideways, her eyes widening, questioning words forming silently.

'Am I dreaming this, Alex?' Ingleby stuttered. 'I'm hearing riddles. What are you talking about? A murder half a century ago. I'm not hearing you very well. The line's cracking up or something. What's this got to do with the NN Air crash?'

The drone of a powerful engine rose to a dull thudding clatter not far away above the car. Phyllis lowered the window and caught the belly of a helicopter, its rotor blades flashing through a patchy break in the thick canopy of leaves shielding them. She leaned back towards Alex who was cradling the handset. 'The crash was the catalyst. It's opened a bag of old ghosts.'

'You're not making sense,' Ingleby said. It was obviously far too early for rational thinking.

'And I don't have time to enlighten you. Just listen and do exactly as I say. Got it?'

'Yes, sir,' Ingleby mocked.

'The crash was just symptomatic of the airline's negligence and Nippon Nagasaki's general mismanagement. Phyl Wakai's writing a book about it. We're not talking just money, Richard, but from what I'm picking up now Miyamoto's empire's barely solvent. No, it's all about control and ownership and keeping the truth well and truly buried. You remember the old document with our company's name on it?'

'Yes. You were going to give it to the president of NNC for his scrapbook.'

The lined blipped. 'I didn't. The old Japan hand in Hayama, the chap Bill we're worried about. He reckons it's a valid recognition of ownership. It transfers thirty per cent of the original entity, Jonsson Nagasaki, to Shinichi Miyamoto, the current president's father, and changes the name to Nippon Nagasaki as required by the military government of the time.'

'And?'

'The Miyamotos are not the legal main shareholders of what's Nippon Nagasaki Corporation today. Unless there was another deal selling the rest of the company to them, NNC still belongs to Roland Jonsson or his heirs.'

'Shit! That won't please the Miyamotos,' Ingleby said sardonically. 'You mentioned another murder.'

Phyllis tapped her watch where Alex could see. He raised a placatory hand.

'NNC started out as Jonsson Nagasaki in the thirties.'

Ingleby interrupted. '"Yonson?"'

'For fuck's sake, Richard, just listen. It's spelled with a J but I think it's pronounced like a Y in Swedish. Jonsson sells thirty per cent of the company to Shinichi Miyamoto, Hiroshi's father, according to the new nationalisation laws. Then Jonsson, although he's the citizen of a neutral country, ends up in a military prisoner-of-war camp in Nagasaki, in the same room as an English sailor who refers to him simply as Johnson and records their life, if that's what you can call it, in a diary.' He looked at Phyllis and held her eyes as he spoke. 'The Miyamotos claim the Swede Jonsson was merely an engineer with the company and he died as an ordinary foreign citizen in the atomic bombing on August ninth, 1945. He didn't. I think he was murdered in the camp they called Nagasaki Six.'

Phyllis reached for his arm. 'What?' she mouthed.

'It sounds preposterous, Alex,' Ingleby was saying.

'So why did somebody at NNC go through my papers and copy the old diaries?'

Ingleby juggled with the question. 'God knows, but look, Alex, I really do think you should come back here and sort things out.'

Alex was imagining the scent of fresh coffee: his injured hand throbbed and he could smell the sour clamminess on his body.

'Not till I find out whether the doctor whose name's on Ed Kidderby's medical certificate is for real or not. I'm not going to sign off on the DC-8 crash until I've cleared it up, even if it does add to Miyamoto's other problems. By great coincidence the hospital happens to be near Miyamoto's private retreat and the old POW camp.'

'Is that where you are?' Ingleby asked. 'In Nagasaki?'

'Right.' He sniffed into the handset. 'We're in a car I stole from the *yakuza* who are working for Miyamoto and are trying to get us arrested and put out of the way.'

'Hang on, Alex, the line's breaking up. I thought you said *yakuza*.'

'That's it, pal. And here's what you've got to do.' Alex thumped the dashboard with his good hand and spoke flatly. 'In five hours, at exactly ten thirty, I want you to call the police. Use your Japanese director, or Yoshi Kanagawa, or anybody. Tell them you've heard from the Nakamura murder suspects again. They are visiting the estate of Hiroshi Miyamoto in Yanagi-cho, a few miles south of Nagasaki city centre. By the time they get here I should have all I need on the guy who passed Ed Kidderby fit to fly and they can have me. I might even be able point them towards the *real* killer of Makiko Nakamura.'

'By the way, that Yoshi chap was trying to get you last night,' Ingleby declared. 'One of many.'

'Know what about?' Alex asked eagerly.

'He just said an Amercan — can't remember his name — wants to talk to you.'

'Was he from the Federal Aviation Administration?'

'Yes, I think that's what he said. Needs to talk to you urgently.'

Alex made a triumphant fist. 'Great! Get a message to him through Yoshi. Tell him I'll have some key information by tonight and be sure to be available to talk.'

'Yes but — '

Alex clamped the handset into its nest and twisted the ignition key in one move. The car vibrated into life.

'How do you know Jonsson was murdered?' Phyllis uttered, her head and shoulders shaking.

Leaving their cover reluctantly, they joined Highway 237 again, the road that twisted between upland gullies carved from the hillsides as it approached the coastal highway. The traffic was fairly light but growing. Alex tugged the shade down against the dawn sun that had burned through the thin mist on the unseen sea. 'It's what Bill said to you yesterday, before his line went dead. About the diaries. Wasn't he trying to explain why they ended up stuck to the old Jonsson letter?'

'Yeah. And have you figured it out as well?'

He pressed a scanner on the radio. 'I woke up about two or so. Wide awake. You were dead to the world so I took the diaries to the bathroom and went over the last few pages. You know, where Bill said he'd found something.'

'Did *you* find it?' Phyllis pressed, disbelief rising in her voice.

'Take a look yourself. They're in the bag, I hope.' His scalp suddenly bristled from a surge of anxiety. The diaries had been clipped to Ed Kidderby's dubious medical certificate and he couldn't remember whether he was carrying the package when he dashed from the bathroom. Hand against the pocket, he had kept the fragile Jonsson document dry when the hem of his dirty, bloodied jacket dragged in the water as they splashed in the stream under the road. Phyllis twisted in the seatbelt and lifted the bag to the front again, coming up with the clip of papers and brandishing them with a triumphant flourish.

'I can see the sea again,' Alex commented as she arranged the pages on her lap. 'We can't be far from the coast road.'

'Go ahead,' Phyllis said finally. 'I'm in 1945.'

'I've circled the entries,' Alex said. The bends and turns were coming up suddenly and sharply. It was painful to grip the wheel with his injured hand and he really needed two in the narrow lane. Oncoming vehicles startled him, forcing him to jerk the unfamiliar car uncomfortably close to the verge. He swore silently as he struggled to drive and think at the same time. 'The British prisoner talks about the civilian, the man called Johnson. Find the bit where he says he's ill again, near the end.'

She gripped the head of the seatbelt to steady herself. 'It's hard to read when you're driving all over the road. 'Do you

293

want me to drive?'

'No. Your glasses are cracked.'

Phyllis sniffed irritably and ran a long finger down a page, then turned to the next. 'July 1945: *"Most of us have been ill. Murphy and Johnson are the worst."*'

'So Johnson's alive in July,' Alex confirmed. 'Now go over to another page, to my next circled bit.'

'Got it.' The ink had made a deep triple circle around a date and a patch of words. '"*The Navy guards in the yards beat up eleven men for nothing,*"' she read sadly, '"*an Able Seaman and the civilian from our room were among them.*" The poor guy's either sick or getting beaten up.'

'That's not the point here,' Alex persisted. 'Look at the date.'

'Eleven August,' she read. Puzzled, she looked at him. 'So?'

'When was the atomic bomb dropped on Nagasaki?'

Her eyes skirted backwards through the entries. 'Ninth of August,' she reminded herself. 'Jesus Christ!'

'So Johnson, or Jonsson, is alive *after* the bomb fell.'

Her eyes were distant, as if mesmerized by the flashes of sun through a short roadside border of cherry trees. Her head rocked. Can I believe this? she was asking herself. 'He's still alive two days after the corporate history book of Nippon Nagasaki says he died.' Then she said to Alex, 'I'd love to believe Johnson's really the Swede Roland Jonsson.'

Alex loosed a hand towards the pages on her lap. 'Yuriko Shimada, or someone at Nippon Nagasaki, went through my things and found something in there worth copying. And it has nothing to do with the air-crash.'

The sea shimmered in rippled pearl and filled the windscreen as they descended. Stark, weathered housing blocks crowded the intersection with the coast road. 'That's the business end of Yanagi-cho,' Phyllis said, indicating across the harbour to white, flat-roofed buildings protruding on piers into the sea. A tanker, five monstrous balloons of liquid natural gas lumped along the deck, pulled against its anchor. 'Take a left at the bottom, where it's signed for the four nine nine. A couple of miles to go.' A red Mercedes with tinted windows was not a regular sight among the docks and factories and they took knowing, wary scowls from the drivers of refrigerated fish trucks and the busy little utility vans making early morning deliveries. Phyllis removed her glasses and brushed a hand tentatively around the swelling above her eyes. 'You told your guy in Tokyo Jonsson was murdered. But if he was alive on the eleventh of August . . .'

'Go forward a couple of days, to the twelfth of August I think. I've marked it.'

She read, "*A party sent to Nagasaki to clean up. Johnson has not recovered from injuries but was forced to go.*"

'Now look at the last two pages. Where I've marked.'

She read silently.

'Got it?' he asked. He was holding the road where it crossed between an area of factories around the harbour piers and low-rise apartment blocks filling the lower slopes of the hills.

'Yeah. Thirty August and eight September.'

'Read it.'

"*I still have not seen RJ so I am keeping his personal things for safekeeping like he asked.*"

'He calls him "R J" for the first time and for all intents and purposes he's disappeared from Nagasaki Six. Tom Humphrey never sees him again. Look at the last entry.'

She read an underlined tract. "*I found a couple of letters the civvy left. I will look after them in case we meet again.*"

"*Civvy*" is slang for "civilian",' Alex explained.

She folded the diary. Her eyes were misting as she leaned back into the curve of the seat. Vapour from a cluster of red-and-white-striped chimneys sprouting from a complex of giant chemical vats filled the car with an acrid, suphorous odour. Alex grimaced and checked the windows were closed. Phyllis's expression was rigid, fixed on the road, and the approach to the Yanagi turn-off. 'Can you use a gun?' she said at last. Her voice was dull, toneless.

'What?'

'Can you shoot a pistol?'

He blinked away a mental cobweb. 'What kind of question is that? Of course I can't shoot. We don't go in for them in Britain, apart from a few gun-club psychos.'

She sniffed silently and reached to open the spacious glove compartment again, her hand behind a slim box of tissues, then under a soft leather cloth, and appearing with a matt-black handgun in her grip. 'Tokarev nine-millimetre semi-automatic,' she said flatly. 'The *yakuza's* favourite gun. Made in China from an old Soviet design.'

The car skewed rightwards when his glance hung a second too long on the sinister toylike object. A truck horn blared, shaking him alert and forcing him to overcompensate the finely balanced power steering. The car grazed the strip of corrugated barrier metal separating the road from the narrow corridor of pavement and then bounced back across the lane. Something fell off, rattling against the inside of the wheel well. A van behind flashed a warning. The gun slipped between Phyllis's legs; Alex regained control, his heart racing, sweat rising to his scalp. He slowed behind an early bus and a heavy-duty lorry stacked with steel tubing, both also heading for the sliproad to the industrial landfill site joining the Kyushu mainland to the former island of Yanagi-jima.

Alex was shaken. 'Throw the bloody thing away,' he hissed. 'I thought this country was a gun-free paradise.'

It was not clear where the mainland ended and the causeway, shared by plain blocks of flats and the workshops and dockyards and split by the road, began but it was obvious from the rear-view mirror that the mountain behind them had been scooped and the earth used to fill in the channel, building the land-bridge and expanding the shipyards. The now defunct Kawaminami shipyards and the old Nippon Nagasaki engineering works, where a thousand allied POWs built ten-thousand-ton tankers for their Japanese captors, had been rebuilt and stretched to their right. Pride of place went to the million-ton dry dock they had seen through binoculars from the Glover gardens above Nagasaki. There was no doubt about the source of the community's prosperity. Many of the buildings and factories, even the *danchi* housing blocks, sported the NN letters in bright green paint on the roofs and walls.

The two lanes of light traffic slowed on the approach to the former island, almost all of it drifting to the right and the turn for the factories and shipyards. Phyllis lifted the roadmap, which had fallen to the floor, and reached into the bag between her feet for the harshly creased pages on which Bill Littleton had written his theories about the location of the primary school where the old prisoner-of-war camp had stood. She placed them on her crowded lap, with Ed Kidderby's medical report and the diaries, using the moment to add a different dimension to Alex's two-week store of knowledge. He was right: Japan *was* a gun-free paradise, at least compared with her grandparents' adopted homeland, and she had been paid by a San Francisco newspaper to write an article about it as recently as last March. She'd heard that Stateside gun killings ran to over a hundred a day and informed her readers there that in 1995 there were only a hundred and sixty-two shooting incidents for the whole year in Japan, three quarters of them involving the *yakuza*, and only thirty-two people had died, six fewer than the year before.

'But it's big status if these creeps carry a gun,' Phyllis declared. 'They go to Hawaii and other places in the States to practise on the ranges, then buy weapons smuggled in from the Philippines and China. They use them pretty rarely, almost always against rival gangs with ambitions on their territory.'

Leaving the broad industrial causeway they turned at a light onto what was the old island's main road along its long western side. They knew from the diaries and Bill Littleton's research that it was an uncomplicated place: an economic network of narrow roads linking the main settlement of Yanagi with a few scattered hamlets, outdoor recreation parks, the Miyamoto estate and the life-blood marine industrial complex occupying a third of the total area. Phyllis pointed to a row of shops and a stand-up noodle bar at one end with space at the side to hide all but the boot of the loud Mercedes. Her damp feet were itching and splashes of dirty water from the sluice had left her with matted hair. 'Let's eat something, drink some *ocha*.'

The sea was out of sight behind a knoll of buildings and houses but the brisk breeze carried, reaching them with a sharp, reviving tang of fresh, salt air. She gathered the papers and maps into the travel bag while Alex inspected the car. Its condition didn't bother him: the more he learned about the thugs they called the *yakuza* the more damage he felt inclined to inflict, but walking around the car confirmed a badly scuffed edge on the driver's door where it had struck the black Mercedes and a broad gash which ran along entire length on the other side. The bang he had heard was the front light casing, smashed free and somehow rebounding and bouncing around inside the wheel well.

They could smell the bland, saporous noodles before they reached the dark-blue, shoulder-length split *noren* curtain. The old woman behind the pine counter was stirring a steaming tub and relaxed when she saw a Japanese with the horrifically tall *gaijin*, her eyes disappearing as her face broke into a pinched smile which revealed a row of gapped, uneven teeth. Phyllis ordered two bowls of *ramen* while Alex retired to wash his hand and replace the soaked handkerchief with a wrapping of lavatory paper. The inch-long cut was open but thankfully the bleeding had stopped for the moment.

'What I don't understand, Phyl,' Alex said, scooping, sucking and slurping the soggy strands of flat vermicelli noodles like a professional – he was imitating a young construction worker who wore a frayed towel headband and split-toed shin-high boots over dusty, loose trousers gathered at the knee – is how the men who've been following us, characters who may as well have "gangster" stamped on their foreheads, can hang around within yards of the police who are trying to arrest *us*? Why aren't *they* the fucking suspects?' He had been thinking about this in the rare gaps when sanity made a fleeting, elusive return. Was it only a few hours since he untangled his body from the delicious warmth of hers, to go on the run, hounded by the police and the local mob, and cursed on the other side of the world by a boss who was probably putting together a strong case for his dismissal?

Phyllis drank up the bitter green tea greedily. 'It's a careful balance. Not easy for you *gaijins* to comprehend.'

'Try me,' he demanded. The worker folded a tabloid newspaper, grunted at the old woman and left.

'The underworld syndicates have a neat, unwritten understanding with the police. The gangs run the sex industry, drugs, bars and the casual labour market and they don't usually strong-arm the public. In fact they act as a kind of pseudo-police in the entertainment quarters. The six big syndicates split the country into territories and that's when the shooting starts: when they cross into somebody else's patch. There's not much of an underclass here so there's no real coercive drug dealing or prostitution and not much street crime and rape. Everything's for pleasure in return for money, and the *yakuza* fill the demand nicely. They're well organised, nationalistic, with strong connections to right-wing groups and by extension to politicians and business. Like I told you. Everyone's working for Japan.'

'So why are the *yakuza* helping the police catch us?' Alex

asked, sucking in the last twisted vine of noodles.

'Because Miyamoto's asked them to,' she said in a voice that barely controlled her anger and told him she was repeating herself. 'They're probably from a local syndicate, if not Nagasaki, certainly Kyushu. Kokura and Fukuoka have very strong gang networks. Miyamoto's contacts must include the underworld because they're a major, powerful economic force. They'll help him and score a few credit points in the mutual book of favours.'

Alex persisted. 'But they're gangsters.'

'All Japanese companies have connections with the *yakuza*,' she said patiently. 'Always have. They pay *yakuza* corporate blackmail specialists to smooth over shareholders' meetings; they fund right-wing lobby groups and down among the hundreds of subsidiaries and affliates there'll be a few with a chunk of *yakuza* money invested in them, now nicely laundered.' She glanced at her watch. It was close to six forty-five. 'Corporate–*yakuza* connections are probably stronger than they've ever been. You've heard about the Japanese "bubble?"'

'Sure. The eighties boom and bust. We had a taste of it in Britain.'

Phyllis finished her last twist of noodles and sipped a little of the salty, miso broth. 'The banks went wild. They had money to burn at giveaway rates of interest. Where to put it all? In real estate, of course. There are bits of Tokyo worth more than the total land in twenty American states. So the banks lend trillions to real-estate companies and golf-course speculators, many of them *yakuza* fronts. The syndicates are now into legit business like land, art, stocks and shares, borrowing and dealing through so-called respectable companies. When the bubble bursts at the end of the eighties and land prices fall by fifty per cent and the stock market implodes, the borrowers, including the *yakuza,* of course, can't repay. Have you ever tried to get money back from a *yakuza*? It's a miracle the big banks in Japan are still in business.'

Alex said, 'So Miyamoto's connections with the syndicates are no big deal?'

She gave an ironic grunt. 'He runs a hundred companies like a dictator. Look at what he owns in this city alone. No. Where there's money and land you'll find the *yakuza*. I'd only be surprised if he didn't have any connections.'

The woman squinted as she watched them turn to leave. Alex split the *noren* curtain then held back, his arm swinging out. Phyllis followed his eyes through the narrow break. A pearl-grey, top-range, 5-series BMW sulked on a verge fifty yards away, pointed towards the dockyard complex as if undecided which route to take. 'Maybe I'm getting paranoid,' he said. 'But I can't see the fishermen round here driving racy cars like that.' As they watched, the German car let a truck pass and U-turned violently, crossing a light and disappearing onto an upland road.

'They know where to find us,' Phyllis said calmly, when they were sitting in the Mercedes, letting time pass.

'That means we're in the right place.' He drew the local map of the erstwhile island onto his lap. 'So where are we, Phyl? Where's the clinic, and the Miyamoto house?'

'It looks like there's only one fairly large settlement,' she said, a fingernail on the Japanese writing for "town hall". 'There are a few clusters of houses scattered around but they all come under the Yanagi Town district.' She gestured through the window. 'And this is it. According to this map, the town admin buildings are about a mile along this road. I expect the clinic's down there among them.' She held the medical certificate over the map. 'It's probably the main hospital for the community. There's one marked on the map, in the area of city hall and the school.'

'What's it called?'

'It doesn't say.' She showed him the medical report, with

the sheets of figures, notes and the dark orange seals of authority at the end. 'We're looking for the Yanagi Community Health Centre – in particular, a Doctor Naito.'

'The POW camp can't be far from here either,' Alex said, starting the Mercedes and backing cautiously into the road. 'The diaries said the prisoners walked about a mile to the dockyards.' He threw a thumb towards the low warehouses, with NNI painted strikingly in green on the sloping roofs, which shielded their view from a complex of dock facilities and repair yards. 'This had to be the prisoners' work site when it was an island. The rest of the place looks too hilly.'

'Measure out a mile from here on the odometer,' she suggested. 'Bill says there's a school on the site of the old camp. Let's take a look at it first.' The digital clock on the deeply inlaid panel of dials told her it was a few minutes after seven. 'Let's give the hospital another half-hour.'

They followed a mass of overhead cables along a road that cut through the foot of a cliffside and dipped over a low hill. What had once had been a roadstead channel leading to Nagasaki harbour was now a bay and it was visible from the rise. 'Pull in here,' Phyllis snapped.

Alex jolted, his eyes flying to the mirror, gravel spitting from the wheels as he braked between the concrete posts of an open gateway.

'"Yanagi High School,"' she read on the signboard.

Slipping the gear stick into neutral, he let the car drift into a hard-earth quadrangle with dismal, weather-stained ferro-concrete blocks on three sides. It was too early for students and if a caretaker had seen them he was assessing the intruders from a hidden corner somewhere.

'This must be it,' Phyllis said softly.

Taking the diaries from the bag and pulling himself from the car, Alex scrutinised the layout of the school and its surroundings against the photocopy of the picture taken from a B-29 when it swooped to drop emergency supplies over the

POW camp a few days after Japan's surrender on 15 August 1945. Stapled to the final page of narrative, the photograph had come into the hands of the prisoner Tom Humphrey from the US National Archives, giving him a constant reminder of the Nagasaki Six slave labour camp. Alex turned it round. 'You sure Bill said the camp became a school?' he said to Phyllis, who stood, hands on hips, by the car.

'Absolutely.' She came over and stood at his shoulder. 'Why do you ask?'

He showed her the picture, with the ghostly black shadow of the B-29 captured forever on the roofs of the prison buildings which appeared exposed in the copy as white images on a black background. Tom had long ago made some jagged pencil notes on it and they were just legible. The sea was marked along the lower edge and there was a road at the top. Alex swept an arm to the furthest of the school buildings and the curve of a low hill beyond it. 'That should be water,' he complained.

Back in the car, they slumped in dejection. Phyllis massaged the lids over tired eyes and leaned to meet a compassionate kiss. 'We've got this far,' he declared. 'We'll find it. Do you remember what the POW wrote? He said that he once dropped out of the lines on the way to the dockyards and stole paper from an empty school for his diary. It could have been on this site.'

If they had not been deceived into stopping at the first sign for a school they would have found Nagasaki Six only a hundred and fifty yards further away, where the road bent around the bluff that created the hillside backing the high-school. The car had not left second gear in automatic mode before Alex braked in front of a shuttered general store flanked by vending machines. He pulled onto a slope paved in pink and blue bricks between the shop and a wire perimeter fence and turned a corner out of sight of the road. '"Yanagi Shogakko",' Phyllis read. Yanagi Primary School.

He could not read the board over the gate but the panorama told him they had found the place where a thousand Allied prisoners of war, and a few lost civilians, lived and died. He pointed to the wedge of placid, turquoise water, which seemed to touch a corner of the plain, white, two-storeyed school, and to the mainland opposite. As it used to be during the war, when it was an island, Yanagi was still connected to the other side of the bay by cables stretched between pylons planted on the highest points.

'The diary said the American pilots used to fly under the bloody cables to drop supplies. Some feat!'

The school and the camp were trapped by the same geography: the sea and the island's eastern route on the broader sides and the bluff and a culvert guiding a stream into the bay at the narrower ends. The small school today was a modern airy building on two sides, leaving the central open space free for playgrounds and sports facilities. Holding the grainy photograph beween them, they easily located the points where, contrary to the conventions of war and the safety of prisoners, the Japanese had built sand-bagged anti-aircraft batteries for the defence of Nagasaki. They were standing in front of a corner shop which would have been the guardroom cells, the school building facing them the site of the living quarters for thirty military guards and the officers. 'It sounded like a bigger place in the diaries,' Phyllis remarked, fascinated by the gentle, morning tranquillity of a place still stalked by the ghosts of the brutalised inmates. 'Can you imagine a thousand men trapped in here?'

Alex eased the gate open and they stopped at the head of a flight of steps leading into the school to plot the rest of the positions of the buildings marked on the old aerial photograph.

'They've gone inside the school grounds,' Hinohara said, focusing the binoculars on the foreign couple and then back to his car. A night of highs and lows had left him tired and mean. 'If they've fucked up my Merc . . .' he muttered to himself.

A narrow, single-lane road, paved in concrete slabs with weeds thriving in the joints and cracks, gave access to blocks of public housing apartments, each with an identification number blazed in black paint on the side and built in clusters on sites hewn from the wooded slopes. The panorama took in the main Yanagi settlement with the primary school on the seafront and the misty shoreline of the mainland across the bay. Two slim muscled footsoldiers idled against the dark silver BMW. The younger, with the sunglasses and greased hair, flicked at a new coat of ochre-coloured powdery dirt on the bonnet with a long feather duster.

'Let's take them now,' Hinohara said to Kamei. The senior man stood stiffly, his mobile phone in the cradle of his folded arms.

'You'll get your fucking car back,' Kamei growled. 'We've been told what to do and we'll do it. The police in their stupidity couldn't harpoon a frigging whale in a bathtub.' He snatched the binoculars. 'Now it's our turn.'

'There's a gun in it,' Hinohara complained. 'The cops'd have to go for us if they find it.'

Kamei's eyes followed the foreigners out of the school. 'They're moving on.' The bored *yakuza* pair pushed themselves off the car, the man in the oversized black suit and collarless white shirt sliding behind the wheel. 'They're on Yanagi now,' Kamei grinned. 'They belong to us, not the National Police Agency. If the *gaijin* get within farting distance of the house we take them.'

They were pensive as they drove along the shoreline, made by the causeway into a sheltered harbour for the weathered, low-sided squid and sea bream fishing boats which lay embedded in the glass-still water. Before reaching a tier of simple white houses where the shore become a slender promontory, they turned into a district of official-looking buildings: the neat, modern town hall with a covered bus stop in front, a squat post office, the modest police station with a single balcony thick with potted flowers, and an older, plain structure. As they waited for the light to change on the town's only traffic light, a lightweight refrigerated van bearing the green Nippon Nagasaki logo crossed the intersection with the morning's catch from a pier on the opposite side of the near island.

'Over there,' Phyllis said, indicating the grim, weathered façade. 'The Yanagi Community Health Centre. A long way for a Tokyo *gaijin* to come to have his blood pressure taken.' She guessed the hospital served a Yanagi population of around four, four and a half thousand.

The parking bays were arranged at the back of the hospital, around an island of thin, leafy trees where a row of tall evergreens blurred a view of the funerary columns in the municipal graveyard. None was visible from the road and only two of them were occupied and when Alex had the Mercedes aligned he exhaled loudly. 'If I'm right about the situation the closest Ed Kidderby got to Nagasaki was when he flew over it.'

'I guess this makes or breaks your case,' Phyllis said, adjusting her cracked glasses. 'And maybe I can get something for this bruise.'

Alex leaned over and brushed the tender welt with his lips. 'And this cut.' He picked the shredded pieces of damp, pink lavatory paper from his hand and rolled them into a ball.

'Do I look as goddamn awful as you?' she said, smiling, running her eyes over his damp, creased, dirt-flecked clothes.

'You look worse,' he shot back, trying to force a smile. 'Have you got the story?'

'I guess so.'

They walked round to the front entrance, which was in a newer annexe. Alex clutched the travel bag like a patient arriving for a short stay; Phyllis fluffed life into her hair and dusted down her jacket and jeans. 'Do you think we're too early?' he asked her, leaning into the stiff door.

She glanced at her watch. 'It's almost eight. We'll have to bluff it. We got a lot to do before the police arrive.'

'Or the *yakuza*,' Alex said drily, backing into the hospital. 'I hope Ingleby doesn't screw up.'

The night receptionist in a dark nurse's uniform and a frilly hat pinned to the crown of her head was near the end of her shift. Two corridors led off the dimly lit semicircular lobby and she sat behind a counter between them. She had read a couple of fresh weekly magazines under a lamp, drunk six cups of green tea and processed a single admission, a salaryman with alcohol poisoning. She was tired and bored and had to blink twice through the weak light to believe the strange man in doorway was not an apparition. She managed a strained, suspicious smile for her first white *gaijin*, easing when she saw what she thought was a Japanese woman with him.

Phyllis affected the high-pitched deferential whine of the department-store lift operator, introducing Alex as a newly hired NN Air pilot with an appointment for his medical check-up and herself as his interpreter. She apologised for their early arrival: Mr Briggs had reached Japan only thirty hours earlier and his body clock was still on American time. They could wait, if she didn't mind, or they could go back into Nagasaki and come back later. The receptionist crooked her head, looking for inspiration, then swivelled behind a computer monitor and tapped the keyboard, turning once to check Alex's name. She tried several options but finally released a noisy hiss. 'We don't seem to have any record of your appointment, Mr Briggs,' she said to Phyllis.

'How unfortunate,' Phyllis complained politely, with a touch of mock irritation. 'To come all this way and find there's been a misunderstanding.' She translated unnecessarily for Alex and said in a low voice, 'Show me a piece of paper.'

He fumbled in the bag and produced the diaries and odd notes. She pretended to read. 'Well, it clearly says Thursday, nine o'oclock, today. Doctor Naito at the Yanagi Community Health Centre.'

Placing Ed Kidderby's medical report on the reception desk, he watched Phyllis manoeuvre it under the arc of light, her hand splayed over the page, covering the pilot's personal details. 'This is the correct name and address?' she asked meekly, indicating the heading.

'Of course it is but— '

Phyllis folded the flimsy pages back, directing the tired nurse's attention to the two orange circles after the last row of figures and comments and the awkward childlike way somebody had written 'Dr T. Naito' in roman script for the benefit of the US civil aviation authorities. 'And this is the hospital's *hanko*, isn't it?' she said, her voice deepening, dropping down a couple of levels on the politeness scale as she indicated the larger of the signature seals.

'It is but— '

'We're in the right place then,' she said abruptly. Her eyes caught Alex's. An elderly couple entered the hospital, read the sign board laboriously and sauntered into a corridor, clutching a box of freshly made breakfast for a sick relative. 'I can't make out the characters in this one,' Phyllis said, forcing a pained expression and offering the other seal for the nurse's examination. 'Is it the *hanko* of the doctor who conducted this particular examination? Doctor Naito. Perhaps we can speak to him briefly, or the hospital's *tantosha*, the person in charge of NN Air personnel.'

The receptionist blinked her sore eyes over the sphere. 'It

is the seal of the general administrative department,' she confessed. 'I'm afraid there's no reference to a particular doctor.'

'Fine,' Phyllis conceded. 'We'll wait here for Doctor Naito.'

Flustered, the night duty nurse fiddled with the diary schedules on her desk and ran through a thin, loose-leaf file. Her face pinched in apology, she hissed, 'This is a small hospital and I am sure, and I've checked, we have no doctor Naito here.'

'Don't get excited,' Phyllis commanded calmy before she translated. She gave him a triumphant wink and a squeeze to his elbow as she listened earnestly to the next rehearsed piece from him.

'Mr Briggs politely suggests you input NN Air into your computer system. That's Nippon Nagasaki Air. It will probably show an appropriate method of procedure for this kind of eventuality.'

Eight o'clock was some kind of watershed. Individuals from the night shift drifted into the reception, nodded a weary farewell towards the reception desk and left. A porter with an unlit cigarette in his mouth pushed gratefully out into the sunlight. A small-faced dark-skinned woman draped in a purple cape arrived, glanced at the rough-looking couple and exchanged a greeting with her relieved colleague before moving behind the desk. They talked about the situation out of earshot and set about the monitor, prodding the keyboard and muttering a comment or two when the screen flashed alive. Whatever appeared on it made them suck air noisily, nod knowingly, their faces close, and mumble something. Phyllis was straining to hear. 'I don't like it,' she uttered to Alex, looking ahead.

The newcomer turned, giving them a hard, controlled look. 'As she said, we have no record of Mr Briggs's appointment. And I'm afraid there's no reference to NN Air in our database.' She beckoned to a bank of plastic seats by a drinks vending machine. 'If you would like to wait over there I'll some further enquiries.' She draped her cape over the second chair and disappeared into one of the corridors.

'Are we talking plan B or what?' Phyllis uttered under her breath, backhanding a crumpled cigarette packet and a book of matches to Alex. 'Could you direct me to the rest room?' she said brightly to the nurse at the desk. Twisting her neck to follow the directions, she said to Alex, 'Go and sit over there and smoke.'

He balked for less than a second before taking the cigarettes. Phyllis always seemed to produce a packet at a moment of tension but he couldn't ever recall her smoking one. He watched her move away with a jaunty swagger, her cotton jacket creased, her jeans, stretched tight over high buttocks, streaked with mud, still damp from the stream. Remembering the strange character in the baggy dungarees and red baseball cap, he almost chuckled. Alex had noticed that Japanese company women wore either uniforms or designer fashions; Phyl looked like a woman who had lived in the same clothes for two days and had climbed a crusty, dirty wall in them, crawled through a filthy tunnel, ankle-deep in water, before helping to steal a car. She looked terrific, but not exactly like an interpreter from the prestigious multinational conglomerate that seemed to own the Yanagi district and control a big chunk of the industrial activity in Nagasaki. His own sour smell of sweat hit him when he slumped into the hard bucket seat. He blinked and shook his head alert, picking a cigarette and finding his mouth after his knuckles had brushed against the harsh stubble on his chin. He sucked tamely on the Hi-Lite until it lit and then held it close to his mouth, blowing at it. He heard the receptionist's muted cautions and ignored them, holding his head low to stare at the floor, the cigarette smouldering in his fingers. When he heard a chair scrape and an exaggerated cough of frustration, he knew she had left her position. A direct approach was the only way to stop the *gaijin* from disobeying the no-smoking rule.

Phyllis turned at the arched doorway to the corridor leading to the general wards in the older building and watched his part of the silly, desperate charade from a shadowed corner. When the exasperated nurse gave up trying to get Alex's attention in Japanese and left the enclave of her desk to admonish him with gestures, she edged back into the lobby, along the wall to the reception counter and the monitor, still flashing its last message into the void. Phyllis encroached behind the desk, peering at the lines on the screen, praying she could understand the reading of the Japanese *kanji* writing and read the message.

'*Pureezu, pureezu*, Briggs *san*,' the woman tried in a thick attempt at English, stooping low, a hand extended tentatively to catch his attention.

Alex raised his head slowly, leaning sideways enough to catch the torso of his *sansei* conspirator, her face close to the screen. The woman was pointing at his smouldering cigarette and flapping the other hand across her mouth, a gesture he took as a protest and met it with a blank, dumb look. Phyllis had picked up a pen and was writing on her arm or hand. Then she was out of his view. '*Sumimasen*,' he stuttered, the all-encompassing apology he had been quick to learn, and held her attention with a futile search for an ashtray until Phyllis joined them and added an apology for his stupidity.

The other woman returned and they all gathered again around the desk. Her small, dark face broke into a lifeless smile. She lowered her chin and turned up the watch suspended on a chain. 'Our special consultant would like to see Mr Briggs but he will not be available until eight thirty. May we ask you to wait?'

Phyllis thanked her and translated for Alex.

'Did they find anything in the computer system under NN Air?' he asked her to enquire again. Phyllis had not bothered to translate their first negative reply.

The two women craned earnestly at the machine again. It hummed flatly, hidden from the visitors' eyes. One of them pressed a key. 'As I told you before,' she said to Phyllis. 'I'm afraid nothing at all came up under that reference.' She smiled thinly.

'Try Nippon Nagasaki Corporation,' Alex persisted, his mock annoyance rising. The medical certifications for NN Air crew were a total sham, but there had to be a record of the connection between the clinic and Miyamoto's company.

The desk staff were huddled around the computer again. 'There's nothing,' the fresher woman said, her impatience beginning to show. 'If you wait for a while our consultant will be here soon.'

Alex bristled. 'How about this?' He showed them the gash in his hand. 'Can you do something for a cut? While I'm here.'

Phyllis tugged his sleeve and led him to the chairs. 'C'mon Alex. You got what you came for.' She was rifling in the pockets of her jeans. 'Have you got a ten yen coin?'

'For chrissake, Phyl,' he growled, shouldering the travel bag. 'Let's get out of here. You're right. I've got enough to raise an investigation. Now we've got to get into safe hands.'

'I've got to make a call first,' she muttered urgently, 'so if you haven't got your cellular give me ten fucking yen.'

He jiggled a few coins in his hand and stood near as she fed the red telephone on its stand by the entrance, watching the women at the desk. One was occupied now with a genuine patient, the other had turned away with a telephone clamped under the hair swelling from her bonnet.

Phyllis stabbed the buttons while reading a number written on the hand holding the telephone. 'They lied to us,' she told him. 'NN Air's on the screen as a specified sub-group of Nippon Nagasaki Corporation. There's an "access prohibited" warning and an emergency number to call.' She flashed him a view of her hand. 'It's engaged. Is she still on the phone?'

Alex's eyes jumped to the desk. He nodded.

'She got there before me then.' She pretended to be occupied with a conversation, nodding and shaking her head blatantly.

Alex saw the woman hang up and moved to shield Phyllis by propping himself against the wall. 'Try again. Quickly.'

She pressed again and almost immediately the corners of her mouth moved and her eyes flashed him a signal. Taking the pen he gave her, she spoke, her voice a childish, subservient whine. 'I am sorry to cause so much trouble,' she lamented, apologising for the unfortunate hour of the day. 'This is the Sanyo Department Store in Nishihama-cho. We have a delivery held over for you but are unable to read the forwarding address instructions left by the customer.' A pause. 'It's the number we were given. Please understand our situation and forgive the inconvenience we have caused you.'

Alex wondered what she had said. She was listenening now, puncturing the silence with a chain of 'hai, hai' responses, the ballpen tapping against the telephone, as if she really were taking down an address. She was playing it so well she was instinctively bowing at the red box when she laid the handset gently on the rack.

Gathering the bag, they reached the broad doors when the relief receptionist cut them off. Her face was mean and full of tension. 'She wants us to respectfully wait for the chief consultant,' Phyllis translated. 'He will take care of you personally.'

'I bet he will,' Alex said, giving the woman a brittle smile. 'Let's get out of here.'

'We'll return at eight thirty as you request,' she said in Japanese in her best subservient voice. 'We'll take coffee

313

first.'

Outside, he said, 'Where did the phone number lead?'

'You have one guess.'

'Group headquarters in Tokyo. Yuriko Shimada maybe.'

'I only used ten yen. Local call.'

Lines deepened on his unshaven face. 'Here, in Nagasaki. On Yanagi?'

The brilliance of the sunlight seared his tired eyes and it was Phyllis, behind him in his shadow, who saw the flash, the sudden glint off the boot of the BMW as it turned into the light. She pulled him back into the recessed doorway. The silver-grey car had slowed to pass a bus parked in front of the hospital where four people waited under the shelter. As they watched it turned into the drive that led to the rear car park.

Phyllis swore. 'Didn't take them long to find us. Did you leave anything in the Merc?'

Alex patted the bag. 'A map. A guidebook. Nothing important.'

'Good. I think it's about to be repossessed.' He turned and thought about a dash through the hospital. He still had the key and might get to the car before the *yakuza*.

The driver had checked his watch and the bus rumbled to life with a blast of black diesel exhaust, the doors closing with a hydraulic hiss. Apart from the four people on the bus and early workers approaching the town hall, the compact town centre was almost deserted. Stooping, they made a dash for the bus, surprising the driver by thrashing on the doors until they crumpled apart. Phyllis paid and talked as the bus drew away. The number seven was heading for Nagasaki City after making the short circle route around Yanagi to pick up city workers. The drawn-out stares of the other passengers hardly surprised or bothered them.

'Does it pass the Miyamoto estate?' Alex asked.

Sitting at the back of the bus, Phyllis drew the sun-bleached blind across the window facing the hospital façade. She laced her arm through his. 'I already asked. It does.'

Hinohara had taken the call in the passenger seat of the BMW and screamed a command at the driver, who immediately threw the car into a handbrake turn. The tyres bit into the earth on the shoulder where the road ran into a sharp downward curve towards the town. Shards of gravel pelted against the inside of the wheel cover like bullets.

'For fuck's sake!' Kamei bawled from the back, shoving the fourth man off as they lurched sidewards.

'They're in the hospital,' Hinohara seethed. Hidden by the dips and overhangs Miyamoto's *yakuza* had lost sight of the *gaijin* when they left the site of the old prisoner-of-war camp. Assuming they had turned back towards the causeway, heading for Nagasaki when they had seen enough, Hinohara had called the black Mercedes idling on a verge near the narrowest point before the road turned onto National Highway 299, ordering it to stop and reclaim his burgundy Mercedes with the least possible damage. To the car – not necessarily to the *gaijins* in it. They had been cruising gently along the hillside with the windows and sunroof open, overtaken once, by a newspaper delivery van. The slim thug in the suit next to Kamei had been scratching an itch behind his ear with the fin-shaped sight on the barrel of a .38 Smith and Wesson revolver when a relayed telephone call told them the foreigners had triggered a confidential telephone number at the Yanagi Community Health Centre. They sped past the dockyards towards the town, Kamei urging the driver faster with a stream of curses. A bus filled the narrow forecourt between the hospital and the town hall. Kamei's driver slowed, waiting for instructions.

Kamei smoothed the lapels of his suit jacket, patting the bulk behind the pocket for reassurance. Deciding it would be easier to take them in the relative privacy of the car park when they returned to the red Mercedes, he ordered the BMW to the rear of the hospital. An elderly leathered gardener in a straw hat and with her head wrapped in towelling against the insects leaned on her rake to watch. Foreign cars were a rare sight on Yanagi, except for the occasional black-windowed machines people didn't talk about. Like these two in the hospital car park.

After waiting five minutes, Kamei nudged his companion and spoke to Hinohara. 'We'll check inside. You two stay here.'

Hinohara left the BMW as soon as his boss has disappeared into the hospital. He was bending to examine his Mercedes, seething as he ran his fingers along the gash and around the smashed light, when the slick-haired, jittery *yakuza* appeared at the rear entrance, gesturing fiercely. They ran round to the plaza where Kamei stood on the pavement, hands on hips, his eyes raking the few faces around it.

'They wrecked my car,' Hinohara told the group.

'A broken light and a few scratches,' the driver scowled.

'Shut the fuck up, both of you,' Kamei barked, a hand splayed over his forehead. 'I'm trying to think.' A pensioner on a bench outside the town hall searched through dim eyes for the source of the noise. 'They tried to keep them here with some crap about a doctor seeing them but they saw through it and pissed off about ten minutes ago.'

'There was a bus here when we came,' the driver remembered.

Kamei swore at their collective stupidity. 'We've got to stop the *gaijins* now,' he growled, and hurried across the road to the bench. The other three watched their leader, his mouth close to the old man's ear, his hands chopping as he emphasised a point. When he returned he was gesticulating wildly, issuing orders as he bustled them to the rear car park. 'We assume they're on the bus. The old guy saw nothing.

Hasn't seen a live white foreigner since the war.' He fingered Hinohara. 'You got the spare key?' Hinohara grunted and dangled a ring. 'Good. Take your Merc and go straight to the house. I don't know what those shitheads intend to do but the bus passes the gate and I want you on the inside.' They reached the cars. 'And don't piss around with them. Take them and hold them somewhere out of sight of the guys in suits with the president. We're going right after the bus.'

'What about Uemura?' Hinohara's driver asked. They had left the other Mercedes, the black model with two more Okudaira syndicate *yakuza*, at the Yanagi–Nagasaki turn-off.

'Call him. Tell him to stay alert. He might have to stop the bus on the causeway or we might need him here on Yanagi.'

The bus rumbled past the old camp, following the coast and turning onto a modern two-lane road where it forked at the potholed approach to the sinister-looking mouth of the old trans-island tunnel.

'First piece of luck all day,' Phyllis crowed. 'The bus's going the right way.'

Alex glanced at the empty road behind. 'Let's hope it holds for another two hours.'

The bus stopped to pick up a solitary passenger by a settlement of flat-roofed two-storey blocks of flats facing the open sea. The man unslung a rucksack, patting around for his wallet while he laughed and chatted to the driver. 'C'mon,' Phyllis urged, the map of Yanagi open on her lap.

Then the road was filled with cars. Alex spun, reaching for the bag and seizing her arm.

Four black executive cars, all Mitsubishi Presidents, bunched as they slowed to overtake the stationary bus. Each held two grim-faced executives from the Nippon Nagasaki conglomerate, only minutes from facing the harsh reality of the group's financial plight from their president.

'Take it easy,' she advised, when they were finally under

way again. 'They're the harmless guys. I told you Miyamoto has ordered all his chief executives together for a crisis meeting. They must have stayed in Nagasaki City last night.' The road twisted inland, rising sharply between the thick, richly green, undisturbed slopes, the cars and their apprehensive passengers disappearing quickly ahead of the lumbering bus.

It was soon the bus's turn to slow and proceed with caution. It wanted to pass a high copper-coloured ornate wooden gateway in a wall obliterated by climbing foliage. It was operated mechanically, allowing entry after an interphone security check, and the last two chauffeur-driven Presidents were using the full width of the road to make their turn. A uniformed security guard received each car with a bow and gestured politely towards the interior.

Their faces peered from the rear window as the bus stopped within sight of the gateway to pick up a mother and her children. 'This chunk of Yanagi all belongs to Miyamoto,' Phyllis said. 'It's the *honke*, the main house for the whole family structure. Old Miyamoto bought it when he was building up the business around Nagasaki and it's one of the most beautiful spots in Kyushu.'

Alex scoffed. 'It'd be suicidal to get off here then,' he concluded.

'We've got to lie low somewhere,' Phyllis said. 'This bus isn't safe, and it's going to start circling back toward the dockyards. What time are we expected to be airlifted out of here?'

Alex glanced at his watch. 'Ten thirty. In a couple of hours, if Richard gets it right.'

They left the bus at the next stop. It had climbed to the island's highest point and pulled onto the verge by a neatly laid-out and broad, deserted parking area. The land had been cleared to make a picnic site and a hard-earth floodlit sports ground. A wild, shrub- and tree-encrusted knoll had been left

318

between the two and an arched-legged viewing platform erected on its peak. They walked briskly towards it under the cover of the low-hung canopy from a row of zelkova trees. A stairway made of half-buried logs cut into the wild hump took them to the summit. Their breathing was fast, from exertion and a creeping feeling of isolation and anxiety, when they reached the platform at the top of a spiral staircase inside the cone-shaped tower.

Shielding their eyes from the sunlight, which dazzled from a cloudless sky, flaring on the aluminium handrails and the white tiles of the floor and wall, they shared Alex's compact, powerful binoculars as they circled the platform, locating the dockyards and the cluster of Nippon Nagasaki warehouses and workshops, the prisoner-of-war camp and the town of Yanagi, and the hazy distant image of the city of Nagasaki. Beyond a ridgeback promontory spiked with pylons, they saw a string of small uninhabited islands surrounded by fish-farm netting, straddling the Pacific across the wide approach to Nagasaki harbour. Phyllis trawled the road they had travelled in the bus until it disappeared beneath ranks of tall willows, the *yanagi* tree of the island's name, and then refocused on a point below them, towards the southern tip. She swept the area and offered him the binoculars. 'Take a look.'

She guided his eyes to patches of open space among the dense greenery and to a part of it enclosing what looked like a compound of solid houses bordering the sea above a stretch of cliffs. 'Can you see the business block? To the left, kind of hidden by the trees.'

He levelled the lenses on the distant angled white roof of a modern, stylish three storey building. A driveway passed under a porch supported by three columns and he could see, in grainy image, one of the black limousines and a clutch of silent, minute figures in the doorway. Having dropped their passengers, the cars drove to a park behind the offices.

'Now look to the right,' she commanded. 'Not far. To the private compound.' Joined by a path to the office building but hidden behind a strip of cherry trees, the luxurious houses were made of ferro-concrete to face whatever the Pacific Ocean could throw at them while retaining the flavour of Japanese traditional style in the curving corners of the roofs and their thick, overlapping mock-earthernware tiles and the stacking of a squat, smaller second floor. 'The big place must be Hiroshi Miyamoto's. I expect his family lives here all year round.'

Alex's sight was drawn to the smaller house, an annexe joined by a short corridor to the other, and by a flash or a reflection at a corner overlooking the ocean. 'Somebody's at home. In the smaller place.' He handed her the binoculars. 'On the veranda, where it sticks out a bit.'

'Sitting on the *lanai*, having breakfast I guess,'

'What's he doing? Is he waving out to sea?'

Phyllis skewed an eye but the figure remained a fuzzy imperfect shadow. 'Could be a woman,' was all she could add. But the real activity was taking place beyond the cherry trees, in the detached, secluded office building where Hiroshi Miyamoto – with Yuriko Shimada not far away, Phyllis had scoffed – was preparing to reveal his masterplan for the salvation of Nippon Nagasaki Corporation and its satellites. The flow of cars had stopped, the occupants were inside, the drivers, even at this distance, obviously dusting and rubbing their vehicles in the car park. Phyllis shifted her gaze a touch. Her body stiffened. An arm flew and she transmitted the rush of tension as she gripped his. She pointed as she stared and then thrust the glasses at him. 'It's our car. The red Merc. It's in the damn driveway.'

Alex followed the jerky, silent movement of the car roof as it glided between trees. It passed the business centre and reversed into a position beside a four-wheel-drive Suzuki on a gravelled forecourt in front of the Miyamoto residence.

Phyllis watched without glasses, her mouth hanging open. 'Christ! Look at that,' she snarled. 'That takes balls. A *yakuza* power wagon sitting right in front of Miyamoto's house.' She caught a puzzled glance from Alex and said, 'We all know the biggest business leaders have got *yakuza* friends but you'd never, ever flaunt the connection like that.' She took another long look throught the binoculars and tugged at his arm, heading for the doorway at the head of the steps. 'We've got to get a picture of the Merc in front of the door. I could really get that sucker Miyamoto into trouble with it.'

Alex had packed the binoculars and lofted the bag. 'You're making me nervous,' he grumbled to the head disappearing below him on the spiral stairway. 'I've seen enough of Miyamoto's home town. Let's keep our heads down until the police take us out of here.'

Phyllis turned on him. 'But I haven't got anything yet.' They were on the knoll, at the foot of the viewing tower, and her pained outburst was a retort in the stillness. A pair of hawks lazing on the high branch of a white birch scattered noisily. 'You've got what you need to nail Miyamoto's airline but I came for the whole goddamn empire.' She pointed aimlessly in the direction of the estate. 'We were in that fucking mobster's car, Alex. Can you imagine the picture on the front of *Time* or on CNN? The tycoon and the gangster. No way the police'll be able to say they've no evidence. They'll have to investigate the connection properly.'

'We can't risk it, Phyl,' Alex said, pulling ahead towards the log steps.

She held back. 'Okay. You stick around here. Just lend me your Nikon.'

He opened his arms to press his objection when they both heard the noise: tyres skidding, braking on loose gravel, the muted thump of doors closing. He dropped the bag and skipped up to the summit of the viewing platform.

Returning, he motioned with a finger against his mouth for silence. The silver-grey BMW was idling by the entrance to the empty car park, he reported in a whisper, two men propped against it, taking stock.

Alex did not know that Kamei had blocked the bus at a stop on the seaward side of Yanagi and the frightened driver had volunteered the information that the *gaijin* had left the bus at the Yanagi Community Park. And he left the platform without seeing Kamei spin the chamber on his .38 revolver or the sun-shaded slim hood remove a metal baseball bat from the boot and practise a few swings.

There were no options: the *yakuza* could see the tower and were already meandering towards the vantage point, as Alex and Phyllis had done. They sidestepped gingerly down the smooth log steps and stooped under the low tree cover lining a forest path, away from the park and its facilities towards the sea. The path petered out and they were scrambling through undergrowth, the light under the forest canopy an underwater deep olive. Phyllis slipped and swore at her clumsiness; the travel bag was swiping the densely stacked tree trunks and snagging on brambles and Alex thought of leaving it hidden somewhere. She seemed to read his mind and when they rested after a rough descent from an outcrop of black volcanic rock she offered to carry it. He shook his head. The gash in his hand had opened again and they were both mentally on the edge, freezing whenever a bird they disturbed flapped away, squawking angrily.

They pressed on and thankfully reached a narrow trail. It was hardly more than a depression in the undergrowth but it let them move more comfortably. The sky was opening ahead of them, the trees thinning as the shore came nearer. Before it merged into a craggy downward slope, the path brushed a three-metre-high, heavy-duty steel mesh fence, painted green and almost obliterated by climbing vegetation and overhanging branches and ferns. 'Just high enough to keep the hikers out of the Miyamoto estate,' Phyllis said, her eyes following the course of the barrier until it was swallowed by the forest. 'But I reckon we can get over it somehow.'

Alex managed an ironic scoff. 'I suppose you could say in a perverted way we'd be safer inside the wire,' he said, giving a glance backwards and up. The viewing tower was not visible.

'Give me a hand,' Phyllis called. 'Lever me over.'

He dropped the bag and was positioning himself against the fence, his hands cupped togther at his knees, when he saw the box. It was discoloured, almost blending with the foliage around it. 'Don't touch the fence!' he barked, angered at the noise he made. 'It's electrified.' He backhanded a cover of fern leaves and indicated the wire running in both directions from the switching box. 'It's not a very strong current, wouldn't give you a shock.' He had seen the system used as a mild deterrent around some airport facilities. 'The vegetation doesn't bother it but if you put human bodyweight against it you'd trigger an alarm in the house somewhere.' He looked along the line of the fence. 'And maybe a camera.'

'Shit!', She released a deep breath and ran her fingers soothingly around the sockets of her tired eyes.

Alex gave her a hug and lifted the bag. 'Let's go down to the beach and follow it back to that village where the bus stopped first. We'd be safer among people. Can't be more than a mile or so. We'll have to risk the tract under Miyamoto's house though.' He checked his watch. 'It's almost nine.'

It wasn't necessary for Alex to persuade her. She knew the two armed *yakuza* were not far behind them and there was no immediate answer to the barrier thrown up by the alarmed fence. 'What a waste,' Phyllis groaned as they slipped down a short slope at the tree-line. The beach was a narrow strip of fine, ivory coloured pebbles broken in places by an outcrop of rock. Sunlight snapped on the water, the breezy air musty with the smell of wet, mouldering seaweed. Leaving the cigarettes and matches in a pocket, Phyllis shed the ripped, dirt-stained cotton coat and jammed it under a rock. Alex thought about abandoning his own ragged jacket but he touched the Jonsson letter inside it and chose to keep it.

They walked as quickly as the loose sand and pebbles allowed, hugging the shade from the wooded slopes: there was a chance the shoreline was visible from a point above them on the Miyamoto property. They skirted an outcrop of rock and came to a set of concrete steps, badly eroded by weather and salt water. Halfway up the short, steep flight, a plain, weather-pitted, concrete *torii* gate, its lower crossbar no taller than Alex, straddled it, leading up to the summit where a wooden Shinto shrine, the size of a small hut, had been cut into the hillside. The forest had thickened around it, almost smothering it. Alex was in front, and when he turned, after she had called out to him in a low, conspiratorial murmur, he saw her taking the cracked steps in twos, beckoning him to join her from beneath the *torii* gate. Breathing heavily from the strain, she explained that the shrine was just the fishermen's offering to the gods of the sea, and, as she expected, the little open-fronted hut protected a statue of Ebisu, one of the seven deities of good fortune, clutching his symbolic fishing rod and miniature wooden sea bream. She cast a glance inside, then pulled herself by a low branch up the incline at the side of the shrine. Alex paused for breath: he had read her intentions and he could see the green wire when he strained his eyes at the morass of foliage.

Propped against the shelter, her hands and clothes filthy, she beamed at him. 'I was right. The shrine at the top of the steps reaches the perimeter of the estate and they had to build the fence over it. Maybe there's a gap we can get through. Check the other side.'

A minute later they were back in front of the statue, Phyllis sitting on the top step, her head forlornly in her hands. 'It was worth a try,' she told herself. The meshing was attached to a solid steel frame which embraced the shrine with half an inch of leeway.

Alex tapped the outside of the sanctuary as if he were sizing it up to buy, then snapped a piece of rotten wood off a corner. With sweat rising again, neck and shirt soaked, he leaned inside and bent a strip of loose chipboard from the wall until it broke away. 'Are these places really holy?' he said without looking back at her. Straining to reach past the old statue, he tapped the backboard of the shrine. It was so thin it sounded hollow. Retreating, he slipped off his jacket, folded it carefully around the precious Jonsson letter and dropped it on the top step.

'What?' She turned. 'No, not really. Not in a Christian way. But they deserve respect. The fishermen probably come here now and again and leave a gift for the gods.' She pointed to a glass sake flask, tumbled on its side and covered with dust below the statue. 'Why do you ask?'

'I hope they forgive me,' he grunted, his words aimless as he eased himself feet first into the enclosure. 'It needs repairing anyway.' Supporting himself on his elbows he drew his legs up to his chest, clenched his teeth and lashed ferociously at the frail rear wall. The dense shroud of foliage drowned the sharp crack of splintering wood.

'Wow,' she uttered, peering in admiringly at the undergrowth filling the gap where the sheet of wood had collapsed in a single piece.

Alex pushed himself through the hole and turned on his stomach. 'Pass my jacket and the bag and come on through. 'Welcome to Chateau Miyamoto.'

They had seen or walked most of the ragged contour of the estate, and Alex had taken an aviation engineer's practised appraisal of his bearings from the viewing platform, and when they finally emerged from the forest they were so close to the gravelled car park and the burgundy Mercedes alongside the four-wheel-drive Suzuki that they had to duck back into the thick undergrowth and the cover of the low, leafy overhang. They could the see the front entrance of the main house beyond the foreign car and the terrace of the adjoining annexe where it faced the sea. The figure they had seen from the viewing tower was not there but a fold of curtain blowing onto the veranda hinted at an occupant. A hard, artificial surface, sprayed in green, made a path around the buildings and across the car park, finally merging with a ramp leading to the terrace. A spur path led to a gate, and a set of steps down to the shore. The office building was hidden beyond the trees but a car door closing and a revved engine in the thin air fixed its location.

'Give me the bag,' Phyllis hissed. She removed Alex's Nikon, set it to automatic exposure and made an early focus setting through the viewfinder. Hanging it around her neck she doubled up behind him, creeping under shade to the edge of the car park. She fell to one knee, level with the broad, ribbed leaves of a fern, and examined the camera. 'Has it got a date printer?'

He dropped beside her and whispered. 'Yes. I like to remember when my site pictures are taken. There should be six or seven exposures left.' He cast a glance behind them, wondering if the *yakuza* had tracked them to the shrine. He'd had the presence of mind to jam the piece of wood back into the break but the repairs wouldn't pass close inspection. 'Would you hurry please?'

The first picture was the safest. Kneeling against the trunk of a tree she captured the Merc's Fukuoka number plate with part of the house's lower cladding unimportantly rendered in hazy perspective. Then closer, sitting on the edge of the tarmac, still with a good level of lateral screening from a

326

patch of thick hedgerow planted as a border, she caught the damaged passenger side of the car in alignment with the roofed portal of the Miyamoto house. She moved sideways, between the Suzuki and the *yakuza* car, capturing the framework of the doorway with the sweep of the red bonnet and its famous three-pronged symbol. After snapping a three-quarter-view profile of the car with the façade of the house in the background she stooped and fixed it in the viewfinder with the white, soft-topped Suzuki on the other side.

Alex rose from behind the hedge, sweeping the compound with urgent darting eyes. 'That's enough, Phyl,' he uttered from a corner of his mouth.

She backed into him, relieved, releasing her breath noisily, and held out the camera. 'Just one more,' she said, her voice a command, her eyes fixed ahead. 'Me with the Merc and the house.'

'Forget it,' he gasped, a hand reaching out to her. Too late. She was stoop-running alongside the car and stood upright, her fingertips on the bonnet, the other hand indicating the Miyamoto house.

Alex sighed painfully, took a hop forward, steadied himself on one knee and breathed in deeply to arrest the thumping in his chest. He twisted the focus a touch and pressed.

'Who are you?' a hoarse, strained voice demanded. It was more fearful then threatening, and instead of racing for cover Phyllis spun towards an old man in a wheelchair who emerged from behind a richly crimson azalea where the specially surfaced pathway followed the sea line above the cliff. An armed *yakuza* would have screamed his command in his peculiar guttural corruption of street Japanese, sneering, menacing and commanding. A wide-brimmed, soft cotton hat and a pair of wide sunglasses shaded the parched, sallow skin on his skeletal, twisted face. His thin lips were cracked and purple and saliva bubbled in the corners of his mouth. 'I said, who are you?' He spoke in flat, breathless gasps.

He was in an electric-powered wheelchair, a woollen rug drawn up against his chest. A hand, its forearm and wrist thin and blemished, protruded from the sleeve of a *yukata* gown gripping the braided hilt of a Japanese long-sword. The blade was unsheathed across his lap, light reflecting along its length. Alex caught Phyllis's eyes, both recalling the distant shadowy figure and the reflections they had seen through the binoculars. He hadn't been sitting on a corner of the veranda waving out to sea: he had been practising his sword strokes. The chair whirred and moved easily on the hard surface towards Phyllis: Alex stepped from his cover onto the path, looking round for a weapon. The chair skidded to a halt. A second hand left the controls and caressed the spine of the sword.

'We're journalists,' Phyllis half lied, her Japanese faltering.

The figure grunted.

'We write articles for newspapers, about famous people. We're doing a story on Mr Miyamoto. With his permission.'

The covered head turned awkwardly towards Alex.

'From an international perspective.' She wondered whether the body in the chair understood what she was saying. There was no nurse or servant in attendance. He was physically capable of guiding the chair alone, using the controls on the armrests and a bar for manual steering, and he had the strength in his wrists and arms to lift the samurai sword. She looked past him at Alex, both knowing they were in the presence of ninety-year-old Shinichi Miyamoto. He was flexing his fingers around the hilt, his eyes darting unseen to them behind the sunglasses.

Alex listened to the exchange, Phyllis responding calmly to the rasped, short barks. 'What's going on?' he drawled, joining her.

'He says we're stupid. His son sees nobody here and we're trespassing. He's got an alarm on the chair and we've got fifteen seconds to walk to the gate.' They watched his clawlike hand leave the hilt of the sword and grope along the handlebar. Phyllis's voice became a corner-mouth slur. 'Let's walk away slowly. I want to get out with the camera and the film.'

'We wouldn't make it,' he uttered, taking a step towards the chair with the palms of his hands held out in placatory surrender. 'There'll be security at the gate and the crew of the BMW and two Mercs are going to be lurking somewhere.'

'And we can't go back the way we came,' she sighed.

Alex approached the old man as if he were trying to pacify a frightened dog, his eyes on the finger twitching above a button, his thin smile pleading, oozing harmlessness. He dropped to a knee, knowing a neat, sideways swipe with the sword would take his head off. He did not hear Phyllis catch her breath behind him.

'We want to talk to you about Jonsson. Roland Jonsson,' Alex intoned in clear, separated words.

Any animation in the cloudy eyes, any change in Miyamoto's expression, was lost behind the dark glasses and the shadows they cast over his face. A sharp grunt deep in the throat made his head twitch. Alex turned from his shoulders, giving Phyllis a brief resigned smile. Facing the old man again he repeated the Swede's name, pronouncing the surname with a hard j, then correctly as 'yonson'. 'He was your partner in— '

'I hear you,' the figure croaked, in English.

Phyllis sprang forward, her face wide, confused.

'I was expecting you,' Miyamoto said, steering the chair into a reverse swivel. 'Follow me.'

Alex retrieved the bag and caught up with Phyllis and they scurried after the hunched figure in the electric wheelchair, the purpose of the slip-proof path criss-crossing the estate now obvious. 'We're safer inside,' Alex concluded dourly.

She took his arm, pulling him closer. 'I'm sorry, Alex. I

shouldn't have insisted we came here.'

He squeezed her hand and tried to sound convincing. 'Another thirty minutes and we're away.'

The path led under the terrace and Miyamoto activated a remote control on his machine, opening a door where the path ended. The house had been designed for the chair and the invalid, built on a single level, where there were no steps or awkward screen runner rails, doors could be operated from the chair and lights and locks from controls in the rooms. Alex nudged Phyllis, shaking his head urgently when she bent reflexively to untie her muddy Nikes. They passed a doorway and saw an elderly woman in a kitchen. She wore a kimono and was staring towards the sound of visitors, her hands twisting a towel nervously. The old man steered the chair into another broad corridor and when they turned into it to follow he had disappeared.

'In here,' a rough voice called, drawing them into an airy room floored and panelled with dark hardwood and spread with bright Afghan carpets. A large-scale model of an early Nippon Nagasaki steamship in a glass case dominated one side with a panoramic photograph on the wall depicting Yanagi when it was an island, the old dockyards clearly visible. Above it, a clock in a barometer frame told them it was almost ten. Shinichi Miyamoto had powered the mobile chair behind a polished rosewood desk and, still wearing the sunhat and the beach glasses, his shrivelled form sat hunched like a freakish doll. The sword now lay unsheathed across an open newspaper and some other loose papers on the desk. He poured water from a plastic bottle into a tea bowl. The window-doors to the veranda were drawn aside to the width of the wheelchair, trapping the breeze into a cool draught that ruffled the soft fabric of the drapes. Miyamoto pressed a button on a panel of dials sunk into the desk and the doors to the room slid together soundlessly. He motioned them to draw a pair of tubular-steel chairs closer.

Phyllis lifted the damp and smudged travel bag and clutched it in her lap. Not daring to look down, she drew the zip open, slipping a hand inside until she found Alex's dictaphone recorder with trepidant fingers. Holding it below the level of the desk, she handed it across to him and coughed at the moment he pressed its record button. Alex wondered if she'd noticed the spread of typewritten pages on the desk. He caught her eyes with his, flicking, leading her he hoped to the familiar pages, laid out with generous spaces between the dates and the bursts of short and longer text. He knew how close she was to exhaustion, and with the photographs trapped in the camera, she craved an end to the torture. She was missing his message. Was she hallucinating? Did she realise she was sitting in front of the man who'd fathered the evil she saw in his son, the man who'd swindled his foreign partner out of a company now worth billions and let them put him into a hell-hole of a concentration camp and then promote the lie that he was killed by an Allied bomb.

'Tell Mr Miyamoto the papers on his desk belong to me,' he said, clearly enough for the old man to understand.

'What?' It was Phyllis.

'He's got the diaries somebody in Nippon Nagasaki took from my briefcase and copied.' He grunted, his scalp bristling as the anger rose through him. 'It also means he knows about the Jonsson letter. His son must have told him.' He resisted an urge to touch the envelope in his pocket, to check he still had the letter the Miyamoto family were willing to kill for. He suppressed the urge to tell him, wondering what the old man would do if he knew how close he was to touching it. Was he totally dependent on the chair? He didn't doubt his strength: wielding the sword was his exercise, perhaps his obsession.

Miyamoto's head rocked. He nudged closer to the desk, a dark, thickly veined mottled hand upturned below it, jerky fingers searching for the button.

Phyllis opened her mouth to translate.

Miyamoto ignored her. 'I do not speak English for a long time.'

'But you remember enough to read the diaries from Camp Nagasaki Six,' Alex said, the recorder clammy in his palm.

The sarcastic praise from the foreigner provoked a discharge of phlegm which Miyamoto contained with the sleeve of his *yukata* and cleared with a sip of water. His other hand slipped off the knob under the desk. He leaned forward, searching for it, at the same time straining through the dark glasses at the papers. His dry cheeks were cratered with brown cancerous lacerations. Was his scalp so hideously scarred that he always wore the ridiculous hat and big sunglasses, Phyllis wondered. Finally, he spoke to Alex. 'You are from London. You must now help my son buy a new aeroplane.'

'Something like that,' Alex said, with a short-lived smirk. 'But there's a problem. Your son inherited his understanding of truth and honesty from you.'

Miyamoto drew a piece of paper closer and leaned forward. 'Your name is *Bo-ru-ton*,' he read impassively. Clearing his throat, he crooked his head towards Phyllis. 'And you are Wakai. A Japanese *gaijin*. My son tells me you are trying to destroy our company. You write many lies.'

'I'm American,' Phyllis spat. 'A *sansei* from California. And your son's destroying the Nippon Nagasaki group himself. He took money from the profitable companies, like transport and marine engineering, to pay for his real-estate and stock speculation during the bubble. When land prices and the Nikkei collapsed in eighty-nine he lost billions of yen from his stocks, land, golf course shares, his art collection. They're worth a quarter of what they were five years ago. Nippon Nagasaki Corporation, his flagship, the company Jonsson started and you took from him, is virtually bankrupt.'

The old man fidgeted, the position of the warning button

still frustrating him.

Alex was saying, 'So he had to squeeze the subsidiaries making money or with cash flows he could milk, like his airline. He ran NN Air on a shoestring, kept maintenance to a minimum and was criminally negligent regarding the pilots' health checks. He could be under arrest within hours.'

Miyamoto burst into Japanese, spitting invective, his frail body shaking in the wheelchair.

'Miyamoto *san* rejects the allegations,' Phyllis said to Alex neutrally, a warning in the eyes behind the cracked glasses.

'Possibly,' he said amiably, showing Miyamoto a brittle smile. They needed twenty, twenty-five more minutes. 'Can Miyamoto *san* tell us about the diaries? It was Roland Jonsson in Camp Nagasaki Six, wasn't it? The man the British sailors in his room knew as Johnson. If it was, we know from the entries that he was alive after the atom bomb exploded on August ninth, forty-five, but he wasn't there when it was liberated by the Americans a few weeks later. What happened to him? Does Miyamoto *san* happen to know? Just out of interest.' He eased the recorder closer to the desk.

Shinichi Miyamoto watched the blurred images through his tinted glasses. The foreigners confused him. More than sixty-five years had passed since he had met the aggressive, devious Swedish engineer in Tokyo, with his money and his dream of adapting the latest European marine turbine technology to an emerging, greedily receptive industry. And he made it clear when Miyamoto became his technical partner that the creation of wealth, not Japan's national interests drove his ambitions. Shinichi Miyamoto himself was three years out of the Imperial College of Maritime Technology and after a year in happier times at a British shipyard he had returned to Japan, fired with ambition, well connected but penniless. The Yanagi workshops they built were only a start: Jonsson Nagasaki attracted so much military and civilian business that by the time Japan engaged China in full-scale military conflict in 1937 they had bought or rented facilities at all major naval production sites south of Tokyo. It was unreasonable for the *gaijin*, even if, like Jonsson, they were not designated enemies of Japan, to possess so much of her wealth and so it was logical to enact the nationalisation laws, forcing these foreign-owned companies to divest part of their investment to a Japanese national. Jonsson had, with ill-feeling, transferred thirty per cent of the stock of Jonsson Nagasaki to Miyamoto in 1938 and changed the corporate name. But how could a situation continue whereby a foreigner owned a majority interest in a company whose output was vital to a country embarking on a war of national survival? Couldn't these *gaijin* understand this? Jonsson, in his stupidity, resisted requests to reconsider his anti-Japan posture and bring the company under full Japanese ownership. He was totally responsible for the regrettable consequences of his obstinacy. Of course, he knew that he would have to cede executive management to Japanese control during hostilities but expected to regain it when normality returned after Japan's victory.

What did the foreigner from London ask? Do I know what happened to Roland Jonsson? Whatever happened during wartime is irrelevant today. *Kako wa kako*. The past is the past, as we say sensibly in Japan.

Until Hiroshi had sent him these pages of nonsense about Camp Nagasaki Six and talked vaguely about a *gaijin* with one of the old Letters of Recognition he hadn't thought about Jonsson for twenty-five years, since the last time he had left the family compound. His old friend the prime minister, Kakuei Tanaka, had just been indicted for taking a million-dollar bribe from Lockheed to smooth the sales of their Tristar aircraft to Japan and it was considered an expedient moment for Miyamoto senior to use the diversion and retire himself to his Yanagi estate with a serious, possibly terminal, illness. But the chance for a brief, secret excursion was irresistible. He was driven the short distance to the dockyards to watch through blackened windows the launch of two container ships with the NN maritime logo emblazoned on the funnels. He had cried with pride. Two buses ferried a contingent of *gaijin* bankers to witness the triumphant fruit of the project they had financed and as he studied the big, prosperous figures, sweating and smirking in their suits on a quayside, he recalled another group of men at a differeent time. Lean, ashen-faced, flea-ridden sick men in rags, standing a few steps away from where they were now all admiring the majestic merchant ships taking to the waters of Nagasaki harbour. Jonsson was the sickest. He was still stubbornly resisting Miyamoto's instruction to divest the remaining seventy per cent of Nippon Nagasaki KK in spite of strong, persistent pressure for an amicable compromise.

When war broke out with America and its European allies in December 1941, Jonsson removed himself absolutely from executive management of a company now geared totally to military production, opting not to cooperate personally in Japan's war effort and instead perform voluntary work as a citizen from a neutral country. He still refused to sell down his majority holding in the company to Shinichi Miyamoto and this was finally unacceptable to the junior partner. In the paranoid world of Japan, where the *kempeitai* secret police demanded that its citizens denounce anyone they suspected of anti-Japan activities, it was the simplest act of patriotic duty for an important industrialist like Miyamoto to intimate that a supposedly neutral Swede was transmitting details of Japan's merchant fleets and technical capabilities to the enemy.

Jonsson was arrested in April 1942 and confined to a soft internment centre for foreign civilians on the lower slopes of Mount Fuji near Kawaguchi City. Miyamoto visited the old

335

converted school occasionally, offering the Swede the chance of freedom in return for a letter of recognition, like the first in 1938, handing over Nippon Nagasaki KK to full and proper Japanese ownership. Jonsson always became enraged, screaming abuse at his tormentor and the liar who had put him in prison. It was too much for Miyamoto to hope that Jonsson would be executed – he was still legally neutral – but when Camp Nagasaki Six opened in October, providing prisoner-of-war labour for the Kawaminami shipyards and the Nippon Nagasaki marine engine workshops on the island of Yanagi, Shinichi Miyamoto seized the opportunity. The war effort could still use the expertise of his 'treacherous' partner, he argued before the military authorities, and recommended he be confined near the company's factory facilities. He might also be persuaded to confess his spying activities and denounce his confederates. In May 1943 Roland Jonsson was transferred under guard to Camp Nagasaki Six on Yanagi Island.

The old man's withered, insensitive fingers found the button under the lip of his desk. Yes, *gaijin san*, I know exactly what happened to Roland Jonsson.

12 August, 1945

A short, violent thunderstorm in the night shook the huts, rousing the prisoners who thought it was the first air-raid since the big explosion in Nagasaki on the ninth. It forced a million mosquitoes into the barrack sanctuaries, to feast on the five hundred sick and starved bodies still in the camp. Men trying to doze until their night-time trip to the latrine slapped and swatted uselessly as the bites of their tormentors joined the welts, the open sores and boils they carried with barely a complaint. There was a good turnout for the five o'clock tenko, *many of the chronically sick struggling in the mud in case the rumours were true and it would be their last roll-call as prisoners-of-war. Leaving the sick and the officers as usual, the work gang left the camp at six thirty under command of the Sergeant Major, whom the prisoners knew only as Bo Ku Go, with the Weasel, the Calcutta Barber, Dead Pan Joe, twenty-five civilian guards and a pair of Koreans in attendance. It was going to be hard to point the finger of retribution at these bastards after the war, and Lieutenant Colonel Horrigan of the US Army Air Force, and the senior officer in Camp Nagasaki Six, instructed the men to do their utmost to discover the guards' real names and commit their faces to memory. Meanwhile, every military guard had a universal nickname. Flip, the cookhouse hancho, who had personally ordered the Weasel to force a fire-bucket of sea-water down the throat of the most senior British officer for accidentally drawing water from the wrong storage tank, would be close to the top of the retribution list. Bo Ku Go was the nearest the prisoners could get to pronouncing the Japanese for air-raid shelter and he was the most violent in a clique of clinically pyschopathic guards who found the inflicting of pain a duty and a pleasure. For some reason today, he had forsaken his bamboo pole and carried a service rifle with the bayonet fixed.*

On the rise outside the camp, the sour-smelling ranks in the three-year-old shit-stained fatigues they wore without underclothes and rubber pads strapped around their bare feet strained for a sight of Nagasaki, about five miles away. The gas and dust over the city had thinned but it had not shifted completely. A party sent to the city yesterday reported burnt corpses and limbs in the harbour and people wandering about, mouths frozen in silent screams, holding on to dripping bits of their own skin as they walked. They said there were thousands of people lying about, just about alive, waiting for help, and there were burning heaps of bodies in the streets. The guards ignored the mutterings, their staves and bats carried loosely across their shoulders. They were as keen as anyone for information, for the smallest understanding about what had happened to the port city of Nagasaki.

Cyclops and his enforcer in the dockyard, a flat-faced ultra-violent twenty-one-year-old the prisoners called the Kid, were waiting at the Nippon Nagasaki gates with a detachment of mixed army and navy guards. Cyclops was a civilian but he wore a plain naval uniform when he came, usually once a week, to the worksites and seemed to be in charge of all production facilities. When he was there the yard rules were brutally enforced: no sitting down, no conversation, no standing near the fires in winter, no smoking and a half-hour for lunch. The day before the raid on Nagasaki the Kid laid out Able Seaman Williams from HMS Exeter with a wrench, smashing most of his teeth. He hadn't bowed low enough. Japanese civilian workers were also allowed to inflict punishment beatings and exercised this freedom liberally.

Cyclops watched the prisoners trudge through the gates for another roll-call. The Kid patrolled near the head of the column, occasionally reaching out with a short bamboo pole and jabbing a POW sharply in the ribs, a signal to fall out and muster by the quay. Beethoven, the dockyard interpreter with an extremely short temper, explained that another party was to be dispatched to Nagasaki to help open up the roads. Roland Jonsson was two days out of the camp hospital after his latest bout of dysentery and was in the deepest trough of a throat-searing dry retch when he felt the jab.

'*Good luck,*' Tom Humphrey uttered from the corner of his mouth. '*Find out what you can, mate.*'

The civilian was in his late thirties, about the same age as Petty Officer Humphrey. He had scratched the mosquito bites on his ears and arms until they bled freely and painlessly. A boil behind his left knee had burst but he didn't feel the chafing or notice how it made him limp. He even tried to joke with the friendly sailor from the bunk below his. In his lightly accented, almost perfect English, with its soft Scandinavian lilt, he said, '*I'll tell you first if you promise to call me by my real name for once.*'

The other man dared a broad grin. '*I will, I promise. But you sound more English than us Cornish lads.*'

'*Tom.*' The Swede dragged his thin frame alongside the sailor, his mouth against the taller man's shoulder. '*Tom. You've been kind to me for two years. I have not reciprocated or expressed my feelings. It is my character.*'

'*Easy, Johnny. Get moving for chrissake and look out for the Kid.*'

Cyclops was looking at them, his head crooked towards a guard, gesturing with his stick.

Jonsson's breath was foul, his breathing uneasy; he had something to say. '*I have a few things in my mattress. A letter or two and a document. They took everything else when they brought me here. If something happens to me please take care of my papers. Don't let—.*'

Neither of them had seen the interpreter sneak towards them behind a wall of prisoners. The blow from Beethoven's boot slammed into the back of Jonsson's knees, his incoherent ranting drowning the single scream from his victim, who collapsed, scattering the prisoners around him.

Forming lines for the next inevitable roll-call, Tom

glanced back at the quay where the mainland detail were helping Jonsson into the broad-bottomed barge the Japanese military used to ferry people and supplies between the island and Nagasaki. He saw Cyclops talk to the Kid, whose stabbing nods of acknowledgement ended with a low bow before he hoisted his rifle and disappeared down the steps. 'Ichi, hachi, yon' Tom ennunciated, almost missing his turn to shout 'one eight four' as he dwelled on the taciturn, remote Swede. It would have earned him a slap from the naval guard patrolling the ranks. A cultured civilian among the rough and ready military prisoners, Jonsson had broken the first law of prison camp survival: stay together. He had no natural friends in the camp, no comrades from battle or battalion, and had made no efforts to attach himself to a pod of men who shared the same strong will to live. He was put in room five with forty-eight tough British seamen, survivors of the battle of the Java Sea and already six-month veterans of Camp Nagasaki Six, taking the bunk of one of their comrades who had died in a dockyard accident. The conditions, the filth, the rats and lice, the beatings and the dying horrified and traumatised him and he soon stopped complaining about the small things, like his room-mates' habit of anglicising his name and the quality and amount of the food. For a while after he had come to the camp he tried to take his professional grievances to the camp commandant through the interpreter. His first appeal was met with a discouraging slap; for the second, and last, Beethoven broke his nose. To the Japanese in the camp mess, where he was first put to work, Jonsson was just another cowardly gaijin. The honcho Flip, whose real name was Iwata, was the worst: when Jonsson and an Indonesian mishandled a two-hundred-pound barrel of miso paste on the gangplank to the ferry barge, allowing it to smash on the quay, Flip and a man called Yamada used the pair for ju-jitsu practice in the guardhouse.

He was often sick, debilitated by diarrhoea or tormented by lice and fleas and the bites and lesions that turned septic or refused to heal. He survived the dysentery outbreak of August 1944 and the pneumonia epidemic of the following February which killed twenty-two prisoners and it was probably only his superhuman will to right an injustice and exact some unspeakable revenge that kept him alive. Tom and others in room number five noticed how his unexpected transfer to tough dockyard labour in the middle of 1945 seemed to aggravate his mental torment and arouse in him an increasingly forlorn and hopeless desire for freedom. There were times when, in the delirium of yet another bout of sickness and dripping with sweat in the bunk above Tom's, Jonsson would mumble and scream in his own language and in only semi-coherent English about betrayal, conspiracy and revenge.

The barge's engine was running on a desperate concoction of low-quality oil processed from plant roots, and coughed uneasily, a trail of noxious black exhaust settling on its wake. Jonsson and fourteen other prisoners, all light-skinned Dutch-Indonesians, squatted silently on the damp, leaking planks, their backs to the prow. The Kid, the Weasel and two armed naval guards sat at the rear, talking earnestly, arms thrusting occasionally towards a spot on the changed, darkening landscape of the eastern shore. The two Korean guards watched the unfolding scene of the tragedy sullenly and silently. Passing the promontory on the northern tip of Yanagi, all eyes fell on two of the big steamships that served the inshore islands of

341

southern Kyushu and now floated on their sides like harpooned whales. Across the harbour, the buildings in the Mitsubishi shipyards looked intact, the low sharp noses of two destroyer-size warships visible and safely protected between the high dry-dock walls. But for the first time in decades there were no spirals of smoke from the foundry chimneys and no rumble of freight trains along the docks. Roofless, half-wrecked buildings appeared nearside as they approached Dejima after forty minutes and scorched ground made broad desolate swaths on both sides of the Urakami River, blackening the slopes as far as the water line. The boat shuddered, striking solid debris in the malodorous, filthy water. Passing the patchwork remains of Nagasaki Station and tying up at a pier by the Inasa Bridge they surveyed a wasteland of rubble, twisted iron and still-smouldering ruins where bundles of humans in rags wandered between makeshift canvas-covered aid stations and the fires where they assembled to cook whatever they found to eat. Three days after the bomb had fallen on Nagasaki, bodies were still being pulled from the river and the city's canals, where the injured had staggered to try to relieve the unrelievable pain on their heat-skinned bodies. Thousands were still being dug from the rubble, and approaching the hypocentre they were extracted in pieces, carbonised, disintegrated or fused to other corpses or masonry. As the bodies emerged or the injured died, they were carried to improvised funeral pyres which had been burning for three days. Priests or relations gathered a pathetic handful of ashes to commemorate the end of a lifetime.

With the rubbish-filled river on their left, the Kid ordered the POWs into a single file for a numbed march across the lunar landscape of destruction, their

eyes drawn to huddled groups of sick and injured. The
cool off-shore breeze in a cloudless sky had quickly
given way to fetid, hazy humidity over the remains of
the city. The Kid dropped behind the sweat-soaked
stinking column, unable to comprehend. As far as he
could see, the city of Nagasaki on either side of the
Urakami River, to the mid-slopes of the mountains
bordering it, had been devastated, stripped of almost
every manmade and natural feature that had existed
before eleven o'clock on 9 August. A few remained,
defiant in the stagnant layers of haze and smoke: the
warped steel frame of the Mitsubishi steelworks and its
chimneys, sturdy terraced walls on the slopes, the
imposing shell of Urakami Cathedral and a few
skeletal, blackened trees. It was his first sight of the
city since the bomb and it wasn't what he expected.
The West Japan Army's Nagasaki Fortress Command,
across the water from Yanagi Island and four
kilometres from the hypocentre, reported light damage
from the bombing and the Kid had believed it. In front
of him the fifteen gaijin bent around the rotting carcass
of a horse. Were they smiling? Were they enjoying the
atrocity, the butchery everywhere? He ripped the
bayonet from its sheath and rammed it onto his rifle,
his eyes burning with hatred. The Weasel dropped back
and spoke to him, but the Kid was transfixed, his rifle
in two hands across his body. He felt a back-hand rap
on his chest and it snapped him conscious. The Kid
blinked, thanked his comrade, and slung his rifle over
a shoulder, issuing orders to the Koreans as he moved
along the column. They had reached a road which
three days earlier had run between the packed houses
and businesses of Senzamachi but now had its course
delineated by the heaps of rubble and burned wood
piled beside it. All along it, groups of civilians and

soldiers were clearing a passage for the relief convoys, stymied by the blockages three kilometres away on the main routes into the city. It was obvious to the prisoners what their job was to be and they followed the Korean guards, clambering over the shells of vehicles and the wreckage and rubble already hauled off the carriageway.

Roland Jonsson lagged behind the work gangs as usual and when he paused for breath after another bout of retching he failed to notice the Kid and the Weasel drop back to him. The force of a rifle butt cracked three ribs and left him heaving in the dust, his scream trapped by his fight to breathe. Without words, the Weasel pulled the Swede to his feet by his trousers and sent him lurching and stumbling across the scorched terrain, past the sturdy remnants of buildings and huddled survivors who neither noticed nor cared about anything. Jonsson clutched his side, chancing a backward glance at his fellow prisoners but they had gone, their minds and concentration centred entirely on their own survival.

Nine hundred yards from the atomic bomb's hypocentre, the Mitsubishi steelworks complex close to the Urakami tram station was a frame web of twisted heat-blackened steel, a useless shelter for the smouldering heaps of corrugated roof, crushed equipment and the half-melted stock, clotted and fused and scattered in piles. Still entombed were most of the corpses of the Japanese workers and the bands of Korean, Chinese and POW forced labourers. The Kid led the trio to a gutted, roofless brick building flanked by two cracked chimneys standing between the fragile ruins of the foundries. The stench of death and acrid smoke filled the rubble-strewn rooms of the shell; and the silence was awesome. The party entered the building warily. Rats scurried away and a filthy soot-black dog reluctantly released the lacerated piece of rotted flesh it had been tugging from the debris. Jonsson spoke good, almost fluent Japanese and having lived in Nagasaki to supervise the construction of the marine engineering works on Yanagi Island he even understood the harsh Kyushu dialect. His ability to understand the enemy was his only weapon; Cyclops knew about it, of course, and was always cautious when he was near, but the Kid and the Weasel didn't, and when Jonsson heard the young brute with the rifle describing how he was going to kill him, he fell painfully to his knees, hands together, his eyes pleading up at the open sky between the beams and splintered rafters that remained. When the scream came it was silent. The Weasel had taken the rifle from the Kid and moved behind the whimpering foreigner, his legs apart, feet dug into the dust. He was a short-legged, stocky country lad whose mental instability rendered him unfit even for front-line military service. His cap sat uneasily on his square, cropped head as he measured the lateral sweep and drew the rifle across his body. As Jonsson begged at the Kid's feet the Weasel brought the steel-plated butt-end of the stock against the base of the prisoner's skull, stunning him with a single blow, silencing him, ending his pain. Consumed by a lust for violence, his face contorted and his feral eyes burning, the Weasel raised the gun again. The Kid sprang at him, shoving him backwards, praising him for his work, for his restraint, for not spilling blood. The Weasel's smile flickered as his face twitched uncontrollably, but he backed off. The Kid took a length of rope from a pouch on his belt and snapped it taut in his fists. Then he leaned over the still figure and doubled it around the neck, bracing himself once before choking what little life was left in Roland Jonsson.

345

They hauled him in a canvas shroud from the ruins of the steelworks to the nearest funeral pyre where the Kid scowled at a sallow-faced man with a notebook who was recording whatever details were known about the bodies brought to the fire. 'A foreigner,' the Kid scoffed. 'A Westerner.' He produced a piece of paper written in roman script with a katakana phonetic transcription beside it. 'Roland Jonsson,' he intoned awkwardly, throwing a thumb over his shoulder. 'Found him over there, in a trench. Must have suffocated under the rubble.' The official transcribed the name perfunctorily into his book and motioned to a position in the body line. The inconsistences in the story, the way the weak-brained soldiers had managed to interpret a foreigner's name and even write it down in Japanese, were meaningless in the endless nightmare of carnage. Twenty minutes later the corpse of Roland Jonsson was tipped onto the burning logs, just another sad victim of the enemy's savagery from the sky.

Shinichi Miyamoto's arthritic fingers closed thankfully on the button under the edge of the table and depressed it, but the effort forced a change of expression when he clenched his teeth and it was caught by his visitors.

'You killed Roland Jonsson, didn't you?' Alex said flatly, his eyes flashing to the spools on his recorder. They were still turning. Answer the question, for fuck's sake, he hissed silently. The frail-looking figure sat impassively in his chair, his secrets still his own. His hand had returned to the desk and rested on the long, ribbed hilt of the sword. 'Or you had him killed,' Alex insisted. 'Like your son had an innocent woman murdered in Tokyo.'

'And a man,' Phyllis said in Japanese. 'An employee of Nippon Nagasaki Corporation who wanted to tell the world your son was buying politicians. It wasn't a traffic accident.'

'So how did you do it?' Alex spat. 'Were you in Nagasaki during the war?'

A few minutes, the old man pondered, the flurry of words starting to confuse him. In a few minutes this silly episode will be over. Just hold their interest. His thin maroon lips parted, exposing his absurdly perfect false teeth in a gruesome smile. His hand left the sword and moved slowly to his head. It took him a moment to grip the soft fabric before he could peel off the sun hat without dislodging the sunglasses. His scalp was blotched with scar tissue, patterned like a map, and wispy strands of sparse grey hair grew in short tufts from the few healthy patches of skin. Then he took both hands to the frames of the sunglasses and lifted them carefully off his ears. With the hat, they had hidden a black patch over Miyamoto's right eye. He raised a shaky finger to it. 'My shipyard in Kobe was bombed. I lose my eye.' Phyllis helped him convert from the Japanese calendar. 'Nineteen forty-three. In spring.' He made a gesture at the pathetic state of his body. 'And the night of March nine, 1945. I was leaving Tokyo by train when the B-29s came. They killed a hundred thousand people in one attack. Did you know that? More people than the atom bomb on Nagasaki.' He brought a finger close to his face. 'I was lucky to escape from the train with little wounds.'

Alex hardly heard him: he wasn't listening. He was staring at the sinister patch covering the old man's eye socket and had lifted a finger quizzically towards it. He looked at Phyllis who had also remembered something but was finding it impossible to believe. He said, in a voice hoarse with tension, 'You *were* in Nagasaki during the war. You're in the diaries.'

'Cyclops,' Phyllis remembered. 'The POWs gave the guards nicknames. They didn't know your real names. You were the bastard in the dockyards they called Cyclops. Now we know why.'

'And we know why you were so hard on Roland Jonsson,' Alex said. 'Poor sod. The other prisoners must have thought he was raving mad when he said he owned the factories he was being made to work in.' He scoffed ironically. 'But the factories and workshops *did* belong to him. There never was another agreement selling you the rest of his company.'

Miyamoto cupped an ear at the torrent of English, his head angled towards them.

'And I suppose,' Phyllis concluded, 'you realised the war was almost over. You knew about Hiroshima, you'd assumed the role of company chief executive so you travelled, talked to people, and you'd seen what happened to Nagasaki yourself.' She changed effortlessly into Japanese: she wanted him to understand. 'But Roland Jonsson didn't die in Nagasaki Six like you wanted him to do, did he? In spite of the beatings, the diseases and accidents. But if he wasn't out of the way when the war ended, and Japan inevitably lost, he would finger you not only as a war criminal but as the man who swindled and cheated him out his legitimate ownership of Nippon Nagasaki. You had to kill him.'

The old man's hands began to shake on the desk, rattling the sword and scattering papers. 'Of course I had to kill him,' he shrieked. 'He wouldn't sell. The company belonged to me, to Japan, not a *gaijin*. I gave him many chances to save himself, to leave Japan. He was stubborn, he refused every time. I killed him for Japan, for the future of my company.' Saliva frothed from his mouth as his speech stumbled into incoherent gibberish. 'And you will also die. The Emperor understands what we must sacrifice.' His dim, good eye blinked behind a heavy, warted lid; his frail, ruined body shuddered as his hands thrashed on the desktop for the dark glasses and the weapon.

Phyllis shivered and carefully, soundlessly, eased her hand into the travel bag on her lap, level with the rim of Miyamoto's desk. She wondered about the light. Alex

348

clicked off the recorder and spoke to her, facing forward. 'It's time to leave. Let's go for the window. I think he locked the doors.'

'One second. Take the bag.' She had the camera in her hands, engaged it and swiftly adjusted the exposure. Miyamoto's chair whirred and shuddered against the desk as he jabbed demonically at the controls. He looked up, suddenly aware of the figures across the desk. Phyllis aimed, twisted the focus and pressed.

The cypress-green doorway to the shelter-like hut blended quietly with the foliage of the copse and opened by security card onto a stairway. From it, a tunnelled passage led under an asphalt spur path to the machinery room below the compact, modern business building Hiroshi Miyamoto had erected on the estate as his private operations centre. It was the route used for discreet entries and departures and was taken by Hinohara and his black-suited colleague, Takada, after they had driven directly from the hospital. Still seething and cursing at the damage to his car, his head muddled by a night full of unreleased tension and empty of sleep, he had carelessly forgotten the instructions governing the Okudaira syndicate's security role with president Miyamoto's family and parked the Mercedes in a forbidden zone in front of the main house. From the boiler room, with the heating and humming air-conditioning equipment and generators and the smell of oil, another secure door gave onto a basement corridor where the storage spaces and the estate's security room were located.

A young electronics engineer employed by a security firm owned by the syndicate through a front operation sat before stacked screens, telephones and recording devices, watching on one of the monitors the fuzzy image of a man climbing the steps from the shore to the estate. 'Where's Endo?' he asked Hinohara, whose approach he had been following on a

349

screen since admitting him through the main entrance. 'He's not with Kamei *san*.'

Hinohara pulled a chair across and slumped gratefully onto it, laying his cellular telephone on the operator's worktop. The other man tossed his jacket aside and sat himself in a corner with a tabloid, a yawn soon breaking across his face. 'He went back to the sports ground for the car,' Hinohara explained. 'The *gaijin* are hiding somewhere in the fucking bushes. We've called in more help. At least they're not inside the fence.'

The security controller indicated a screen showing pictures of the building's parking area above them, the executive fleet and their drivers caught in the camera's sweep. He pressed a button and the image changed to a secluded patch of paving with a light-coloured BMW parked on it. They could just make out a figure in it. 'He's back. The car wasn't there a couple of minutes ago. 'Where's your Merc?' he asked Hinohara.

The *yakuza* slapped his forehead. 'Shit. I left it at the house. Wasn't thinking.'

'Can't check it,' the operator complained. As the vulnerable access points to the grounds were reasonably covered, Hiroshi Miyamoto demanded privacy in the area around the main house and annexe. No one ever talked about the real reason: the old man, seen occasionally from a distance through the trees as he took the air on tracks specially laid for his motorised wheelchair. 'You'd better shift it before the president sees it. They're due for a break soon.' He switched to a panelled corridor hung with paintings and a closed double door at the end.

The lock to the security room door clicked as a card was swiped through the scanner and Kamei joined them. His skin was clammy, his face pale. He rubbed the soreness in his eyes and scratched at the itchiness on his scalp. 'Fucking insects.' The double-breasted suit was creased and the gold cross-chain on his Italian shoes remoulded in mud. He stood behind Hinohara, scanning the screens and nodding sceptically. 'They're probably hiding under a bush somewhere, maybe following the shore back to the town. 'We'll get them when they surface.' A telephoned buzzed. The security man answered and gave it to Kamei. 'It's Endo,' he said, motioning to a screen and the figure of the *yakuza* propped against the BMW, looking towards the camera, mobile to his ear.

'Talk to me,' Kamei growled.

'The boys called from town. Probably nothing, but there's a pack of police cars and an ambulance or two grouping around Nagasaki Station. Three more black-and-whites seen coming down the thirty-four, by Nakajima Bridge. They thought you should know.'

'Get them on the line and keep them there,' he ordered. It was ten thirty-seven on his watch. 'Let me know if the cops as much as fart out of line.' He had hung up and was standing immobile, pondering the situation with his cheeks between his fingers, when a red warning lamp on a console of lumpy bulbs and dials began to flash. The controller stared at it disbelief. It had never been engaged before.

Hiroshi Miyamoto was an hour into his discourse. He worked without prompt notes but frequently delved into a stack of papers to find a statistic or illustrate a point with a quote. With Yuriko Shimada at the door end of the oak-panelled room's oval conference table, he had gathered the twenty-two principal presidents from among the ninety-two subsidiaries and affiliate companies, all interlocked by mutual shareholdings and common goals under the Nippon Nagasaki banner. They were universally glum, and some, like Shigeo Onoda, president of NN Marine, angry and resentful at the way Miyamoto had drained his company and the other profitable divisions of cash and mortgaged their tangible

351

assets to finance five years of extravagance and waste by his headline operation, Nippon Nagasaki Corporation. NN Marine was the direct descendant of the original marine engineering company and its business remained the prestigious core activity of the group. Now, all its valuable assets, its land and holdings of securities, had been used as collateral or guarantees for Miyamoto's vast borrowings, ruining as he pillaged the balance sheet its reputation as well as its independent financial credibility. Many of the big-ticket speculations Miyamoto found irresistible were, by 1995, worth a fraction of their original price and were delivering no significant investment income. His struggle to raise cash to meet debt repayments attracted the critical attention of the banks, whose own generosity in lending their shareholders' funds to legitimate business and crime-syndicate front companies in the first place was almost criminal in itself. And finally the authorities: the trade and industry regulatory agencies and the national tax bureau. They were particularly interested in the dubious financial transactions among Nippon Nagasaki's *keiretsu*-connected companies. And now the Civil Aviation Control Bureau of the Ministry of Transport were taking their investigation into the crash of the NN Air DC-8 a big step forward to a major inquiry into the airline's procedures. And at the Tokyo District Prosecutor's Office, a small team had been quietly assigned to open a file on Nippon Nagasaki Corporation's alleged connections with proscribed organised-crime syndicates.

'We must face this severe situation with the same dynamic spirit and determination that my father displayed at the end of the war when our country was in ruins,' Miyamoto announced, his pen pointer stabbing at the growth lines on a flip-chart graph.

Onoda caught the eye of Sakakibara, the silver-haired president of Nippon Nagasaki Transportation, another core group business. He had been forced to announce a one-point-seven-billion-yen pre-tax loss in the last financial year, which ended in March, the first time in forty years the company had fallen into the red. Even the least observant analyst might question why NN Transportation bought two Chiba golf courses and a Shikoku hotel development from Nippon Nagasaki Corporation. Only the stupidest analyst would not know the answer.

'The first objective of our restructuring will be NN Air,' Miyamoto said flatly. 'It has nothing to do with the regrettable crash at Haneda two weeks ago. I have been considering it for some time.' He sipped from a glass of water. 'The world economic situation concerning air transportation has turned against Japan and I have decided to reorganise the airline accordingly.' He turned a chart. 'I have instructed brokers to initiate the purchase of NN Air shares starting Monday on the Tokyo Stock Exchange.' He nodded towards the silver-haired man opposite Onoda. 'The buyer will be Nippon Nagasaki Transportation. My own block of shares will be transferred in due course. I leave it to Sakakibara *san* to coordinate the financing of this arrangement. NN Transportation will then enter into discussions with the Miami owners of the five remaining aircraft to cancel the leases on at least two of them and renegotiate the terms for the others. Incorporating the airline into our mainstream transport unit will enable us to trim staff levels by at least four hundred people in operations and support.'

Sakakibara's sigh was almost audible; he exchanged another rueful glance with Onoda. It was now absolutely clear NN Transportation was to become the cesspool for Miyamoto's group shit. The buzz from the pager on the belt covered by Yuriko Shimada's lilac half-sleeved jacket was loud enough in the stupefied silence to turn the heads of the delegates. Miyamoto caught her eye and made the slightest of nods. He had left instructions with his secretary and with security that the meeting was only to be interrupted in severe

emergency circumstances. Leaving her president distantly
visible in the gap between the double doors, Yuriko called
the security room from the corridor, her expression stiffening
as she listened to the urgent, excited voice. She snapped the
phone shut and beckoned to Hiroshi Miyamoto. The eyes of
the sombre, dark-suited men followed him to the door.

'The gentleman pressed the alarm button,' she breathed.

Miyamoto almost doubled up. 'What?' He spun, said
something terse to his executives and pulled the doors
together fiercely. 'He's never done it before. What's going
on?'

Yuriko bustled in his footsteps towards the stairs.
'Perhaps he's unwell.'

'I pay that old woman to look after him. She's there to
wipe his backside. Everything.'

'The security team's on the way.'

'It's the damn *gaijin*,' Miyamoto cursed, his frame jolting
as he took the stairs in twos. 'Why can't I rely on the police
or those idiots from Fukuoka?'

A car waited at the entrance to rush them across the
compound.

Kamei, Hinohara and the third man Takada hurried across
the gravel. 'Get your gun,' Kamei ordered, holding his own
.38 in his belt as he ran. Hinohara broke away to the
burgundy Mercedes.

The elderly housekeeper was holding a towel to her
mouth when the two men rushed in. She was speechless,
hysterically pointing along the corridor, incapable of
distinguishing the hard-faced *yakuza* who bundled and
jostled her from the rare, formal visitors to the annexe.
Kamei drew his gun, the other man a short sword. They
found a switch and the doors slid apart. Kamei swept the
room with a two-handed grip on the pistol. At first he
thought the room was empty: the unoccupied electric

wheelchair was on its side against the wall, its motor whirring, and the flapping curtain drapes beckoned to an escape route along the veranda with the ocean view. Shinichi Miyamoto was lying on the floor behind the desk, his thin, short body curled, his mouth an agonised contortion. The wraparound *yukata* gown and the rug were saturated with fresh blood. Crazed and desperate, he had lunged for the sword, seizing it blindly along its razor edge, his grip so fierce the blade stayed embedded in the bones of his hand as he fell, severing the tendons and veins. He was not dead: the scream that had paralysed the housekeeper had faded to a low murmur with each weak saliva-wet breath he emitted. His son clattered into the room, followed by Yuriko Shimada. He pushed the *yakuza* aside and bent over his father, pressing his neck.

'He's alive,' Yuriko breathed with relief, seeing the movement in the lips. She started to press her cellular telephone.

'Not the ambulance,' he barked. 'Get that doctor here, from the hospital. Just give him a rough details. I want no one else to know about this.

'Somebody knows,' Kamei said, patting the sunken impression in the leather seats stretched between the tubular frames of the chairs flanking the desk.

Hinohara burst in, his eyes flashing at the chaos. 'They took my fucking gun. The *gaijin's* got my Tokarev.' Then he saw the feet behind the desk.

Miyamoto looked up, his fingers stained with his father's blood, his face buckled with rage. 'The *gaijin* again! Well, go and get them, like you were supposed to before.' He turned on Yuriko, who was talking into her mobile. 'Go with them. You understand foreigners.'

If the *yakuza* hadn't been so focused, so determined to smash their way into the annexe, they might have seen the shadows protruding from the terrace onto the path that bordered the building. Leaving old Miyamoto screaming in the electric wheelchair, which swivelled maniacally to the demented jabbing of his uninjured hand, they had fled through the window doors, shielding their eyes against the glare from a cloudless sky as they stooped along the veranda. Hearing feet on the gravel and urgent voices out of sight, Alex blocked Phyllis with the bag, then pressed hard against the wall as he risked his profile to watch aghast the play of mingled shadows spreading across open ground. 'I can't take much more of this,' Phyllis breathed. 'What time is it?'

'Ten fifty.'

'So where's the frigging cavalry?'

Sweat stung his eyes, and a surge of anger-driven adrenalin overcame his fear. He was in a world of madmen and he wanted to survive. 'I don't know,' he groaned, putting a narrow profile round the corner again. 'We could run for it, cross the car-park. But I don't know what's on the other side.'

'What about going back the old route, down to the shore?'

'I'm not— ' There was a noise behind them: windows on runners slammed apart.

'Let's go,' he said, grabbing her hand. They stumbled into the sunlight, only the red Mercedes and the Suzuki between them and the shelter of the woods across the open space that seemed to stretch away into the distance like a desert. Phyllis saw the shoulders of a figure in a grove of trees. They'd have to pass him. 'Shit,' she said pointing on the run.

They reached the first, familiar car, and Alex remembered. He was crouching against the grille, his back to the verge of bushes. 'I've still got the keys.'

The passenger door was unlocked. 'Let's go for it,' Phyllis stammered. She slid inside, flicking the glove compartment shut. The papers, tissues and other odd cloths from inside were scattered around. Alex dropped into the driver's seat, heaved the bag across to her and rummaged in his jacket for the ignition key. Phyllis twisted: three men and a woman could be seen in the sun by the gate to the steps that led to the shore. They used a flat hand to shade their eyes as they searched. 'C'mon *gaijin san*. They're looking every which way but here.'

'They can't see us through these black windows,' Alex drawled, his hands deep in his coat pockets. The key was attached to a furry mock paw. He revved the engine alive. 'Hold on.' A reverse turn and a biting forward surge which spat grit into the bushes gave them a start. Yuriko Shimada spun, screaming a command. Kamei set off towards a curtain of dust, pistol drawn. Hinohara slapped his thighs helplessly.

Alex braked as the private forecourt to Hiroshi Miyamoto's mansion narrowed to a gap leading to an arc of asphalt where the grille of the silver BMW they had seen at the noodle shop and the hilltop sports field faced them. It blocked their exit to the car park behind the business centre and ultimately the main gate of the estate.

In his black suit and sunglasses, Endo was propped against the door, a telephone clamped to an ear. He turned at the sudden racket, the noise of an abused engine and the harsh barked shouts searing the air. The Mercedes was skewing towards him. He dropped the mobile and threw himself at the BMW's open boot.

'Move, move, move,' Phyllis urged. 'Don't stop for him. He's *yakuza*.'

Alex's eyes hung on the space between the trees, an escape route beyond the car, and he missed the swift movement as the man snatched a pump-action shotgun from the boot and stepped out to face the foreigners. Alex would remember only a dull thud and shards of glass rapping the windscreen like hail. The car's forward movement met resistance, not so much from the discharge of the cartridges'

357

contents but the body of the *yakuza,* who wrongly assumed the driver of his colleague's car would swerve away. Phyllis had seen the danger and wrenched the steering wheel over as the man pumped up another shell. The car veered into him, the impact propelling him into the windscreen, blood erupting from his face.

'Stop the car!' Phyllis shrieked, her hands wrenching apart the zip of the travel bag. Alex braked instinctively.

She flicked the door catch and kicked it open. The matt-black Tokarev semi-automatic was gripped so tight her knuckles were white; she was muttering in Japanese. The *yakuza* foot-soldier had rolled off the bonnet, a scream choked in his throat. He was trapped between the Mercedes and his BMW, clutching his face in two bloodied hands. He recognised the metallic rasp when she snapped and released the automatic's slide to load the chamber.

'Don't do it!' Alex bellowed. Running figures filled his rear-view mirror, but Phyllis had swivelled in the bucket seat, the gun in a double-handed grip against her cheek. Endo's bloody face filled the space, his eyes pleading at the woman snarling above him. Alex heard three sharp, loud thuds, and at each one Phyllis jolted backwards. The three ejected shell cases smacked the windscreen inside the car, the last one singeing Alex's cheek as it ricocheted around inside.

'Go, go, go,' she commanded, dragging the door shut.

'Christ, what have you done?'

They were skirting the business centre, approaching the drive that led to the estate's gate. The sound of urgent voices and strained engine noises had filtered into the building, drawing curious Nippon Nagasaki executives and a clutch of office workers into the open in time to see a red Mercedes struggling to hold to the narrow exit road. There was more shouting, out of their sight.

Yuriko knelt beside the prostrate, wriggling, groaning figure of Endo, holding a handkerchief to his face. The car had run over his sunglasses, the cellular telephone and his feet. Kamei was gathering the pieces and the shotgun while his footsoldier was already behind the steering wheel of the BMW. They hadn't seen what Hinohara had: a neat triangle pattern made by three bullet holes in the front offside tyre. He brought two fists crashing on the bonnet. Endo spat out a tooth with Kamei's name. Kamei left the sinking car and leaned close to the young *yakuza*'s mouth.

'The police crossed the causeway,' Endo spluttered, aiming an arm at his shattered cellular phone. 'They're coming here.'

The narrow drive curved downwards, in permanent semi-darkness from the interwoven canopies of the packed trees encroaching from the forests on both sides. The rear-view mirror was mercifully clear, thanks to Phyllis.

'I thought you chucked the gun away,' Alex said, when he felt safer.

'I almost did. It kind of fell in the bag when you went into your zig-zag pattern this morning and trashed the car.'

Their long-overdue smiles of relief evaporated when they turned a bend. He was driving too briskly for the terrain, elated by the escape and determined not to stop again until they were off Yanagi. The uniformed guard they had seen guiding in the limousines a couple of hours earlier would be persuaded to open up, with the weapon in Phyllis's lap if necessary, but when Alex slowed they saw the double gate barring their departure There was no keeper. His little roofed hut was deserted.

'Hard to ram our way through,' Alex said, stepping from the car. 'They're solid.' Measuring the climb, he looked up at the top ledge of the gates and the wall that ran from either end at the same height.

Phyllis called from the hut. 'There's an interphone gadget. Probably connects with a security room somewhere in one of the buildings.'

'I guess you need a remote control or you have to call from your vehicle.' He ran his hands over a side-door by the main vehicle entrance. 'Pedestrian's gate. Works on remote like the main ones.'

'We could try,' Phyllis suggested, tugging the familiar spiral cord from the car. 'Pretend we're Miyamoto's business pals.'

He indicated the cameras sitting atop the gates, covering both sides. 'They're watching us. I don't think we can get away with it. Look at the state of us.' He held up a hand. 'Can you hear something Phyl?'

Phyllis came to a stop and looked up to catch the air currents. Birds fluttered and twittered.

'Is that a siren? he asked.

She made a face. 'It could be. It's definitely a car. But it's coming from the estate. Let's ram the gate, Alex. My turn.' She jumped behind the wheel and drew the seat belt across her body. Alex's face filled the opened window.

'Let me do it, Phyl.'

'Stand back, *gaijin san.*'

He looked towards the sound, and trudged backwards. Then he saw the mess on the asphalt: viscous lime-green fluid spreading like a yolk in the puddle of oil dribbling on the incline.

Phyllis turned the key. It sprang back, soundlessly. She swore and twisted it again. 'Got a problem,' she called, her neck stretched through the window.

'I know,' Alex groaned. 'The car's been shot. The whole bloody cartridge must have gone through the light, fucked up the works.' His head flopped on the door rim and he exhaled grimly. 'Stick it in neutral, Phyl, and get out.' The E320 was a monster, wide and heavy, and even when Phyllis lent her shoulder to his against the boot they could only force it into a limp roll towards the stout barriers. It struck solidly, stressing but not breaking the bolts connecting the two halves. They spread a fraction, like a pair of badly closed lock gates. Apart from the twisted mascot, the damage to the car was hidden. Its grille nuzzled the entrance.

They turned together. A car appeared on the driveway, its headlights catching the sunlight and flashing a warning. Alex heaved the bag onto the bonnet and followed Phyllis, who found that the teeth of the electronically controlled bolts, now bent and rendered inoperable, made a decent, if narrow, ladder for the last few feet to the flat top edge of the gates. 'Easier without the broken tiles,' she uttered, her body slithering over the rim.

Alex could see her on the ground through the slender gap in the broken gates. 'Catch it,' he said, hoisting the lumpy bag over. 'Break the fall at least.' He was lying on the top of the gate, like a fallen high-wire act, pain throbbing through his lacerated hand as he clung to the flat, narrow ledge of wood. Phyllis was urging him to jump, to join her in Yanagi's orbital road. On the estate side, he saw the faces of three men emerging from a black Toyota Crown. They dodged warily towards the cover of the trees along the road: the *gaijin* were armed and strangely unafraid. The big *yakuza* with the zip-up jacket and the flat, mean expression ducked for lateral cover with his injured friend's shotgun.

'Get your ass down here,' Phyllis urged. 'What's the matter?' A bus growled up the incline and with no passengers in the bus shelter proceeded without stopping. She bit the tip of her tongue. Another thirty seconds and they could've been on it.

'I've got a problem,' he said, immobile. 'Can you get back up here?' The left side flap of his jacket, which had absorbed most of the blood from his hand and was badly torn, hung over the gate, facing the estate and the *yakuza* hardmen creeping towards him, slowed only by the perceived threat from their stolen semi-automatic. The flimsy, priceless document Roland Jonsson had protected in the face of violence and threats during years of imprisonment was in a plain, white envelope in Alex's inside jacket pocket. He had reassured himself it was there every few minutes since they had left the inn six hours earlier. Now the entire envelope was exposed, except for one corner tip still snared in his pocket. He could see it, trapped in his armpit, and any movement, any attempt by him to lift an arm and bend it backwards or roll over the gate, would dislodge it, sending it fluttering into the hands of Miyamoto's heavies.

'Say again, Alex.'

'Get up here for chrissake!' The gates were split to the width of Phyllis's trainers; and the raised horizontal struts gave her a knuckled grasp as she stretched for the three bolt steps. Her head reached his prone body, level with his waist. 'Can you reach under me, through the gap, and get the letter? I'm going to lose it.'

'Oh, God.' Her head sagged and butted the wood while she drew breath. Then she spread a leg and an arm to take a tenuous splayed grip against the gate. Lifting the other side of his jacket, draped on her side of the gates, she lowered her head, pressed an eye to the space and saw the other hem of Alex's jacket and through a thin space the front of the black car.

'Careful, Phyl. Take it easy.'

A man's voice called out, urging caution while encouraging unseen companions forward.

'Have you got it?' Alex breathed, feeling fingertips grazing his ribs under a sweat-damp shirt.

'I can see it. Can you ease up a bit? You're trapping it.'

He was facing the estate road and the trees which gave cover to the *yakuza*. Then he saw the man whose car he'd stolen from the road by the inn: he had stepped from the tree line, a shotgun across his chest. He heard the snap as the man pumped the gun. When the explosion came Alex was actually looking into the eye of the barrel. Hinohara had taken a few steps forward and aimed from the hip when he fired. The payload hit the gates three feet to the left and below his head, splintering the wood with shallow penetration and sending ricocheting shot and splinters at his arm, which stetched along the gate, protecting most of his head and face. He felt the stings as pellets stabbed his wrist and pierced the sleeve of his jacket. Something slashed his cheek and he tasted blood. His bowels loosened, and as his senses lurched between reality and disbelief his grip on the rim weakened and he rolled over the edge, dislodging Phyllis with the sweep of his feet, managing instinctively to cling to the rim by his fingertips, stupefied and numbed.

'Let go, Alex,' she called from the ground, her ankle twisted. 'It's only four or five feet. Let go of the fucking gate!' She scrambled upright and hopped to him, reaching and gripping a leg. A patch of grass broke his fall. Phyllis was trying to haul him to his feet. The harsh voices were approaching the stalled Mercedes cautiously.

'Did you get him?'

'Get over the gates the same way.'

'Careful, they've still got the gun.'

'Get security to open the side gate.'

The fugitives were hop-running, following the course of the leaf-covered concrete wall down the road, away from the Miyamoto estate. Her ankle throbbing, she draped the bag across his shoulders and forced his hand around her waist, while she gripped his belt. The blood from his arm was warm and sticky against her skin. They turned a bend, the breeze blowing from the distant shimmer of sea rousing Alex a few degrees closer to awareness.

'I was out of it for a while,' he breathed, touching the cut on his cheek gingerly. The blood was smudged across his face, dribbling thinly. Then he remembered. 'Christ! They shot at me. And I dropped the letter.' A car approached from behind. Phyllis spun to face it but it passed before she could decide if it was safe to try to flag it down. Another came at speed from the front, its driver hunched in a flash of white coat. Phyllis raised an arm limply but it was clear he was on an emergency call.

Phyllis pulled him closer and patted the bag, beaming. 'I caught the letter. It only cost me an ankle.'

It put a spring in their three-legged hobble. Alex closed his eyes, smiling as he shook his head clear. The flat roofs of the barrack-like apartment blocks they had passed in the bus appeared below them and, on their left where the modern road flattened towards the sea, the short, neglected road which led to the arched southern entrance of the old cross-island tunnel. And what they could hear now *was* a siren, several in fact: the techno-whining echoed through the straight, single-lane tunnel, from the direction of the town of Yanagi.

'We can hide in the those buildings,' Phyllis suggested, pointing to the settlement.

Alex hesitated. 'We won't make it that far if they've got over the gate. They're in better shape than us. Let's get off this road and let them find us in the dark.'

There was no raised pavement along the narrow, unlit tunnel; pedestrians were expected to hug the walls, keeping inside a faded blue line while the one-way passage of traffic was controlled by lights at either end. The ancient concrete cladding on the walls was cracked and stained with seepage and half a century of grime, the air musty, heavy with stagnant exhaust gas. They could see the shrunken arch of light five, perhaps six, hundred yards away where the Yanagi entrance opened onto the shore by the fishing harbour and close to the site of Camp Nagasaki Six. They hurried gratefully towards it, pausing for breath near a funnel of pale, broken light from a narrow ventilation shaft.

'I thought the police were in the tunnel,' Phyllis remarked, with a touch of anxiety.

'I guess they took the new road,' Alex said, 'like we did

364

when we got here. We heard the echo.'

They rested in the darkness, Phyllis propped against the damp wall, taking the weight off her sprained foot, Alex lowering the bag, dabbing his face with a ragged jacket sleeve and stretching his aching limbs. Then more magnified sounds penetrated the silence, reaching them from the direction they had come. The beautiful, liberating, subdued hum of sirens. Alex caught her smile in the thin light. It told him the madness was over. She offered him an open palm which he met with a high-five slap from his uninjured hand, then let him take her in a hug which generated heat, squeezing the tension from them both. They were still in the embrace, touching and kissing tender cuts and bruises, promising all sorts of soothing recuperation, when the headlights found them. They were frozen in the beams like rabbits. The vehicle was approaching tentatively from the Yanagi Town direction. Separating, Alex lifted the bag and its precious contents; Phyllis squinted into the blinding explosion of light, then joined him in the recess of the air vent.

'Is it the police?' he asked hopefully.

'Can't tell. No siren, warning lights.'

'Could be turned off.' He looked up the ventilation shaft, following the course of a rusted ladder bolted to the wall. The passage was narrowed by dangling vines and roots that had pierced the walls. 'A normal car would've reached here and passed us by now.'

Phyllis peered into the tunnel again and tossed her head towards the low echo of the sirens. 'We can wait here for it, or we can go back the other way.'

'We wouldn't make it, even if you had two good feet. We're halfway along the tunnel already. If it's a *yakuza* car it'll run us down. We can hear the police down the other end but why don't they come in and get us?' The beam was broadening on the tunnel walls.

She breathed out noisily. 'So we go for the ladder.'

His blood-streaked face, with its fatigue-shadowed, bloodshot eyes, moved into the thin shaft of light. 'I'm knackered, Phyl.' He threw a thumb upwards. 'It's about eighteen feet. Even if I get to the top there's a grille that's probably been up there for years. It'd take a pickaxe to move it.' He looked towards the car: it had stopped. Two figures were silhouetted by their own headlights, moving cautiously towards them. 'Give me the gun, Phyl,' he said, his voice croaked with dust. As he turned, his hand outstretched, a movement at the other end of the tunnel snagged his vision. There were two figures there as well. He blinked at the gloom. Something was wrong. They weren't police. Phyllis reached across his shoulder and took the Tokarev from the travel bag.

'Give me the bloody gun, Phyl,' he pressed. 'They're coming at us from both sides now.'

'Move out of the way,' she ordered. 'You need two good hands to use it.' She flicked the safety catch, remembering it was still cocked after her three-round volley earlier, and took a position at the corner of the recess and the tunnel, her cheek pressed to the edge, her eyes on the black figures trapped in the light. 'Stay in cover,' she growled.

He knelt behind her without a protest, only his head exposed, staring the other way towards the light where the tunnel breached the hillside. 'What are they doing?'

Phyllis risked a look in the direction they had come from and held it. 'They're walking backwards. I don't get it.' Her head flew back to the men approaching from the car. They were almost linked, the shape of their weapons sharp in the headlight beams: the starkly angled outline of a semi-automatic held high and the length of a baseball bat, perhaps a sword, over a shoulder. 'Watch the other two,' Phyllis said. The echoed whir of the sirens had died: the silence was shivering. One of the men from the unseen car broke it when he removed his sunglasses with a clack and shoved them in his jacket pocket.

'*Gaijin san,*' he called, with tense, friendly irony. 'It's over. We need to talk.'

'What does he want?' Alex uttered.

'Our asses.'

'They're gutsy. Standing there like that. I don't suppose they know you can shoot.'

'I don't think they even know I'm armed,' Phyllis said gravely. 'I guess they're the guys from the other Mercedes. They won't know what's been happening.'

Then the two *yakuza* noticed the movement at the other end of the tunnel and stiffened. Their friends from the Miyamoto estate were not closing the trap: they were fleeing in panic. There was a shout, a command and more figures filled the entrance. The unmistakeable crack of a single discharge from a revolver resounded through the tunnel, followed by a concentrated firecracker burst of gunfire which echoed like a swarm of thunderclaps. Shrieks, orders and demands from a voice reverberating from a bullhorn exploded in a bedlam of confusion. The two *yakuza* retreated, moving backwards at first, and when the realisation hit them, they turned and ran to their car. Phyllis followed them along the sight of the gun until they disappeared behind slammed doors. Tyres bit into the rutted tarmac, the wheels screaming as the car skewed into a desperate reverse surge. A black-and-white Nagasaki prefectural police car had been drawn across the mouth of the tunnel and vacated by its crew moments before the black Mercedes careened towards it. With the rear lights of the car emitting a useless, low, almost infra-red glow, the driver raced the car backwards in virtual darkness, seeing the police car at the last moment, too late to avoid impact.

Phyllis and Alex winced at the echoed crunch. There was a flash but no explosion.

The *yakuza* inside the Miyamoto estate lost time when Hinohara tried to start the car blocking the gates and Kamei ranted uselessly when his call to the security room went unanswered. Thwarted, Hinohara slammed his way out of his Mercedes and blasted the key-card entry device on the side gate with a single shot from the pump-action gun. It didn't open to his kick. The doctor called to aid Shinichi Miyamoto was talking into the interphone, his green Honda hatchback drawn up to the gates on the outside. The report from the gun jolted him and his face collapsed when three angry thugs scrambled over and fell beside him, two of them armed with guns. Yes, he had seen two people, one obviously a *gaijin*, and they were heading downhill, and yes, they could borrow his car.

They were trapped when Kamei and Hinohara left the Honda to check whether the foreigners were hiding in the tunnel. They had turned back, satisfied, knowing the headlights at the other end belonged to their black Mercedes, when the roads erupted. Before the driver, Takada, could react, he found himself caught between a convoy of armoured riot-control vehicles and police cars approaching from the east coast road and three units from the north whose main complement had broken off to search the Miyamoto estate for two foreigners wanted on suspicion of murder. He stumbled from the car, his hands already pleading. For the others, the tunnel was their last refuge.

Kamei fired first, from just inside the lip of the tunnel. It was an aimless shot from his .38 revolver, a gesture of utter frustration which also might gain him a few extra seconds of flight. He ran, stooping instinctively, towards the distant lights, and when he felt the burning sting in his back and his legs grew suddenly heavy and unresponsive he knew it was over. Three more shots were fired and he was hit again. Before he fell he thought he saw blood behind his eyeballs.

Hinohara swung round the body of his chief, hugging the wall, moving his heaving, heavy body in short jerks. Sweat filled his eyes. He slowed: there were shadows ahead, elongated, stretching from a recess into the illumination from the Mercedes. Then he stared at the headlights in disbelief, oblivious to the threats and calls from the police who tracked behind him at a prudent distance. The boys were leaving him. The shadows faded as the two points of light grew smaller in a pandemonium of squealing tyres and the stench of scorched rubber. The impact of the crash that caved in the police car and sent it into a crunching spin rumbled down the tunnel. He stumbled forward, blinking as his eyes adjusted, and almost ran into his own Tokarev. It was aimed at his broad chest. He forced a weary smile which turned to a scowl and he slumped almost gratefully against the wall.

Her forearms ached. Mass-produced by the Chinese from a Soviet model, the semi-automatic was built for heavy-duty mischief. It quivered in the grip of her long, agitated fingers. The wall gave her the support her twisted ankle didn't. There was a round in the chamber, she kept telling herself. She swallowed and held her breath, wondering if she had the strength to draw the trigger and still keep the gun on the target. The *yakuza* was a dim outline. He was perspiring; she could almost taste the sour, garlic reek above the acrid drifting smell of cordite and gasoline fumes. He was backed to the wall, his dirt- and sweat-blotched face still full of malice as his mind fought for a solution. The short-barrelled shotgun dangled loose on a stubby finger. His left hand was moving slowly across his body to reach it. She sensed a movement in the corner of an eye. Alex, still unseen by the *yakuza*, was inching in a painful crawl from the deep recess to the open tunnel. What was he going to do?

'Don't move, goddamnit,' she hissed through tight teeth, her eyes on the shotgun as the barrel began to move. The trigger was slippery to her touch and she knew the weakness in her fingers would defeat her.

Hinohara ventured a flashing glance behind him: the police had retreated. There was no movement or sound until the growl of a powerful engine soon filled the tunnel, followed by the sweep of its headlights. The armour-clad riot-control wagon, its bulletproof windows encased in steel mesh, lumbered through the entrance, armed officers inside and others following behind, crouching in its cover. A matching model that had pushed by the wreckage of the black Mercedes was approaching the tunnel from the Yanagi Town entrance. Hinohara trembled with corrosive rage and desperate frustration. When Phyllis shot him she couldn't tell whether he intended to use the pump-action gun he suddenly snatched in two hands to blow her to pieces from ten yards, or to make a traditional *banzai* assault on the superior forces closing in from all sides. But she fired, blinking at the recoil and the flash that momentarily blinded.

They waited for the headlights to meet before stepping with hands raised into the glare. When they were safe from the risk of deadly friendly fire, limping under escort to the sunlight and giggling and squawking with relief and shock, Phyllis gripped his arm, clutching the bag with the photographs and the tape of Shinichi Miyamoto's confession. 'I've got a lot to tell Bill Littleton about. Let's get to a telephone.'

EPILOGUE

15 August
No more dockyard work today. The rumour must be
true, so only worked half the men cleaning the camp.
16 August
Same routine as yesterday. Issue of Red Cross meat
today - half a tin per man. The war must be over.
17 August
No working parties; also no air activity for three days
now. Japs turned over all Red Cross food to our officers
today. Some of this was sent to Camp 14. (See attached
list of food.) Some of the guards have gone and five or
six of our men are still missing. Must have died in the
big bomb.
18 August
Received official notice from Japanese Camp
Commander that hostilities had ceased today.
Apparently Japs surrendered on the 15th. I wonder how
long it will be before we start the long journey home.
Everybody was excited and cannot sleep. Some of the
military guards have left the camp.

19 August
*Held a Thanksgiving Service today and at the end of it
we sang the National Anthem. First time for three years.*
20 August
*Got my ring back today. Japs made an issue of soap to
all. Our Officers have also taken over control of the
Camp. We painted the letters 'P.O.W.' on the roof of the
two-storey building so that the camp can be located
from the air.*
24 August
*Allied aircraft overhead all morning. Hope they can
find the Camp. Received mail today. One letter
contained photo of Kath and the children. How they
have grown! They look well.*
25 August
*We have been allowed outside the Camp today. Went for
a walk and saw some Japanese who had been burned at
Nagasaki. It seems the hospital is full of injured from
the town.*
26 August
*American aircraft flew over camp at 0830 hrs today
and dropped cartons of Old Gold Cigarettes. At 1020
hrs one plane named* Headliner *dropped eight ration
parcels. Three were badly damaged. We had spelled out
the word 'NEWS' with clothing on the potato patch and
the Leader of the Squadron dropped a medical kit. In it
was the following message:*

> *WAR IS OVER. JAPS SURRENDERED
> UNCONDITIONALLY TO ALLIES AFTER
> ATOMIC BOMB DROPPED ON NAGASAKI
> AND AFTER RUSSIA ENTERED WAR AGAINST
> JAPS. McARTHUR WILL ARRIVE TOKYO IN A
> FEW DAYS TO ACCEPT HIROHITO'S
> SURRENDER. AMERICAN TROOPS SOON BE
> HERE TO FREE YOU.*

29 August

Spent afternoon walking round the island, picking up US Airforce supplies which had fallen outside the Camp. Jap Field Army are acting as police. Civilians are stunned over the Atom Bomb. I think they knew the end was not far away, but it came quicker than they thought. Surprised to hear that people who had coloured clothing on were burned worse than those that had white clothing.

30 August

More supplies received today. Better drop as nearly everything fell in camp area. One box came through roof of sick bay and injured two Yanks. I still have not seen RJ. I am gathering his things for safekeeping like he asked. They probably transferred him to another camp with some others. I hear there are other men missing.

1 September

I must say the American pilots are good. To drop supplies to us they have to approach the Camp from the south between the mainland and the island. About half a mile from the Camp are high-voltage cables from the mainland. They give a clearance of about 100 ft from the surface of the water. If they fly over the top of the cables the supplies drop outside the camp, so they bring their superforts in under the cables and after dropping their supplies have to give full power to their aircraft so that they can clear the hill behind our camp.

4 September

Super Fortress crashed south of us today. Fourteen of the crew of fifteen were killed. The survivor is in hospital in Nagasaki. American Navy started sweeping the approaches to the harbour today. Home is getting nearer.

6 September

Saw people who had been burned. An awful sight.

8 September
*Supplies are coming in every other day. I use the
wrapping paper for my diary. No sign of land forces
yet. We're all impatient to leave. I'm getting my things
together. There's not much to take home. I found a
couple of letters the civvy left. I will look after them in
case we meet again.*

9 September
*Memorial service held at Oura Catholic Church for the
dead US aircrew and all the men who had died in the
Camp during captivity. Tried to signal a minesweeper
today. No joy. Arch and I will try again tomorrow.*

12 September
*American warships entered harbour today. Also a large
hospital ship. No. 33 Recovery Squad entered Camp.
Sick men were transferred to the ship. Told we would
leave Camp early tomorrow.*

13 September
*American landing craft took us into Nagasaki and we
were processed, as they Yanks say. After medical
examination we were kitted up with American Naval
clothes and then embarked in the American aircraft
carrier to the tune of 'Don't fence me in.' The carrier
was called USS* Chenango, *a small fleet carrier. How
good to be with friends!*

14 September
*Left Japan for Okinawa. Have started homeward at last
after more than three and a half years a prisoner. I am
no longer a guest of the Emperor of Japan, but free at
last.*

William Littleton's body was washed up on the beach a mile
to the south of his beloved Hayama house, two days after the
police were summoned there by the representatives in Japan
of a British insurance company acting for the suspects in the

374

case of the murder of the bar owner, Makiko Nakamura. After a police investigation prompted by the testimony of the American journalist Phyllis Wakai and corroborated by the aviation surveyor from London, Alexander Bolton, the Yokohoma affiliate of the Okudaira-*gumi* surrendered three of the gang to the Kanagawa prefectural prosecutors for the murder of Littleton. Wataru Hinohara from the syndicate's Kyushu base confessed to the strangling of Makiko Nakamura under instructions from Kazuo Kamei after forcibly taking her from her apartment and confining her against her will in the Sanya district of Tokyo. With Kamei dead, and if he ever walked again, Hinohara would face the prosecutors' demand for the death penalty. The charges of attempted murder of the foreign journalist and her companion were almost secondary. A file was opened on the untimely death of an employee of Nippon Nagasaki Corporation in a supposed traffic accident and several early depositions implicated the president's office in a conspiracy to silence him. Yuriko Shimada was questioned with the rest of the boardroom of protesting Nippon Nagasaki executives found in conference at the scene of a major disturbance at the home of their president. No charges were ultimately made against her and after resigning from Nippon Nagasaki Corporation she now teaches Japanese to *gaijin* businessmen in Tokyo.

And then there was Roland Jonsson. The Swedish government, through its embassy in Tokyo, demanded an investigation into the death in Nagasaki in August 1945 of their neutral citizen in consideration of allegations made by the American journalist Phyllis Wakai in a *Washington Post* article and later in a television documentary. Ms Wakai transcribed the text of a recorded conversation with Jonsson's former Japanese business partner in which he appears to confess to a conspiracy to murder the Swede. She also claims she was led to the murderer by the reference to Jonsson in the fifty-five-year-old secret diaries of a British prisoner-of-war in which he was known to his fellow inmates in simple Anglo-Saxon as Johnson. The chronicles say he was alive after the day of the atomic bombing of Nagasaki, when official records claim he died. The breaking of the story forced the cancellation of a memorial service for the pioneer industrialist and patriot Shinichi Miyamoto, who died suddenly in the study of his retirement home in the Yanagi district of Nagasaki. The Prime Minister, three cabinet members and several hundred politicians and the gerontocracy of the business world had already accepted an invitation to attend the solemn event.

The dissolution of the Nippon Nagasaki Corporation began soon after the arrest of its president, Hiroshi Miyamoto, following an intensive investigation fuelled by the allegations made by Phyllis Wakai in her book on the conglomerate and its business practices. Raids by teams of prosecutors and tax officials unearthed secret internal accounting books which documented the extent of the company's abuse of the Commercial Code and a hundred and sixty charges were ultimately brought. Banks withdrew their lending facilities and refused further financial support when it became clear the company could not service the interest payments on its borrowings and discovered that much of the collateral put up against it was worthless. Two months after its spurious founder died, Nippon Nagasaki Corporation applied for protection under the Corporate Re-organization Law, coincidentally within days of his son Hiroshi having conspiracy to murder added to the charges against him. Three and a half weeks after the old DC-8-71 crashed, forced onto the runway at Haneda Airport by its sick pilot Edward Kidderby, NN Air made its last commercial flight. Many charges would ultimately be brought against the management: it was as if a fleet of Boeing 747s had been flown contemptuously through the complex and comprehensive civil aviation laws of Japan and America. The prosecutors already had compelling evidence for the charge that NN Air had deliberately falsified documentation covering their pilots' regular, statutory medical examinations. It had been obtained by the British surveyor, Alexander Bolton, in life-threatening circumstances.

Survivors of Camp Nagasaki Six still drift back to the primary school by the sea, their bitter memories eased by time. It's a long way from home but not hard to find: the district of Yanagi is a prosperous place and the people are happy to assist the process of reconciliation. When they left the camp in September 1945, after liberation by American forces bearing clothes, medicine and more food than they could eat, they took little with them, anxious as they were to get home, far away from the disease, the beatings and the constant smell of filth and death. Apart from memories, Tom Humphrey's only possessions on the long trip home were the pair of matching school textbooks he had gathered on Java and scraps of paper scrounged around Camp Nagasaki Six and the dockyards on Yanagi Island in Japan. It took him more than a month, travelling to the Philippines and Vancouver, across Canada by train and then by a French liner from Halifax to Southampton, finally reaching the picturesque fishing town of Padstow in Cornwall, south-west England, on 1 November 1945.

Ten years later, three years after the peace treaty with Japan had been signed and reparations agreed, Tom and the other survivors of the Asian camps received £76 each from a grateful government.

On his way to Nagasaki, Tom might stop at Yokohama and visit the immaculately tended lawns of the cemetery where his shipmates from HMS *Exeter* and all the two thousand or so British and Commonwealth soldiers who died in Japan rest peacefully. On his arrival at Nagasaki Station, the taxi to

Yanagi might take him first around the beautiful city, to the Peace Park and the stark, black monolith pointing to a spot six hundred metres above it where Fat Man exploded and obliterated sixty thousand people in an instant.

His first big surprise will be to see the narrow straits between the old island and the mainland filled in and replaced with a broad causeway of houses and factories. If he feels fit, and desperately nostalgic, he might want to leave the car at the end of the landbridge, very near the gateway to the site of the old dockyards where he worked, and walk the mile or so to Camp Nagasaki Six. There's a shop on the corner now, where the road meets the camp. It is on the spot where the guardroom and the punishment cells had stood and is run by an old lady with a broad smile who actually moved into the camp temporarily after Tom and the others had left. She can point him to a few of the surviving civilian guards who were recruited from the local populace and still live nearby, but if revenge is on his mind after fifty years he will not track down the military guards who tormented him. The US Eighth Army went after them, an extremely difficult task since the names of most of them were not known to the prisoners and many melted away into the general mass of defeated, demoralised people.

The interpreter Tom knew as Beethoven – his real name was Sumioka – was caught and tried at Yokohama and was hanged in November 1946 for war crimes committed at Nagasaki Six and two other camps. Flip, the brutal mess sergeant - his real name Iwata - got twelve years in prison. Donald Duck, the medical orderly whose name was Kuroiwa, was fingered by many POWs for the ferocity of his assaults on the sick and for sending them to the yards when they were unfit. He was also given twelve years. Sergeant Masaaki Murai, a graduate of the Waseda University School of Law, and known as Napoleon to the prisoners, was given nine years. He administered punishments individually, a sword in one hand, his heavy, buckled belt in the other. The power in the camp, the man who ran it and led the administration of punishment by example, was Sergeant Major Hideo Yasutake, the one they called Bo Ku Go. He was sent to Sugamo prison for twelve years but he was probably insane.

Evidence given at the trials showed that the average POW population at Camp Nagasaki Six between October 1942 and its liberation was one thousand one hundred and twenty and a check of survivors revealed that only two had not been beaten during their imprisonment. All those charged with war crimes pleaded not guilty to every charge and were found guilty on almost all of them. In his own evidence, Captain Nozaki, with his receding hairline and full moustache – who was commandant of the camp for eighteen months until its liberation – said he had seen only one incident of a guard slapping a prisoner. None of the guards from the dockyard was apprehended, although there was a search for the Weasel and the Kid, who had been named by more than two hundred prisoners for their brutality. The one-eyed civilian supervisor they obviously called Cyclops was cited as an instigator of violence and an occasional perpetrator, but the dockyards on Yanagi were deserted when the Americans got around to checking. A hundred and six men failed to survive internment in Camp Nagasaki Six. Roland Jonsson was just one of them.

AUTHOR'S NOTE

I came across the diaries of Tom Humphrey in 1995 at the time of the 50th anniversary of the end of war with Japan. They are written in two notebooks scrounged from a deserted Indonesian school soon after he was captured following the sinking of HMS *Exeter* and the destruction of the rest of the Allied fleet in the Battle of the Java Sea. Displayed in the Imperial War Museum, London, they form at once a sad and defiant testimony to the human spirit when a British prisoner of the Japanese had a one in three chance of survival. Looking for a new story, I saw in the meticulous records Tom wrote at his peril whilst a captive in Indonesia and Japan for over three years, a modern tale that drew on his accurate and fascinating historical details. It was only when I did my research at the site of the Nagasaki POW camp and looked through the prisoners' evidence and war crimes trial testimony, held in dusty old boxes in the US National Archives, that I understood how accurately Tom had recorded the details of his captivity.

Eighty-nine years old, and living with Kath who waited years without news of her husband and who appears often in his diaries, Tom lives in the same house on the coast of north

Cornwall. He still gives talks to local schools and the new generation of sailors at nearby naval bases. The grand scale of his experiences fascinates them: surviving a fight to the last ship in a three-day sea battle, incarceration in two of the infamous labour camps and, just when he thought the world owed him and his fellow inmates a break, he watched a B-29 bomber peel away, high above the camp, leaving an orange fireball of destruction over the city of Nagasaki, five miles away. Had the world's second atomic bomb found its intended target, a dockyard complex two miles from the camp, Tom would not have survived. He kindly allowed me to dig deep into his vivid sketches and reproduce many of them in my novel. Although I have seeded the diary extracts used in the book with elements of my story line, and condensed them in places, they are, in form, language and style, exactly as he wrote them.